Servant

An Unnatural Series

KATLYNE MARIE

Published by Katlyne Marie

Distributed by Bublish, Inc.

ISBN:(paperback) 978-1-64704-308-7
ISBN:(eBook) 978-1-64704-307-0

Unnatural Series

Servant

An Unnatural Series

Chapter 1
Cinder

"Lift her!" I heard a new voice command. I could barely see these newcomers through the barred cell I had been holed up in since that night. I had to believe I had been locked away inside the stables located not far from the main house. Tiredly observing the lackeys storm the stall, I could not help but let these strangers pick up my once more paralyzed frame. Slowly being lifted off the straw bedding, I had been calling my mattress for who knows how long I worked on eavesdropping in on the conversation occurring between the two leaders.

One of the leaders who was now thanking his associate I knew was supposed to be the Unnatural who was supposedly in charge of the Vampiric Syndicate. "I really appreciate this Calem." The Vampiric who was wearing the same suit I had last seen him wearing, making me wonder if he ever wore anything different. Despite the exhaustion I was still broadly fighting, I glanced my sights over to the person he was talking to, who was another Unnatural I assumed. "We just don't have the means to take care of her anymore."

"As I said, we would happily take her off your hands." This Calem figure returned with what I felt like was an English accent. "Although

I have to admit she looks a lot worse than I had originally imagined, especially considering that she was under your diligent care."

Braedon huffed. "Well, she was in good health up until an incident a few months ago."

"I had heard about that. How is everyone doing?"

My stomach dropped. I too wondered as to everyone else's well-being, but I knew that they were not going to tell me. Why would they, when I couldn't even tell them why to begin with? Even though I had desperately tried several times to tell them my reasoning, everyone thought I was just being arrogant. However, they didn't understand that because of the energy I had exerted on that night I had temporarily lost my 'humanity'. My ability to speak in the human tongue was gone. But, even with all that, was this really the right thing to do? I knew what I did was wrong. I knew because of my actions, I had no right to refute the consequences which were now bearing their weight upon me. There was just something off about this. Something wasn't right.

"Just put her in the bed of the truck." The other Syndicate Leader continued to command his kin. With my sights still fixated on the men, I took in Calem's traits. He resembled a proper Englishmen from the way he talked to the way he held himself, to even the type of clothes we wore. This Unnatural too wore a suit like Braedon, however, the fabric seemed to come right out of the old Victorian Era. As my surroundings changed, I also took note that we had left the dimly lit stables and were making our way around a hidden drive that I figured had to be on the other side of the connection to the Garden. Trying to intake the lain pebble drive, I felt my gut once more drop. The reality of my situation was beginning to hit my limp body. This was a custodial transaction; I was being exchanged from Vampiric Syndicate who had taken care of me for nearly two whole years and being handed over to the Lycan Syndicate.

Braedon took a heavy sigh, followed by a long pause before he finally answered his fellow high-ranking Syndicate Leader. I hope I too could have my questions answered. I needed to know their conditions. I needed to know the condition of the man who had admitted his love for me. After his long pause, the Vampiric spoke up, "Well Jakob..."

"Jakob-?" I whined remembering the way I had left him lying on the snow ridden ground. His jacket's sleeves scorching, exposing the burned skin beneath the exquisite material. His stomach and neck lacerated and spurting blood.

Watching out of my peripheral sight the two men stop and stand there for a few seconds while my large, yet thin canine frame was dropped into the back of the riddled truck's bed, I tried to stay focused on them. However, one of the new Syndicate men's silhouette blocked my view. His brutish height quickly jumping up into the truck and proceeding to stand over the top of me. I could feel his hands hastily grab and pull the newly dressed collar I was wearing around my neck. Baring my fangs at the man, I rounded up my remaining energy to give this man a fair warning. Throwing my head up I felt my long front scissors scrap the skin of his arm. Their sharp edges barely puncturing his muscular arm just as he pulled the collar up behind my jaw. Not phased a single bit, he hastily grabbed at my tented scruff before dragging my entire body further into the truck. The truck's bed suddenly appeared a lot longer than I had originally thought. I could feel my medium-length shedding winter coat get hung on the rivets it was passing over. The bolts savagely ripping out the fine hairs causing me to erupt in pain. Depleting what little reserved energy I had; I dropped my head back down onto the cold steel floor. With everything gone, I adverted my attention to the second Unnatural who had carried my large canine frame and was now handing a very short lead over to his companion. I could see the leash was tied to a clasp that had been bolted into the steel frame of the truck. Hearing the leash's hook clasp itself around the keyring of my nylon choker, I continued to helplessly watch from the terrible vantage point the two Unnaturals exit the bed.

Once their heavy boots had stomped out of the truck, I was finally able to return my hypersensitive hearing towards the conversation Braedon was having with Calem, hoping deep down that I had not missed out on the condition of at least someone. Though just as I had feared, the Vampire had already told the story from that night.

"She managed all that?" Calem shockingly asked.

"Somehow. We still don't know why?"

"Has she given you an explanation?"

I couldn't see Braedon's image over the truck's lifted gate but guessing by his heavy sigh, I believed he had shaken his head in denial to the question. "No. All we know is that she kept saying how she had to leave but that she didn't want to leave. We tried to interrogate her once she had woken up, however, once she had awoken, this is all we were left with."

"Normally with shapeshifters they can still communicate to some degree in the human language." Calem attempted to scientifically explain.

"Nope. She must have lost that ability."

"Can't transform either?"

I didn't hear Braedon respond to that question. "Everything about it seems off. She even seems to be acting more...I don't how to explain it...more feral..."

The Lycan's Syndicate Leader's tone went quiet. "That's not all that uncommon when something like this happens. It's unfortunate, but it is still manageable, nonetheless." Slightly altering the tone, Calem now asked. "This can't be the only reason why you're giving her up so easily? I mean it wasn't that long ago that you guys were refusing to hear out our offer because of her high risk."

"Originally, yes, I refused to hand her over to anyone else because she was such a high-risk, but now...now she's simply too dangerous and too unpredictable for us to keep her housed here any longer," Braedon answered. His tone growing darker, more assertive than what I would normally hear. "And the only reason I chose your Syndicate over Saylene's or any of the other Syndicates and Sanctuaries in the area is that I believe you guys are better prepared. You have better precautions and procedures to deal with these types of things." The Vampiric took another pause. "I would've made other decisions if she was still coherent."

"The Hellhound still seems coherent to me. It's obvious she can understand what's going on around her." My ears overheard another voice enter the conversation. I was unsure of whose it belonged to, however, I assumed it could only belong to one of the lackeys. "Damn thing nearly ripped its fangs into my arm."

"Well, it's not exactly what I was meaning." Braedon frustratingly interjected. "You will see what I mean once you get her situated."

"Right." I heard the newcomer groan, obviously not knowing about my psychotic dreams and blackout attacks.

"Alright then, I guess we will be returning home." Calem deeply breathed. "Do not worry about sending any of her belongings to the Estate if she indeed returns to her human form, we have plenty of things we can fit her in."

"Fine by me." Braedon ended as the engine of the truck revved, filling the eerie silence of the early morning hours with its heavy roar.

I felt so sick to my stomach about the uncertainty that was now standing before me. Something still seemed very off. I could feel the vehicle change its gears from park to drive, its sudden motion jolting my body around, jerking the collar encompassing my neck up behind my jaw before the chain choker part tightened. Once the vehicle remained at a steady constant, I felt the choker steady, and the leash too loosen the tension. Taking a quick breath of relief, I adjusted my tired body so I could lie directly on top of my stomach. My long overgrown canine nails trying to grip the sheets of coated metal in the bed of the truck. Looking off into the speeding by forest which encased the property I had been calling home for quite some time, I quietly murmured my goodbye to the Manor. Wondering deep down in the darkened abyss of my mind, was this all part of your plan, Shadow? Did you know that this was all going to unfold as it had?

Chapter 2

Cinder

Once the vehicle had come to a complete stop, I rolled my weakened body around to attempt to get itself to stand up on all fours. The pads of my feet could feel the cold floor of the steel bed, they could also sense the weight of three Lycans in their human forms exit the four-door vehicle. Their brute strength shaking the truck conceding the moment the doors were slammed shut. Keeping my nauseous sights locked on the Unnaturals I debated what the proper response to this situation was. I was in a location that I did not recognize, surrounded by people who could overpower me, and completely exhausted both mentally and physically; all those variables meant I had very few decisions. I could either fight them, or try to yet again flee from my problems, or allow them to do what they were planning on until I decided I had enough. Observing the same guy from before crawling into the bed while the Leader and his other Syndicate Member waited at the end of the tailgate, I decided to stay submissive. Submissive with a hint of aggression.

Folding my ears flat against my skull and keeping my head low, I allowed my tail to slightly tuck. Unfortunately, my movements were limited by the short leash still attached to my collar restricting head, but it did not mean I was completely immobilized. However, the limited range was better than none. Continuously watching everything that was unfolding around me I felt the large hands grab at the lead. Vocalizing my argument, I shot out a low growl and quickly flashed my gums at the man just as he had untied the leash from the bolted plate. As soon as the tension was relieved I threw my maybe ninety-pound body around in an attempt to maintain the maximum distance allowed.

"I do not want to be here. I do NOT want to be here!" I pleaded to my ramped thoughts. Sustaining the distance, I continued to roll around the rising panic in my head consuming all of my rational thoughts. The longer I reacted to the events unfolding, the more my thought process continued to run rampant. "I know what I had done was wrong, but I didn't know what else to do. Why couldn't they understand that?! Why can't anyone ever see my side of the story?!" Dragged over to the edge of the tailgate, I had to jump out just as those demanding thoughts began to dictate my actions.

"You know where to take her. Get her situated, then come report back to me." Calem spoke to his lackeys as if I couldn't sufficiently comprehend what they were saying. "And for now, I wouldn't underestimate anything the beast does." The Syndicate's Leader warned per leaving me alone with his two associates.

Looking around the property I saw a pretty modest Colonial Estate which was covered with growing ivy and other plants I could not identify from where I stood. The house where Calem had disappeared off into was the largest on the property, though not the only one. The building the truck had parked nearby must have been the updated garage because I could see several other vehicles parked, and a couple in one of the open doors. My eyes following up the half-circle pebbled driveway then noticed there was another large Colonial Manor beside the House their Leader had wandered off into. I still had not a clue where we were, but I could tell that this place was not smaller than the previous Syndicate, it was also hidden away deeper into the woods. We could still be in New York for all I knew, but my gut felt like we were in a whole other state. Being tugged off into a specific direction I unwillingly fell in line and followed in behind. Still taking in as much little detail as I possibly could. As I examined the surroundings, I noticed an all too familiar figure.

Granted it was just a glimpse of the character, I didn't need a second glance to know exactly who it was. The cold dark Aura I felt wafting off from it, alone told me. It was that cruel being I had not seen since that night. Pulling on the brakes so I could try and get a stronger look at the shadow, I fought against the short leash.

"Come on." The man growled tugging on his end. Creating a tug-of-war game with me. "Stop fighting me."

"Wait-" I barked back trying my hardest to win the game. My paws kicking up a ledge of pebbles along the driveway. Looking back in the direction where I had seen the Shadow, I noticed the being dart behind the larger Manor. I knew I needed to track him down. I needed answers to the ravaging questions I had. Pulling heavily on the short lead, I forced all the remaining energy I had and easily broke free. The leash burning through the skin of the Unnatural's palm. Ignoring the hungering growl in my stomach, and the craving primal instinct I had, I managed to gain quite the distance between me and the Syndicate Members. Kicking up more pebbles I swiftly darted around the back of the larger Manor. "I said wait, Shadow!" I angrily called out to the entity who was gradually drawing me away.

"Cinder get back here!" I could hear the Lycans call out to me, using the name that sweet Jakob had given me. Pushing the haunting image of the Vampiric lying on the melted snow bleeding out, I fixated on getting answers to my questions. I had to catch that thing before I was caught by the Lycans I knew were chasing after me.

Catching the black dancing shadows, I angrily snarled "This was all a part of your damn plan!" Challenging the Shadow, without a care about his 'consequences'. "Was this all a part of your plan?!" I again repeated my tone lower with more uncertainty.

Once the skeleton turned around to face me, his ember dancing eyes locked onto my blue pupils, forcing them to change just like any other conversation the two of us had. Ignoring the harsh burning sensation behind my color-changing eyes, I stared directly into those hatefully calming eyes of his. Once more aggressively interrogating him with the question I desired answers to. "Naïve Reaper. I am surprised she has yet to lose her sanity."

"Answer my questions!" I snapped flashing my fangs and gums at the supernatural being.

"Such fierce vigor." The black cloak wearing Skeletal Shadow hissed back. His tone told me that I was overstepping my boundaries. Quietly strolling up to where I was holding my ground, he resumed, "If you want answers, then my Reaper, finish your assignments." The tone now forcing me to shroud down in a semi-submissive pose whilst he changed subjects. My ears uncontrollably locked in the same position as my tail began tucked further in between my legs, along my thin abdomen. "Just get over what happened to them and do your job."

Looking away from his eyes, breaking my challenge, I furiously growled in my head, "Easier said than done." Not caring that he could still hear my snarky conscience. Taking a small breath, I upsettingly submitted, "Who do I reap now?"

"I will tell you in due time, my smart Reaper." He returned placing his bony skeletal hand on top of my head, "For now just fall in line with these wolves."

"I understand." I conceited, giving him the one response he always sought after making his puzzling demands. Although I despised our traditional line of authority, I was content that I finally got an answer to at least one of my questions. This was indeed all part of his annoying plan to mold me into this perpetual image of his 'Reaper.'

"Good." The being said, simultaneously disappearing into the shadows of the house seconds before the pursuing Lycans rounded the corner. Surprisingly they were both still in their human forms.

Quickly one of them grabbed at my scruff so his other hand could grab for the short foot long lead. My body tensed up, trying to fight the large hand that tightly gripped the dehydrated skin along the back of my neck. Refraining myself from snapping at the fellow Unnaturals, I attempted to 'Fall inline' permitting them to lead me towards wherever it was they were supposed to hole me up in.

Coming around the front of the house, I was led up the concrete steps attached to the foundation of the second house. My starving stomach churned with this sickening feeling as soon as we were beginning to pass through the threshold. I felt like I was about to enter an awfully familiar situation, a situation where I was going to be locked away all over again. Stepping into the extensive foyer, I was instantly greeted with the massive amount of free Unnaturals freely moving around the house. I could see that many of them were free or recently liberated, but unfortunately, I could also see how cramped this place was. Compared to the Manor, this was like walking into a small house meant for a family of four yet holding every possible person it could. Being dragged around the property, I also noticed that a majority of these Unnaturals were Lycans. It wasn't that much of a surprise to me, as just like their human counterparts, Unanturals were naturally drawn towards their natural species. It was instinctual. Making our way past the double staircase, the Lycans now dragged me down a long hallway. Pulled again in another direction, I was forced to go down a set of stairs into what I assumed was the basement. Awkwardly crawling down the stairs in my tired canine form, my eyes caught onto the attentive care of the living space beneath the main floor. The furniture was more modern than the Regal Victorian furniture I had grown accustomed to seeing.

Once all four of my mutated feet had touched down on the laminate-lain floors, I noticed that the frontman was now leading me into an offset room. With my eyes locking onto the off-shoot door, I instantly felt a nasty déjà vu. The unsettling feeling made my fatigued body freeze. I did not want to go in there, but I knew I had very little choice in the matter. Entering this off-brandish room, I noticed that inside was a couple of bald chairs, some wall counters, and cabinets on one side of the room. Slightly craning my head to see what was on the other side, I saw there was the object my instincts had forewarned me to avoid. Sitting at the far end of the room was a large seven-foot-tall black-iron rodded cage nestled inside these four nine-foot-tall walls. Eyeing the cage, I noticed that all of the rodded walls were stationed far enough from the parallel exterior walls as to not damage the room despite the bars themselves telling a long story of its previous captors. There were hundreds of marks created by both claw and fang were embedded deep into the iron.

Applying the breaks again, I burned my paw pads along the wool-rug that laid on the floor as the more powerful Lycan dragged me towards this interior room. I had gone through enough cages; I did not want to be put in another one. Stating my refusal in that universal canine language, I snapped my jowls at the man.

"Stop fighting me!" the man who was holding the leash shouted back to me as he fought to overpower my traumatic block.

"Hold up, Lucious." I heard the voice of the second man clearly order over the sound coming from the hushed voices above us, as well as my cries of refusal. Looking back at the second man, I watched him walk over to the massive six-inch thick wood door conjoining these two rooms. Using some of his supernatural strength, he then forced the door gently shut, locking me inside this undesired room, on this undesired location with two men I did not know.

Chapter 3
Cinder

Groaning my answer still in the canine language, I simultaneously flattened my cropped ears. The action aroused a soft chuckle to erupt from his throat.

"Yeah, that's your name. It's alright if you don't trust us, I wouldn't expect you to, especially as of right now." Lurching my ears forward as my churning gut finally relaxed its unending nerves, I proceeded to avidly listen. "But, we have our reasons why we must do this, Cinder. One, we are completely overfilled with Free Unnaturals, so filled that we have one too many bunking up together. Leaving us with only one place where we could keep you until we get to know you more ourselves, and that place just happens to be in there." The man paused for a quick second so he could point back at the massive cage standing behind him. Although I did hear him quietly mumble, "We would have had an actual room for you if it weren't for that incident which happened three months ago."

Swallowing quickly, I grumbled my deliberation. Flashing my fangs and the tops of my gums, I raised my hackles and squinted my locked gaze. Telling him that I had heard exactly what he had said, and opposed the Unnatural's very words. "It wasn't like I exactly had a choice."

The man neither heard nor understood what I said, but that was okay. He at least understood my growl. "And for two, it's because of the information our Leader received from your Syndicate's Leader that we must keep you in that cage. I know it's something you don't want to do, but regardless of whether or not you want to go in there, you do not have a choice here. This is for the safety of both you and everyone else who lives here. " Opting another sigh, he took a quick breath before advancing. I knew that he was trying to explain what was going to happen to me while I was going to live here at this Syndicate, however where I currently stood, his words were not going to deride my denial. "While you are in there, you will be seeing only a handful of our trusted members as you did back at those blood-drinking hissers' place."

"That includes me, Joseph, and a couple of our other Beta ranks." I overheard Lucious's anguished voice bark, throwing his two cents into the conversation.

"Yeah, you will be seeing a lot of us during the duration of your visit." I heard the second man shot back, his choice in vocabulary telling me just exactly who he was. "Now I have to get you in there..." Joseph painfully sighed. Instinctively I pulled back, putting as much space between the two of us as the leash would allow while he stood up. With the leash completely extended, I began to transcend in a half-circle, doing everything I could to still fight. But compared to his companion, Joseph was a lot stronger. "I know you don't want to, but stop fighting us!" As I was dragged closer and closer towards the massive cage, I refuted the idea of yet again being locked up behind bars. I had already spent over half of my life holed away in one and I did not want to ever go back. Tossing like a fish out of water, I began to jump up and down on hind legs, swinging my front legs up over the lead. I felt I had to do whatever I could to make my voice heard.

Just as I went back up on my hind legs for the fifth time, I felt something tightly wrap around my emaciated abdomen. Thick arms coiling around the upper part of my stomach, and lower part of my chest. Right under my raised front legs, it proceeded to lift me off my feet. Relying on the creeping irrationality, I swung my squared skull with its long muzzle around to chomp down on the other man who had snuck up from behind me.

"Just let go of the leash, Joseph," Lucious growled to his companion whilst vertically carrying me towards the kennel. Stubbornly letting go of the leash, Joseph speedily switched places with the other Lycan. As the more aggressive Unnatural carried me closer towards the cage, I tried to revert to my human form for more leverage, but just like before it was a failed attempt. Passing through the iron rods, I felt my heart drop, the déjà vu scenario flooding back to the front of my deranged mind. Once I felt the arms release their grip from around my chest, I dropped down onto the floor. Unable to land perfectly, my front legs sprained themselves as I harshly fell on top of the hard-laminate tiles. Fastly standing myself back up on all four of my paws, I attempted to dart past the two Lycans, but I was too slow. The gate was slammed shut in my face.

Pacing from one corner of the cage to the other, my long-overgrown nails clapping on the tiles. "You didn't have to do that, Lucious." I witnessed Joseph argue with his fellow kin.

"What was your plan then, drag her in there and sit with her for who knows how long?" Lucious bit back with just as much ferocity.

"Don't challenge me, Lucious! It is none of your damn business what I was going to do."

Rounding around to pace in the other direction now I curiously watched the two argue, reminding me of how much more laid back Mhykal and Jakob were when they argued. The memory desperately made me miss those simple things. I missed the place I just beginning to call 'Home'. Why did I have to leave it in the first place? Pushing those cursed memories I was reliving, I zoned back into the argumentative conversation occurring between the two Lycans.

16

"So, what if I was going to stay in there for a little bit? You have-n't done anything to your comrades like she had." I heard Joseph furiously sigh. "When you could not control yourself, you had this cage to turn to, you didn't have to worry about ever possibly killing someone."

"Whatever-" Lucious gave in.

"Go report to Calem that we got her situated for now." I heard Joseph order the other Lycan. Informing me that he was of higher rank. Pacing from corner to corner, I watched the lower rank unlock the door and open it back up to go tell the Syndicate leader that the job was complete. After Lucious had exited the room, I reduced my pacing down to a slow walk but refused to take my eyes off Joseph. I could see in his gaze that he was trying to pull apart the rumors surrounding me. Deeply trying to understand more of who I was. Exhaling another sigh, he steadily strolled closer to the corner I had conformed to before he again slumped down to my eye level. Halt-ing my pacing, I parked my haunches down on the cold floor. Once the two of us had situated ourselves, I quietly awaited Joseph's calm-ing voice to break the minuscule silence. "I am sorry about that."

Flashing my fangs, I rolled right on by the apology. I wasn't in the mood for apologies. Making a swift roll of my eyes, I awaited the next statement.

Softly chuckling, Joseph continued, "Let me at least take that lead off, please Cinder."

Hearing my given name spoken by someone I had just met made my heart drop. Painfully causing me to reminisce the memory, I innocently pushed my head against the rods. Depressingly skipping through the painful memories of betrayal, I felt the soft-skinned hand reach in through the rods and press against the top of my skull. His palm resting on my forehead. Pressing my head further into the palm of Joseph's hand, I felt my eyes start to water, the tears starting to stream down my cheeks and muzzle.

"It hurts, doesn't it? The memories?" I could hear him very softly ask. His hand remaining steadily fixed in its position. "It was something you did not want to do." There was just something about his presence that made me feel slightly more comfortable. Acknowledging his statement, I felt a whimper escape from my throat. My heart heavily hung above my hungry upset stomach. "Yeah, it hurts." Joseph continued to calmly express. Noticing his hand reaching towards my collar, I unsteadily pulled away from his soothing hand. I knew what he was doing yet I had no control over my own body. Once more it was acting on its own. "It's alright, I am just going to unhook the leash." Staying put in the same spot, I allowed him to use his free hand to unhook the leash's clasp from my blue nylon choker's keyring. "See, that's all I was doing." He returned as he cautiously removed the second hand from beyond the bars. Pushing my large head into the palm of his hand again, I returned to desiring all of his comfort, which he thankfully granted for a few more minutes of silence.

Chapter 4
Cinder

Upon waking up, I felt more hands running through my still dry bloody fur coat. Shaking up to my aching feet, I tossed myself around the small man-sized cage to attempt to attack whomever it was swiping their hands down my back through the black rods. As my sights caught onto the figures moving around the other side of the bars, I noticed the familiar figures of the two Lycans, Lucious, and Joseph. Adjusting my tired eyes to focus on the one I did not recognize; I quickly captured this male's 'human' characteristics, every single detail.

This man was around six feet tall, maybe six foot two. A well worked-for toned body obviously hid under the modern casual athletic wear he was wearing. Scanning my eyes up towards this man's facial expression to figure out his true identity. The unusual scented man with a soft-faded square face, a masculine nose, and unusual emerald green eyes which almost radiated under the shining light of the rising sun's rays poking its heads through the small high-rise windows part of the basement's Colonial-brick foundation. Those green eyes were hinting at a very familiar side of comfort I had felt from somewhere before, yet for the life of me, I could not remember. Scanning around the open skinned parts of his loose muscle tank shirt, I noticed many small healing scars were resting along his upper arms and shoulders. While I did wonder where the scars had come from, my curiosity was more centered on what was this modelic man with an unusual scent was doing here? Who exactly was he? I knew I had seen his face all over several magazines, and posters hanging in Valyerie's room, but I still had not a clue as to who he was? And all that made me wonder what did he want with me?

Paying closer attention to the three men who were standing on the outside of the cage, I lied back down on the hard laminate floor I had spent the night on. Huffing a sigh, I rolled my body back towards the bars, my black fur pushing in between the bars. Still unable to get comfortable, I crawled myself a little bit forward, sprawling out a tad more. When none of it worked, I flipped sides and went back to avidly watching the men who too were watching me.

"Still uncomfortable, huh?" I heard the unknown man mock. The words just smoothly running off his tongue as he spoke in this soothing yet deep voice. "Oh well."

"Just take it slow and easy." I heard Joseph casually command. Recalling the obvious from last night's events before my fatigued body had crashed on itself. "The memories are traumatizing her more than what had happened to her yesterday."

"Is she still coherent?" The man then casually demanded as he abruptly changed the subject on the Lycans.

"From what I saw, yes." Joseph returned, his amber gaze strongly fixated on my bright blue stare. The staredown lasted only for a few seconds before I passively turned away.

Turning my gaze back over to the new male character who I had suspected was an Unnatural, I now locked my gaze with his supernatural green glare. "Can she answer questions?"

"For the most part, yes."

"Most part?"

Shrugging his shoulders, Joseph heaved another sigh while the lower-ranked Lycan huffed a very audible growl. "Lucious, why don't you go see if Nycola is done preparing her breakfast, while I discuss what needs to be done here."

"Whatever, I don't see why we need to devote so much of our time to her. I don't see what Calem, or Braeden, or what you even see in that Hellhound that makes her so damn special." Lucious responded with a similarly savage snarl. Expressing not only his transforming fangs but his undeniable hatred for me.

"Go now." I noticeably saw the other bi-pedal wolf shifter coldly snap at the lower rank. Once more clarifying the difference in their rank, and their Specieal Powers while my stomach quietly savagely cried its hunger out to the world.

Once Lucious had left the room, slamming the thick door shut behind him, I lied my head down on the cold floor relaxing some of my nerves from the heavy tension. "I apologize for that Mr. Gale."

"No. It's alright. Irritating, but alright." This unknown man now called Mr. Gale gently returned. "So, she can understand and answer questions?"

"Yes. It's not in the English Language, but it is in a universal nod or cry. I'm sure you will be able to understand her just as much as she does you." A small pause occurred while the Unnatural I, unfortunately, had let in on my painful mindset started slowly strolling up towards where I lied. Lifting my head to stare at him, I followed his smooth-masculine hand slip past the bars. Allowing it to enter inside the cage again, I allowed it to rub along my square-head and pull against the top of ears. Reminding me of the same way that Jakob had often comforted me. Whining out my frustratingly painful reminiscent memories, I proceeded with forcing myself to overhear the subject at hand. "Just take it slow."

"Alright-"

"I will leave you to do what Calem brought you here for," Joseph stated with a clear and defined tone to the still unfamiliar gazing green-eyed man. Whining again the painful deliberation, I tried to refuse being left alone with this strange and untrustworthy man: though I barely knew Joseph either, I at least was more comfortable around him. "It's alright, Mr. Gale is a trustworthy individual. Despite not working in any local Syndicate, he has helped us out in more ways than one. He's never worked in any Institute either. All he needs to do is have a simple conversation with you."

"Really?" I sarcastically inquired to myself. "A 'simple' conversation? Nothing is ever just a simple conversation."

Removing his hand from my black fur, I observed the Lycan leave me alone in the room with this mysterious Species of Unnatural who I now knew went by the surname, Mr. Gale. Once the door had shut itself off from the adjoining world, I proceeded to fixate all of my waning focus on this male who was sauntering towards the cage.

Stopping in front of the barred wall, he sat on the nearby wooden coffee table. "Now, if you can truly understand me Cinder, allow me to tell you what is about to occur while you stay here."

"While I stay here? What is about to happen?" I questioned. Interested in these so-called possible events that were to unfold during my stay, I sat myself up on the floor and turned myself around to face eye to eye with this unclassified Unnatural.

"So, you do understand what I am saying? That's good. Alright then, Calem asked me to help him out on a few things. While all those tasks do revolve around you, regrettably said they are not for your benefit." The man said his smooth voice going cold. His eyes darkening while he rested his chin in his left hand with its corresponding elbow resting on his knee in this expressionlessly bored position. Receiving confusing signals from this man, I now stood myself up to represent my own altering behavior. Raising my hackles and swishing my tail from side to side, I vocalized both my confusion and apprehension strictly based on his emotional posturing. "You obviously don't like what I am here for, nor will you like the task, that of which I can assure you, Cinder." Rolling my eyes at him, I huffed another low bark making the man laugh. "But be happy that in the least I am telling you this. I had to lie to those Lycans just to get some privacy for this conversation."

Flattening my ears as I saw another uninvited character involve itself in the darkening, one-sided conversation Mr. Gale was having with me. Flashing my fangs under my curling lips, I mentally interrogated the being, "Now, what do you want?"

Chapter 5
Cinder

Locking nearly my entire focus on the Shadow being, I again questioned it, "What do you want?" Getting no answer right away, I reeled back my aggressive interrogation before asking the question for the third time. "What are you here for?"

My ears that were sensitively attuned to his hidden presence capable of understanding his dialogue from the otherworld unfortunately also caught onto the previous speaker, making this a two-subject conversation. Mr. Gale seemed to endlessly ramble on about something. My hearing tried to drown him out but was unsuccessful in the endeavor, so I had to keep listening to this newly acquainted man speak until the Shadow had finally decided to speak up. "Calem ordered me to keep this on the down-low, but being the kind of acquaintance I am, I hope you can learn to trust. I believe you have a right to know this." With the sentence being on repeat, I shook my head while my sights remained locked on the being who was hiding behind the casually sitting man. "I know trust is the last thing you are expecting to build up-"

"You would have to be right about that. Trust is the last thing I have on my mind as of right now." I thought to myself before savagely growling out in the direction of the Shadow, "I want an answer."

"Listen to the man first, and then after he leaves, we will discuss what happens next, my still little Reaper." I heard the Shadow sternly tell as he traveled through the Unnatural and towards the cage. Stopping in front of me, his thick black silhouette casting out Mr. Gale's figure before he put his skeletal hand through the bars and finally on its resting place on top of my boxed-shaped skull. The boney fingers rubbing over the top of my short black hairs. It was an unwelcome feeling, yet also the only recognizable comfort I had here.

"Fine-" I mumbled, "I understand." The Shadow removing his hand from my canine transformed head, then swept off to the side of the cage allowing me to revert my entire focus to this man. While tentatively observing this man, I wondered in my head, "What is so 'special' about him?"

Ignoring the mumbling for a little while, I shifted back to the conversation we were having prior to the respawn of the Shadow. "Calem is after your 'Blood Trait'. Why? I do not know. After a few weeks, I will be back to start drawing your blood."

"Why my blood?" I questioned my eyes hastily averting their gaze back over to the Shadow, hoping for an answer. Forgetting that the task at hand was to wait until Mr. Gale was done talking. With the exhale of another sigh, I proceeded to wander in my mind, "What made my blood so special?"

Flattening my ears, I returned to painfully listening to this man who now was standing himself back up. Coming off the coffee table, I heard him resume, "I know you have an abrupt habit of making your point heard, but let me tell you this regardless of what your point is, I am here to tell you that I have a job to do." Observing this blonde-haired man saunter up to the front of the cage, Mr. Gale

25

knelt before me, his eye level lowering to match mine. "Now onto the conversation that they believe you and I are having." Flattening my cropped ears, slanting my blue interchanging orange eyes, and flashing my teeth at this man, I refuted the next part of this 'conversation/interrogation'. "Although, I can see you have had enough of me-" Mr. Gale sighed standing back up to stretch his back just as the temperamental Lycan, Lucious, and the soft-hearted assertive Lycan, Joseph both returned. My nose easily caught a waft of something that smelled like food drafting off the Auras of both men. Alerting my ravenous stomach to the hidden sustenance, I presumed they were carrying on a dinner plate.

"Did you get what you wanted, Mr. Gale?" Joseph casually probed as his lower-ranked associate brought forth the delightfully smelling dish. I could smell a strong stench of meat and that was enough to override any sense of rationale I was using. Every inch of my canine instincts was demanding him to hurry up, demanding me to devour the high-protein content as fast as I could, so I could survive my next ordeal.

"Well as much as she would tell me." This still very unusually scented human sighed. I felt like there was a lot he was hiding from not only me but the Lycans as well. Shoving off those creeping thoughts, I further indulged Mr. Gale as he spoke to the two slightly taller Lycans. "I will be back in a few days so I can do those 'tests' Calem asked me to prior to the blood draw."

"Okay, we will see you then." Joseph sighed while he simultaneously hinted towards his companion to bring forth the plate.

"You can feed that mongrel." Lucious upsettingly professed to the group before he stormed out of the room.

"What's his problem?" Mr. Gale inquired the higher up a second after the thick door was slammed shut. "Why does he dislike her?"

"Personally, I don't know why. Though it could quite potentially be because you are looking at the murderer of his older brother."

"How can you be so sure she's the murderer?"

"Who was it?" I thought, hastily looking back at the Shadow, wishing he would stir some memory of some poor Unnatural or some poor human I had 'Reaped'. Of course, the entity was of no use. Glancing back to Mr. Gale and Joseph, I anxiously awaited the answer to awaken something while my poor starving stomach continued to savagely demand it be fed.

"A while back we had received a call from Braeden about an incident revolving around his brother. Apparently, when one of his Vampirics had mind-shifted with Cinder, the member had witnessed her kill Lucious's brother." Joseph answered, sternly staring down at me with that supernatural amber gaze. The hard-cold gaze starting to make me feel on edge, almost as if I needed to prepare myself for a fight.

Still trying to wrap my exhausted mind around the details, I began to read around the lines, retracing what physical memories I had involving those exact details. Luckily it did not take long until I finally figured out who this mysterious brother was. With my mind belatedly wrapping around the digesting material, I bitterly struggled with the facing doubt, "That guy deserved it. He almost killed Valeryie. Screw being told to kill him ahead of time, he deserved everything that had happened to him."

"So that Syndicate leader ratted out someone who he was supposed to protect?"

"Unfortunately, he did," Joseph stated. "But it wasn't that moment that brought her to us. There was another incident that happened, and it was then that we were granted custody." The Lycan momentarily halted, to inform Mr. Gale that his Syndicate had tried multiple times before that one incident to be granted custody over me. Eventually, he came back around the point. "Despite Calem having expelled Logan for obvious reasons, he was still a member here."

Joseph again paused, his hard glare suddenly softening, turning almost empathetic. "Although…" Joseph continued, finally beginning to carry the plateful of semi-cooked food.

As he approached the cage, I uncontrollably began to lose myself, ecstatic to finally eat. Shooting up to all fours, I began to eagerly pace the front wall feeling those canine instincts of mine consume me. The hunger overpassing my hard depression. Hunting every move the Lycan made, I watched Joseph place the plate on the floor and gently skid it beneath a gap in the bars. Intently eyeing the food, I noticed it was a partially cooked venison, a meal I once was accustomed to eating back during my last institutionalization in that awful Government-funded base. I wasn't thrilled to eat it, but I was overjoyed to eat something. Offering space for the food, I held back my biting urge to eat until his fingers were well out of my fangs' range. Eagerly diving in, I lost sights of the men, however proceeding to eavesdrop in on their conversation.

"Although-?" Mr. Gale questioned, urging the Lycan to finish his statement.

"I would not blame Cinder for what happened. Braeden told us that she acted in order to save the younger sister of a Vixen whom she had befriended at the Syndicate. Cinder is a good-person. If anything, I am sure she too has her reasons for the event that had unfurled a couple of months ago-" I heard Joseph sigh. As my mouth was overwhelmed with all the blood and juices the finely cut piece of meat offered, the Lycan continued, "I know that Hellhoundism has its sides of unconscious primal instincts, and all that...but I cannot imagine her doing what she did without a fluent reason."

Chapter 6
Cinder

"Now what was it that you needed to discuss with me?" I interrogated the empty room the second I had been left alone. Or supposedly alone. Looking straight ahead, my eyes were locked on the black mass standing about a foot away from the bars of this black steel cage. "What was so important that I had to wait until after he had finished talking?" I probed, standing on all four of my paws with my head raised high to assert my dominance.

"I desired your full attention for this, my Reaper. That is why." The Shadow coldly stated with an unusual softness this time ringing in his voice.

"I was already planning on giving you my full attention." I quietly snarled back, my tail twisting back and forth. "It was just easier for you to wait, so you could slowly torture me."

Apparently, my ill-tempered observation had made him lightly chuckle. Eventually, returning to his normal dark and gloomy demeanor a few moments later. "Say what you wish, my little Reaper. Whatever makes it easier for you to understand your purpose."

"What is it anyway? My purpose?" I hastily interrogated. "I've had that question for years running rampant inside my head, and each time I have wondered the answer, you only ever tell me 'in due time.' Well, I think seventeen years is long enough."

"Do your job." The Shadow growled back, the softness in his dark voice quickly snapping back to the masculine coldness it frequently held. The same cynical tone that sent chills down my spine and made my body freeze completely over. Staying completely paralyzed with uncertainty. "Your purpose is to do your job."

My ears tightly fell flat against the back of my skull as the statement flew out of the moving gap where his mouth was supposed to be. Fearfully digesting the order, he had just demanded of me, I aimlessly wandered around the endless abyss of my mind. Coming to an understanding that in that harsh exclamation was the answer. "MY ONLY PURPOSE WAS TO REAP?!"

"Now you are getting it, my intelligent Reaper."

"THAT WAS MY ONLY PURPOSE!" I furiously snapped.

"Onto your assignment..." the Shadow attempted to move on. But I was unwilling to submit so easily. I wanted a better answer than the one he had given me. Captivated by his dancing orange ember eyes shift into a dark amber red, I felt body become overrun with a sudden incense of pain flowing throughout my dying nerves. Focusing on his movements, I noticed the Shadow raise his left arm before extending it out in front of his cloak-wearing skeletal body and form a tightly wound fist. I didn't understand what was happening, but I could feel my back begin to savagely burn. The cross-shaped scar embedding itself further into my flesh. Flinching from the pain, I instantly came out of the trance his vague answer had left me in. Savagely crying out in agonizing pain, I listened to the being's dark voice ring inside my outer eardrum. "Now that I have my Reaper's attention once more, your next assignment."

"Not yet-" I argued. Unwilling to roll over just yet, I pushed through the incapacitating pain. Ignoring my weak and shaky legs, my lungs having difficulty breathing, and the block he had put on my intelligent rationality, I bared my fangs back at my 'Master.' Flashing him the dehydrated pink gums and white fangs I kept hidden beneath my curled lips, I locked my mimicking color-changing fiery gaze on the being. "I want my answers first!"

"NO!"

"NO ANSWER MY QUESTIONS!" I snapped. "You told me that if I broke away from them that my questions would be answered-"

The last bit of strength I had was rapidly drained out of me, forcing my body to tiredly collapse onto the laminate floor. Forcing my body to once more regain a solid footing, I stood myself back up. Completely upright once more, I was suddenly thrown back. My burning back pressing against the extremely frigid bars in the back of the cage. Staring straight ahead, I saw the Shadow standing directly in front of me. His skeletal hand tightly wrapped around the bottom of my neck. The boney fingers steadily cutting off my ability to breathe. As I struggled to breathe, I barely heard the harsh words he was curing into my throbbing ears. Just as my vision began to grow spotty, and I was about to pass out from lack of oxygen, I was released. My body was free. Crashing on to the floor, I hurriedly worked to breathe. Trying to soothe my sore throat, I reignited the staredown between some excruciating coughs.

"I ha-have no prob-problems with 'reaping'" I cried as the terrible burning sensation in my scar became manageable. "Just pl-please answer-answer my questions. That-that's all-all I want."

The Shadow took a heavy exhale before his complete skeletal frame bent down beside me. His intimidating frame standing directly over my position on the floor. "Fine. I will answer a couple of your questions, Reaper. However, the rest will have to wait until you have done your job. Do you understand me?" Feeling his frozen fingers push under my lower jaw, I observed my level of sight begin to lift a few inches.

Blinking a couple of times to wash the tears free from the filling ducts, I could feel the burning orange fade. Swallowing, I hoarsely returned, "Ye-yes I understand."

"Good-" he growled, releasing my lower muzzle allowing it to fall back to its resting place. Free once more, I rustled my feet out from beneath me and tried to stand back up. "You won't be able to actively move for a few hours, I nullified a few of the nerves in your legs and paws."

"I see that." I huffed, succeeding my third failed attempt. Adjusting myself on the floor to an upright lying position, I glanced back up at the Shadow with a much softer approach, content that we had at least come to some sort of deal. I knew I couldn't win a fight against him no matter the subject, but I at least had a right to challenge. If I was to be his 'Reaper' and fulfill my 'purpose' then it was my right to do just that. I could better do my job if I knew more.

"Now, Reaper, what questions do you have for your 'God'-" he snared with a creepy lipless smile. Using an accurate term for the type of relationship we had. However, upon hearing the word, I couldn't but compare it to the stories Peylith often told regarding the relationship he had with his 'God' Anubis. It was clear to me that the relationship we had was not the same and would never be on that level.

"Why me? Why- choose-choose me?" I asked in between painful pants. Receiving no response, I took the hint and moved on to another question I had scouring through my head. Taking a calming breath, I relaxed "Was this all part of your plan?"

"You could say that." The being said surprisingly in an unusual narration. The text was different, untraditional. "Now onto your next target, who is unsurprisingly sanctioned here. I guess one would say he is unusually scared of what he knows is coming."

"Death?" I asked, following up with the same subject.

"Most people are afraid of Death, especially when their Death is supposed to be painful."

"Why is that?" I asked. "What turns them into an assignment, a task for a Hellhound like me to deal with?"

"The laws of life and death have existed for as long as life itself. And Immortals are a counted variable." The Shadow simply told whilst he exhaled a long sigh. "Enough questions for now. Back to the assignment at hand, Reaper."

"Fine-" I growled. "Who is it?"

"The Leader of this Syndicate, Calem."

"What for?" I questioned baffled. "I mean, yeah, the Lycan came across as a shady person, wanting my blood and all, on top of locking me away in this cage, but he seemed also to be a decent man. Well at least in the eyes of the Lycans he did. So, why was he next on the list?" I proceeded to imagine inside my deranging head.

"You will figure it out in due time, my naïve, little Reaper." The Shadow whispered into my ear like he typically did just before vanishing into the emptying mass particles of the surrounding shadows.

Chapter 7
Cinder

Alone again in the offset room lying under the base foundation of the Colonial house, I laid my head over my paws. Surveying the thick door impatiently waiting for the next person to enter the room and hopefully appease my social desires, I wondered to my deranging mind, "How was I supposed to 'reap' my target when I was stuck behind bars and stuck under an excessive watch?" It was useless to devise such plans right now. I still knew too little about the man and this place. There were too many possibilities to consider, and even if I could've been granted the perfect opportunity, I knew it would just envelop into yet another failure. Frustratingly yawning, I concluded it was time for a break and leaned over onto my right side. Falling over into a full lie so I could stretch out my still numb legs, I continued to eye that bolted door.

After a while of blankly staring at the door, I finally heard the handle jiggle. Paying closer attention to the doorway as it commenced to swing open, I impatiently anticipated the visitor who I knew was standing on the other side. Electing to not use my gifted nose in hope of a surprise, I was greeted with crushing defeat. The person who was walking through the tall archway was the same old, same old Joseph. Flicking on the lights to see, the tall Lycan nonchalantly called out, "What are you doing back there, Cinder?" Obviously noticing that I was resting in the back of the cage instead of the front left corner I fancied. Responding with a low moan, I aimlessly patrolled the man who was now casually wearing some faded blue sweatpants and a form-fitted off-white long-sleeve shirt stroll towards the black rodded cage. "Well, whatever the reason, it does make it a bit easier to retrieve the plate." He callously joked. "Because if you were up here, I would've had to sneak in somehow."

"Mmm-sure," I growled. "I have no grudge against you," I growled, reflecting aloud in the still versed canine-language. Which, I had surprisingly learned this specific species of canine-shifters could not comprehend. "Besides it's not like I could move anyways."

Joseph opened the cage's door to reach for the licked-clean porcelain gold-trimmed plate that was right beyond the threshold suddenly stopped. Catching a glimpse of that supernatural glow in his darkened gaze intensely staring back at me, I overheard him ponder aloud, "Cinder, are you okay?"

"Exhausted-" I ironically complained, completely understand that it was impossible for them to understand a lick of what I was saying.

Placing the plate back down on the floor, the Unnatural who appeared to be maybe in his mid-thirties now wandered towards me. Unsure of his next move, I began to count the steps it took to get from the gate to the location where I laid. After almost twenty steps, he finally reached my paralyzed frame, where he again bent down in front of me. Pressing his hand on top of my head the same way he did yesterday, Joseph proceeded to wonder. "You aren't just coldly lying here, are you?" Pushing my forehead back against the palm of his hand, I replied with a deep whine. "No, huh? Are you in any pain? If so, we could give you something for the pain-"

"NO-" I growled, fiercely flashing my fangs. "I do not want to be given any drugs-"

"Alright, alright..." Joseph acknowledged. Maintaining a front of no fear, the Lycan kept his hand in the same position, his fingers gently caressing my ear. I could hear it in his voice, he was not afraid of me, but I knew it was only temporary. Everyone became afraid of me at some point in time. "We won't give you anything man-made, but you should still get something for the pain. Now, where does it hurt?"

"You catch on much faster than everyone else," I smirked, ramming my head against his palm to shove it back. Swallowing some of the formed saliva residing inside my mouth, I felt the soft-skinned hand slide down my shoulders. Gliding towards the raised scar resting over the top of my spine. Showing my teeth again, I cried out, "STOP-" The words flew right out of my mouth. This time in direct English, shocking both of us.

Rapidly removing his hand, he shot upward and took a few steps back. A second later, Joseph hastily questioned, "You-you just talked-"

Taking another swallow, I clarified my previous response, "I don't want you to touch my back-"

The sentence took him another few seconds to comprehend before he retorted a simple 'okay', his hand gliding over the top of my head.

"My back hurts-" I repeated, trying so hard to not cry at hearing my soft voice speak once again in its primary tongue. It had been so long since I had heard myself.

"Okay, well we can get you some herbal remedies for it-"

Quickly interrupting him, I again rebutted "No! I do not want any form of drugs...It will go away, just give it time."

"Okay, Cinder-" he continued, thankfully understanding my desires. Once more rubbing my squared skull, the Lycan stood himself back up and wandered back towards the gate. "I will come back in a few hours with your dinner." Joseph then foreshadowed as he leaned over to pick up the plate.

Nodding my head, I softly acknowledged. It seemed that during my stay here I was to receive two meals and that during my lock up, I was going to see more and more of this ranked Syndicate member. Just before Joseph had made it out of the cage, I abruptly asked, "Why did Braeden give me up?"

Apparently speaking the questionable thought aloud, I noticed that the Lycan halted in the doorway of the cage. With my world turned on its side, I surveyed the Lycan turn his head slightly off to the left as if to look over that corresponding shoulder before replying, "I can't say why. It doesn't make sense to me either, and Calem has yet to tell us-"

"Oh-" I mumbled, looking away from his accosted gaze.

"You can't change what has happened- It sucks, but you can't change it either way." Joseph continued to speak while he returned to his prior obligation. The way he spoke, it seemed to me that he too, at one point in time had done something similar. Altering the subject, he repeated, "I will be back in a couple of hours with your dinner, hopefully then we can have an actual conversation." Looking back up at the Lycan, I observed him finish closing and locking the gate to the cage. Focusing on his facial features, I noticed under the bright fluorescent lighting Joseph had a soft smile on his face. A very familiar expression that I had felt I had seen prior. The expression waved off a calming aura I had not felt since the weeks before the break-away incident. Loosely carrying the plate in his right hand, I proceeded to tentatively eye Joseph take his leave.

Once the door had shut, I wondered to myself, "Why did I regain my voice, now of all times?" Staring into the bleakness of the horribly arranged contemporary furniture and dusty countertops beyond the bars of my prison, I watched the dust particles which were dancing in the lights of the sun shafts poking through the high-rise windows of the foundation. "A conversation with a third-partisan may help me come up with ideas to complete my recently given 'Reaping' assignment." I quietly pondered to my still contemplating mind. "Although-" I sighed as I started to regain the feeling in my front paws, "Where am I supposed to go after that?"

Chapter 8
Cinder

Joseph did indeed return a few hours later carrying a similar plate that this time smelled of a different food source. My nose alerted me to the nutritional scent of chicken, seasoned with maybe some thyme, or some rosemary, I couldn't determine. As he walked inside the room and towards the cage, I stood myself up. My slightly numb feet eager to walk the rest of my body towards the gate in excitement for another meal.

"I see you are feeling better-" I heard the Lycan joke while he gently pushed the food under the cage.

Ignoring him, I quickly sparked my sly snarl before commencing to devour the food. My taste buds suspended with each bite I savored. The drool uncontrollably frothing and fleeing out of the corners of my mouth by my third swallow.

"I know it isn't much right now, but with having to feed as many people as we do, we have to ration what little food there is."

Swallowing my mouthful, I used my recently regained ability to speak, "It's fine."

"You have a very feminine voice for someone who's a Hell-hound." The man realized while I hurriedly devoured my meal. Rolling my blue eyes, I simply groaned a low growl after swallowing another mouthful. Standing over my meal, I finished up the large portions and began to lick the plate pristine. A bad habit I had picked up since being starved many times over in this 'form' of mine. "Done-?"

"Yes. Thank you." I sighed, exhaling a deep breath. Using my muzzle, I attempted to happily push it back under the edge of the gate.

"You didn't have to-" Joseph politely excused.

"I may not be able to transform back to my human form yet, but at least I can still act civilized." I returned with an 'obedient' sit to tease my civility. Hoping that he was going to stick to his previous promise and the two of us could have a decent conversation.

Picking up the plate the Unnatural man with mid-length brown hair gently placed it down on the coffee table and returned to standing in front of the black-steel rodded cage. "If I may ask, why can't you return to your human form?"

"I don't know" I sighed, giving my best guess. "I haven't been able to revert to that form for a while now."

"Since that night?"

"Seems about right."

"You don't remember all of it, do you?"

Holding back the pain of the memories, I squinted my eyes together and grimaced as I remembered wrapping my fangs around the neck of the man who had only minutes earlier confessed his affliction to me. Eventually finding the energy and confidence to answer his third question, I muttered, "Not all of it. I remember running into a field of lavenders while trying to outrun Peylith, but after that, it's all hazy."

"Either someone blocked the memories, or your mind has sub-consciously locked it away."

"You talk as if you have gone through something similar," I smirked, glancing back at the Lycan, locking our gazes. Observing the usually wolfen amber gaze soften before shying away, I quickly asked for forgiveness, "I didn't mean to say it like that-"

"No, I asked you the same thing, so it's only natural for you to question me in return." He coughed, trying to pull on a fake smile as he sat down on the Laminate floor. "I had indeed gone through something familiar at one point in time." Joseph hesitated, the fake-ness falling through. "I was around your age when I too had lost control over my own 'cursed' powers." Avidly surveying the Lycan's mannerism while he stared deep into the palm of his hand, I listened to Joseph tell his tale. "My wife and I were being chased down by Hunters. The humans were hunting us down to catch my wife's Blood Trait."

"Blood Trait?" I asked, not wanting to interrupt his story, but I was curious. I had heard the term before, back at the Federal facility, but nobody had ever defined it for me. It had to be self-explanatory right?

"It's a trait that runs through the host's bloodstream, creating usually high-healing capabilities and unique characteristics." Joseph clarified.

"What was your wife's trait?" I further probed, hoping my in-quisitiveness wasn't overstepping its boundaries.

"Her blood trait had something to do with altering the presence of one's perception. It only took a single drop to come in contact with the skin of another for it to activate." The Unnatural spoke, his tone going dark before returning to the painfully depressing soft voice. "She refused to flee to a Syndicate for the protection of their Sanction, so we continued to run from place to place, and state to state. Eventually, we were surrounded, and instead of conceding our surrender, my wife came up with this crazy antic to ensure that neither one of us would have to pray on having the Rebels to come save us as normal Unnaturals do. Cutting her wrist with a piece of broken glass, she distressingly triggered my still yet to be controlled primal wolf instincts, forcing me to change into a full wolf. From there she wiped her bloody fingers down my skull while I fought to not harm her and keep the Hunters at bay. The blood quickly soaked its way through my red-fur and into my skin- and then-" Joseph once more hesitated. Pausing for a long moment, I could see it in his eyes, the questioning of 'Why he was even telling me this?'

Standing myself up, I started to slowly walk towards the barred wall that separated us from complete interaction. Pushing my head against the bars, I softly whined a low cry. My voice acting as a trigger to bring him back from that dark corner of his mind I knew was venturing off into. Feeling the same extended hand get pushed back into my head, the palm forming along my rounded squared fur-covered skull.

"You remind me of her, in SO many ways. In so, so many ways." I heard him cry, breaking down in front of me. The wall coming crashing down. Hearing him breathe in a heavy sigh, I waited for him to continue, "She didn't want to die, but she ordered me to kill her under the oath of her Blood Trait. I killed my wife because I was forced to-"

"That's why you joined the Syndicate?"

"When I regained complete consciousness, I was at the door of this Syndicate, standing in the pouring rain, still in my complete wolf form." He sighed. "But even twenty years later, I still don't remember all of the details that happened that night, but regardless of what I couldn't recall I knew what I did was still horrible. I knew I didn't want to do it, and I knew I had no control over what I did." Pushing my head further into the palm of his soft-masculine hand, I could feel the coldness of his soul that was aching for his life to be over, so he could return to his wife. The Aura he was giving off also told me that he had a job to do, like the job that Yalu had told me she had to do. Using my own 'body-heat', I attempted to try to warm his freezing soul. "Cinder-"

Hearing my name get said in that same manner that Jakob had called out to me, I quickly jumped back. The hackles on my neck and back raised as high as it could go. My tail slowly tucking its way between my legs and under my lower abdomen. My 'Fire' abilities no longer in contact with his skin to attempt to warm his dark and cold mind. Shaking in anxiety, I could hear my heart rapidly beat out of fear.

"Woah, easy." The Lycan quickly returned, trying to calm my raised nerves. "I didn't mean to scare you-"

Trying to calm my heart, I panted back at him with a low snarl, flashing the edges of my long fangs. "It wasn't that you scared me, it was that you speak and comfort me in the same way he did, the exact same way Jakob did. And-" I paused. "I don't want to hurt anyone like how I hurt him-"

"Oh-" he said, his calming, low, soft voice returning. "Well, we will do what we can to-"

"NO!" I snapped, chomping my jaws together, and flattening my cropped ears. "You don't get it! No matter what anyone has ever done to attempt to stop me from harming anyone, it never works! IT HAS ALWAYS FAILED!"

"So, what are you saying? Have you done this before? Have you harmed people like what happened at the Vampiric Syndicate?"

Looking away from his interrogating gaze, I hastily rambled, "I was sixteen when I killed my first person. The first person I killed was a nurse who took such good care of me. A person who acted more like a mother to me than my biological mother ever did. I remember it so vividly even now that it horrifies me, and yet, I remember not having the ability to stop myself from it. Then it happened again a few months ago. And I still don't know their conditions, and it-"

"It hurts. It pains you the more people bring it up, the more-"

"I am so afraid to sleep now. I am so afraid of hurting more people that attempt to help me." I cried, turning my head towards my chest to face the ground.

"Cinder- it's okay." Joseph tried to comfort me, using the same words that everyone else has, using the same words I had grown so numb to.

"Stop saying that! I am a Hellhound! And this is what happens to us! We destroy any path of peace just as soon as we pave it-"

"What are you talking about?"

"Just leave me alone, before I do something to you too- please-" I cried, feeling that psychotic itch racing towards the surface. "Please, Joseph..."

Chapter 9
Cinder

"Alright just hold still now-" Lucious growled aloud, his words directed at me while his large tightly wound arm was wrapped around my neck. I wasn't trying to fight, I really wasn't, and yet my body was acting on its own impulses. I knew what their plans were for today, but I still couldn't help myself. I had gone stiff; my legs were as straight as a board, holding firm on the unusually familiar behavior that these Syndicate Members were portraying. "Just hold still-" the Lycan again fiercely shouted into my ears.

"It's involuntary movements." I finally heard a second voice pike in from behind me. "The mongrel cannot help it. The same would happen if you were stuck in your full canine transformation and someone came up behind you, sat over the top of you to hold you still while we prepare to do this 'draw'." The voice was low yet calm, passive, and yet also orderly. The distinguished accent, however, quickly gave away who this unknown character was, Calem. While the British Lycan came into my line of sight wearing that old-time European suit, I avidly listened to him continuing to talk; "I know it's been moved up a bit sooner than expected, but according to Mr. Gale, he has a few other jobs lined up which unfortunately are taking his primary concern, so-" The werewolf in his human form paused, turning around to face where his subordinate was holding me stationary out in the middle of this unusually barren room. My eyes started to burn as I focused on this Unnatural. "So, we had to move ahead with the blood draw that I'm sure he had foretold you was coming, young Hellhound."

"What is wrong with your body?" I thought, timidly confused in my head. My burning eyes were seeing the wrinkled wolfish face of his apparent Lycanized form. The fur was gone, nothing but dried up dark skin. His lips were so sunk in and malnourished I could make out his canine teeth and exactly where they sat underneath the moving jowls. The wolf's ears were gone, almost as if they were torn from his head. "What am I seeing?" I further inquired, debating if my poor sanity was starting to wane all over again. "I know I had just seen the Unnatural in his human form a minute prior, and he had not changed while he was talking, or else his lackey's behaviors would have become more submissive. Key pack mentality."

Feeling a hand tightly grip at my leg, I snapped back to reality. The burning in my eyes ceased for the moment as they scanned downward to see who else was aggressively grabbing at me. The hand felt a lot softer than the brute one I knew belonged to Lucious, as it held my stiff left leg out in front of me. Quickly noticing that it was this Mr. Gale character again, I huffed a slight groan while raising my curling lips. "The blood test won't take any longer than a few minutes to run through, then I can start the draw." The man with stunning green eyes explained to the now normal-looking Calem.

"And how long will the draw take you?" The Lycan sighed as he leaned against the nearest wall.

"No more than a couple of hours, all depending on how much she struggles against the needles, and if I can get a good vein."

"Good luck with that-" I thought, refusing to speak aloud to any of these characters because of my conformity with them.

"That may be difficult with the abrupt past she has had with Institutions, and years of sacrifice, but I guess I can leave you two to it for the time being. Lucious, call me back once he is finished with the drawing, I don't want to wait for this one-"

"Alright-" the lower-ranked wolf depressingly sighed. Of course, I now knew the reason why he had been treating me so cruelly and I didn't hold it against him. His actions were just as reasonable as mine were when I had killed Logan.

"Here we go Cinder- a quick prick here and we will see if we hit the right vein." Mr. Gale spoke up as the Syndicate Leader excused himself from this darkly lit barren room. Feeling the needle quickly stab into my leg, I tossed a little from the pain that was now shooting throughout my entire working nervous system. "I'm surprised you still have such good veins after the abuse your body has endured." This still very suspicious man continued to ramble on while he slowly but swiftly removed the needle now from the injection point. The syringe full of the thick and dull colored blood rising in the air as he stood himself up to walk over to a small dining table that sat randomly off to the far side of the room. Out of the corner of my eye, I proceeded to observe this person who I was beginning to believe had lied about his true species calmly maneuver around the table. "Lucious, you can loosen some of that hold on her, I doubt Cinder will put up much of a fight right now. I mean, she knew this was going to happen and didn't react then..."

"No, I think I will hold onto her for a little while longer, can't trust her kind! Can't even tell what she is thinking even with my years of studying canine behavior!" the Lycan argued.

"Do as you wish, but I doubt it will let her build trust up with you either, and if she can't trust you, she may kill you in the blink of an eye." Mr. Gale chuckled to the Lycan whose grip had suddenly tightened around my neck. "I'm just joking, damn Lucious, you really think she could kick herself out of another Syndicate?"

"Right, and that's why the Shadow told me to kill their Syndicate Leader-" I sarcastically groaned, rolling my eyes and readjusting myself from under this straining grip. "And for one, I did not kick myself out of the Vampiric Syndicate. I tried to leave, and they wouldn't let me so..." I educated.

A few hours later, we finally were coming to the end of this exhausting blood draw and my body was completely drained. The effects of having the blood drawn out of my veins had left me dazed from the anemia, on top of utterly flaccid. Everything had grown limp from my normally upright cropped ears to my strong legs all the way down to the tip of the long tail.

"I think you can drop her now." I faintly heard the man who was again standing over the dining table trying to finalize the 'Blood Samples' for whatever it was that Calem had planned to do with them. The more I wondered what these mysterious plans were, the more that unsettling feeling was swimming back to the surface. My poor gut was violently spinning as it tried to piece his secret identity in with all of this. That form and the blood felt all too familiar to me like I had seen this before. However, I still could not for the life of me figure it out, nor could I shake that god-awful image. "It will probably take her several hours before she regains all of her strength."

"Lucious, just let go of the Hellhound!" I heard the Lycan command to his lackey, who had yet to release me from his impenetrable grip.

Falling harshly down onto the ground, I barely managed to catch myself with my numb legs. My paw's toes spread far apart in their own attempt to hold up my regaining weight. Lifting my tired blue eyes to adjust my line of sight and stare directly in the direction of wherever Calem had wandered off to, I began to wonder if he was the one who the Shadow had been referring to. Was he the false Immortal? Stalking the Lycan who had taken a hold of one of the vials and begin to pull out the small plastic cork lid, I steadily pieced together the entire puzzle. I wasn't entirely sure if it was him or not, but my gut told me to take the risk. Refusing to jump the gun, I held back for a few seconds. I needed evidence first. A definitive reason to kill him. Intently eyeing the man, I watched the Lycan bring the vial up to his mouth before cocking his head back and finally dumping the collection of my 'unique' blood cells into his mouth. Instantly I felt that terrible burning sensation singe my eyes. The same sensation that turned the color of my eyes, the same feeling that alerted me to the premonitory image of a nearly mummified Lycan in the Syndicate Leader's place. Holding back the urge to let out my whimpers, I tightly clenched my eyes shut, digging my claws into the tiled flooring which was still fighting to hold up my deadweight lower half.

Upon opening my gaze again, I saw the same image. That same unusual half-dead old face. Dried skin. No fur, nor hair. No ears. Lots of scarring. I could even make out the layout of his canine morphed skull and fangs again under the tightly wrapped wrinkly skin he had. As soon as I had laid my eyes on all of the washed-out traits, I terrifyingly watched this thing fade away and the identity of Calem I had grown accustomed to seeing, return.

Making a hard swallow, I surveyed the Lycan pick up the third vial, and once more drink every single blood cell he could. It was here that I finally made my decision. "It was time that I 'reaped'."

Chapter 10
Cinder/Mr. Gale

Taking advantage of my recent freedom, I shook loose the warring thoughts and darted off from a dead-beat run. Pushing past the anemia that my body was fighting through, I forced my paws to strike the ground and my legs to stay steady while I ran towards the assigned target. Moving at my fastest speed, I swiftly closed in the gap between the tall human-formed wolf and me while simultaneously distancing myself from the harsh short-tempered Lycan who held a deep grudge against me. As I prepared my legs for the jump upward, tightening the hamstrings in my hind legs, I hurriedly darted the sights of my left eye over to Mr. Gale, expecting this man to attempt to intervene. But instead of predicting him moving closer towards the target, I saw this strange man appear to have an unexpected look on his face as he stayed put. Unsure of this unusually scented human's true position, I put the worrying thought out of my head and jumped up for Calem's throat.

The Lycan, of course, lifted his hands in an attempt to shield himself from my forward attack. Yet, I still had other plans up my sleeve. Placing my front paws onto his shoulders, I tossed my exhausted and lightweight heavily into his frame. Throwing Calem off of his balance just enough that it forced him to fall backwards and onto the worn wooden floors with my body falling on top of him.

Fighting around his throwing arms, I zigged and zagged my snarling jaws, trying to reach for his throat. Becoming frustrated, I began to feel the psychotic itch consume more of my rationality while the burning sensation of my eyes returned.

"GET HER OFF OF ME!" I perceived Calem's voice shout, the scared tone ringing deep down into my eardrums. "DAMN IT!"

Chomping my fangs down and snapping my jaws together, I felt my long canines grip past the skin, slice a small amount of flesh or clothes, I could not interpret. The more I tried to reach for his throat, I more I began to sense a change in his Aura. Paying closer attention to the morphing pheromones my nose was smelling, I noticed before my very own color-changing eyes that Calem was beginning to mutate into his werewolf form. I watched the old wolf begin to de-age. This almost mummified bi-pedal canine was steadily reversing. His wrinkles were fading. His skin was moistening, even the color was returning. The hair loss was patching over with new fuzz. Even the malnourished atrophy was vanishing before my very eyes. I was watching Calem turn young again!

"Now I understand-" I finally figured out, although I was interrupted when brute hands harshly grabbed at the skin around my neck and the skin around my hips. Lifted off the ground, I was hastily tossed aside. Thrown into the nearest wall off to the far right of my target with such force that I coughed up a bit of blood and collapsed onto the ground. Forcing myself back up, I continued to theorize everything the Shadow had previously told me. "The balance between Life and Death is what makes these my assignments. You are overthrowing the balance by drinking the blood of Immortals and because of the extremely heavy Iron Counts in their blood. That's why you wanted my blood-" I stopped mid-thought as the two Lycans were now standing in front of Mr. Gale and both were completely transformed into their Lycan forms. Snapping my jaws and flaring my fangs, I frustratingly charged back into the 'ring'.

Reaching the Lycans, I pretended to charge for the Syndicate leader, however, as soon as I jumped up for my assigned target's throat, a swinging fist came right for me. Hit directly in the side of my square jaw, I was thrown back by the brute force. Catching myself, I skidded back for a bit. My poor pads burned along the polished floors as I tried to come to a standstill. Falling a few feet short of the same wall, I finally brought myself to a complete halt.

"Thank you, Lucious." Calem gratefully expressed. "I was not expecting her of all people to be the bloody fucking 'Reaper'! I have to say you hid yourself pretty well, Reaper."

"How do you know about that name-" I growled inconspicuously in the canine language, unsure about how well these 'wolves' could understand their true language.

"Here to claim my life, are you not, Cinder?" The Syndicate Leader questioned, his English accent coming through that false Northern Accent of his.

Lifting my head to show my assertiveness in our little break, I rolled my eyes over to check on their fighting behaviors. I needed to quickly evaluate and predict what these two tall timber werewolves were planning. Lucious was a hothead who held a grudge against me, so I knew he would stay in front of his leader, following the pack protocol. Glancing over to Calem, I noticed his annoyed behavior, although I also witnessed he was maintaining a calm and collected behavior, making him that much harder to efficiently read. Scanning my eyes over to the still unknown Mr. Gale who I was starting to believe was some type of Unnatural, I noticed his cold green glaze glaring right through me. I couldn't read his moves nor could I establish what threat he opposing to the mission.

"I should've known that when those Vampirics suddenly sanctioned you they were hiding something from us. Who would've thought that it would have been the 'Reaper' all this time?" Calem sadistically mocked, licking his lips clean from the blood he recently had drunk. To be more precise it was my blood!

"Don't you dare bring them up-!" I bit back to the Syndicate Leader, chomping my jaws together and raising my unsure tail into a confident aggressive position.

"Oh? did I singe a nerve-"

"SHUT-UP! YOU ARE STARTING TO PISS ME OFF!"

The two Lycans just chuckled at the Hellhound, as if she was all bark and no bite, deeply underestimating the person that Lord Zachariah had chosen for the title of 'Reaper'. Their teasing only seemed to irritate the Beauceron more. Looking between the two seven-foot-tall transformed werewolves, I could see that the canine had her ears pitched forward, her tail raised so high it was starting to curl over her onto her spine, and her teeth were nearly all exposed. The room was beginning to get warmer the longer everyone stood at this tense stalemate. I knew things were going to get worse, things were even going to get dangerous for me the longer I stood here, especially if that 'thing' was going to lose control over her emotionally unstable sanity. Attempting to step away from the pair of soon to be victims, I began to see the transformation I feared.

Her body was starting morph into the Alter form. Those beautiful amber-orange eyes of hers were darkening in their shades. Maturing into a deep red. Her Blood Trait was weaponizing, forming those Blood Scythes she had out of her wrists. Although I could not see behind her raised head, I knew that her bone spikes were also slipping outside of her spinal vertebrae. The form took less time to grow than the last time and thus told me two things about our, or his 'Reaper's' mind. One was that she was losing control over her sanity, and the other was that the Hellhound was developing the exact way Zachariah had wanted her to. No matter what way I was looking at her awe-inspiring transformation into that psychotic blood-crazed Alter form, I knew this wasn't going to be good news for any of us. We all were targets.

"What is that-" I heard Lucious snarl, his fangs also exposing themselves to the still-warming air. The tone of his voice sounding paralyzed with overwhelming confusion and fear.

"It's a Hellhound's Alter form-" I answered as calmly as I could.

"What-?" Calem questioned, taking his eyes off of the animal who was now licking away the foaming drool from the corner of her lips. "What the hell is that?!"

"It is the image of one's Death. " I answered. "A form where the Unnatural loses control over their rationality to do whatever it takes to complete their task. Or at least that is what all the books on her species tell."

"You knew this was a possibility?!" The Leader continued to snarl, now turning his back completely away from the being who was going to lead to his death. "You knew all of this-"

Shrugging my shoulders, I sighed, "I did. But if I were you, I would not focus all of your attention on me, Calem."

"Huh-"

Before the Lycan could complete his sentence, his comrade howled out in agony. Moving around the large-furred half-naked were-being to see what was going on for myself, I watched the Hell-hound called Cinder chomp through his shoulder. Those long fangs ripping right through the thick built muscle. Her small emaciated weight forcing the Lycan to saunter backwards. The sound of her low growl sounding very overdrawn the longer she clamped down on her chosen target. Grabbing for the black and tan-furred large dog's neck in an attempt to either break her neck or throw her off, Lucious hastily let go of the animal.

"You see your comrade needs you." I jeered.

"Why you, sly bastard-" Calem snarled, spinning his attention again off of his Beta Ranked Syndicate Member. Backing myself up, I continued to slyly grin at the Lycan, before pointing behind him. Just as the Lycan turned his head around to attempt to find the source of my emote, the transformed canine, attached her fangs into his thick neck. Her head turned horizontal to fit between the shoulder and jaw space. Dragging her paws over each side of his collarbone, I saw the trick Zachariah had told me she used in her last transformation; Stabbing her Scythes into the upper pectorals of the Lycan just like a mountain climber uses his picks to climb and hold at a cliff, Cinder held on to her target. Her red eyes were locked on me as the wolfman was stumbling forward by the force of her weight crashing into his back. Quickly dodging out of the way, I lift my foot and tripped the seven-foot near two-hundred seventy-pound shapeshifter. Calem fell flat-faced into the hard floor with the hundred pound, two and a half feet tall canine falling on top of him. Her hold remaining stubbornly strong through the jolt. Doing the canine shake, she managed to spurt blood out of his throat. The werewolf erupted in pain. Howling for his comrade to rip her off, however, Lucious did not come. Again, the wolf called for his aide, and again his fellow species did not come.

Taking my eyes off of the kill happening before me, I noticed Lucious was lying on the floor, doing whatever he could to get up, yet failing at every attempt. There was something wrong with his nervous system. "How did she do that?" I questioned myself. Rapidly returning my attention to the two breeds of canine shapeshifters who're fighting, I observed Cinder had broken her scythes off from her wrists and were using her paws to maintain steadiness over her anemia. Releasing her insane grip from the Lycan's neck, she stepped off the wolf's back. Curious, I stayed put and made myself as little of a threat as I could to this deranged mentality. "What do you have planned?" I continued to wonder to myself. "What is running through that crazy head of yours?"

"YOU BI-BITCH!" Calem shouted out to the female Hellhound who I do believe was a bitch by scientific terminology. Blood was spewing out of his wounds, yet because he was able to talk, I knew that the Hellhound did not rip through his vocal cords or his trachea.

"What is she doing?"

The dog just smiled back at the Lycan while he gravely fought to get back up to his feet. His long nails scratching the wood floors as he transformed once more. The thumbs breaking apart from the joint to form into dewclaws. His fingers formed together, notching, and knuckling into the identity of paws. The hips and shoulders rolled to complete the assuming painful transformation into his true wolf form. Completing this altercation, I noticed a few characteristics I could not see from his were-form. His skin was poking through his paws and muzzle in places where the fur appeared to be bald. Trying to investigate without moving any closer, I listened to the Lycan Leader savagely snarl, "It has been decades since I the last time I had turned into this... "

Glancing up over to the Hellhound, I saw her red ember dancing eyes avidly watching the wolf steady himself under his now four-legged form. Her smile exposing every single one of her fangs that it possibly could. The snarl raised so high that it was hard to count the number of ripples in the skin wrapped around her muzzle. The cropped ears were pitched even more forward than prior, and her tail was happily wagging instead of stationed straight up. The be-havior I analyzed was almost like Cinder was toying with her target instead of hunting and completing her assignment.

"HOW DARE YOU SMILE AT ME LIKE THAT!" Calem snapped as charged straight for the smaller Unnatural.

Chapter 11
Mr. Gale

Remaining as still as possible, I observed every distinctive detail in the fight between the two four-legged creatures' resume. Each attack Calem made. Each dodge Cinder danced. Each counterattack the Hellhound made, and each flaw the Lycan missed. His fangs only once or twice successfully skimming over the smaller canine's fur, meanwhile, his opponent's fangs triumphantly ripped through every inch of flesh it met. The longer this fight drew on, the more frustrated the Syndicate Leader became, and the more the 'Reaper' enjoyed her mission.

With another split, I was able to observe Calem's welfare. The Lycan was still in his true-wolf form, barely managing to remain on his feet, his timber fur markings soaked through with blood by the many wounds he had. Deep gashes straddled his shoulders and hips. From head to toe, throughout his entire body, I could see the flaps of skin Cinder's fangs ravaged through. The bones easily peeling through the muscle. He was either going to eventually bleed out, or he was going to get murdered by the 'Reaper', nonetheless, he was going to meet his demise sooner or later.

Swinging my gaze slowly over to the hunting Unnatural, I noticed she too was covered in blood. I felt like more of it was his than hers judging by the location, however, when blood is the same color all around, it can become difficult to tell who's was who's. The other hint that told me the Hellhound was most likely not wounded was her strong energy level. She was not panting, not struggling to stand, not acting unsure, Cinder was purposely drawing out the fight.

"What is going on in that head of yours?" I wondered just as the female canine darted out for another attack. Impressively after fifteen minutes of pure dog vs dogfighting, the Hellhound was not at all winded or exhausted. Moving at the same speed, she reached Calem in no time. Her smaller frame allowing her to easily slip in under his throat and grab the Lycan's jugular. The fangs chomping through the area with the least amount of muscle and fur to protect. Holding on tightly, she proceeded to shake at the throat while simultaneously throwing her weight into the wolf's chest. The small hundred pounds easily pushing him back, however, it was not enough to overthrow him. Calem angered by the futile attempt, swung his jaws down onto the Beauceron's back. Although, he was quickly obstructed. The bone spikes protruding out of Cinder's spine quickly stabbed the roof of his mouth, and the bridge of his muzzle. Howling out in frustration and agony, Calem continued to try to shake off the smaller canine, yet that too proved futile. "Was this where his final breath was going to be laid?" I imagined then paused when I surveyed the Hellhound release her impenetrable grip from the Lycan's neck. Expecting her to make a gap between her and her prey, I saw Cinder sidewind, darting off to the non-dominant left side of the Lycan and kick her front feet off of the blood-stained wood floors. Dancing around Calem's swinging neck, she proceeded to lift higher up off of the ground and attach her jaws to the side of his throat behind his skull. Her jowls spread as far as they could go while the incisors attached to the skin under the jaw and behind the cheek. Knowing from my experience with these forms, there was a massive collection of vital nerves and arteries she was chomping through. The wolf attempted to scream out another cry of pain, but with Cinder chomping down on the vocals, nothing came out.

While she held the choice of life and death in her hands, Cinder continued to once more shake her body. Vigorously swinging her body around in a rigorous game of tug-of-war, Cinder surprisingly managed to exhaust the Lycan enough that he decisively collapsed down onto the floor. Falling on top of the heavily breathing animal, the Hellhound relentlessly continued to shake her head. With a clear view finally, I could see the smile spread across her face. A psychotic grin that exposed every-single blood-stained tooth she could through the short fur.

"Calem!" I overheard a voice shout over the savage snarling of the two canines. "Calem!" Swinging around to find the source of the voice, I quickly remembered that the target I was supposed to watch over per Zachariah's orders had immobilized the short-tempered Lycan.

"Shit!" I quietly complained to myself. "Why can't you just sit there-" I was cut off from redirecting my frustration when I felt a massive heatwave spread across the room. The temperature viciously increasing by almost thirty degrees. Profusely sweating, I was forced to redirect my attention back to the fight at hand, seeing a line of orange flames shootout between where I stood and where the Hellhound was standing over her target. "Well there went my view-" I now frustratingly criticize. Turning over to the other Lycan, I proceeded with walking closer to Lucious. The werewolf snarled back at me, but I was far from afraid of his ill-predicament. "Growl at me, all you want, wolf, but your Syndicate Leader has already met his demise. And if you want to meet your demise the same way he did-" I pointed back over to the two canines poking out between flames, only seeing the Beauceron who I assumed was still standing over the Lycan. "I guess it's all up to you-" I paused for a moment before deciding to rephrase the statement, "Well more like it's up to her whether or not you also die today." Looking down at the Lycan who was still angrily snarling at the flames, his amber wolf eyes reflecting the wall of fire. The flicker of the embers reflecting in that golden gaze. Watching him slowly reform into his human form, I continued to speak, "It's obvious she didn't want to kill you because she understands and accepts this grudge you have against her. She left you unable to move instead of ripping your stupid life from that pathetic body of yours. Now, if you still want to possibly get your revenge for her killing your brother, I would suggest you bite your tongue and keep yourself as submissive as possible."

"WHO THE HELL ARE YOU-?!" Lucious shouted back at me.

"It's not my place to tell you, nor is it your place to know my true identity," I answered, leaning against the table and attempting to once more return my full attention to the last fleeting moments of this fight.

"You were in on this weren't you-" The lower-ranked Lycan calmly snared. "You are working with that bitch!"

Shrugging my shoulders, I ignored his proclaims. Examining the flames dissipate, I noticed a strong stench rise through the warm room, and it wasn't sweat that was filling my nose. Sweat would not burn. As the last few embers faded away, I finally saw the source of the stench. Cinder was no longer standing over the wolf, but the blackened remains of bones. The scalding stench of burning flesh lasted for a few seconds, proceeding the image of the Hellhound's true form. She hastily turned her glare over to the two of us who had so far survived her Alter Form. Those crimson eyes cruelly deciding our fates. Expecting to fight for my life against another one of his 'minions', I kept my fists down low. "This is where you don't move-" I whispered aloud, reminding myself how dangerous a 'Reaper' was when they had been consumed by that lustrous level of blood lust.

Avidly surveying every movement, the Beauceron made, I observed an unusual change in her already bizarre behavior. The red eyes dissipating into a faded soft yet warm orange amber. The boney spikes molded back into her vertebrae, retreating without leaving a single sign of ever protruding from her spine in the first place. The female Hellhound then miraculously proceeded with yet another surprise, the return of a form thought lost. Watching the four-legged canine rise up on her hind legs, and the fur begin to shrink back, exposing the soft white skin hidden underneath. Glancing over the completely exposed skin, I saw the Cross-shaped brand, Zachariah gave every one of his Hellhounds. It was embedded deeper than the previous Unnaturals before her, but it also folded nicely over her petite female physique. Scanning over the nude woman, I noticed there were many more scars on her clean skin. Many of which were contained to her legs, stretching from her thighs down to her ankles. As she finished standing up, I oversaw the woman grab at something secluded deep under the cremated corpse of the Lycan Syndicate Leader. While she straightened herself up, I noticed the object that she was callously holding and was horrified upon realizing it was Calem's huge wolf skull she was elegantly holding by the nasal cavity.

"YOU BITCH! WHAT ARE YOU DOING WITH HIS SKULL!" Lucious angrily shouted over the deafening silence. Before I could even swing my glaze over to the surviving Lycan, he was standing up on his own two humanized feet and was running towards the transformed Hellhound.

"Lucious, stop!" I called back. "Great-" I sighed when of course the Unnatural did not listen to my words of advice. "I do not want to have to explain another unwanted soul-"

"This is my trophy, Lycan." The woman coldly snared. The tone of her voice sounding much darker, and if I had heard her actually speak before, I would say that this was still the Alter speaking.

"Where is he when you need him-"

Chapter 12

Cinder

"Jakob, just let me go-" I cried out aloud, attempting to break away from the tough grip the sweet and caring Vampiric had on my wrist. Doing whatever he could to keep his hold of me, to keep me close. "Please-" I cried, staring into his gorgeous soft greenish-hazel eyes. Seeing the look of confusion and refusal tore on all of my heartstrings. Clenching my eyes shut, I felt my body get dragged closer to the lean physique of the seven-hundred-year-old Unnatural. Opening my gaze, I awakened my sights to see a whole new sight.

Glancing around my surroundings, I saw I was standing over the same man. I was standing with my body perpendicular to his, standing in my canine form with my left paw over his right shoulder, and my right paw stamped in the freshly fallen snow beside the left side of his neck. My nose could smell the strong stench of iron. My tongue could decipher the metallic taste of blood rummaging through my mouth, drooling down my long fangs.

"Cinder-" I could hear his memorizing deep voice call out to me. Looking down to locate the voice, I saw more blood oozing out of his mouth and down his chin. Dribbling onto the white snow, painting it red. "W-why?" He coughed.

"Jakob-" I cried, or deeply desired to. My body turned on its own. Backing off of the man I had just attacked, my legs turned and ran off into the darkness behind us. I had no control over what was happening. I wanted to stay beside him. Swallowing a mouthful of tears and blood, I cried out the name of the man who had made my life so much better since my regained freedom. Pleading for forgiveness the further I went into the backwoods. "JAKOB!- I'm so sorry. Please forgive me- Please-"

"Hey, wake up-" I heard an unusual voice call out to me. The tone wasn't full of complete urgency, but it was still a tone of concern. A deep tone that abruptly shook me from my slumber. Springing my eyes open, I saw an unwelcoming green glare staring right back while the attached body stood directly over the top of me. I could make a familiar face that belonged to someone I had only previously seen on a few magazine covers. With my sight adjusting, I made out the slightly round face, the squarish cheeks, and those smoldering eyes I recalled from a particular poster I had seen back in Valyerie's room. This man had the same messy blonde-hair gelled back as if he simply ran his hand through the locks of hair and it held. Taking in all of these awfully familiar characteristics, I finally pieced together that voice of his, recognizing that deep soulish voice of his as none other than the Mr. Gale. "There you are-"

Interrupting the man who had been hired by Calem to draw my blood, I swiftly spun around and rushed to my feet. Jumping off of the comfy slick-back modern sofa, I assumed Mr. Gale had chivalrously let me sleep on, I hastily grabbed his arm and pulled him in. Mr. Gale flopped right down on the couch. Without delay, I saddled my physique over the top of his infamous hard chest and drew my Blood Scythe. The weapon's blade swiftly spawned out of the pores around my wrist, falling in line with my forearm I propped it against his throat.

"Woah-Woah, woah-" Mr. Gale cried, trying to place his hands out. The palms facing outward in surrender.

"You better explain everything to me!" I demanded, pushing the blade closer to ripping into this flesh. I may have only been half-awake, but I was completely prepared to kill him. The freshly sharpened edges decimeters shy of slicing those fine hairs lining his neck.

"Okay-okay! Just put down the blades first!"

"Answer my questions first!"

"Release me-"

"Do what he says, Reaper." My sensitive ears heard a terribly cold voice echo throughout the surprisingly bright room. Scanning around the living area to find it's owner, I upsettingly complied. As I proceeded to remove the red blade, retracting the Iron Blood back under my skin I overheard the voice further exclaim. "Allow him to explain without the threat of you taking his life."

"Fine." I sighed to my conscience. Staying stationary, I leaned back over the top of the Unnaturals broad chest and trained abdomen. "But you can explain it from down there." I snarled down to Mr. Gale. I needed a bit more on this man before I was going to let him up, realizing that whenever Gale was around, the Shadow was also nearby, always telling me to listen to this person. What made him so special?

"That's fine by me." The model-like man returned. His square-face creating a very triggering grin. "What's your first question?"

"What did you just say?" I interrogated. My eyes squinting to fixate on the next words he would attempt to speak. A sneaking hunch biting into my gut.

"What-" he shockingly returned. "What are you talking about?"

"Your vocabulary, you talked as if you also heard him-"

"Him? Him who..."

"Stop lying!" I demanded.

"Explain." the Shadow growled aloud. That cold voice no longer whispering in my ear but filling the entire room.

"What are you saying?" I barked, my body craning around to see the Shadow I had finally realizing was talking from behind me. "What the hell is going on?"

"Now? You want me to explain it now?"

"Yes, I do." Both the Shadow and I shot back in unison.

"Fine-" Mr. Gale complained, throwing his head back against the arm of the sofa. "That black mass that has been barking orders and assignments to you goes by the name Zachariah. He once had a mortal form and like your other Hellhound friend, he represents your Deity-"

"How do you know about them?" I snarled glaring back down at this unusual human who deep down in my gut I was really starting to believe was an Unnatural. After all, he too could see the being. However, knowing he could see the being was nowhere near as shocking to me as the news that Mr. Gale knew of my past, my second family. Recreating the Scythe, I demanded more answers, completely blinded by the loyalty I still owed.

"No." the Shadow lowly denied. His commands as always uncontrollably driving my body, forcing it to comply.

"I know about everyone you have had in your life since you have been liberated from the Institution. That was my true job." Mr. Gale softly answered. "Zachariah didn't let me observe, you nor them in person, so I do not know how they look, however, the Rebels aren't as good at hiding their valuable information as they should be."

"Don't talk about them like that!" I growled, this time successfully drawing my left forearm's blade against his neck. "I will only warn you of this once..."

"Okay, okay! Jesus Christ, he was not kidding when he mentioned you had an attachment."

"Just relax, Reaper-" the Shadow ordered, this time physically bringing me back. His boney fingers were tightly wound in my long black hair as it painfully pulled my head backwards. Eventually, I could feel the bones wrap around the lower end of my skull and restrain nearly all of my movements. The muscles temporarily contracting. "Listen to what the man has to say."

"Fine-" I growled. Sheathing the blades much to my demise, I fell in line.

"Continue, Valkyrie."

"Valkyrie?" I questioned. "So, you are an Unnatural."

"Yes, I am a Valkyrie, in particular an Archangel." Mr. Gale explained with a deep sigh. "Now's not the time to explain that whole fiasco." Taking another breath, I saw the man's eyes physically lock onto me. "To answer your first question, you completed your mission to kill Calem. But to be precise, you did a lot more than just that. You essentially cremated the poor bastard, burned all of his flesh, and a majority of his bones. After that, you clung to his skull for some weird fucking reason." Observing the newly acquainted Valkyrie Unnatural point over towards the adjacent metal framed coffee table, I saw that indeed sat a large wolf skull. Though only the top half was there, sitting on top of the glass table.

"I clung to a wolf's skull?" I inquired confused. "I don't recall ever even touching it-"

"Yeah, kind of figured you wouldn't remember, given your whole behavioral change and all..." Gale said, rolling his eyes at me.

"I blacked out again..." I mumbled, looking over to the Shadow, hoping for some of his insight. Though I felt deep down that just like all the other times, I was going to be shot down with more confusing dialogue.

Chapter 13
Cinder/Mr. Gale

"It was more like you were consumed." The Valkyrie, Mr. Gale spoke ahead of the Deity, which apparently, he too could interact with. That was going to take a bit of getting used to, though it did make me happy to finally know someone else saw the same spirit I did. Swinging my vision back around to see the model-like square face and astounding emerald green eyes, I continued to listen to his low voice clarify. "You became consumed by the blood-crazed psychotic conscious that resides deep down in your subconscious. It sounds more complicated than what it is, but in simple terms, you didn't blackout. Instead, you were consumed by the itch, by your lust for blood."

Instantly I recalled the memory from my first assignment, recalling the exact feelings the Unnatural had just explained. Remembering how lost I had gotten in the hunt and the kill when instead I was supposed to protect Logan's victim. Thankfully, I wasn't able to dive in too far before the hovering black mass interrupted, "That memory Reaper, has nothing to do with what he is explaining to you."

"While I'm sure you have felt this a few times before..." Mr. Gale once more exhaled. "That itch that consumed you back at the Syndicate was more like the one that had consumed you when you had attacked your friends a few months ago. It's more fear-based..."

The Shadow quickly scolded me with a strict 'uh-uh'. His cold words freezing any plans I had of ripping this man to pieces. "Valkyrie, hurry up."

"I'm working on it, but there is a lot to explain!" The Archangel shot back with a deep annoyance. "And while this is nice, could you please get off of me? It's already hard enough to hold back when you're already completely naked!"

Glancing down at my breasts, I saw that I was completely nude again. I was naked. Every inch of skin I had was exposed. Standing myself up from the clothed built chest this man had, I stepped off the couch, my bare feet firmly placing down on a cool sleek dark-brown wood floor. "What happened to my clothes?" I softly questioned, falling for the subject change. Scanning around the large open space living room, I noticed that the entire place was above and beyond modern. Everything had been color-coordinated with black and white furniture, beautiful potted plants. Large floor-to-ceiling windows were allowing the most beautiful view of the surrounding cityscape to flow in. Distracted from the gorgeous view, I hastily noticed I was somewhere in New York City, I believe Manhattan to be accurate. I could make out from the view we had a straight-line sight of Central Park in the distance. This place was a far cry from the 'place' I had grown up in, and the seclusion of the Syndicates which I now knew were miles away.

"Thank you." The Valkyrie happily returned while I wandered over to the windows for a better view. "And to answer your question, I don't have a clue where your clothes went. When you transformed back in your subconscious, you were already nude. It could be a possibility that during the loss of sanity they were lost." The charming masculine voice returned, his charismatic tone taking full attention over the fixation I had with the gorgeous sunrise view from this high-rise apartment.

"I see..." I sighed, looking away from him and intently staring at the unique parquet layout of the floor.

"I've got some clothes I can give you for now."

"I want answers first; the clothes can wait," I ordered the Valkyrie now as I left the windows. "But...

"I can see that I will not be able to get the right answers unless you are thinking steady." The female Hellhound returned, her long-overgrown bangs falling off from behind her left ear to cover the corresponding eye. Hiding that brilliantly intelligent blue color behind her dyed blue-black hair.

"Let me go get you some." I hastily responded, standing myself up from the suede black couch. Walking around the furniture, I disappeared down the hallway and ventured towards my room, where I knew I at least had a shirt and some sweatpants for her. They may be a bit too big for her, but at least it would cover her defined softly-skinned feminine frame.

Passing through the open doorway that connected the suite's Master Bedroom to the hallway, I swiftly strolled towards the dresser. Opening up the drawers holding my sweatpants, I proceeded with searching for the right pair of pants for her. Ones that were not only form-fitting on me but also had a drawstring. Finally finding the right pair, I pulled out a solid, dark black, athletic pair of soft-fabric sweatpants. Placing the pants on top of the black-stained sleek wood dresser holding four round metal pegs which held the furniture up by three inches. My fingers gripping the metal tag acting as a handle to the drawers, I proceeded with pulling open the drawer that held my shirts and eagerly grabbed the first one I saw.

Taking out the shirt, I closed the dresser drawer, stood myself up onto the palms of my feet, grabbed the sweatpants, and left the master suite. Pairing the shirt and pants together, I anxiously walked down the hallway. Passing the beautiful white potted plants adorning the corners of the dark corridor to lighten up the penthouse's monotone colors, rounding the corner, I locked sights on the open-concept living space. Scanning my eyes around the kitchen and dining spaces which were almost adjoining, I brought them back onto the living area where I overlooked the Hellhound. I had to make sure everything remained as it was, that nothing was out of place and that nothing was well...burned in my absence. After my rounds, my eyes laid its sights back on the Hellhound who was submissively challenging Lord Zachariah in a way that almost seemed normal for them. Trying my hardest not to get dragged into the heavy conversation, I leaned against the corner's wall, my back nearly brushing over the large twenty-inch by thirty-inch horizontal oil canvas painting of abstract green and white paints in some sort of splatter pattern and patiently waited for the vulgarity in the conversation to die down.

Counting the time go by on my new silver Rolex watch, I noticed after fifteen minutes the tone in the frustrated Hellhound had simmered down, and the Shadowed Deity's black mass stopped foreshadowing the cursed God's emotions. Looking over to his orange-eyes residing deep inside his scarred human-skull, I finally spoke up. "Are you guys finally at a stalemate, or what?"

"I will leave you to explain what is left." Zachariah hissed before vanishing into the bleak darkness of my floors, like always. His voice succumbing back up through the air, it's cold tone frustratingly barking the defined orders clearly in my ear. "Explain what her purpose is for now. DO NOT go into detail with it, but explain it enough that she understands that she has no choice in it."

"I understand, my lord." I consciously expressed to the hidden Deity.

"Good. I will be back after a while. Until I return, keep her here."

"I will try my best, but I cannot make any promises."

"I have faith in you." The voice lastly spoke.

"Sure you do," I smirked, leaning off of the corner of the wall to finally attempt to clothe the nude woman standing in between my living area and dining room.

"Soooooooo, what still needs to be explained?" Cinder requested with a familiar look on her face that told me the Deity didn't explain anything to her at all. The same expression that was organizing what was true and what was false into their separate subconscious folders. Her left black eyebrow arched, her lips stuck in a calm, stern position, and her body arched in the cocky, aggressive position with her right hand positioned high on her hips.

"Assuming by the way you are glaring at me, there's a lot." I sneered, stepping around the furniture.

"So, explain."

"First thing first." I continued, pushing the stacked pile of neatly folded clothes up in front of her face. "Please get dressed, I cannot keep ignoring the temptation."

Chapter 14
Cinder

Pulling my hair out from under the white fabric man's tank top, I walked back around the black sofa where minutes earlier I had attempted to kill the Archangel. Holding my short tolerance for run around questions, I sat down on the soft, firm cushions and proceeded with my first question as the model bachelor sat in the opposing white living chair. Although, before I could open my mouth to speak, I was already interrupted by Mr. Gale.

"Thank you for getting dressed."

"Sure." I confusingly accepted. "Where-?"

I was interrupted again. Holding my tongue and my boiling blood, I managed to keep my temper's short fuse under control while he broke, "I am just going to do a quick run-through, so we can get this over with."

"Okay-"

"As you know, you were marked at an early age, by Zachariah, your Deity."

"Marked?" I thought. My eyebrows furrowing as I not only tried to digest these new terms but also digest the long-awaited answers to my numerous questions.

"That cross on your back, it stands as a mark of ownership per each Deity. Your other Hellhound friend, the Pharaoh Hound, is marked with a Golden Ankh tattoo, that tattoo represents his Deity, Anubis. Meanwhile, yours is a representation of the Deity, Zachariah." Mr. Gale continued to explain. "Most of the time, Deities assume a Hound's marking once they accomplish a certain task or survive for a certain amount of time. You happened to survive not only under some of the cruelest conditions in today's world, but you survived thirteen consecutive Blood Moons. Not many have survived long enough to see their Fourth Moon, let alone their Thirteenth."

"What made him choose me?" I growled, desperate for an answer to that one question. The Shadow had been so evasive every time I brought it up, and personally, I didn't understand what made it so hard to answer.

"Lord Zachariah chose you for multiple reasons that were once explained to me." The dirty-blonde haired Angel replied.

"And?" I eagerly probed, hoping for a stronger answer.

"You were originally chosen as a test. Something he was curious about. You were nothing more than a lab rat." Gale paused so he could read my comeback. I could see his facial expression become sorrowed. "Judging by the stationary expression, you already knew that." Relaxing my furrowed brows and pushing back my fallen bangs back over my left ear, I kept engaged. "He wanted to test if age and gender increased probabilities of survival to a Reaping Hellhound."

"So that was one reason. What were the others?"

"Well, through the research he had me do, we found that you had a Genetic Blood Trait and a rare one at that. We also found out that your intelligence level was superior to the other children we had picked. Those two things were what sealed the deal in his eyes. I assume there are more reasons, but those were the reasons he had told me."

"Okay, so what about my purpose?" I inquired. "If I was only used as a lab rat, why keep me? Why brand me with a scar that covers the entirety of my back?" I frustratingly interrogated. "I heard him tell you that you needed to explain my purpose to me."

"Your intelligence level is indeed high." He snickered, leaning himself into the square back of the open-backed chair. His chin again resting in the palm of his hand while his elbow rested on the arm of the chair.

"Why act so surprised? I thought you already knew I had a high I.Q.?"

"I knew that on file; however I wasn't expecting it to still be that high because of all that time you spent boarded up in that Institution."

"You and everybody else." I groaned.

"Anyways..." He hastily tried to push on. "Yes, you heard correct, I am supposed to explain your purpose and why you are here? But what's the rush?"

"The rush?" I snarled. "I have been asking the same question to that thing for years, and all he ever told me was that my only job was to obey and reap."

"Okay, okay, calm down." The Angel said, his position in the chair changing so he could freely use both of his arms to mimic the calm down motion. "I will tell you your main purpose to Lord Zachariah, just try not to go ripping the messenger's head off."

"You seem more like my babysitter than his messenger," I smirked, repositioning myself on the couch. My body twisting around more and more in these baggy clothes that barely fit my petite frame.

"Yeah, that's what it feels like." Gale chuckled for a minute. Taking a deep breath, his voice returned to a serious tone as he moved on. "While I cannot explain the reason why Zachariah looks like a

Shadowy Skeletal Mass, I can tell you that your purpose is to Reap and collect the souls of the dead just as it suggests to your Breed of Hellhoundism in several works of literature, including the Book of Demons does."

"Collecting Souls?" I queried.

"It is something that you haven't done physically. Each time you kill someone, whether or not it was your assignment they manifest their spiritual presence from their physical mortal body. Most of the time the soul is collected by the Reaper, however, thanks to the change in the laws of the Natural Order and Balance, the Reaper's Watcher is the one who collects the Souls. Traditionally, it would be the Deity, however, as I am another one of his servants, collecting those escaped souls is my task."

"Okay-." I stammered, understanding the explanation surprisingly easily. For some reason, it felt like I was being told something I already knew, although I knew this was the first time I was ever told about 'Soul Collecting'. And while I was curious about this whole collecting souls, I was okay with the knowledge I was being let in on, so I ignored the urge to pry deeper.

"Going back to your purpose, you are to kill all those assignments and aide Zachariah's return to his seat of power." Mr. Gale explained in such simple verses.

"Seat of Power? I thought he was already in a higher seat?"

"He was one once, however that is a story for another time. For now, I suggest you push that question out of your mind and try pondering other questions to ask. Like, how your life is going to be from now on, or something like that."

Hastily interrupting the Angel, I blurted out, "Was it that urgent that I left the Manor?"

Mr. Gale readjusted his position in the chair, moving his elbows around so they could firmly sit on his knees while he hid his chin behind his hands that were clasped together. I heard him take another long sigh before coldly speaking in that lowly 'I don't care' tone. "Yes, it was quite urgent that you left."

"Why?!" I snarled, bouncing off the sofa.

"By staying there, you were endangering more people than you thought you were." The Valkyrie resumed in that same icy tone of his. Sending freezing vibes down the back of my neck to dare me to argue. "Grant it, Zachariah originally believed that you staying there was for not only the greater good of your mental and physical health but for the greater good of the Syndicate and Unnaturals who resided there. Allowing them to understand what a Hellhound's purpose was in the world and support it, as well as for you to regain those lost socialization and motor skills. However, the longer you stayed there and the closer you got to the members, the more you put them in danger. According to Zachariah, the night he decided you were to come and live with me, instead of those Rebels was when that Vampiric saw you not only bleeding out under the Blood Moon a few months after your return to the outside world but also when he saw you beginning to show signs of your Alter form."

"Alter form?" I confusingly questioned. I recalled Peylith talking once about his Alter form and exposing the bi-pedal canine form, however, the sinking feeling deep down in my gut left me with worry that our forms were not alike. The way Gale talked about my 'Alter form' was as if it was a lot darker than the Pharaoh's.

"A Hellhound can only awake an Alter Form after years of experience and the collections of hundreds of souls, at least that is how it is for Reapers."

"How does that work, I mean sure I was changed almost nineteen years ago, however, I was hardly ever able to transform, let alone control my form that well."

"It is difficult to explain when I was not present for the event, nor when I can barely understand how you accomplished it myself."

The Angel shot back, his deep voice softening as he leaned his head off to one side, locking it inside the palm of his right hand after he broke the tight grip it had on his left. "Anyways..." He pursued, trying to return to his previous explanation. "After you had exposed those signs, you also began to not only expose certain mannerisms dictated with that form, but you also began to lose control over your rationality. I don't know what exactly Lord Zachariah meant by his choice of words, however, once he has set his mind on something there is no way you will be able to debate your involvement or your choice."

"Because you don't have one." I groaned, plopping myself back down the sofa.

"He expects your full support whether or not you want to give it."

"If you refuse, you get forced into submission through punishment. I know the drill, quite well."

The comeback must have been funny or something because Mr. Gale lightheartedly chuckled for a brief moment. Calming himself down, he proceeded, "When Zachariah saw a break in the chaos that was unfolding in your other life, he gave you the choice of you watching the demise of your friends or leaving and saving them."

"It was not much of a choice in the matter."

"It was but not in the way you think."

Chapter 15

Cinder

Jumping over the coffee table, I altered my appearance. Reappearing back in the large Beauceron canine form of mine and landing all fours down onto the wood floor, I quickly kicked off and lunged for the man. Keeping my front paws outward, I hastily gripped the target's shoulders while the rest of my body came in for the landing. My hundred-pound emaciated body thrusting all the deadweight into the man. Crashing him into the chair, causing the chair to fall onto the floor, I remained headstrong over the top of him. Baring my teeth into his face, I hesitated for his next explanation before deciding to pull his head off its broad shoulders and forever staining the beautiful sleek floors. "Explain!"

Getting nothing but a sly smirk on his cocky square jawline, I planted my left man-sized paw along his throat. Slowly and steadily dropping the weight of my mutated hand down on his trachea.

As he coughed for air and tried to remove my paw from crashing through the skin, I once more demanded an explanation, "Explain that to me! Now!"

O-okay!" He mumbled, still coughing for more air. "OKAY! Just get off of me!"

Folding my cropped ears flat against my square head, I released my grip and placed the paw back on top of the floor beside his head. Using the placement to steady my weight while simultaneously holding him down, I steadied my voice, "Explain."

"Are you going to get off of me?!" Gale continued to shout.

"No, I'm not." I snickered. "I haven't decided whether or not I am still going to kill you."

"Really, after all that I have already done for you?!"

Transforming back to my human form, I sat my sweatpants wearing butt on top of his abdomen once more. "What exactly have you done for me?"

"Oh, I don't know, how about keeping you alive after you lost consciousness following your murderous rampage, or what about the time Hunters were following you and your friends in the woods, or that other time when you-"

"I get it." I groaned, before slyly smiling and leaning forward, bringing my head closer to his. "But no, I am still not going to get off of your so well-chiseled abs." Speaking in the soft feminine voice I had learned to use to my complete advantage over these recent years of my freedom, I proceeded to inquire. "Just answer me this. What did you mean by I had a choice? I had no choice with that matter."

"Well, you kind of did." He paused for a long second. I could see that he was debating how to explain the answer to the question, or at least rephrase his harsh words. Those green eyes avoiding my direct sight.

"Tell me." I femininely flirted. Doing what I could to keep my temper under control, I proceeded to use all of my trained expertise. Recalling every moment, I had both seen and heard occur between the two lovebirds back at the Vampiric Syndicate, I accurately portrayed it all. I had to admit it was quite empowering.

Awaiting his answer, I was forced to wait a few moments. The torture was unamusing. "Zachariah didn't properly explain the choices, which I am sure you already know is pretty typical of him." The Angel casually spoke. His voice slightly cracking to hide the tone of temptation he kept rambling on about. Rolling my eyes in agreement, my sight observed Gale swallow prior to voicing the next statement. "You could've stayed with the Syndicate, with your friends, but at the rate you were heading into physical insanity, well let's just say that you would have let loose that 'Primal' psychotic side of yours and would've two to one killed them on top of reaping who knows how many other 'undesired souls'."

"It still wasn't a choice." I summed up.

"I guess you could say that, yes, but you have to see now that it was for your benefit, I mean you still did end up severely hurting them, right?" The Unnatural with that famously cocky smile jeered.

"Do not push me!" I hissed, throwing my left wrist up against his neck. My dark-red, Iron Blood Scythe uncovering itself from the soft underside of my forearm.

"I am not wrong, though." He further pushed. "You attacked that Vampire. You almost killed him-"

"He's alive?!" I sobbed, holding back my tears when the awaited answer finally surfaced. Removing the blade, I took a long sigh of relief. My hands cupping up around my mouth as I gasped a soft 'Thank god.'

"You didn't know?"

"NO! I didn't! The members all turned their backs on me, and the Lycans wouldn't even utter a word about his condition to me." I shot back between tears.

"Ouch."

"He is okay though?" I requested, desperate for an answer to Jakob's condition so I could try to soothe my traumatized heart.

"Your little Vampiric is okay. The last I heard, he was still comatose, but he was stable. His wounds have scarred and healed, so now, can we get back onto the main subject at hand?"

Repositioning myself over the late twenty-year old's chest, I took one more longing sigh. Holding my hand over my heart, I felt the muscle start to soothe, returning to its regular 'human' beat. "Yes, I am ready."

The Valkyrie tried to begin, but I could see in his eyes that he was now hesitant. Eventually, I heard him speak, "I think we've already hit the main topics...we discussed your purpose and all, right?"

"Yeah, my purpose is to reap and steal souls." I moaned while I finally stood back up, giving the man his chest back. "Though, it doesn't seem like that much of a..." I veered off, trying to keep some of my true feelings deep down.

"It may not seem like that important of a job, but your job is exactly what is going to help him return to-."

Interrupting Gale I hastily ordered, "You didn't want me to ponder about his 'Seat of Power', however, if you keep bringing it up, then how can I continue to keep my questions to myself."

"You're right, my bad."

"What is your purpose here? I mean, you're an Angelic Unnatural, what binds you to someone like him?"

"A shit load of stupid obligations is what binds me to Zachariah, which I am not obligated to tell you." The man growled back as he accepted my offer to help him back onto his feet. "And my purpose here is to watch over you, make sure I record any signs of you losing more control over your 'Primal' urges."

"Again, you're my babysitter."

"Pretty much." Gale chuckled. "But unlike a regular babysitter, it is my job to do whatever it takes to ensure your sanity."

Returning with a slight snicker of my own, I jeered to the Valkyrie, "That must be difficult to watch over, especially with everything that has happened in my past and is returning to haunt me."

"Yes, it is quite hard, but it does not bother me, because you are not the only Hellhound I have 'babysat'." He quoted, using his fingers to form the bunny-ear motion and mock the title. "Over the years, I have been bound to that Deity, I have overseen my fair share of Hellhounds. And let me tell you it's not pretty to see what happens when one loses their sanity. It's an inevitable thing that happens to you guys, but I'm sure I didn't need to tell you that, huh?"

"I already had a feeling it was going to happen to me one day." I sarcastically shot back trying to keep the fears on the down-low.

My arms were harshly gripped by his calming masculine hands. Staring into his stunning green eyes, I locked my gaze onto his as he talked, "I promise you I will do whatever it takes to keep that from happening to you anytime soon."

"Why even bother with it? You don't even know me." I coldly questioned.

"Because..." the Angel stuttered, acting as if I had said something he wasn't prepared for. Guess I had gone off-script. "Because it's not just your life that is on the line. You represent a massive shift in the balance if you are to lose your sanity too soon..." Mr. Gale stopped, rephrasing his statement. "I care because you hold the life-line of hundreds of thousands of lives in your hands-"

"Are you lying to me?" I interrogated with much disbelief while I shook off his strong grip.

Chapter 16
Mr. Gale

"Why in the fucking world would I lie?" I shouted to the female Hellhound who was starting to become more and more intimidating the longer we had this debate/conversation. "I have no reason to lie to you." I proceeded while standing a few feet back to give her some space.

Observing her gaze harden, I saw the growing doubt of whether or not she could trust the words I just said. I could see it was hard for her to trust, but it seemed she was more willing to at least consider it. Awaiting a response, I studied every little movement her small frame made. Reading her stance to hopefully counter another attack I was expecting to arouse, I noticed that there wasn't anything to go off from. No twitch. No contraction. Nothing that read predictable. Cursing to myself as I recalled what Zachariah had prior told me, I understood the other reason why he kept her. Cinder's movements were unpredictable. She could swing at me at such a speed that I could never properly brace myself. "This Reaper stands as a valuable Hunter." I could hear the shadowy being's cold voice echo inside my head. "It took her, less than a few spars to learn how to 'fight' in both forms."

"I guess I can trust you, for now, that is. But that's only because, I currently don't have anywhere to go." I heard the female Hellhound finally utter. "Although, if I'm supposed to trust you, I am going to need to know more about you."

"Yeah, I guess I should tell you more." I agreed, turning my back on the transformed woman who was dressed in my house clothes. "So, what do you want to know?" I inquired as I went over to pick up the befallen chair from off the floor.

"Well, I already know you are a babysitting Valkyrie." Cinder snickered. "I guess we could start with your name. The only alias I ever heard the Lycans call you was Mr. Gale, and I know that you have a real name."

Strutting over to the kitchen to grab some ingredients and attempt to prepare some lunch for the two of us, I shot back with another chuckle. "Yeah, when I 'sell my work'" I paused, grabbing some refrigerated farm fresh eggs, before moving up to the freezer for some frozen sausage links that I could microwave. "I prefer to use my surname and hide my first name just in case things go downhill."

"Stop stalling, I don't need a full backstory on why you do it, I just want to know what it is so I can call you by something else other than Gale." Cinder interjected midsentence. Turning my head slightly off to the side, I noticed through the side of my eye that the Hellhound was sitting on the modern black iron-rodded, white-cushioned barstool.

Placing a skillet on the stove, I agonizingly answered her hasty bark, "It's Augustus, but I was telling you that story so I could get you to understand when we are out in public-"

"When we are out in public!" I overheard her shout. "Who said anything about us going out in public together?!"

"I did!" I bit back.

"You may be my babysitter, but you are not my boss!"

"No, I am not, but Zachariah is, and he is the one that told me to watch over you wherever you go inside and outside of my house!" I shouted back as I worked on cracking the seven eggs I had collected from the carton.

"Alright, fine, but it still doesn't give you the right to order me around like some 'dog'-."

"Well, you are some 'dog'." I chuckled, "Some dog with unusual shape-shifting abilities."

"Whatever."

"Anyways, per his orders, I have to follow you and you have to follow me unless it is out on calls. I will not follow you on most of your assignments, and you will not follow me out on most calls from clients I receive."

"So that is our contract?"

"That is our contract," I confirmed whilst breaking the yokes and mixing the eggs to prepare them for the ready-to-go skillet.

"Fine."

"What else do you want to know, Cinder?"

"How is it you have been able to live like this and not be found out by the Hunters and Institutions?" the woman scowled. "I mean there are only a handful of Unnaturals I know off the top of my head who's living the life of wealth and freedom, but they all fall and hang their heads around the humans to hide their true identity. Making them nothing more than cowards in my eyes."

"Call them what you want, but that is the unfortunate reality of our world." I responded to the Hellhounds question, keeping my back turned to the 'Reaper' I tried to wrap up cooking our meal. Stepping away from the stove to put the sausage links in the microwave and quickly nuke them for safe eating. "It's either blend in and shamefully hide your real identity or face the same torture you had to endure. Sacrifices have to be made in order to stay alive and if all someone has to do is kiss a few feet here and there to stay out of the prying eyes of the cruel Government, then why not."

"You sound as if that is how you did it?"

Sliding half of the scrambled eggs onto the plate I had assigned to her, I moved over to my plate and repeated the motion. Simultaneously concepting an appropriate way to answer her question without turning her against me all over again, I continued. "It's not exactly how, but I guess hiding my identity is how I have been able to survive all of these years." Reaching for the warmed sausage links, I proceeded to place three on each plate. "Unlike shapeshifters, my species can expose their characteristics whenever we choose to. I can even hide my genetic DNA from being exposed when I go for Blood Draws." Handing the Hellhound her plate, I returned to the far end of the counter island, deliberately putting space between us. "But to answer your question about how I had come into this lifestyle." I sighed. "I used to be a property entrepreneur both commercially and residentially. After I had sold some huge companies, I decided to retire and invest my money in some large stocks. The money tripled soon after. Eventually, I pulled out of that and well ended up creating the massive organization that helps fund the Syndicates in their cause to change those stupid fucking laws." Stabbing my sausage link, I ripped off a bite, taking notice of the woman's revised attitude. She now looked more intrigued instead of pissed off. A good sign, I hope.

"You are still a coward."

"Huh?" I questioned with a mouthful of crunched meat.

"You heard me." Cinder chuckled as she began to eat my hastily made breakfast. "You. Are. A. Coward."

"God, you are a complicated person to figure out." I chuckled back.

"I know I am, why do you think I was used for nearly twenty years of my boring life as a lab rat and a host. Everything about me is hard to figure out, I can't even understand it. However, we aren't talking about me, right now." Swallowing another mouthful of food before she returned, "I am calling you out-."

"I get that but why-? I have not hidden anything from anyone, well except my true identity, but other than that I only use a surname when I am working with Syndicates. It's easier to stay on the down-low that way. I mean, I'm sure you already know that unfortunately, I'm a pretty popular guy..."

"I could care less about your infamy, nor do I care about how you hide the fact you are an Unnatural from even other Unnaturals. Sure, it took me a bit to figure out your real identity, and in our world, if you resemble human then, of course, you should play that off as much as you can, however, the reason I called you a coward was because you have no pride in your species. Now don't get me wrong, all the charitable work you do in shutting down those horrid places all over the world is grand, and I commend you for it, but in the eyes of an Unnatural whose suffered there is no pride in having a 'HUMAN' do that. I would rather see an Unnatural take the credit. And until you do that in my eyes you will be a coward." Cinder argued from the other side of the counter. I had to admit I was thankful for the few feet of space because I was completely expecting her to jump over the marble top and throw me against the stainless-steel fridge behind me.

Locking my sights on her stern blue eyes, I kept my mouth quiet, proceeding to silently evaluate what the Hellhound had just said, "I completely understood where she was coming from, but-." I hesitated, even my poor mind had a hard time finding a good point to debate this woman on. "If I was proud enough to live a life like this. Flaunt my money whenever I got the chance, then why was I so scared to flaunt my species' characteristics. Why was I so timid to expose the truth of who I was? GOD DAMN IT!" Blinking my green eyes slowly, I finally came up with at least something to tell her. "How about I show you then?"

"How about after we are down eating, I don't want whatever you are about to show me to get in my food." The woman teased, expressing a genuine smile that told me that the Hellhound had won her argument and was content with my request. At least I hope that was the case. I did not want to have to try to yet again pry her large hundred-pound canine form off of my body.

Chapter 17

Augustus

Harboring what little physical energy it took to unsheathe my Unnatural species' key trait, I spawned the Valkyrie Wings out from my shoulders. Rolling the shoulder blades around, I flexed the quickly formed muscle. Fluffing the feathers that were plucked into the mass, I exposed the glorious snow-white angelic wings to the entire outside world from my high-rise patio. Glancing back over to the female Hellhound who was standing a few feet away from me, I lightheartedly interrogated, "Happy?"

"Sure am." Cinder smirked. Stepping closer towards my fifteen-foot extended wingspan, I avidly eyed her fingers begin to play in between the feathers and their quills. Before I could pull my left-wing away, the woman had plucked one of the smaller feathers from around the armband.

"Ow!" I acclaimed, grimacing in slight pain.

"Sorry, did that hurt?" Cinder jabbed. "I had to know."

Isn't it obvious that hurt? It's no different than when someone pulls on your hair." I answered, folding my large wings along my back like how a bird sheathed theirs.

"Sorry, Augustus." She once more apologized.

Hearing her speak my first name in her soft feminine voice as if she was apologizing, yet trying to talk as if whatever she had planned had worked; sent grieving chills down my neck and through the feathers. Quickly shrugging off the aimless chill, I hid away the wings quickly hoping that she was not going to spot the one flaw my gorgeous wings had. Looking at her surprisingly still dressed in my clothes, I returned, "It's no problem, I understand why you did that, though it still hurt."

"Oh, stop being a baby." Cinder still teased as she swindled the white feather between her index finger and thumb. "I had to see if they were attached to your flesh, or if it was some nasty ploy you had to gain my trust. Now, onto my other questions." She paused, looking away from the feather before letting go of it, allowing those individual quills to freely float along the strong draft echoing through the city. The white feather quickly disappeared into the early afternoon backdrop. "Do your feathers heal at the same rate, or do they heal at similar speeds to other Unnatural Species such as myself?"

"My feathers heal at a rate of speed a tad faster than the average human hair does. It is nowhere near as fast as your healing process, but it is still quite abnormal."

"Well I don't think many species can heal as fast as I can, but I am glad you are willing to answer my questions." Cinder continued as she once more pronounced in that highly flirtatious soft tone of hers. The voice still sending frigid chills down my spine.

"It was what I was told to do." I jabbed back at her, trying to counter this unusual mannerism of hers.

Seeing the hurt in her eyes, I, however, observed the woman's lips curl back into a smile, "So if he didn't tell you to answer my questions than you wouldn't have-"

"Yes." I swiftly answered. Scanning around the large penthouse balcony I had, I decided it was time we moved back inside. "We should head back indoors before any humans decide they want to make a possible report." With my eyes looking over several rooftop topiaries, greenhouses, and other apartment patios where I could locate some humans lounging around, I prayed they did not look up at the right moments. Peeking back into the Hellhound's boundless blue eyes, I knew it was time I put my charismatic powers to use. "I don't want any of those people down there to sniff you nor I out-."

"There you go again. You are such a coward!" Cinder hastily snarled.

"Call me what you wish, however it is my job to ensure you stay out of the Institutes and Hunters prying eyes and arms." I bit back.

"Call it whatever the hell you want to." she waved, strolling right past me. Her shoulder ramming into my left arm. "But in my eyes, you are still a coward."

"Well, I got you back inside at least." I sighed. "Keep calling me whatever you wish, but I will put my job and your life above all else." Turning on my heels, I spun back around to head back beyond the massive sliding glass doors, stopping when the familiar feeling crept up from behind me. The hurried rush of frigid wind, and bloodlust. "I thought you had things to do, Lorde Zachariah?"

"I still do, I'm just checking in. See if my 'Reaper' had killed you yet considering her previous demeanor...and I guess I have my answer." The Shadow Deity danced, speaking in his natural vocabulary. "Seems like you have managed to gain her trust, good because I was beginning to wonder if she had any left to give."

"It will take some time to gain the level of trust you want me to have with her."

"Gain as much as you can for now, until my 'little' Reaper has ascended her duty." Zachariah slyly smirked.

"So, why else are you here? I know it wasn't just to see whether or not I had been murdered by your Reaper." I inquired, locking my gaze into those fiery orange pupils.

"Still as observant as always, Augustus." The being complimented. "Yes, I am here to also give her a mass assignment."

"Mass assignment?" I questioned. "As in tons of souls for me to collect as well?"

"Yes and no. This time around she can collect them. My Reapers body will act on instinct. Back to the assignment, you and I both know that they exist. Deep underground, hidden from plain sight, a seemingly cruel yet legal treatment for those so-called 'Unnaturals'."

"Black Market? You want me to send someone like her to the Black Market?!" I blurted.

"There is a collection of seventy-four souls that needs to be collected. If there are casualties, there are casualties-"

"Why the sudden rush?" I asked, understanding that there was a reason why now of all times he wanted to send her out to reap such a large quantity. Quickly sliding shut the glass door, I remained outside before continuing to pry, "I mean that was something we planned a little further down the line, like after she had learned to control her Alter Form."

"It's because of the Council-"

"Are they back to hunting us again?"

"That last incident where she killed Calem, alluded a light in our direction. So, I need to get my physical form and my powers back before they track us down."

"Okay, okay, I get the idea. Though, I don't know why you could not forewarn me ahead of time about this, like start the conversation with how the Council is after us before handing out the mission." I questioned in as submissive of a tone as I could muster. Swatting away the rambling, I mimicked the motion with my right hand, hoping to wrap things up. "What part of the Black Market are we talking about, my Lord?"

"The Pits."

"As in the Fighting Rings?" Getting no response from the lurking Shadow, I pressed on. "Don't you think that will only further speed up that loss of sanity you keep pressuring her about? That place is for true killers and even then only the darkest of minds make it out. It's not for someone like Cinder, especially when she is already one step closer to slipping into a psychotic break."

"That is the plan. Besides she is a lot stronger than you think."

"But won't that amount of souls she has to collect alert the Council to our location..."

"Not exactly."

"What?" I confusingly probed. "What do you mean by not exactly?"

"You have been down to the Pits before right, my stupid Valkyrie?"

"Yeah, I went there last week to continue scouting the location out for you for back when the plan was supposed to happen a few months down the line?"

"So, you know the rules of the Fight Ring?"

"Yes, I do my Lord," I growled, looking away from his harsh orange glow.

"Good, come next month take her there. Until then, continue to work on building up your trust with her. Do whatever you see fit, even ensuring her rising intimate tensions if you must. Whatever you can manage to keep her under lock and key. To keep her under your control and their cruel prying eyes."

"As you wish, my Lord." I sighed.

"When the time finally approaches, I will fill you in on more of our plan until then, keep up with your life and your job here."

"Yes, my Lord. I understand."

Chapter 18
Cinder

"There you are. I thought you flew away on me." I jabbed to the Archangel as he finally sauntered inside the apartment. Getting no quirky remark, I called out to him, "Did your conversation with him, go well?"

"How much of that did you hear?" Augustus quickly sparked. His tone full of worry, and yet serious anxiety.

"Hear? Nothing. That glass is a lot thicker than the regular sky-scraper window." I returned, telling the truth. I couldn't even hear the drafty winds hit the windows. "But whatever it was, I can tell it was about me, wasn't it?"

"Yeah, it was. More like about your Alter Form than about you in particular."

"Okay-" I softly sighed, sensing that there was something else more serious afloat. They couldn't have just discussed my Alter Form. Sure, the form was powerful and could be very bad if improperly controlled, I got that, but with that Shadow, there was always more going on. "I guess I won't prod too deep."

"Thank you." The man sighed, recollecting his unwinding nerves. "Let's get you some clothes ordered, so tomorrow when I am out on calls, I can pick them up and you can have something to wear besides my sweats."

"Okay." I submissively returned, still unsure about what was going on. The scent wafting off of his Aura was telling me that whatever they were talking about had piled in deep. I wanted to question this further, but this feeling stirring deep in my stomach was telling me not to. Forewarning me that whatever the answer was to my egging questions, it would not have satisfactory results.

Watching the man with the model appearance quietly stroll off to an offset room for a moment before coming back out and closing the doors behind him. I was curious about what secrets that room held, but again I didn't pry. As intriguing as it would be to see a flustered Augustus, for some reason it felt like that would be taking a step in the wrong direction. That it would be worse for me than it would be for him and all his angelic prefectures. Avidly eyeing Augustus, I noticed him walk past me to sit on the couch.

"I will start up my laptop, and from there, I will let you buy a few outfits. You should be able to buy what you need with only a few hundred dollars, right?"

"Yeah, I can manage with a few hundred dollars." I mindlessly answered, plopping down on the black sofa. As I sat down beside him, I felt my nose burn from the unusually scented Aura he had. I could sense he had a build-up of pessimistic emotions.

"Good." He returned as he hastily typed in several websites of a few different stores which I could only assume were local. Leaving the laptop on the coffee table, Augustus then stood up and wandered off down one of the two halls I had yet to explore. Disappearing for a moment. When he returned, I could see he was carrying a nicely woven but worn man's black leather wallet. Digging around, the Archangel pulled out a tiny plastic credit card and explained, "This card is yours. I've put five hundred dollars in your account and will continue to put an allowance in it from time to time." Examining the card's numbers, and the unique etching of the bank's name on the front, I proceeded to take the credit card from him. Upon further examination, I instantly became shocked when I saw that the unique three-digit security code, ran four-hundred, ninety-seven on the back of the plastic card.

Fighting to control my nervous shakes, I snottily sparked, "Are you trying to buy my affection, Mr. Gale?" Flashing him a sly grin, I further jabbed, "Because if you are, you know that there are so many other ways to go about it besides giving me money-"

"Oh, I know many ways to get a woman's affection." Augustus jeered back, mocking my grin with one of his own. "I'm only doing this because Zachariah believes you having some free money will help you attain a bit more 'freedom' and dependency. Though I doubt, unlike other women, you aren't easily sleuthed by money."

"It's a nice asset to have, but no, money isn't everything." I agreed while I tried to scroll through the websites. I hadn't used a computer since I was a kid, and while not much had changed it was still a big deal. Easily adapting, I sped up my window shopping and scrolled through the numerous pages of women's clothing. "But it's still appreciated, the last time I ever had any money in my name was back when I was a kid."

"Really? That was what twenty years ago?" the Valkyrie questioned me, his level of doubt written all over his face. Shortly after he saw I wasn't lying, his demeanor returned to it's calm and serious mannerism. "Once you have bought what you want, let me know, so, I can then pull up a clothier's website, and we can get you some clothes set aside for when you go out 'Reaping'."

"I need a special uniform for 'Reaping'? Since when?" I returned.

"Don't ask me, it's per his orders, and it's my treat. But I will leave you to pick out your clothes. Remember to get some under-garments, some casual, and some formal." Augustus told before he began to stroll towards that locked room, the same one he had pulled this fancy laptop out from.

"Wait, why formal?" I questioned. "Are you talking like formal for meetings or formal like dresses?"

"Formal like dresses, and I don't mean cocktail dresses, I mean formal like evening gowns and luxurious party gowns." He responded with his back still turned to me. "As I said earlier, there will be some events that you are to be arranged to come with me, and most of those include dressing up a bit."

"Do you even know the last time I wore a dress?"

"Yes, I do. And I know it will be uncomfortable for someone like you to adjust to wearing something like that again, but you wore a hospital gown for almost sixteen, seventeen years, so I can assume that it shouldn't be too hard for you to adjust."

"Fine." I reluctantly sighed. "Anything I should not look into? Considering you are already dictating what style of clothes I need to buy?"

"Not in particular. I would prefer for you to have at least two formal outfits, and at least a couple sleepwear, then the rest I leave to you."

"Okay." I agreed, understanding some of his anxious stenches. Waiting for him to leave the open-concept living, kitchen area, and return to the secretive room of his which, I assumed was some sort of office just by the layout of this place, I pondered, "What to shop for first?"

"Are you done yet?" the blonde-haired green-eyed man spoke as he fell onto the black-fabric sofa. His body sitting beside mine.

"Yeah, just finished the checkout," I answered, adjusting the laptop in my lap. Uncrossing my legs, I proceeded to put the sleek HP computer back down on the glass coffee table.

"And how much did you spend?"

"I spent close to the max you put on the card, but I managed to buy everything from this one website. Two 'gowns', two pairs of sweatpants, a pair of yoga pants, four pairs of skinny jeans, some shirts, and tank tops." I paused, counting the outfits with my fingers as I tried to remember the numbers on the receipt.

"And any undergarments-" the man questioned with a look in his eyes that made him dread ever speaking the words.

"Of course, I bought some underwear and bras." I chuckled. "Only a handful, but I did buy some. Matter of fact, I bought everything you told me to, so don't bother asking if I bought shoes and accessories."

"Good, now let me see the computer."

"It's your computer, go right on ahead." I continued as I pulled myself back to let Augustus scoot over on the sofa.

Watching the man swiftly type another address with a bunch of unique backslashes and semicolons into the bar, I wondered what this special clothier's website was. This special place that supposedly sold clothes designed for my 'Reaping' Uniform. Once the sight loaded up, I saw the immediate uncontrolled darkness. The website was gothic and nothing but sleek black, red, and pale white colors. Looking around the website, I watched the Angel quickly log into what I assume was a sign-in box for some sort of membership. Keeping quiet, I fixated on the many loading screens and reloads before the website eventually came to a unique array of dark clothes. Still intently eyeing the few clothing items I saw him scroll by, I completely spaced out his voice.

"Hello, Cinder?" I heard the man call again, speaking the name that Jakob had so dearly given me.

"Sorry, I zoned out."

"Yeah, I could tell you zoned out. Daydreaming, or just caught up in something else?"

"I don't know." I sighed, blinking my sore blue eyes, I looked away from the bright computer screen. "So, these are the clothes I'll need for my 'Uniform'?"

"I don't know why you keep calling it a 'Uniform', but yes, you can choose whichever ones that appease you, however, this is the style of clothes that Zachariah wants you to wear when you are 'Reaping'."

"Alright, well considering I don't have much of a choice in the matter, just go ahead and pick out the uniform yourself for me, Augustus. I could care less about what he wants me to wear." I returned to him, standing back up from the sofa. "Where is the bathroom? I want to take a shower, get all of this dried blood out of my hair, and my fur."

"Down the hallway, and second door to the last is where your bedroom is, there is a bathroom just through the walk-in-closet." He responded while his quick fingers manhandled the keyboard and its touch-pattern mouse, alerting me to the fact he already had an idea in his head about what I was supposed to wear. Rolling my eyes, I softly strolled down the hallway to begin my search for the second to the last door, the door that was assigned to be my bedroom.

Chapter 19
Augustus/Cinder

"It's too quiet." I sighed, looking up from my computer after finishing the thorough item checklist of the Hellhound's 'Reaping' gear. I didn't know why he wanted her to have a uniform for just reaping, but there was no way I was going to question his lordship. Glancing out towards the hallway, I looked past the setting sun's warm rays peeking through the windows and noticed that one of the fluorescent lights was on. Standing up from my seat on the sofa, I left the computer to go check in on the Hellhound, noting it had been a few hours since she had left to go shower.

Creeping around the potted fern plants that sat along the floor of floor to ceiling windows, I crept towards the guest room I had set aside for Cinder. As I neared the second to last door, I noticed the door was ajar, not completely closed, but not completely open either. Gently knocking on the door, I softly called out the woman's given name.

No response came back.

Putting my hand on the modern slick handle, I slowly opened up the door, and before my very eyes, I saw that lying on the queen-sized, sleek-black bed was the large rising and falling black shroud of wet fur belonging to Cinder's Beauceron form. She was sprawled out across the middle of the bed, lying on her right side with the stomach completely exposed, absorbing the fading orange lights of the gorgeous sunlight. Creeping up on the dog, I stepped inside the room taking in the characteristics of this species' primary form. While I surveyed the woman's transformed physique, I noticed there were fine scars along her front and back legs. They were decorating the limbs like the stripes of a tiger, or tabby cat. I couldn't decipher what had caused them. Some looked like they were caused by sharp blades while others looked like severe burns. She also had plenty of healed needle scars from the torturous years of abuse. To any normal human, these scars were barely noticeable unless you were right on top of her and examining the skin through the short strands of fine hairs.

Cautious about comforting the sleeping animal, I simply smiled before glancing around the room. Expecting her to make herself completely at home based upon her personality, I was taken aback by how she kept everything so tidy in the room. The clothes I had given her to wear were neatly folded up on top of the matching sleek black dresser counters inside the walk-in-closet, straining my eyes, I scanned over the bathroom that was on the other side of the closet. Blinded by the shining bright rays of the sun echo off of the gorgeous white tiles, I relieved a sigh seeing that at least not everything about her was a complete contrast to her personality. Lying on the bathroom floor was the soft marble grey towel, informing me she had dried herself off then dropped the towel and altered appearances.

"Well, at least you know how to pick up after yourself-" I sighed with a soft chuckle. Stealthily sneaking back out of the bedroom, I left the door ajar in the same spot I saw it in and returned to the hall. Quietly thinking to myself, "How can someone who sleeps so peacefully, and acts with such a childish heart possibly ever survive the Pits? What are you truly planning, Zachariah?"

When I awoke from my short nap, I noticed that the sky was changing colors. The midnight blue was fading into the bright yellow haze of the morning dew above the city skyline. Setting a gorgeous cloudy haze down on the view of the park which lied beneath this 'apartment'. I had unsurprisingly slept through the night. As I stretched my long legs, I recalled that last night I was too lazy and too tired to redress myself with those baggy clothes after my shower. Instead, I altered forms and crawled up into the bed for the night. Sitting upright, I dropped into a downward dog pose and slid myself out of bed. Coming down onto the soft white throw rug which covered a third of the bedroom's dark wood floor, I made myself do one more long stretch before shifting back into my human form.

Strolling through the empty closet that I knew by the end of today would not be so empty, I strode into the bathroom and began the process of relieving my bladder, trying my hardest to attempt to be civil. After I washed my hands, I was taken back to find a large hairbrush sitting by the sink. It was an item I hadn't even thought he knew to have put in the bathroom. Aggressively pulling out the tangles from my long hair, I placed the brush into an empty drawer and walked back into the bedroom. Happily returning to my large canine form, feeling more comfortable in the species' main form rather than my beautiful pale human form, I slipped past the ajar door. Noticing that while I passed through, the door had been shifted a few centimeters further away from the doorway. Knowing that there was only one other physical person in this apartment, I choked out the worrying thought of what he could have done to me while I was unconscious and trotted back into the hallway towards the living/kitchen area.

Finally entering the room, I noticed that everything had been picked up. The laptop had disappeared, as well as the wolf skull I had so questionably clung to. The dishes had been done and put away from the meal Augustus had cooked for the two of us yesterday. Everything was spick and span. Matter of fact it was so clean it reminded me of Yalu's kitchen and her impulsive cleaning habits. Cringing at the memory of her betrayed facial expression flash through my eyes, I grimaced bringing my head closer to my heart. Those amber yellow fox eyes coldly glaring at me, judging my uncontrollable actions with such cruelty. The painful memory clung so heavily to my heart that it felt like the poor muscle was attempting to rip itself in two when the other faces flooded to the forefront.

"Breathe," I told myself. I had to breathe. I needed to relax so I could calm down. I needed to calm down before Augustus, or that damn Shadow saw me like this. "Breathe." I again commanded. Taking a deep inhale, I slowly exhaled, finally feeling my streaming heart rate calm. The tranquil rate returning.

Returning to looking around the apartment so I could potentially map out all the crooks and crannies this property beheld, I hastily realized how confusingly simple the layout was. The entry was through a closed-off private foyer, separated by gorgeous black French doors. The foyer's doors were located a few feet down the first hallway, connected to the kitchen and farthest from the balcony's massive sliding glass doors. As I ventured down the first hallway, I noticed that was another set of familiar closed doors. There were three doors down this long hallway. Two of them were pretty close making me wonder if one was a half-bath or some sort of small room. Of course, I could figure it out if I truly desired to, but I decided to not pry. The third door was across the hall from the second farthest door and based upon the feeling my instinct was explaining to me, I assumed this was another bedroom, or at least something similar. Scrolling further down the corridor, I noticed that there was a sharp turn leaning towards the direction of my room and the balcony. I was surprised to see double doors that again were closed locking me out, but using my adjusting scents I wafted the scent of Augustus having come and gone from this room as well as a few other scents. They were faded, but still there. Possibly weeks or months old. Taking a long sigh, I danced around some more potted plants, a small wall shelf adorned with unique trophies and awards, then around a modern rectangular shaped ottoman, that wrapped around another sharp turn taking me in a complete 'U'-turn. As I rounded the corner, I came upon a row of interior glass windows that looked like they connected to a sunroom or atrium of some sort.

"How did I not see this room prior?" I questioned upon realizing the last floor-to-ceiling window was about ten feet away from my bedroom door that was now swung open from my earlier escape. Taking the possibility that I missed it when I was so exhaustingly eager for a nice hot shower and a comforting nap, I turned my attention to the unique interior room. While sunlight poured through the ceiling, I could not believe that it was a roof-top atrium. The Triangular ceiling allowed the still-rising sun's rays to soak through once it hit a specific angle. Absorbing all of the detail, I saw that there was a nice squared out glass fire-pit adorned with black and blue rocks to contain the flames it could shoot out, some modern black and white cushioned patio furniture, and plenty of ornate tropical plants that I had to assume were either fake or something because I knew there was no way something could be planted this high up out of the earth. Although, a further investigation would have to wait because, yet again, I was locked out of the room.

Hearing the alarming sound of a doorknob clinking, I craned my ears to listen to where the sound was coming from. I suspected it came from the room I had only assumed was Augustus's I, however, did not let my guard down in case it was someone else who was coming through the foyer's front doors. When the scent of the Arch-angel stirred, I relaxed and returned my focus to trying to identify what orange, red, yellow, and white flowers were poking themselves out from between the massive ferns and small bamboo trees.

"Oh, there you are?" I heard Augustus's soothing masculine voice call. "I saw your bedroom door was open-"

"Yeah, I have only been up for a little while." I softly expressed in my canine form. My long fangs poking out through the jowls as my mouth moved.

"Want breakfast?" he spontaneously sparked. "I can cook some more eggs, or-."

"No, I'm fine for now." I returned.

"More for me," Augustus smirked, trying to obviously alter my focus from exploring the rest of the place. Keeping an eye out on his roguish movements, I eyed the man swing open the massive glass doors, pulling them open like awning doors. They had to be an accordion-style or something along those lines. "There you go, I'm going to go cook me some food before I have to get ready for work. Feel free to explore the entire apartment if you wish."

"An open invitation-" I wondered to myself as I continued to watch this unique bachelor stroll down the hallway before disappearing into the open area living space.

Chapter 20
Cinder

Feeling the absorbent sun soak through my soot-black canine fur, I could feel its glorious heat keeping my canine frame naturally warm, making me feel drowsy. It would be so easy to slip back off into a deep slumber the longer I calmly laid on the patio sofa that sat before a glorious fire pit, however with all that was going on, I simply had too much on my mind to even think of sleeping now.

"I figured I'd still find you here." I heard Augustus's voice come out of nowhere, forcing my 'adjusting instincts' to wake up and stay alert.

Making a tired nod, I dropped my head over the wicker armrest of the modern patio sofa. "Where else would I be when you've got me locked in here?" I teased, trying my hardest to stay awake.

"Well, there isn't much here, but despite that, you have just as much access to everything in this place as I do." The Angel expressed, sitting down on one of the adjacent chairs that sat on the other side of the atrium, "It's funny though, I would have never pictured you to be a nature lover?"

"When you spend your entire life locked away in a cramped windowless hospital room, you learn to appreciate the sun as much as

I." I shot back, keeping my attention fixated on every single move this 'Valkyrie' made. I couldn't figure out just how exactly should I be treating this Unnatural. Was it really okay to trust him? Was I supposed to fall for his charismatic charm? Or was he just going to be another 'target' that I would have to reap later on? And if so, should I even try creating a relationship? Hearing the man chuckle, I snarled, "What's so funny?"

"Oh, nothing. I completely understand what you were saying, but it's the fact that after all these years I have spent serving Lord Zachariah, and seeing all the Hellhounds I have come and go, you are for sure the first Hellhound I have met who loves the light of day, instead of the cry of night."

"About that-?" I softly probed, setting myself up so I could truly give Augustus all of my available attention. "You said yesterday that I was in a set of children studied to become the next 'Reaper', however, you just said that you've seen many come and go. Just how many has that 'Thing' created? And how just how many have passed on?"

Avidly hunting all the movements this man-made, I noticed his facial expression change, the mutation from contentful jitter to the look of 'I shouldn't have said that'. Curious I flashed my teeth in both preparation and warning. I wanted answers and giving me lies wasn't going to make me probe less, but at the same time, I had to remind the man what I was capable of. Several seconds of silence passed before I saw the expression again grow serious. The traditional calm bored expression filling his stern jawline and squarish model-like head. Pulling his hand through his blonde-locks, I watched him sleek back his unusual short-medium length natural spikey dew. Flashing my long canine fangs once more, I finally got the man to speak.

"I truly do not know how many Hellhounds he's created, but I do know Zachariah is among one of the oldest Deities among the Gods, so I can only assume he has a great amount of experience on working with your species. How many have passed on is another thing? All I can say is that a majority of them are simply put out of their misery." Augustus answered.

"Misery?" I thought. "What misery?"

"I can see your head is spinning with what I just said, so I will break it down for you." Shifting in my seat, I moved around my weight as I fully expected to hear another long explanation. "As you already know, Reapers face the loss of sanity, and not many can control their sanity levels. Matter of fact only four have ever been able to successfully serve up to their complete potential while controlling that 'Psychotic Bloodlust' they face with every 'Assignment.'

"Then why the hell would he look for new Reapers if he had those four-" I interjected, furiously snapping my jowls together and showing all of my teeth to the Archangel. "Why the hell would he look into children?"

"That's because he lost his seat of power, and those four are essentially in prison. Sentenced by the hierarchies and whatnot." Augustus returned with a surprisingly short answer. Watching him roll his wrist with the 'what not' phrase, I began to wonder 'what hierarchies'. But the more I wondered who these people could be, my gut spun with a harsh warning to not dread any deeper. Veering away, I noticed the man's eyes and facial expressions were telling me to move on. "I'm not going down that road of bullshit." He sighed giving me a slow blink. "Now you remember how yesterday I had told you, you were only chosen to be nothing more than a lab rat for a test of sanity and blood lust control, right?" I nodded, recalling the conversation from the day before. "Well, that was only half of the reason. The other half was because he needs someone to help him return to his seat of power. You were chosen because you were the best option."

Pushing past the 'ouch' feeling, I tried to return to the previous subject, "So back to the whole being put out of their misery thing, just how many have you seen 'put down'? How many have you put down yourself?"

"Again, you are too intelligent for your own good."

"Well, you should've known that coming into this, being my babysitter and all." I snickered, slyly smirking, "But, I don't think that's quite the right term, you are more like my executioner, aren't you?"

"I guess in some ways you could say that, though it's sort of like I'm both babysitter and executioner. I do the initial watch and I pull the 'final trigger', everything in between that is Zachariah's work." He replied, the tone in his voice becoming a familiar shroud of freezing air. "And to answer your other question, I have unfortunately lost count of the number of Reapers that have been 'euthanized' since I had joined. Now there have been a few who've lasted a couple of decades, but when it came down to the final phase, they couldn't suffice, and they too died."

"Final phase?" I wondered aloud.

"Your Alter form-"

"No, the way you said those words were as if it goes beyond the Alter form. You cannot lie to me." I returned, yet again flashing those pure white fangs of mine.

"I can see that," Augustus smirked, leaning back on the sofa. "To put it bluntly, it's a form beyond the Alter form, but it's not my place to explain that. If you want to know more, you'll have to ask him."

"There goes my chance of ever figuring that out."

"Anyways, I am about to head out. I shouldn't be gone longer than four maybe five hours."

"Why bother telling me?"

"Because we need to build up our trust in one another and since I don't trust your overbearing 'curiosity' I'm telling you when I'll be back."

"You make it sound like I'm going to destroy everything you love and admire." I teased back at the now standing man.

"It is a possibility."

"Well, I won't destroy anything of yours if you stop treating me like I am some child." I bribed, taking a moment to dissolve all the probabilities of comebacks with my next statement. "I mean, I know the maturity of my mind was massively slowed down by all the drugs and time I spent in the Institute, but it still doesn't' mean I don't know when to touch things that do not belong to me."

"The heart of a child." I heard the man quietly mutter to himself as if he was trying to say it in his head but spoke it aloud instead. That statement made my head hurt, and my poor heart stop. Was I supposed to take that as a compliment or an insult? I was so hurt and confused that I didn't even give a counter, nor did I notice the man leave the Atrium.

As my blood pressure returned to normal and my heart began to beat regularly, I jumped down from the sofa before I too took my leave. Heading around the sleek hallway, I turned the corner and wandered towards the closed-off foyer. As I laid sights on the interior room, I watched the final image of the tall man disappear behind the elevator doors on the other side of the large French doors. Gritting my teeth, I morphed myself into my human form curious about a gut-wrenching instinct.

Placing my feminine hands around the matching levee door handles, I felt my stomach churn as I pushed down on the mechanism. The doorknob wouldn't budge. My instincts were right on the money as usual. "Asshole," I called out. "How the hell were we supposed to trust each other when here you are locking me away like some princess in a damn tower?"

Chapter 21
Jakob

"Cinder what are you doing?" I excruciatingly thought to myself as the animal's fangs tightly clenched around my throat. Trying to put my hands inside my sweatpants pockets, I was trying my best to wrap my head around the unfolding events. The woman I had just admitted my love to had her murderous fangs wrapped around my throat, her heavyweight pressed along my chest. Not leaning into my tired chest, but still so close that I could feel the natural warmth wrapped around this canine form of hers. "Cin-cinder?" I managed to whisper. My voice was barely audible as I coughed up blood, the red liquid spewing out from the corner of my lips.

When the tips of my fingers finally grasped the GPS trigger button on my cell phone, I felt the fangs pull out of their positions in my flesh, warm blood oozing out along with them. Focusing what conscious attention I had on the Hellhound before me, I noticed her solemn expression. The sadness just fled out of her beautiful icy-blue eyes. Entranced by that stunning stare, I couldn't help but begin to feel guilty over something, however, I couldn't say why?

"Jakob, I'm sorry." The dog whispered as she removed her hundred-pound canine body from the top of my chest. Her stunning black frame stained with my blood, sulking off into the shadowless night cast by the bright full moon.

As I slipped into the darkness of my subconscious, wondering if this would be my last day alive. "Was this why she had distanced herself from us so she could easily disappear from the safety of our Syndicate? Was it something the Shadow had told her to do? Was she doing this for our benefit?" I aimlessly thought, horrifyingly peering into the varying depths each one of these questions offered. Oblivious to the severity of my condition, I attempted my best to cling to the edge of my consciousness. I needed to stay alive, so I could find where Cinder was heading off to. My purpose was to make sure she was safe. Cinder was the love of my life, and I would do anything to assure she was safe, that she was not hurt, and that she could live the life everyone had stolen from her. Just as my sensitive hearing faintly caught onto the voices of my comrades, I alluded the promise to myself.

Slowly opening my eyes, I saw that I was not outside in the blistering cold. I could hear the hush tones of people whispering perplexing declarations. Speaking so quietly that I couldn't make out the words. My throat was hoarse and dry. My eyelids felt so heavy that it made it hard to clearly make out the blurred figures coming into my line of sight. Straining to focus on the nearest figure, I eventually realized that my friends were standing around me.

Before I could recognize the rest of my surroundings, or even atone for the numb feeling in the rest of my body, I was rushed by a female figure. Her arms felt like a ton of bricks as they wrapped around my back and neck. Swarming my horizontal body in a hug. "Oh my god. Thank god you are okay." I could hear her soft raspy voice cry. A familiar tone I had spent years listening to.

"Yalu give him some space. I know your hormones have kicked in and all, however, he just woke up. Give him some space." My sharp hearing overheard an annoyingly familiar masculine tone interject.

With the final bits of my numbing nerves unwinding, I saw the figures refine themselves, allowing me to make out all of their characteristics. The similar sightings of my fellow friends. The woman who easily let go of my sore and tired body, I hastily realized was none other than our one and only Yalu. The eldest of the two Vixens we had, and the woman who was pregnant with Mhykal, my best friend's offspring. Her once long beautiful black hair was cut a few inches back, going from the middle of her back to the upper shoulder blades. It was held up in a high ponytail to keep the majority of her loose strands short from falling into her gorgeous Caucasian face. The skin felt as if it was gleaming, glowing with her breaking news. Those amber fox eyes glowering down at me in a soft contentful expression. Further analyzing the current outfit the Vixen was wearing, I noticed that she was wearing an elastic band, black sweatpants, and a loose fit tank top that seemed to be somewhat more form fit than the last time I saw her. Trying to wrap around what I was seeing, I noticed that the woman had unintentionally put weight on. Seeing the bump, I was reminded of the day she had told us all about her Christmas surprise.

Looking over to my long-time friend and fellow Vampiric Mhykal, I noticed that none of his features had changed, unlike his girlfriend. His black hair was still the same length, and his amber eyes were still the same color telling me that unlike his mate, the Vampire had not changed. Well mostly. I soon realized that he had let a little bit of his facial hair grow out. The scruff adding some unique seriousness to the frame of his soft chin and cheekbone structure.

Swallowing what little saliva had formed inside my mouth, I softened the blow to the back of my throat and spoke as loudly as my vocals would allow. "How long-" I paused for a moment, realizing the words were barely coming out of my mouth. Checking my throat yet again, I attempted once more to speak, "How long was I-" Once more I stopped when I realized that behind Mhykal were the other two Unnaturals, the elder Hellhound, Peylith, the younger Vixen, Valeryie as well as the Vampiric Healer, Viktor. They were still too far back to see whatever the passing time had indeed done to their physical attributes, but they were still close enough that their Auras wafted off their specific scents. Swiftly realizing that there was one more missing, I finalized my tone and asked, "Where-where is Cinder?"

The looks on their faces told me almost immediately that there was something off, that her absence in this room was concurrent.

Swallowing the doubt, I once more asked, this time using a deeper tone, "Where is Cinder?"

"Jakob," Yalu said, her voice mimicking a soft cry while simultaneously mastering a low growl.

"Jakob, Cinder isn't here at the Syndicate anymore." Mhykal hastily spoke up. His eyes full of worry, and for some odd reason, when I stared into his Vampiric amber gaze, I saw lying deep down was the disguised look of infidelity and apology.

"Where did she go?" I interrogated, trying to get myself out of bed. Forcing all of my sore muscles to stop complaining and start working immediately!

My friend looked over to Viktor for some silent aid in explaining where the woman I had just confessed my love to had wandered off to. The seven-hundred old vampire who too had not aged a day since becoming immortal brought himself closer. Both Mhykal and I knew that Viktor would bluntly tell you the honest truth regardless of the consequences. Laying my eyes on the pale, slender Vampiric Doctor, I listened to him verify, "After we brought you here to get your wounds treated, a couple of hours later, Mhykal and Peylith returned with an unconscious nearly demonic-looking Cinder in hand."

"Unconscious? Demonic?" I muttered to myself, too tired to speak it aloud. Finding my voice, I probed, "So, she's still here?"

"She was..." Mhykal interrupted.

"Was?"

"Braedon heard about the scenario and wanted precautionary measures put in place.-" Viktor explained.

"Precautionary measures?" I growled, "What measures?"

"At first it was locking her in her room for a little while, but whenever anyone of us tried to go inside to try to ask about what happened, or tell her about your condition, the Hellhound attacked us. Or tried to slip past us, to get out of the room. It felt as if she was two different people-"

"Two different people?" I wondered to myself, recalling the memory of her blood lust when she killed Logan.

"The last draw was when she nearly killed Peylith, and Braedon wanted her moved to the Stables for those measures."

"You put her in the Stables?" I angrily barked.

"Jakob, it was what had to be done."

"What had to be done?!" I shot back, suddenly recollecting the level of fear and timidity in her eyes that night. "Was further traumatizing her really what had to be done?"

"Traumatizing her? What about us, Jakob!" Yalu blurted out. "She nearly killed you, and almost killed Mhykal and Peylith all in one night! I love her like family but when she tried to kill the father of my child, I was not going to stand by and let her do that!"

"SO-!"

"Jakob!" Mhykal hissed, speaking above even my boiling rage. "We had to do it. Although it severely pained us, it had to be done."

"Cinder didn't fight us on it, either. I do believe she understood what happened and the consequences that were to come of her actions." Viktor defended. "I know it sounds cruel, but it was necessary-"

"Let me see her," I stated, forcing myself out of the bed. My numb legs dramatically arguing with my brain's orders.

"Jakob, no! You just woke up from being a coma! You can barely even stand up-." Yalu cried, trying to push me back down into the bed. Her smaller pregnant build, easily managing to press down on my weakened state.

"I need to see her Yalu!" I argued.

"I know you do, but you need to think of your condition first."

"It wouldn't be possible anyways." Another voice entered the clash of many, it's bossy arrogance further pissing me the hell off.

"WHY THE HELL NOT BRAEDON?!" I snapped, catching sight of the man who was still wearing that same god-awful suit he always did.

"Because Jakob," the Vampiric Syndicate Leader addressed. "A week ago, I sent her over to the Lycan Syndicate."

"YOU WHAT!?" I snarled, now pushing my body once more against the hormonal raging woman. Dancing my eyes around the rest of the room, I saw that everyone else's eyes were doing whatever they could manage to look away from my stare. Their glares breaking the minute my amber eyes even looked their way. "YOU ALL KNEW, DIDN'T YOU?!"

"Yes, we all knew about it, and we all agreed it was..." Mhykal's voiced, the first to come forward. "It was better off for Cinder, who could barely speak to us, let alone transform back into her human form, or stay domestic around the slightest scent of blood. We believed if it was anyone that could help her control that crazy itch of hers, it was them."

"We could've managed-." I coughed.

"No we couldn't, and neither could they, it seemed." Braedon sighed.

"What are you talking about?" Peylith spoke up, his brown hair having been cut short against his head as if he was trying to fit into the era. His Golden Ankh tattoo popping up through the firm white muscle tank he was wearing.

"Cinder killed Calem."

Chapter 22
Jakob/Cinder

"What are you talking about, Braedon?" Mhykal blurted out, the shock in his tone of voice very distinguished. "There was no way in such a short amount of time that Cinder was able to kill someone as experienced as Calem-"

"Mhykal's right, Braedon," Viktor spoke up. I could easily sense the level of shock surging up through his typical laid-back demeanor. "Besides, Cinder was not in the greatest of-"

"Of, what?" I questioned.

"We had her starved..."

"Don't you dare lie to me, Braedon!" I ordered, attempting to once more to get out of bed. My heart racing, beating with such deadly velocity, I thought it would return to life and storm out of my chest.

"I had her fed once daily, so we could keep her under a decent amount of control, at least until the Lycans could attain custody over her." The Leader said, using the same level of arrogance that only further enraged my simmering blood.

"She was able to still move, it wasn't like she was starved, but she wasn't in any position nonetheless to challenge the Betas, let alone Calem." Viktor further explained to me, trying to relax my enraged nerve.

"For as long as I have known that Slobbering Wolfman, not even I could pull out many weaknesses from him." Braedon continued, "So I would guess it wouldn't be impossible to spot them if she knew what she was looking for, however, whatever the reason was, he was killed two days ago."

"So how are they handling her custody now?" Yalu curiously asked.

"They aren't. According to Joseph, a hired Client by the name of Mr. Gale, apparently took Cinder after she lost consciousness succeeding her brawl with the Syndicate Leader. Neither has been seen since."

"Mr. Gale?" I pondered as my head wrapped around the thoughts of another man being in cahoots with Cinder. Speaking up, I interrogated, "And they have nothing on this man? This Mr. Gale character?"

Braedon shook his head, his hands coming out of his suit's pockets. "No, the only information they knew was his alias and his phone number. But when they ran a check on the number it seemed that the phone had been shut off hours before the murder."

"Leaving suspicion that this guy knew what Cinder was going to do." Peylith theorized, his behavior abruptly changing from the more concealed and stand-back mannerism into a more comprehensive and confrontational one. "Something doesn't seem right with this picture." The Hellhound further wondered, his index finger and thumb stroking his chin in a manner that usually meant someone was in deep deliberation.

"What's, not right?" I probed, feeling my anger turn into trembling anxiety.

"I need to get a hold of Anubis, see if he knows anything." The Hellhound returned, promptly turning on his heels and wandering towards the exit.

"Anubis?" Mhykal imminently asked. "Peylith wait up! Anubis?! You don't mean the like the Anubis, the Egyptian Deity of the Dead, do you?"

The Hellhound stopped at the door's entryway, pausing so he could answer the rampant questions the Vampiric was asking. Even though all of my heightened senses were still adjusting to the conscious world surrounding me, I could sense the Unnatural's Aura was way off. It was full of both pure fear and yet utmost seriousness. Something was indeed off, here. Listening to Peylith's tone, I heard the man simply answer, "Yes" before slamming the door shut behind him.

Stretching onto my side as I laid once more on the comfortable wicker sofa residing out on the Atrium, I looked up at the dark clouds while they passed overhead. The deep dull grey hues building up underneath the white puffy clouds forewarning its audience of an approaching storm. As I watched the large shelf cloud roll over the triangular glass frame, I couldn't help but feel amazed by the immense power I knew the collected moisture could bring. It was hard not to be anything else, but amazed. Deeply staring into the passing clouds, I eventually felt an overwhelming sense of worry corrupt me. "Was he really okay? Augustus said that Jakob was in a coma, but was he okay? Would he be mad at me when we woke up? Would he forgive me and my intolerable actions? Is he just as worried about me as I am him?"

Rolling myself over onto my back, I brought my muzzle in towards my chest so I could get a strong whiff of the scents still heavily saturated into my Christmas Gift. His scent was so strongly entwined with the nylon fabric that it stood out more than the others did. Inhaling the strong, musty masculine scent of the seven-hundred-year-old Vampiric, I breathed in the distinctive aroma of his testosterone, his high levels of oxytocin, his love for me. It was all there. All of it was there. After a few more puffs, I stopped once my ears alerted me to the sound of rain pitter against the glass roof.

"Did you really love me?" I doubted. "Was that wrenching feeling in my heart really love? Was that kiss the two of us had, a true-?" I stopped audibly wondering when I heard the sound of keys jangling coming from inside the huge apartment. Hastily spinning myself around, I fell off the sofa and nearly crashed into the nearby concrete fire pit. Regaining my surroundings, I made my way out of the Atrium and down the hallway towards the foyer. As I approached the foyer, I growled "Augustus, you better have a good reason why you locked me..." Stopping at the last moment when my eyes realized that it wasn't Augustus who was standing in front of the French doors. "Who are you?" I now quietly wondered to myself, simultaneously debating if I should announce my Unnaturalism or not.

Taking in this stranger's appearance, I overlooked this person. Easily noting that it was a woman who I would say was maybe a year or two older than me. It was hard to say, she may be younger for all I know. So far going by looks, I noticed that her long hair's dye job was fading, its dark roots showing through the washed-out blonde. With her back turned towards me, I couldn't gain much intel on her, so I pressed on with trying to decipher her species. Was she Human or Unnatural? I needed to know what sort of threat she could potentially emit to either me or the absent Archangel. Quickly figuring out that she was human, I attempted to come closer. Analyzing every little detail, I could as I approached, I officially decided that upon her 'attire' and her careless demeanor this woman wasn't a threat.

"You are just one of his wealthy associates." I gratefully sighed, officially stepping out of the shadows to introduce myself as the 'new dog.' Upon completion of my approach, I observed that with her low-hanging beige shirt, this woman had large breasts that smelled off. Honestly, they smelled fake and in my opinion were, unfortunately, a bit too big for her frame. To hold the shirt up, I glanced over a thick chain that was wrapped around her neck, leaving her perfect back exposed to the elements. Though if she wanted, I could easily give her a few etchings into her bare back. Further examining the possibly one hundred and twenty, maybe thirty-pound woman, I noticed she was wearing skin-tight jeans and fancy red-sole heels that I could only assume cost as much as her long luscious hair extensions did.

"Oh, who is this?" the woman wondered, finally realizing I existed. "Come here baby-" She called in this god-awful high-pitched tone. The type of volume I would expect to come from a wailing animal, not some wealthy associate. Eyeing the woman kneel, her large white purse collapsing onto the dark wood floors, I continued to play the part. Trotting up to this still suspicious character, who I had yet to completely figure out I nearly broke character from the amount of perfume she was wearing. She wore so much that I was surprised I couldn't smell it until I was right next to her. My poor nose couldn't smell anything else but that pungent aroma. Trying to get my nose to inhale some fresh air, I heard her shockingly exclaim. "Look at you. My god, you must be eating him out of house and home."

"Oh, you should see how much he eats." I shot back, my head submitting to the toxic smell I could not escape from.

"I'm sorry to intrude, but I came here to bring a few things over before he got home."

"Bringing things over?" I now inquired. "Are you his girlfriend?"

"You wouldn't mind helping me set up a little bit, would you?" she continued to question as if I was indeed man's best friend.

Chapter 23
Augustus/Cinder

Stepping off the elevator and onto the floor of my sleek penthouse, I dropped the two boxes and several bags of clothes I had Cinder order the night before and began to look for my keys. I knew that the Hellhound was going to rip into me for locking her inside the apartment, especially after how we had just talked about 'trust' and all, but my priority was to keep the Unnatural safe under lock and key until the appropriate time to unleash her. Eventually, finding my keys, I went to unlock the Foyer doors and hastily realized the door had been tampered with. Somebody had broken in! Glancing through the lightly frosted glass, I noticed that thankfully nothing else seemed to be messed with. Exhaling a sigh of relief, I stopped midway when the thought ran through my head, "Did she break out? Did she even have the skill to pick the lock?"

Opening the doors, I left them open and strode inside, keeping my eyes out for whoever was either awaiting my return or was not. Thankfully, I didn't have to venture far to get my answers. There, waiting for me in the kitchen was an unexpected guest and someone whom I did not want Cinder to meet.

"This is an unexpected visit, Theresa." I shockingly declared as I ventured towards the kitchen area to set down my household keys in the usual place I normally tossed them before strolling back towards the foyer for the undisclosed clothes.

"Yeah I know Augustus, but there is nothing better than spontaneity." The woman smirked.

"Spontaneity huh?" I sarcastically wondered, "Yeah, right. This is not the time for my girlfriend to be here when I already have another woman living in my apartment." Coming back with the boxes, I used the hallway to off to the right so I could try and hide Cinder's clothes from Theresa. Quickly running the two large boxes and three plastic bags into the Hellhound's room, I noticed that there was no lounging canine in the Atrium. "Great, now where did she go off to?" I growled as I dropped the boxes down in front of Cinder's acclaimed bed. Coming back out of the room, leaving the door ajar as it was before, I returned to the 'fun' that awaited me in the next room.

"So, Augustus, when did you get her?" Theresa questioned me as I came into the kitchen. Coming into the room to see the still canine shapeshifted woman getting her ears stroked by the woman's femininely small hands.

"Two days ago- walked right into my life." I returned, partially exaggerating exactly how I had come in contact with Cinder, as well as her true identity. I couldn't let it come out that Cinder was an Unnatural and not some dog. Looking into those deep blue eyes of hers, I could see that the Hellhound had me practically dancing in the palm of her hand, and I knew she was enjoying every single moment of it.

"Well, that can explain why you haven't gotten her registered or well any actual 'pet' items." Theresa shot back to me as she wrapped herself around the unknown Hellhound's neck exposing the blue nylon choker the Beauceron was wearing. "Such a sweet girl."

"Yeah, I am surprised that she is behaving herself right now."

Getting a flash of teeth from the dog, I heard my girlfriend chuckle, "I don't think she liked you saying that about her, honey.

So, what's her name? I mean you should have a name for her by now."

"It's Cinder," I said, again not lying.

"That's a pretty name. Cinder." Theresa said, locking her hazel green eyes with the dog's blue gaze. "Even though she has the most gorgeous blue eyes that can even put a Husky to shame, I can see how the faded amber dances around her eyes as if they are little embers dancing under the deep blue sea."

The compliment made Cinder pull away from her challenging glare and return the fixation onto me as I walked around the kitchen. "She had the name when I got her," I said. "I couldn't change considering her age and all."

"How old is she? I mean, she looks no older than two or three maybe."

"Yeah, that's what I was told too. You know your dog's quite well."

"I should, I had a few growing up, but none ever this big. Mainly little dogs like Pomeranians and Poodles."

"I believe the people at the shelter called her a King-sized." I lied, trying to give a scientific reason for the dog's massive Dane sized structure. "They also said that she wasn't a purebred."

"I can see why they would say that," Theresa said, breaking away from the dog's side. "So, how about we go get her some stuff, that way we can have some time to catch up?"

"I just got home." I heard the Archangel agonizingly complain. "I really don't want to go back out there. It's a fucking madhouse."

"Oh, come on, honey. Cinder needs some things of her own." The woman named, Theresa, continued to try and persuade. Her high-pitched voice still ringing deep in my ears and giving me a rotting headache. It made me thankful that I only had to be alone with her for an hour before the secretive Augustus had returned. Any longer and I think I would've lost it.

Walking around the counter island, I brushed my shoulder into the Archangel before sitting on my haunches and fastening my gaze with his. Hinting the best way I could without giving myself away. "Oh come on, just go. I've already been here by myself for long enough, what's a few more hours." I mentally snickered. "Besides, with as much time as I'm expecting to be in this form, I might as well have a few things lying around."

"Fine." Augustus reluctantly caved. Either he understood what I told him, or he didn't want to be in the 'Doghouse' with this woman, either way, it didn't matter to me. "I guess it will give us some time to catch up since your trip to Paris..."

"And London. I went there too, remember?" His girlfriend quickly reminded.

"Oh yeah, I forgot about the time you spent there."

"You liar." I jabbed, watching the man proceed with grabbing something from the fridge. My strong sense of smell which was once drowned by the terrible stench of perfume was now overwhelmed with the powerful smell of food. Meat specifically. Watching him take a large collection of raw meat, I knew was wrapped in a white piece of paper, I listened to my poor stomach demand to be fed.

"Is that what you've been feeding her?" The woman interrupted. "You know human food really isn't that good for her?"

Yeah, yeah, I know human food isn't that good for her, but if you cook beef a certain way it can be fed to them." The Angel debated.

"So, you've been cooking her meals?"

"Yup, she eats when I eat."

"Right, keep lying." I snarled. "Hurry up and cook it whatever it is." My stomach was so hungry for the meat, that I was tempted to eat it raw. Tempted. I still preferred to eat a cooked meal, but if I was forced to eat it raw, I would as I recalled all those days I had eaten both raw and partially cooked food back when I was in Federal custody.

"Just let me cook this for her, and then we can leave. She hasn't eaten yet, so I can only assume with it being nearly three in the afternoon-"

"Well hurry up, I don't know when the pet store closes." Theresa blandly ordered in the same way that Yalu ordered Mhykal around. That haunting image making me cringe in pain. Pacing my front paws on the tile flooring, I patiently waited for the expected mashed beef and rice dish Augustus was cooking up. The smell of the sizzling beef made my mouth heavily salivate, so much so that I was allowing drool to escape onto the floor.

"Come on, come on, come on." I anxiously repeated.

Chapter 24
Cinder

"We'll be back in a little while," I recalled the last words the woman saying as she left the apartment with Augustus in tow. I could see the look of not wanting to go spread across those emerald green eyes of his, and smell the odor of anxiety written all over his Aura, although with curiosity biting at my heels for the desired answers to the new questions arousing in my head, I aloofly pushed away his que. Leaving just only one concern left in my head, "Could she be trusted? Could she really be trusted with our secrets?"

As I devoured the beef and rice dish that my canine instincts had so happily savored while the meal was slowly cooking itself, I continued to wonder the worrying thoughts: "I could barely even consider trusting Augustus who was supposed to be my babysitter, so why was I worrying over the trustworthiness of this 'Human'? Was it even worth trying to create a relationship with her when I wasn't sure how much longer she was going to be around? Was it worth telling her secrets if she may not be around much longer? If I told her who I was, or if he told her who I truly was, would she keep the secret? Or, would she blab her high-pitched loudmouth to the Hunters?" Licking the platter clean, it's edged bottom banging against the tile floors as it danced around from the weight of my tongue, I stalled when I suddenly thought, "Does she know what he is? Does this 'Human' even know she's in the presence of a Valkyrie? Had he been lying to her? And if so, then how had he been able to do it for so long? I mean Augustus is a really bad liar…" Now making head-way towards my room, I adjusted my thought process. "I guess only time will tell." Brushing past the door, I noticed the boxes and plastic bags sitting beside the bed. Naturally assuming that this had to be all of those clothes I had bought yesterday; I sorrowfully altered my appearance and returned to my naked human form. As I closed the door to the bedroom, I questioned the rapid speed at which these boxes had arrived. Nothing ever came that fast, but I guess for the right price you could get it overnight. Once the door was closed, I began to dress myself in the baggy clothes Augustus had given me. I knew that I needed to be somewhat 'decent' just in case I was being spied on. After pulling the shirt down over my breasts, I knelt beside the boxes and used my blood scythe to cut open the first box. The thick iron effortlessly slicing through the packing tape.

Opening the first box, I was greeted by the sights of the two 'formal' dresses I had reluctantly bought. Each dress had cost me eighty dollars, but given the cheap accessories I had bought to go with the items on top of my petite frame, I knew I could easily play that 'distinguished look' he sought. The first dress I pulled out had an astonishing deep red color with an open back followed by a long train that flawlessly flowed from the soft red fabric into a velvet-soft black fur. Fur so black that it reminded me of my own. The dress also had long sleeves that belled out into an intricate floral lace fabric to match the center corset. The lace fabric sat low on my breasts to further accentuate my apparently to-die-for hourglass figure. And the last but not least detail this dress offered was a thigh-high slit. I still couldn't believe how I had managed to get such an exquisite gown for such a low price. Although, I guessed I had to thank the Archangel for that. Dropping the dress onto the bed, I dug back into the box for the second dress. The second gown was a dark navy-blue fabric with another low-hanging V-neck with extended fabric wrapping up around the neck area. Where the loose v-neck gap came back together stood a stunningly gorgeous sapphire jewel stitched into the fabric. the other gown was a dark navy-blue with a low hanging V-neck fabric, that wrapped back up around the neck. Now while this gown lacked in complex detail its simplicity silhouetted a gorgeous form-fit figure before falling into a mid-length train. Placing that dress too on the bed, I proceeded to match all of the costume jewelry with each gown.

Taking a minute to absorb each dress, I moved onto the second box where I again effortlessly used my blood scythe to open the sealed cardboard. "Alright, what secrets do you hold?" I mumbled to myself while I pulled back the flaps. This box contained many goodies, the clothes and shoes I deeply adored buying. Pulling out an interior shoebox, I opened that up to see the formal shoes I had bought. A simple anklet black four-inch stiletto heel. Closing the lid, I threw them back up on the bed beside the gowns. Grabbing the next box, I instantly knew that these were my athletic black tennis shoes. Placing the Nike box down on the floor beside me, I moved onto the secluded clothes. The first items to come to the light were my sweatpants and athletic yoga pants. Followed by the spring/fall jacket that deeply resembled the one I had fallen in love with a year ago and had no idea what happened too since the incident. Matter of fact, the jacket was such a spitting image I wondered if Yalu and I had gotten ripped off with our bargain. Shaking that thought out of my head, I tossed the jacket onto the bed as well as the pants. Rolling through the rest of my clothes in the box, I managed to pull out two tank tops, a cool blue and a soft grey, three varying fashionable tops, a loosely hanging collared white shirt with a nice laced back, a beige V-neck t-shirt, and another beige form-fit camisole. Under those shirts were my desired skinny jeans. A faded worn pair with holes at the knees and a dark offset black pair that had a frayed bottom to adorn well with a majority of my shoes. It made me content that the Vixen had taught me everything about this 'outside' world and its worldly fashions to help fit into the socialized civilization, yet those memories also brought much struggle and pain.

"Would any of you ever forgive me?" I wondered aloud, looking out of the tall windows that separated my room from the balcony. Staring out into the rainy world beyond my view, I painfully swallowed. "Would you guys understand if I told you that it was to keep you all safe?"

Understanding that there was no way I could go back and ask; I pushed the worrying thoughts aside. Taking a look around the messy room, I decided it was time I put things away. Standing myself up, I grabbed up the two shoeboxes and wandering into the walk-in closet. Finding a spot for the shoes at the bottom of the closet, I took them out of their boxes and happily placed each pair on each shelf. The heels on the higher shelf and the tennis shoes on the lower shelf. Unsure of what to do with the empty boxes, I tucked them beneath the shelves for now. Strolling back into the bedroom, I embarked on working through the many plastic bags.

The first plastic bag I snatched had all of the undergarments I had bought. Quickly glancing over the undergarments, I counted the several pairs I had ordered. Two soft pinky-beige lacey pairs, then the three black bras and their matching undergarments. "So that's everything I ordered yesterday." Glancing over to the second bag, I inquired "So what's in that bag?"

Reaching for the next plastic bag, I realized that on the front of the bag was the same logo of the one website where Augustus had ordered me my reaping Uniform. Understanding that this had to be that, I hesitated further peering inside. I knew I wasn't going to being 'Reaping' right away per the Diety's demands, and so I simply closed the plastic bag before grabbing its partner and taking both bags to the closet. Standing in front of the dresser and looking into the wall mirror for a quick second, I tiredly sighed. For the third time in two days, I just stared aimlessly at my figure. Taking another breath, I glanced away from the reflective glass and started putting the clothes away in their designated drawers. Leaving the 'Reaping' uniform's bag on the top of the dresser, I easily put away all but one of the undergarment pairs. Leaving the black set on the dresser, I crumbled up the plastic bag and walked into the bathroom where I had seen a trashcan remain. Tossing the plastic bag into the little silver metallic can, I went back to the bedroom to grab both the jacket and those two dresses I had purchased.

After several repeated processes, I had successively put away my entire wardrobe and had also changed into something more decent than my birthday suit. With myself lazily dressed in a pair of the super soft grey sweatpants and the blue athletic tank, I carried the two cardboard boxes out of my room. Dropping the stacked boxes beside the sliding glass door, I returned to my large Beauceron form, comprehending that it wouldn't be much longer before Theresa and the lying Augustus would be back. Falling back onto all fours, I made my way back towards the beautiful Atrium where I hoped deep down I'd be able to find some more peaceful sleep.

Chapter 25

Augustus

You got it honey, or do you want me to help?" Theresa questioned as she tried to grab for a few objects I was barely able to keep ahold of. Pushing away her hands, I kept following the sound of her guiding voice as we stepped off of the high-rise elevator and into the foyer. "I hope she likes it."

"I hope so too." I responded before silently telling myself, "Because I am taking this out of her allowance no matter what she argues." Hearing the doors open, I continued to rely on my girlfriend's voice to make my way through the apartment while she simultaneously dragged me towards the balcony.

"Here's a good spot, Augustus, put the bed here."

Dropping the extra-large dog-bed down on the floor, I proceeded with pushing it against one of the few floor-to-ceiling glass windows which offered a gorgeous view of the balcony and the cityscape beyond. Letting the soft white-fleece fabric that adorned the mattress sit on the ground for a bit, I upsettingly recalled I still had the rest of the bed to build. Though where was the frame? Looking around the common area, I bit my tongue prior to running back for the elevator. "I forgot the frame," I called out just as I stepped onto the private elevator. Once the doors had shut, I pressed the button for the private garage floor and quietly mumbled, "What the hell made Theresa want the bed that badly? When I knew deep down that the likelihood of Cinder even using it was close to never. Matter of fact, I doubted she would use any of the items I bought. Anyone of those things could send her over the edge and would only result in the Hellhound being mad at me and not the woman who made me buy them!" As the elevator finally reached the floor, I ran towards my one hundred and three thousand-dollar sleek black Lexus LC. The suited-up vehicle had been custom made so it could only help endure the tastes of the wealthy but make me fit in more with this society. Opening up the trunk, I was still surprised that the matching dark wood frame was able to fold down and fit into the tiny trunk this vehicle had to offer. Unlike that damn mattress that had to be fitted painfully into the back seat by me and no one else. "I swear that woman can be no help at all, and it feels like she is just in it for my money," I complained while I fought to get the collapsible frame out of the trunk. Winning the game of tug of war, I tiredly shut the trunk and locked the fancy car before eventually making my way back towards the elevator. Preparing myself for the excepted chaos I knew was unfolding back in my apartment.

"Oh, Augustus, there you are." My blonde-haired girlfriend panted from nowhere within my range of sight. Walking over to the bed, I dropped the frame and began to piece together the dog bed. "See, I told you it would fit the theme in your place." The woman jabbed, her arm tightly coiling around my chiseled abs.

"Now only if we can get her to use it." I jabbed. "So, I can get my bed back." I then partially lied. I mean, Cinder was sleeping in one of my beds. But in her defense, it was the bed I had given her.

"Well let's hope so because I don't think I can efficiently commit when we have someone with such human eyes watching everything that I am going to do to you tonight." Theresa purred, her peppermint breath whispering deep down into my ear. Spinning around, I smiled and playfully leaned in for a kiss on her soft lipstick red lips. Unable to contain the hungering crave for her, I dragged her into my room while we continued to heavily make out. With our hormones raging, I barely managed to get the door to the Master Suite open while also trying to not miss a beat. Leading Theresa into the room, I heard the woman's heels kick the door shut behind us as she began to rapidly take off my shirt. Using my hands to help guide her, I slipped out of my form-fit long-sleeve shirt before spinning her around and tossing her onto the queen-sized mattress. Proceeding with the next step, I brought my lips down her neck and towards her firm breasts, while removing that exposing garment from around her chest. Hearing the woman's heavy sighs and moans were moments of pure ecstasy. So much so that it only drove me deeper into the hungering itch for her.

"I don't know how you do it, Augustus..." Theresa complimented, her head lying on her hand as it lied on top of my left pectoral. Remaining silent, I tried my best to now ignore a deep feeling that was choking me out. "What's the matter, baby? Usually, you give some snarky comeback."

"I don't know." I sighed, breaking away from the beautiful woman who remained naked under the dark sheets. As I grabbed for my boxers and began putting them on, I felt something in my stomach was not right. Putting on my sweatpants, I continued, "It's too quiet-."

"Honey, I don't know what you're talking about, it's always this quiet at your place."

"No, I know my place is pretty quiet here, that's the reason why I bought the place." I recklessly returned. Heading towards the bedroom door, I felt my heart stop for a moment. Feeling it freefall deep down in my churning stomach before it flew back up into my throat, I again coughed on the choking feeling. "I just have a bad feeling."

With a heavy swallow, I spoke up, "I'm just going to go check in on Cinder."

"Baby, I'm sure she is fine," Theresa said, stepping out of bed. Her figure dancing with the echoing warm fluorescent lighting of my nightstand as she sauntered closer to me. "Just come back to bed."

"It will only take a minute." I rebutted, shoving her taunting temptation away and leaving the room. I had to make sure everything was okay.

Strolling through the hallway, I noticed that although nearly all of the lights were off except for the overhead kitchen lights that naturally dimmed with the time of day, I soon realized dancing through the balcony windows was that unwelcoming red glow. Craning my eyes over to the windows, I saw that over the clouds was the one truly unwelcome guest. That dreadful red moon.

"Shit-!" was all I could get out before I heard the amusing awe of my girlfriend's voice coo from behind me.

"What a beautiful view..."

Knowing I couldn't waste time, I sped up my search for the Hellhound. I had to find her as soon as possible. There were so far only two spots I could place the black and tan dog at, her bedroom or the Atrium. Taking my shot with the Atrium first, I ran for the interior greenhouse that made this penthouse a huge selling point besides the view.

"Holy Shit!" was all I could get out this time as my eyes absorbed the condition of Cinder. She was lying on the ornate linoleum tile floor that stretched out a simple walkway and pattern around the fire pit. With the shale color of the linoleum, I could easily make a large puddle of blood that the black and tan dog was lying in. There was so much that it was hard to see exactly where it was coming from, although I assumed from the reports, I had read on her, it was coming from her back, nose, and mouth. Strolling into the room, I oversaw the long bone spikes that came protruding out of her spine.

As I bent down to attempt to examine the spikes, I watched the shy bones pull themselves back under the skin. Hiding away from sight. Coming up to the canine's head, I softly finished kneeling on the floor, my knees pressing hard into the still wet but somehow freezing cold blood. Placing my hand on her shoulder and running it down the side of her rib cage, I watched the dog throw her head up. Her fangs bared, streaking the blood down each tooth she had. Her gorgeous blue eyes were replaced with the dancing fiery orange. The Hellhound only managed one warning call before her head collapsed down onto the floor with a heavy thud back into the pool of blood. Feeling her rib cage rise and fall at an unsteady rapid beat, I knew that she was beginning to have respiration problems, something that I had seen many other Hellhounds fall to when they couldn't handle the power of the Blood Moon. Swallowing the fear lodged in my throat, I softly announced my presence, "It's alright Cinder, I'm right here."

"Aug-august-." I could hear the dog cry. The tone in her voice full of pure agonizing terror and pain. "It, it hu-hurts, Aug-."

"I know. It's alright. I will go get you something that will help your breathing-." I hurriedly spoke, trying to stand myself up but stopped when the Beauceron flung her head back at me, trying to send me a clear message. Stamping my knees back down onto the floor, I returned, "Alright, I will stay here, but you still need to take something."

"No-no." she panted.

"Cinder, don't argue with me! I cannot let you die." I argued before taking the risk and calling out for Theresa's aid.

"It, it'll-it'll pass." The Hellhound claimed.

"No, it won't. I have seen this too often to know how it goes, so just let me do my job." I pleaded with her. "THERESA!" I shouted. "Get in here-"

Chapter 26
Augustus/Cinder

"OH MY GOD, AUGUSTUS!" My girlfriend shrieked. "WHAT HAPPENED?!"

"I need you to go into the kitchen, inside the third drawer from the stove, and grab one of the few needles in there. It doesn't' matter which one-." I explained as I continued to attempt my best to keep the arguing Hellhound, arguing. Doing what I could to keep her in the least conscious. "All of them have what I need."

"Alright." Theresa returned, darting for the kitchen in her dark negligée that she had brought with her to the apartment. Seconds later, I could hear her patter around the drawers, completely forgetting which drawer I had told her held the medications I had created for just this moment. I knew that her panic and shock had overridden her sense of comprehension, which I completely understood, my first time seeing this was no different, however, we were in a rush here.

"God that woman, I swear-" I frustratingly teased, trying to keep the female Unnatural still awake. Yet when I got no response back, I hesitantly called, "Cinder?" Still nothing, I rested my hand along her rib cage, waiting for the fast rise and fall, but I received nothing. After a few seconds, I knew that Cinder's respiration levels had turned for the worse, I knew that I needed to hurry up and do something to keep her alive. Cursing at myself, I crawled up towards the canine's large square head. I didn't want to do mouth-to-mouth resuscitation, but I had no other choice until Theresa got back with that needle. "Damn it-" I said, delaying yet another second of Cinder's draining life. Wrapping my fingers around the dog's muzzle, I tightly clung them around her mouth, clenching it shut, I brought my mouth towards her bloody, wet black nose. Taking a huff of breath, I swiftly exhaled all the breath I had into the Cinder's nose. Pulling away after the first puff, I repeated the sequence. I had to do whatever I could to keep Cinder alive, or else Zachariah would have my head for letting his current 'Toy' break on him.

'Here Augustus." I heard the high-pitched feminine voice call out from behind me. Pulling my mouth away from Cinder's nose, I immediately grabbed the needle out of her small hand.

"I need you to leave the room and close the doors behind you," I ordered the human woman.

"Why?"

"Don't argue with me, Theresa!" I snapped.

"Fine!" she complied, leaving the room and swinging the accordion-style doors shut with much haste. I could see out of the corner of my eye that she remained on the other side, her scared eyes eyeing everything I was preparing myself to do.

"I'm sorry Cinder." I apologized as I put the needle with its cap still attached inside the forefront of my mouth, holding it there by the edge of my lips. Moving the longer strands of fur away from the canine's neck up behind her upper jawline, I began anxiously feeling for a vein. "This is going to hurt like hell," I warned as I pulled the needle from the cap and injected it into the soft pink flesh. The needle of the syringe breaking through the meat and into the large vascular system underneath. Pushing the medication into her bloodstream, I watched the canine's stiff blue eyes staring so painfully and sorrowfully back at me. I was waiting for the dilated pupils to retract then grow large from the side effect this drug created. After a full minute, I growled, "WORK DAMN IT!" Another thirty seconds passed by and still nothing. I could see those gorgeous eyes of hers starting to glaze over, and her faint breathing decline into the last remnants of respiration arrest. "Work. Please, work." I now sadly begged, moving my hand around her head. Stroking the soft tear-stained fur under her eyes and on her cheek. "Come on Cinder, wake up."

"Wake up..." I barely managed to hear someone call out to me through the depth-defying darkness. "Please" the voice repeated. "Please, wake up."

"Wake up?" I wondered. "I don't want to. I just want to sleep." I could feel someone's heavy hand press hard onto my face before it glided through my canine-shifted fur.

"Remember everything that your life holds in its hands." The voice continued to tell. It's tone so saddening, so anxious, so fearful. "Remember everyone you need to protect. You can't do that unless you wake up. So, please...please wake up."

"What?" I confusingly questioned, trying everything to recollect any memories of what I had been told, but unfortunately, nothing rose from the endless abyss inside my mind.

Just as I decided to ignore that prying voice who rang deep down into my conscious that shatter feeling again rose into my subconscious. That exact same feeling that had happened on that horrible night.

"No-" I bit down, fighting every dying nerve, I began to wipe away the crushing instincts. "No, that cannot happen again." I cried. "Not again."

"Finally." I sighed, relieving a much-needed breath of my own. The drug was finally working. Cinder's darkened glazed over stare returned full of such vibrant shades of blue, that it took me by surprise. "There you are..." I happily exhaled, slowly removing my hand from her soft fur. "Thank God." Watching the heavy breathing of the transformed Hellhound return, I observed her mouth gape open and that nearly whitewashed tongue came rolling out. The panting motion was another sign that life was coming back to Cinder. However, no matter how great the signs of life were, I knew that this not yet over. We still had to work through the other side effects and sequences which had yet to surface from having that drug enter her system.

"Aug-Augustus." I barely heard the Hellhound cry.

"It's alright Cinder," I assured.

"What hap-?"

"You know quite well what happened and this time it almost killed you. At least for fifteen minutes, it did." I now explained, the words sounding drained and exhausted. "I'm surprised you came back..."

No words came out.

Glancing down at the blood-stained woman who was mutated into a large one-hundred-pound Beauceron, I noticed that her eyes were now softly closed. Although, thankfully, she was still alive. No signs of the other side effects yet, another thankful grace by the Deities above. Rubbing my hand through her fur, I softly petted the sleeping canine. Her fast heart rate was still a massive concern that would have to be watched over the next couple of days, which meant I had to move my schedule around. "Great." I complained, "But your life ranks higher up the chain than my work and clients do. Even higher than hers." I softly murmured into the dog's long cropped ears that flickered as my breath tickled the fine hairs residing inside the oddly angled triangular cartilage. Looking over to Theresa, I flashed a small content smile, silently telling her it was okay to come back in. Hearing the doors pull open, I announced. "She will be fine for now that is."

"Oh, thank god." Theresa sighed with tremendous relief. "I thought..."

"Don't even say it." I hastily interrupted. "She was. And for the next forty-eight hours, she'll have to be avidly watched."

"She will? What exactly happened?" my girlfriend called as she bent down beside the dog's back, doing whatever she could to not step in the blood that was surrounding most of Cinder's unconscious body. "This is a lot of blood."

"Yes, the drug may wear off sooner than expected based upon her tolerance level." I slightly lied. I knew that there was a chance that her Iron Blood Trait would fight the drug and possibly eliminate it like a majority of the drugs she has been periodically put on throughout her life. "But to your second question, it's a medical condition that Vets are having a hard time even diagnosing, and it happens from time to time. Whatever the reason it is, they cannot figure out how, but she ends up bleeding out and as with any living creature, anemia is deadly. Then there is also the chance that she could also suffocate on her blood, or her heart itself could give out from the lack of blood and oxygen flowing to it."

"Which is what happened?"

"Sort of." I sighed. Truthfully, I wasn't sure how to answer that question. Not even I knew why this was happening. "Anyways, I need to get her moved out to the living room, someplace where I can keep a contained environment for her. If you would please go grab some towels from the dryer." I softly asked the woman, who thankfully obliged without a single question. "Alright, Cinder." I called out to the sleeping animal, "I'm sorry to do this to you, but I need to move you." Pushing my hands under the dog's heavy frame, I began to attempt my hardest to carefully pick up the canine. A sharp cry escaped the panting mouth. Saliva and blood just spewing out of her mouth as the jowls were lifted inches up from the floor. "I'm sorry. I really am." I repeated.

Chapter 27

Augustus

"Here we go," I mumbled to the slightly conscious creature as I gently lied her down on the collection of soft grey towels. Theresa had danced them around the floor before the tall windows where the living room and corresponding hallway freely flowed together. Not a peep rose from Hellhound, but I could tell she was biting her tongue and holding her breath to keep from bawling out in agony. Removing my hands from under her neck and interior hips, I stood myself up to take notice of my own condition. Swiftly realizing that I had still wet and cold blood drying into my casual nightwear.

"Why don't you go change, honey?" Theresa offered. "I can watch her for the time being."

"Are you sure?" I questioned. I was defiantly hesitant to leave an inexperienced human to watch over an unknown Unnatural, but I needed to change out these dirty clothes so I could keep myself from becoming shish-kabobbed by the Iron Blood's thick density. Rubbing the back of my blood-stained hand through my dirty-blonde hair, I grimaced at the feeling of Cinder's blood starting to impale the fine bones running through my fingers, pushing their way through like a ton of bricks.

"Are you okay? You aren't hurt, are you?"

"No, I'm fine." I lied. "Cinder just didn't understand what was going on and did the only thing she could to defend herself. It's only a scrape, anyways."

"Oh, okay. Well, go wash up." She now directly ordered me, her tone returning to its normal self.

Observing her plop down on the sofa, in the seat closest to the hurt animal down, I wondered to myself, "Was that every towel I had?" Strolling towards my room, I went for the master bath. Taking off my clothes as I ventured through the walk-in-closet, I tossed them in the adjacent hamper. Turning on the showerhead, I quickly set the digital water temperature to the perfect warmth and hastily stepped my nude build inside. The hot, steamy water ran itself all over my fading tan skin, washing away all the blood which had fervently soaked through my clothes and was merging with the skin. Grabbing the soap, I began to lather the exfoliant over my hands and feet, knowing that I needed to scrub away all remnants of the Hellhound's Blood Trait. Guiding the soaped up scrunchie over the skin for the third time, I finally began to feel the heavy pressure let up. "That's going to bruise," I complained over the high-pressurized water. "But, I guess that's not the worst Blood Moon I've ever had." I continued to tell myself, proceeding to glide the scrunchie over my arms, running the mesh fabric right over the raised ridge of my healed scars. "That cursed breed is nothing but trouble. Guardians, Reapers. Nothing but toys to their Masters."

Finishing up quickly, I grabbed the towel I had thrown onto the towel rack outside the shower's sliding door. Swiftly drying off my frame, drying every inch of my replenished skin, I wrapped the towel around my waist and wandered back into the closet for some fresh clothes. Something more leisure. Upon finding my typical pair of boxers, I hunted around for any shirt and pair of sweatpants I had left clean.

"Of course." I snarled. I had found a nice black t-shirt, but there were no sweatpants. "Figures now of all times, I would not have a pair of clean sweatpants. Fuck." Grumbling, I then walked over to the hanging closet behind me and grabbed the first pair of jeans I saw. Pulling them off the hanger, I turned back around and finally got dressed. Allowing the towel to fall from my waist, I grabbed my black boxer briefs and pulled the slim pair of dull navy-blue jeans over my legs. Staring at my reflection in the mirror, I eyed the cross that had been forcibly tattooed to my arm when I had signed my life over to Lord Zachariah. The immortal ink had slightly faded over the past couple of centuries; however, it was still as noticeable as the first day I had it etched into my skin. Staring at the cross, I noticed that the pattern and shape were practically identical to the scar on Cinder's back. "Why tattoo this on me, and yet mark Cinder with a burn scar? Why put her through that at such an early age? Why make it spread down the entirety of her spine? Why embed it so deep down into her flesh?" I aimlessly wandered, pulling away from the many straying questions in my head, I dragged the shirt over my head and down my chest. Finally dressed, I exited the closet before decisively venturing back towards the living room.

"That was quick," Theresa called as she glanced up away from the wall-mounted flat-screen television. "You even took a shower, damn."

"Had to." I sighed, rubbing my hand back through my wet sleekback hair. The blonde locks were so damp that it resembled a light brown instead. Glancing over to the now sleeping Hellhound, I noticed her breathing had begun to calm down. "Looks like things have finally started calming down."

"Yeah, she's been sleeping like that since you laid her there."

"Good, I wasn't expecting her to be awake so soon anyways." I returned. Walking back over to the sleeping animal and gently placing my hand down on the animal's still heavily breathing chest for a hasty examination. I could feel the rib cage rapidly rising and falling with each breath. Feeling the heartrate through her thick muscle, I

147

counted the beats. Indeed, it was still uncomfortably fast, but thankfully her panting had seized, so things were beginning to look uphill from here. Rubbing my hand down her side, I stood back up and finally returned most of my attention to my girlfriend. Coming up behind her, I watched as she leaned her head back along the spine of the sofa. Leaning my head in for a tender kiss, I pressed my soft-moisturized lips against those lipstick red lips of hers. Our kiss lasted for moments before I broke away and whispered. "You have no idea how appreciative I am for having you in my life. Especially with that little fiasco. No idea, baby, how much I love you."

Chuckling with a soft sigh, my gorgeous girlfriend returned, "I love you too, baby. But there was no way I was going to let her die, even if I had to do mouth-to-mouth myself."

"You saw that?" I embarrassingly inquired.

"Of course I did. And before you ask if I am jealous of your sweet-lips touching a dog's, no I am not." She laughed.

"My lips never touched her lips. It's mouth to nose." I lightheartedly corrected, heading in for one more kiss.

"Oh, sorry." Theresa teased before slipping away from our little romantic moment. "Hey, there is a Café around the corner, why don't I go down there for some coffee, and a few muffins."

"Are they even open?" I wondered aloud, recalling the exact place she was talking about.

Theresa looked down at her cellphone real quick to check the time that flashed on the lock screen of the iPhone's recent store model. "Umm, they should be, it's close to seven-thirty now."

"Already?" I continued to question, now looking out the balcony to see the skyline beyond the glass railing. Seeing the sun pry itself free from the clouds, I was surprised I had not noticed that the horrendous, uncontrollable, creeping Blood Moon had sunk back with the fall of the night. I hated seeing that red glow, especially after seeing the amount of agony it aroused the Unnaturals it affected; Unnaturals like Cinder. And without any way to track the rise in the unusual pattern of the lunar phase, no scientific way to explain it, it only troubled me further. The Blood Moon and the Harvest Moon in our world were completely different and had different effects on the Unnaturals. Could it be possible that was the reason behind Salem Institution's rigorous testing? Shoving those thoughts aside, I quickly remembered that Zachariah had once told me Cinder could accurately track the moons. Pondering, I wondered "If that was, in fact, true, then why didn't she warn me? Why didn't she change forms?"

"Baby-?"

"It was something I would have to ask her later. When it was just the two of us." I growled, returning my sights to the Hellhound. "There is so much I still do not know about you, and yet the more I find out the more I become terrified of whatever he has planned for you."

Chapter 28
Augustus/Cinder

With everything settling down, I somehow ended up apologizing to Theresa for a ruined evening last night and a horrible non-special anniversary morning breakfast. Thankfully, she accepted, however, she kept pushing the fact that she wasn't all the upset.

"What happened couldn't be helped." She repeatedly returned. I knew it couldn't be helped but it still didn't help make me feel any better. I felt horrible for ruining whatever it was she had in mind, and when it came down to our anniversary there was always something planned. Always.

"I know it can't be..." I snarled, taking a bite out of my plain chocolate chip muffin, the heat still steaming out of delicious baked goods. Quickly chewing and swallowing the massive bite, I continued, "It's just hard to let it down when I know you had something big planned for our day."

"Well, it wasn't anything too big." The woman continued. "I just paid for a romantic trip to the Bahamas, although I wasn't expecting to see her when I came here to surprise you."

"A trip to the Bahamas." I acted, trying to sound surprised, however, the tone of exhaustion still spilled over. 'I'll pay you back for it."

"Augustus don't' worry about it. Really, it's not a big deal." She continued, putting her hands up to tell me to slow down. "I wasn't expecting you to have a dog and it would be cruel to know you just got her to then leave her for a week in the tropics."

"A week!" I complained to myself. "I really could've used that trip."

Taking another bite out of my muffin, I heard the little high-pitched beep rise out of Theresa's cellphone. Glancing away from the sleeping Hellhound and to my girlfriend, I waited for her to say something. The only sound that slipped out of her mouth was the traditional growl she admitted whenever her phone rang.

"Work?" I asked after a few moments of peaceful silence.

"Unfortunately. I'm needed for some candids then I have to go to Las Vegas." Theresa sighed.

"I wish you could have stayed longer." I lied as I went in for a quick goodbye kiss.

"I wished I could stay longer as well, but I need this money."

"Alright, then I'll text you tonight, baby."

"Bye, Augustus." Theresa expressed while she fled towards the foyer.

Hearing the doors close, I returned to watching the sleeping Hellhound. For almost three hours Cinder had been peacefully sleeping on the collection of bloody towels. The blood having caked into the fabric, but surprisingly not crushing the floorboards underneath. Straining my eyes, I attempted my best to eye the rising and falling of the Beauceron's chest, however, the attempt was futile. From where I sat, I could barely make out the ribs dancing up and down. Forcing myself to stand up from the couch, I carried the last chunks of my muffin with me as I strolled over to the sleeping dog. Throwing the rest of it into my mouth, I hastily finished eating the baked good and ensued with checking Cinder's heart rate. The beats per second had slowed down to a steady enough pace that I could thankfully take a breather. It was still a bit too fast for a sleeping dog, but it was going to have to do.

"Thank god." I sighed as I stood over the top of her, my knees bent down far enough that I could stay avid on my feet just in case some of those side effects occurred while I was this close to the sleeping beast. It was a result of those side effects that had caused me to get wounds like the one on my arm and the one that wrapped around the side of my stomach. The avid chance of losing one's sanity or rationality when they were under the heavy sedative and painkiller was extremely high and so was the chance of the caretaker becoming their next victim. "Your first kill was done under the effects of this exact drug," I mumbled aloud, recalling more of Cinder's past while I dangerously placed my hand on the smoothly sleeping Canine Unnatural. "Such a tragedy, that they didn't know what was happening, and neither did you." I continued. "I believe your breathing is steady enough that I can at least get some shut-eye after pulling that all-nighter."

Finally regaining the ability to reopen my eyes, I hastily shot them open and swung my exhausted body upwards, trying to shake the feeling of being tied down by some sort of phantom controlling agent. My head spun, and I fell back down onto the believed to be the dry fabric of towels. Moving my legs around, I readjusted my fatigued frame around to a more comfortable position as I thoroughly examined my surroundings.

I was no longer in the Atrium, but back in the center common area of the apartment. I could feel the warm, rays of the sun scorch their way through the wall of glass that separated me from the outside balcony, its glorious heat warming my cold fur. Looking around the rest of the apartment, I caught onto new objects lying around that I could only assume were the 'pet' objects, Augustus and that high-pitched, kind woman went out and bought. My blurred vision located the collection of two large dog-bowls beside the outskirts of the counter island. The dishes running in a parallel line to the island's lower cupboards. Scanning around the other side of the common area, I caught the sight of what I could only assume were 'dog' toys. "Stuff I would never even think of using." I refused. As I completed the scan over my surroundings, I noticed that there was someone lying on the black sofa. I couldn't tell from the way the blonde-haired person was lying there whether or not the person was asleep or watching the television, but I knew all too well those familiar characteristics. The hair alone told me who it was, however, my question was: why was he out here lying down on the sofa, instead of in his own bed?

Attempting myself to stand back up again, I watched as my wobbly legs buckled underneath me. My body still retaining the deadweight negotiated that I was still too weak to use my four limbs. Cursing aloud, I let out a shrew cry as my head banged furiously down onto the dark wood floors unprotected by the layer of soft towels. Flinching from the pain, I blinked a few times. Soon discovering upon my sight's return to the bright apartment, I caught the sight of the dancing Valkyrie. His long legs swinging off of the couch, onto the floor, and darting right over in my direction.

"A little late." I huffed, once more trying to stand myself back up off the floor.

"Sorry." Augustus tiredly apologized, his green eyes absorbing the fading rays of the sunlight. "The sun is already setting." He paused for a moment, checking the hidden cellphone for the accurate time. "Already eight o'clock."

"What happened?" I questioned, bringing my head up so my tired eyes could lock with his.

"You don't recall anything that happened?" the Angel asked as he sat down on the floor beside me.

"I remember it being a Blood Moon, but other than that, I'm drawing a blank." I cried. I was trying my hardest to collect any of my recent memories from last night's events, but I couldn't find a single memory.

"Don't strain yourself." The Angel quickly interrupted me. "You nearly died."

"That's nothing new." I snickered, rolling my eyes at the Angel. "I've almost died so many times that I have lost count."

"Well, you really did stop breathing for fifteen minutes, but thankfully, I was able to resuscitate your heart."

"You-?" I questioned, feeling a thankful rush of gratitude rush over me.

"I had to, or did you forget that your life holds so much in its hands and that Zachariah would have my head if you were to die," Augustus smirked.

"Now he wants me alive?" I rhetorically bit.

"You are his Reaper, aren't you-?"

"I guess so." I sighed, "However, back to what happened last night, I know that it wasn't only your gift of air that had saved me." Crossing my paws, I once more adjusted my lying position to again try to get comfortable.

"I had to end up giving you a drug yet unnamed, and while there are so many positives to this medication, there's also some severe side effects to this drug, so I need to keep an eye on you just in case one rears its ugly head."

"So, you are going back to babysitting, huh?" I snarked, flashing a tired toothy smile.

"Have to, it's my job." The Angel smiled back. The smirk lasted seconds before disappearing and his serious face returned. "As you probably can already tell, your body is still numb from the loss of blood as well as the sedation, I had to give you. So, for at least the next twenty-four hours, you won't' be able to move very efficiently."

"Not like I have anywhere to go, do I?" I ironically pondered.

Chapter 29
Jakob

As I attempted maneuvering myself around the Medical Ward and attempt to get my legs moving, to get my muscles working as they once could, I could not shake the after-effects of what had happened to Cinder while I was unconscious. Everything they had done to her. Everything our Syndicate had done to her. Everything that the Shadow had done to her. All that she had to do to per the sprouted orders. My knees buckled underneath me, causing me to break my train of depressing thoughts. Nearly falling face-first into the small cod's bed rail, I hastily grabbed for the iron rod. My fingers barely kept swindled around the iron while I forced myself to steady again.

"It will take some time for your muscles to learn all of their proper motor functions." I heard Viktor speak up while he kept his back turned to me. "Although you were in a comatose for three months, to someone who was as nearly drained of blood and nearly as dead as you were, it will take a little longer to heal."

"So, what of your healing abilities?" I hastily shot back, flashing my gaze in the Vampiric's direction.

"For some reason, my powers didn't work as they should have."

"As in?" I wondered.

"I was only able to do some immediate field treatment, but the wounds still wouldn't take, especially the one in your abdomen."

"The one where I was stabbed?" I now softly hissed, recalling when Cinder had stabbed me with that Blood Scythe of hers. The firm blade easily pressing through my hardened flesh and driving deep into the muscle underneath. Grabbing for my gut as the muscles relived the memory, I heard the calm man spring up out of his chair. "I'm fine." I snapped back to Viktor, telling him to keep his distance for now. "I'm fine," I repeated. "Just-."

"Reliving it-?"

"Her solemn face. It hurt her more to attack me than it hurt me." I recalled.

"As of right now, I do not understand what caused someone like her to do what she did. However, whatever those effects of her Blood Trait are, it kept the wounds from healing and causing a few of your organs to compress, as well as fracture the nearest bones." Viktor continued to explain. Flashing him a stern glare, I noticed that in his soft-collected gaze he was wanting to say something else.

"And-?" I hastily shot, urging him to hurriedly say it.

Before he could open his mouth to explain, the ward's door swung open. The swiftness of the door nearly being blown off its hinges made both of our heads turn. Noticing that the person who came flying through the archway was none other than the other Hellhound we had liberated a little shy of seven months ago, I relaxed some of my tensions.

"We need to talk, Jakob," Peylith growled, his tone still as serious as when he left the ward two days ago. Quickly glaring at the other seven-hundred-year-old Vampiric, the former King snarled, "Privately, if you would not mind Viktor."

"What is it about?" I asked ahead of time.

"Nothing that he needs to know." Peylith coldly answered, speaking in this unfamiliar serious tone. It was the type of tone that would make someone like me understand how he had managed to become a Pharaoh. His Aura had so much gifted wisdom, so much experience that it made my years of existence feel like child play.

"That is alright." Viktor softly sighed, taking the hint and walking out of his 'Ward' closing the door behind him.

Turning around to face the appalling man, I kept my bracing hands down on the iron railing of the footboard and stayed as calm as I could possibly manage. "What is it that you needed me alone to tell me?" I requested.

Peylith rubbed his hands down his face in a way to extend the dreaded feeling of having to possibly retell the incident. Seeing the color of his wolf-like gaze darken and turn almost a smoldering gold like the sun, I heard him quietly explain. "I had my conversation with Anubis, and what he told me are things that I dare not yet explain to our fellow comrades. At least not yet. None of them are as close to her, as you are. None of them love her as you do, so that is why I appreciated taking privacy with our conversation."

"What did he say?"

"The 'Deity' that Cinder is currently sworn to, the one who changed her from a Human child to an Unnatural, was none other than the creator to the book of Demons, the former Angel Zachariah," Peylith explained. "Anubis knew of this 'God' for centuries before he even created I, and Lord Zachariah was at one time the highest-ranking members on Helya's Council."

"Once?" I questioned, trying to keep my requests short while trying to digest the information of the man Cinder had called the haunting Shadow all of her life. However, the way that Peylith and his 'Deity' Anubis explained this man's characteristics was different than how she feared him.

"Yes, milord Anubis forth explained that Zachariah was creating 'Reaping' Hellhounds-"

"Reaping?"

Peylith took a long sigh before walking up towards the cod that was empty besides my own, motioning me to sit as well. "While there are seven species of Hellhounds, there are two Branches or two ranks. One is the Guardian, a rank such as I that watches over the dead souls and their interaction with the living. We control who crosses, who doesn't, who gets into 'Heaven' or who goes to 'Hell' and so forth, as well as who may receive reincarnation. While on the other spectrum are the 'Reapers', a rank like Cinder's. They are just as they sound. They are the killers of those whose lives must meet their maker. Most souls that Reapers hunt are those who spent their time alive with criminal intentions or had extended their stay in the living."

"So Reapers are the hunters for the kill-?" I interjected upon re-calling the memory of Cinder's lips drawn back, exposing every tooth she had in her canine morphed mouth and the tops of her gums. Her mouth curled in such a psychotic grin while she stood over the Lycan she had murdered.

"To the normal eye it comes across that way, but they are es-sentially those who keep the balance of life and death intact. A job that is even more important when adding how prominent Immortals are in the existence of Unnaturals. Guardians work in similar ways, but our title rarely requires us to take violent actions." Peylith paused, taking another long exhale. "Back to the history of Cinder's Deity, it is said that when Zachariah began creating Reapers, many became lost in the blood lust and his followers ended up-" The Hell-hound again paused as I saw an ember-blaze flicker behind the hu-man-transformed Unnatural.

"Allow me to explain it, Pharaoh." My ears heard a soothing dark callused voice speak as my eyes watched a creature step out of the

159

gazing embers that were surprisingly not catching the Manor's walls ablaze.

"Are you sure, milord? You won't be putting his life at risk, will you?"

"An-Anubis-" I mumbled, watching the bi-pedal black jackal step out of the flames. His long slender snout forming the ideal silhouette around his blue and gold Egyptian headdress.

"No, your comrade's life is not in danger. The Council has deemed my presence in the living world okay." I heard the soothing voice continue to speak. The jackal's jaws moving as he brought out his Golden Ankh staff.

"What is going on?" I asked, trying to wrap my head around the presence of a god appearing before my very eyes.

"Just listen, Immortal Blood-Drinker," Anubis ordered as calmly as he could.

Chapter 30
Jakob

"Zachariah is no one to trust. Everything is for his benefit, including the 'love' of your life. She is nothing more than a pet to that man."

"She is no PET!" I snapped at the God of the Underworld.

"To you, she is not, but to him, she is nothing more than a prized show dog."

"Show dog?" Peyltih spoke up. "Why? She isn't the one, is she?"

"The one?" I asked. "Peylith start explaining."

"Blood-Drinker just listen. Savor your questions till the end." Anubis growled to me. I could feel my lips zip up and knew the god now held the key to me speaking. "Zachariah has had a Reaper at every mass causality event in History going as far back as the Black Plague and Roman Empire. While many Hellhounds have fallen under that creature's name, the former Angel only had twenty-one successive Hellhounds and had used them for every Historical Disaster, including the fall of my follower's Empire." The bi-pedal jackal snarled, flashing me his long white-yellow fangs. Recollecting himself, the god continued a second later. "Zachariah hates men for whatever purpose, and he eventually got caught by the Council for the mass exterminations he plotted against them by having his 'Reapers kill those who did not deserve to die even under the prominent circumstances of man's war and man's hatred of one another, and the natural disasters that unfolded around them in the living plane. As well as for the heavy loss of souls for his many experiments. When he was finally tried at the Courts by both 'Titans', he was deemed Guilty."

The story just pushed more confusing questions to the top of my mind, and I tried my hardest to fight the urge to blurt out the prying interrogations I had going through my wandering mind. Biting my tongue, I held down the crying voice.

"As punishment, the Titans and the fellow 'Deities' who served as the jury of peers, stripped Zachariah of his powers including his physical Angelic form, as well as sentenced his Blood Lust Loyal Hellhounds to euthanasia. However, upon the sentencing of his crimes, it came out the Deity had already 'gifted' one set of his six wings to an Archangel who had recently joined his Cult of Followers, hence allowing the God Zachariah to maintain some of his power."

"Was that Archangel the alluded Mr. Gale?" I wondered to myself. "If not, then what else was this cursed Shadow's purpose for choosing Cinder?" I was so confused. Between trying to digest the sights of seeing an actual God before my seven-hundred-year-old eyes and trying to digest the unfolding story of a whole other realm of Gods, my mind had tons of unanswered questions that desperately needed to get answered so I could fill in those blanks.

"Of course, with the fading sights of the Titans, they did not expect for all the cunning calculative plans he had made prior to his sentence."

"Calculative Plans?" Peylith's consumed yellow gaze shot over to his Master.

The Deity shot a glare back and before his servant could apologize the God continued, "Zachariah went against the Creator's Law, granting Four of his most successful creatures the evolution of the Fiend. That Law forbids us, Creators, from giving that form to our Hellhounds. No matter the circumstance it is forbidden, and that is because while Fiends are extremely powerful, there is no way to kill one. Not even the Titans can kill a Fiend. The best way to describe a Hellhound Fiend is that they themselves are a god. And that takes our situation back to your 'beloved', Blood-Drinker."

There were still so many questions I had, but I fought to keep my lips sealed.

"Zachariah has spent his time stuck in the Shadow form along-side his loyal Archangel for the last two hundred years and had been endlessly creating havoc for the Council in his wake. While trying to contemplate his next Creation, he spent those years looking for the right human to transform. And not only did he go away from the laws of transforming the souls into living Hellhounds as you know of my Pharaoh's past, but Zachariah also began transforming living Humans for some new project of his. The Council has sent countless peers to watch and evaluate what that cursed being is up to, yet none of us has figured it out, that was until now."

No longer able to contain my surging amount of questions, I blurted out, "And? What does all that have to do with her being the one? Is it for this project of his?"

"I can only assume so, Jakob," Peylith answered back.

"The Council does not know for certain and are currently trying to find out where this Mr. Gale is hiding your comrade, the one who does not remember her birth name," Anubis answered.

"What are you going to do if you find her?" I hastily snarled to the god, not thinking the action through. Looking away from the stern canine's gaze, I shot it back a second later.

"She will be sent to the Council." Anubis coldly answered. "It is up to the Titans what to do with her."

163

"And what if you find her too late! What if HE turns her into a Fiend!?"

"JAKOB!" Peylith shouted, his Aura quickly darkening and forewarning me to speak carefully around the God of the Underworld.

"It is alright, Peylith. Your comrade's worry for this woman is understandable. Remember you acted the same when I told you of the demise your son was to face, Pharaoh." The Hellhound retreated, his smug growl retreating. "However, if she is turned then it will not change much of the Council's goals. Zachariah needs to be dealt with and returned before he attempts any severe damage to the balance of life."

"And you think Cinder is the one who will cause the damage?" I softly questioned, my heart dropping deep into my gut at the expected response.

"I cannot answer that question for you, Blood-Drinker, simply because I do not know myself the cynical plans of that cursed God." Anubis softly returned before turning his yellow gaze to his serving Guardian, the former Pharaoh Peylith. "I appreciate you telling me about the scenario that is at hand, and I do believe that the chance of this Mr. Gale character taking custody of the Female Reaper is indeed the Archangel who serves under Zachariah. And indeed, you were right to tell this man about these possibilities and of Zachariah's History."

"It was his plan, to tell me?" I quietly thought to myself my eyes scanning over to Peylith who was already standing back up from the cod.

"Blood-drinker," Anubis called, swiftly redirecting my direction. Fixating on his stern but somehow sorrowful gaze. "I waiver you and your comrade's lives for hearing the news of this confidential case." As the god began venturing towards the dancing orange ember portal he shot out from, my sensitive hearing overheard the god's voice while his back was turned to me. The sleek black fur mimicking the dancing embers. "I will, however, apologize ahead of time for that young woman you so deeply care for. I cannot waiver her life, only she can save herself when the Council finally tracks her down."

"What?" I barked, but the bi-pedal Jackal had already disappeared into the fiery portal. "Wait!" I called again, forcing my fatigued body up from the cod, to follow where he had disappeared. I knew that there was no stopping the god, although my mind argued against all subconscious thoughts. Shooting my fixation over to the sorrowful standing Hellhound, I growled. "What in the fucking hell does that mean, Peylith?"

Chapter 31

Augustus

Almost two weeks had passed since that worried night under the horrid red rays of the Blood Moon, and Cinder had thankfully worked out the remnants of the drug from her near-death experience. Surprisingly the Hellhound had no side effects from the medication, and her body acted as if it had not nearly bled out. I had to admit that the Unnatural was beyond special when it came to that rare Blood Trait of hers, on top of the combination of her heightened intelligence, fast observant skills, and nimble frame, it was becoming less of a surprise that Lord Zachariah had picked her over the other candidates.

"No surprise at all," I murmured to myself as I sat in my dark sleek wood office that I kept locked off from the shapeshifting creature's prying eyes. Sitting in the comfortable modern black office chair behind my glass computer desk, I examined through the numerous files and papers I had made copies of when I began researching the young woman for the confusing Deity. Thinking aloud to myself, I glanced over the copies for the hundredth time since those orders and wondered, "How were they so willing to sign over an eight-year-old child? How could the love that went beyond natural instinct betray the trust of parent and child? The trust of a mother and her child?" Looking over the Hospital file of the small child's picture and info, I easily depicted the facial features that Cinder had yet to mature out of. "Although your hair has grown black and your skin has massively scarred, those eyes of yours have never changed. Still that radiant blue that stares right through one's soul." Cinder's face had thinned, but the soft feminine features of an elegant woman could be found in the child's oval face.

Looking over the pictures the Institution created to observe her growth and maturity; I noticed that despite her body's physical development and her hair self-dying into that deep black color, there was a gradual loss of life in the woman's eyes, a loss of weight and an increase in needle and scalpel scars all over her legs. I could see the willingness to let these people do whatever they were doing to her ensue. It was obvious that she just didn't care anymore. However, the longer I passed through the eight-by-ten photographs, I overlayed the current woman with the past image. "Where was that woman? I cannot imagine seeing someone like her being that broken?"

"It is a miracle, is it not?" I heard the dark voice call. The deafening hoarseness of the cold breath escaping the skeleton's moving jowls. "I must admit I owe those Rebels the benefit of the doubt for saving my Reaper from the depths of that blackness."

"Why? When you are just going to drag her back down into it?" I growled, putting down the pictures and papers to look up at the shady shadow.

"Well, that's because that was a different darkness, my stupid Valkyrie." Zachariah continued as he manifested closer. "The darkness I am hoping to send her down is on a different level. One of hatred, not depression."

"Hatred?" I quietly pondered to myself. My tattoo burned at the recollected memory of how naïve I was when I once held the same hatred his voice expressed. The same demise I wished for man, for this cursed world. Abruptly changing the subject, I sneakily voiced while I interlocked my fingers and massaged the palm of my hand with my thumb, "I know you are not here to discuss your project, so please explain what you have planned for the day's events?"

"There's the smart Angel I recruited." The Shadow smiled. "You are right, let us leave the subject for a better time and return to the date's current objectives. I hope you have gotten her registered for the Pits."

"I am to finish the paperwork once I get her there." I returned.

"Good. What does she know?"

"Nothing."

"Good." He repeated.

"Anything else?"

"Yes, do not explain what the plans are." Zachariah calmly smirked, the orange eyes remaining as stern and serious as per usual.

"Why?" I unwisely questioned.

"Are you doubting my judgment?" he growled.

"No, my lord." I immediately returned with a wavered glare. "I just wonder why you were ordering me to build this level of trust with her when I'm sure you know the second I let that man take custody of her, what little trust I had built up will be demolished. If I'm to press on the with this job, I'm going to need to at least come up with some reason I can give her."

"Yes, I know quite well how my Reaper will respond, but this isn't for your benefit. Nor is it for her." Zachariah harshly denied. "It was for mine. I needed you to not get your head removed by those fangs while you housed her here from both Unnatural and Hunters alike."

"You used me, again." I sighed, though it wasn't that unusual.

"It is what you signed up for, is it not, for your freedom?" the Deity grinned. His words reminding me of the day I had sought him out...going to his temple for sanction after I was...

"It is what I signed up for." I once more sighed. "So, you still want me to keep up with that even after her assignment gets completed?"

"Yes." Was the only answer he gave. A brief moment of silence occurred before I eventually left my chair. "Augustus-" The once highly presumed God of Death darkly called, his tone sending chills deep through my spine. "Do whatever you must to keep her in your arms at all times."

"Yes, my Lord." I quickly responded, my green eyes locking with his for a fast second before submitting to that cold olden gaze of his.

"Good, then I will leave her life in your hands." Zachariah had sternly ordered before vanishing into thin air and returning to the nothingness of the abyss that he had protruded from.

Dropping back down into my office chair, I took a painful breath. "Fuck!" I snapped, throwing my arm down on the desk, scattering the papers everywhere. Only a handful of pictures had managed to remain on top of the glass tabletop. With my hand resting over a distinct picture of the innocent child and her side-by-side comparison with the enormous Beauceron, I realized how even the canine form too resembled her age. Between a child and pup, I could tell in those same gloomy eyes that this kid, this woman, was immensely observant. "How in the fucking world am I supposed to keep 'her' from figuring all that you have planned?"

Running through the file information, I once more skimmed my eyes over the paperwork, desperately trying to strategize a plan for deceiving the Unnatural whose God had just said could easily remove my head from my broad shoulders. Reading the following, I still couldn't imagine myself ever becoming as worthy of her trust as I was supposed to be.

'Patient Number: 0497

'Patient DOB: 12/27/1993

'Patient Diagnosis: Undiagnosed. Hellhound

'Patient-Doctor: Shane Masters.

It was all that I could read, everything else had been redacted for who knows what viable reason. But with each time I glanced over the blacked-out file, I proceeded to wonder to myself, "Why leave all this left open, and yet cover her birth name, or her parent's names, her social security number, her parent's phone numbers, her location, or her room? What were they really hiding? Was everything revolving around you so difficult?!" I complained, rubbing my hands over my face, before once more aggressively cussing to myself, "Fuck! Fuck! Fuck!"

Chapter 32
Cinder

"Cinder-" I heard the Archangel call from the other side of the bathroom door inside my room, his voice surprisingly ringing clear over the roar of the high-pressured water from the updated touch tech showerhead.

Pulling my hands through my wet hair as I prepared to shut off the steady water flow, I answered back. "What do you want?" Getting no answer, I grabbed the soft grey towel from the towel rack and wrapped it around my soaking hour-glass figure. Proceeding to stroll out of the nice bathroom and into the room I slept little in since that Blood Moon, I again asked, "What do you want Augusts?"

"First of all, get dressed, we got things to do." He hurriedly spoke, his eyes looking away from my towel-wearing body.

"What things?" I inquired, strolling over to the closet I had just walked out of for some 'clothes.'

"That, I cannot tell you."

"Oh really? Does it have anything to deal with whatever you two were talking about a month ago on that balcony? Or does it have anything to deal with the conversation you had with that man over the phone a couple of weeks ago?" I probed as I grabbed some clean undergarments.

The silence told me my answer.

"So, it does, huh?" I repeated as I dropped the towel and proceeded with putting on the black lace underwear and bra.

Again, the man was silent.

"But you can't tell me, can you?" I now asked. Exercising a sigh, I now scavenged for some nice skinny jeans.

"If I did-" Augustus tried to speak up, his tone sincere.

"No, I understand." I softly mumbled. "It pisses me off, but I was once in that same boat, so I cannot hold my grudge." I depressingly clarified as I began to wander out of the closet carrying a nice V-neck women's t-shirt.

"About done?" the Angel questioned, immediately attempting to change the subject.

"Just about." I expressed, reaching for the simple hairbrush sitting on the dresser back inside the walk-in-closet, "Let me put up my hair, then we can go." Brushing the wet tangles out of my dyed black hair, I continued to challenge, "What is the hurry?"

"Hurry?"

"Stop beating around the bush. After all this time I have spent living in your apartment, you never rushed things as much as this. So, what's the hurry?" Putting the brush down, I now swept the long locks up in a ponytail before locking my gaze with the blonde-haired, green-eyed Fallen Angel. "And don't you dare lie to me."

"How is it you can always tell when I'm lying to you?"

"It's a secret." I teased, flashing a sly smile as I slid my hand under his stern chin, feeling the short stubble that was growing along his perfect tan skin. "Now let's go. I'll deal with whatever it is when we get there."

"Yeah, that I doubt." I heard him mumble deep under his breath. Deciding to ignore the statement this time, I rolled my eyes and exited out of the large modern bedroom.

Arriving down in the penthouse's garage, I examined the fine art sports and luxury cars all the tenants owned on the property. Augustus's car was such a sleek-black that it made me unable to take my eyes off the repeating reflection I saw through the waxed carbon-fibered door. "How is it that all the Unnaturals I meet have so much money?" I softly whispered.

"Lots of lying and arduous work," Augustus spoke, jolting me out of my fixation. Locking my gaze again with the green-eyed man, I rolled my eyes while easing my body into the passenger side. The Angel followed in not too long after and surprisingly kept his mouth shut for the entire ride up to this undisclosed location.

As we pulled up into a confusing location, I swiftly noticed a change in the environment. The sky had turned a dull grey and cloudy as if at any moment the clouds were preparing to drown the world under its feet with a heavy downpour. The buildings seemed darker, broke down, washed out. Around each turn we took, I saw the unnerving amount of skittish people we passed by and could no longer keep my concerning mouth quiet.

"Augustus, what is this place?" I inquired, wanting at least a little bit of insight.

"Well it's kind of hard to explain, but this is the side of the city you hardly see." He answered me, pulling the car into one of the few empty parking spots.

"I can see that." Still avidly examining the surroundings we were in. Swallowing the fear rising deep in my throat, I continued to interrogate, "How many Unnaturals live here?"

"Lots. Not everyone makes it big, sweet cheeks."

Spinning my head back around I snapped back at him, "Don't you ever call me that again!"

"Okay, okay." Augustus retreated. "Sorry."

"Why are we here anyway?"

"Well, we aren't really where we are supposed to be yet. The location is a short walk-"

"Stop beating around the bush!"

"Alright, alright." The fellow Shadow follower submitted, still holding onto that irritating smile of his. "This is the Black Market, and if I told you everything that goes on here then you would for sure swipe my head off of my shoulders and go on a psychotic hunting spree."

"What makes you think that I don't want to do it now?" I blurted back. "The stench of fear, anger, power, greed, it's all sending my predatory instincts overboard."

"Yeah-." Augustus stumbled before changing the gears and taking the keys out of the electronic ignition. "Let's get this over with." I again heard him mumble under his breath. Simultaneously stepping out of the car, I kept in stride with the angel's long legs.

As we strolled on the sidewalks towards wherever he was supposed to take me, I quickly analyzed the change again in the environment. Surprisingly it was here that I noticed our attire fit in well with the crowd, blending in well with the upper-class society. Getting pulled in every direction, I continued to explore the stands that were selling everything from organs, to personal identities, expensive cars, apartment leases, exotic animals, and even Unnaturals. I could see why the place was called the Black Market. These guys were literally selling anything and everything they could get their grimy hands on.

"Ignore it, Cinder."

"What?" I snarled.

"Ignore it." He growled again, this time ordering me with a stern tone that sent chills down my scarred back while clutching my arm so hard that it began to cut the circulation off.

"Augustus-." I called, sensing that familiar rising gut feeling as I attempted to pull away. But the man's grip remained impenetrable even with my supernatural strength, I couldn't get my arm free. As I was dragged along, I relentlessly fought still trying to get some straight answers out of the Valkyrie. "Augustus, why are we really here?"

The man didn't say a word to me while he dragged me through a crowd full of those filthy creeps, their prying eyes locked on the two of us. Doing what I could to ignore the harsh looks of the potential buyers, my body was suddenly tugged into an empty alley. Before I could gain my surroundings, I was thrown into the worn brick wall with such force that it pushed all of the air I had in my lungs out. Heaving for air, I noticed that the Angel had swarmed my personal space, his hands pressed against the wall, completely blocking my exits.

"Augustus..." I softly announced, sensing this aggressively dark Aura consume his traditionally calm demeanor.

"For once, just shut the fuck up and fucking listen to me, alright Reaper." The man sternly demanded, relaxing the tense expression on my face and drowning the temptation to rip the man in two, I obeyed the commands. Keeping my mouth shut I further listened to Augustus speak. "This is how the world works. Always has, always will. So, just ignore them, keep your fucking head down and your god damn short temper in check. Do you understand me?" I didn't give him an answer. "Do you understand me?" Augustus once again asked, this time using a softer, more sincere approach.

Making a huge swallow, I quietly nodded my head before a second later responding "I understand."

"Good, now let's go. we're already late as it is." The Angel growled, this time following me out, his hand pressing deep into my lower back as he drove me in the anticipated direction Augustus wanted me to walk in.

Chapter 33
Cinder

After seven minutes of speed-walking, we finally reached our apparent destination. The building seemed more updated, and about a whole two blocks wide, one half was the parking lot in general. There were two buildings on the property, both were made up of concrete and adorned with the facial architecture of old bricks and plaster. Large industrial windows adorned the farthest building, and as we stormed upon the property, I noticed that there was a horribly familiar scent floating over the musty saltwater stench that told me we were close to the Atlantic. It was the scent of my past.

Applying the brakes on my nice tennis-shoes, I turned back around only to once again run into Augustus. His hands grabbing me by the shoulders with such harsh control that it made me stop dead in my tracks. All I could manage was, "I can't go in there. Augustus, I can't..."

"Yes, you can. And yes, you will." He said in a tone that while came across as demanding, it wasn't nearly as dark as before. "Cinder, I know you are reliving your traumatic past, and I am sorry that there isn't anything I can do to help you step out of the past, but this has to be done."

"I can't." I returned, trying my hardest to not weep as the scents began to override my head.

"Cinder." Augustus continued, his voice finally returning to the one I had grown accustomed to. Feeling his hand wipe away an escaped tear and push away a loose lock of my bangs back behind my ear, I looked up at his dazzling eyes that always seemed to fixate me. "Yes, you can." The Angel paused for a moment. "Remember, I will not let anyone, nor anything that I cannot control happen to you. I promise that to you, I swear it."

"Augustus?" I barely managed to shockingly ask while my heart stopped beating for a minute. Only one other person had ever made that promise to me, and he broke it.

"I swear it on my life." He continued as he brought me in towards his chest. My body confined to his personal space could feel the sculpted pectorals and underlying muscle. Stepping away, I watched his eyes glance down to the cross necklace he always wore around his neck. The Archangel proceeded to take off the silver chain before slipping it over my head. "I know you don't trust me, and I know you will most likely hate me for today's events, but-"

"Augustus, just stop." I exhaled, feeling the gesture of trust he was attempting to offer. Wiping away my tears, I took another long inhale before finalizing, "I still hate you."

"Alright, let us get this over with." He lightly smiled, obviously catching onto my abrupt sarcasm.

Stepping up towards the building with the lesser amounts of high-rise windows, and large doors, I once more took in the vastly changing surroundings. The rush of loud screaming people who I couldn't decide were either cheering and or booing. The sound of people in pain, and people in the angst of blood. As we walked through the threshold of the large iron gates, I noticed that this was more of a concrete stadium turned courtyard, turned something unforeseen. The scent of sweat and blood overpowered my nose.

Fighting the urge to turn again and flee, I felt the man's left-hand, yet again deeply press into my back before wrapping around my waist.

"I am right here." I heard him speak over the rush of screams.

"What are we doing here?" I questioned Augustus while he steadily steered us through the large crowd. The surrounding audience parted, exposing the hidden secret that was rousing their vocal input. I was immediately met with a mass of thick chain-link. A fence stacked like a cage. Even having a roof. The cage was so large it was hard to believe the possible creatures it could hold. "What is this?" Stepping away from the comforting hand, I pulled myself towards the front of the cage. Stopped by a black guard rail, I noticed that a few feet were separating the north and south sides of the cage while that same separation exceeded the east and west sides except under those standing people were large ten-foot by ten-foot grates showing a hidden passageway beneath the sheets of metal. Placing my hands on the railing, I peered closer to look down the twelve-foot descent into the interior of the cage. Inside the cage, I noticed the subject at the hand of the human's thrill. Two Unnatural Shifters were brawling. Tearing at each other's throats, spraying blood all over the beige white sand and mottled earth dirt. "What is this?" I repeated, trying to swallow my breaking heart.

"I told you to ignore it." Augustus reordered, his hand yet again guiding my body back away from the ringside seat I had obtained at the cage.

"How in the hell do you expect me to ignore that?!" I snapped, breaking away from his soft guide. "I can hear their screams of pain! Augustus, I can understand every word they are shouting out to the world! Every curse-"

"I know you can." He shouted back over the still screaming people. "Did I not tell you that you were going to hate me?"

179

"Yeah, I fucking hate you right now!" I shouted back, still trying to hold back the urge to unsheathe my Blood Scythes and slit his throat along with every single cheering human being here in this building.

"You can take it out on me later, okay, let us just get through this." He continued.

"Through what? Are you ever going to tell me what we are doing here?"

"I can't."

Keeping my frustrated mouth shut, I barged past the crowd leaving the front row seat. Staying close behind the Angel as he strolled up the stairs, I felt my gut churn and crunch with each step. Mindlessly following, I noticed that as we reached the second floor there was a sudden change in the atmosphere. The crowd up here was smaller, quieter, and obviously richer. Before we could step one step off the half concrete, half industrial grate steps, we were stopped by two burly men wearing black uniforms from vests to even firearms. Retaining the quietness, I stepped up towards the blonde-Archangel and awaited his explanation to the guards.

"Mr. Gale and Ms. Salam here to see Gerard." He demanded. "Had an appointment at one-forty."

The Guards spoke into their earpiece as if checking in somewhere out of my line of sight, but a few seconds later they stepped aside allowing us to strut up onto the second-floor high above the main crowd and cage. With the angel's hand guiding me around the walkway, I noticed that the way all these Humans were dressed and were being tended to, these guys were at the top of the one-percenters.

"Here we are." Augustus exhaled as we stopped in front of these immaculate double office doors. Watching him courteously open up one of the doors, I held my breath and took the lead, stepping inside of the decently sized consultation office. The Victorian era furniture blending amazingly with the modern industrial structure of the bookshelves, windows, doors, floors, and technology.

The man behind the computer desk stood up and walked around the dark wood table to greet his clients. Assuming the man was this Gerard character we were to meet with, I swiftly began observing all of his characteristics. It was obvious by his scent that he was human. The gait was confident and masculine, matching the physique and natural facial build. His short black hair and heavy stubble made his hazel eyes stand out along the dark caucasian. His tan was about two shades deeper than Augustus's perfect skin. The casual V-neck firm blue shirt and worn denim jeans made me curious if this man was truly the man in charge here. "Ah, Augustus, what a pleasure it is to see you again." He greeted with a deep raspy masculine tone.

Shaking hands with the Archangel, the human then proceeded with the typical 'bro' hug proceeding the shake. I was confused about their relationship, however with my traumatic past trying to bite through the wall I had put up, I gambled what trust I had created with this Unnatural. Trusting that he knew exactly what was going to happen.

"It's great to see you too, Gerard Hunter. Been a few years hasn't it?"

"Sure has. Sure has." The human chuckled before turning his unique gaze over in my direction and expressing the slyest smirk on his lips. "My, my, who is this fine young woman?"

Feeling Augustus's arm wrap around my hips and draw me in close to him, I overheard the angel's answer, "This is Cinder Salam."

Chapter 34

Augustus

"The Hellhound, right?" The owner of the Pits asked with an extinguished smirk. Something he normally did when he found an interesting subject.

"This is her," I confirmed, trying to hold back my tempting will to punch his teeth down his throat.

"I am right here." Cinder interjected, breaking the small vow of silence.

"Apologies, Cinder," Gerard retracted, offering his hand to shake the woman's and officially greet her. Cinder remained unsure, but eventually unfolded her arms and took his extended hand. "Such soft skin." The man now complimented, when he grasped her feminine hand. "Augustus, you never told me that female Hellhounds could be so beautiful."

"Smooth-talking her, won't get you anything, Gerard." I tried to warn. "She's quite the intelligent mongrel, so much so that without telling her anything about the Black Market, she's already grasped two and two together."

"Yes, so do not beat around the bush." Cinder growled, her body breaking away from my hold. Freeing herself from my arm and my claim as well as the Owner's shake.

"Alright, no beating around the bush." Gerard submitted while leaning against his broad computer desk. "Welcome to the Pits, Cinder."

"Pits?" She questioned, maintaining the same low tone. "As in Illegal fighting?"

"Well not entirely legal no, but with today's society, the Black Market is mostly legitimate minute a few cross-hairs that occasionally gets singed here and there."

"Why did you bring me here, then Augustus? You expect me to fight in that thing? What is this, one of my damn assignments?!" The casually dressed Hellhound snapped, now turning her hostility back towards me.

Rubbing my hand through my hair, I tried to ease the feeling that she had indeed solved that mystery with little difficulty. Looking back over to the infamous Pit Owner, Gerard Hunter, I asked for some help in the illusion. The Manager taking hold of the subject, motioned his hand up calling to his hidden bodyguards who remained outside the office space. The two men stepping inside made my own worries rise. I knew exactly how Zachariah's Reaper acted when she was surrounded, and it was never good.

"Um-." I attempted to warn.

But my opinion was thrown out before I could even attempt to speak another word. "Ms. Salam, I do not know about these assignments of yours, but this is where we register you in to the Pits."

"I am not going to fight for you!" The woman snapped, her full attention adverted back onto the human. "I already fight for one prick, I am not going to for another."

The name-calling only made Gerard's sly smile spread. The tone is his voice shallowed, darkened. "It's not something you get to choose, honey."

"Um, Gerard?" I again called, recalling how the woman despised being called by those pet names, however before I could finish the statement, there she was with those Blood Scythes unsheathed and pressed against Gerard's throat and stomach. "She doesn't like being called by pet names." I managed to finish.

"I can see that..."

"I will not fight for those bastards' pleasure." Cinder snarled, her gorgeous blue eyes changing into the terrifying orange.

"It's not something you can choose, Cinder," Gerard repeated, still flashing the same smirk.

Watching the bodyguards step closer, I knew I had to try to talk down the soon-to-be-slaying beast that was about to be unleashed. Stepping closer to the Hellhound, I hastily grabbed for her arm that was pressed against her victim's throat. Of course, Cinder pulled away, removing herself with enough mobility and elegancy that it explained several other reasons why the Deity had chosen this child from the group. The woman so nimble and lean on her feet put enough distance between the two of us and the two bodyguards blocking her only exit. Despite being as fast and observant as this woman was, she could not foresee everything that was occurring. Before I could even acknowledge it myself, the thick Blood Scythes collapsed onto the marvelously sleek wood floors. Staining the wood with the de-clotted heavy, iron red, blood cells.

"About time it took its hold." Gerard snarled, rubbing his hand over his throat where seconds ago those de-clotted Blood Scythes were pressed against. The avenging orange eyes of the Hellhound retreated, flashing back to their stunning blue, while her athletic physique now seemed to be out of energy. At a loss, her eyes began to look around the office, scanning over the room for exactly what I thought had also happened. That there had to have been some sort of drug injected into her bloodstream.

"Time it took for what?" Cinder growled between exhausted pants just as her human form collapsed onto the ground.

Barely able to catch her in time before she bashed her head on the wood floors, I looked back at the owner and asked myself "Gerard, what did you do?"

"You don't think that I didn't do my own research before having a nearly extinct Hellhound show up at my ring." He smiled, striding up to where I held the barely conscious woman. His callused hands grabbing at her chin to stare into those gorgeous pupils. "Hellhounds aren't like any other canine shifter, they don't have reactions with Silver or any of the other metals like Iron or Gold, no her's is Blessed Salts. That same shit that is used to restrain demons." Moving her still damp black hair strands away from her face. "I always have to take precautions when it comes to you bringing me Unnaturals. So, I had a slight trace of salt spread around the interior border of my office." Dropping her head, the man proceeded to stand up tall and continued as he walked back around the desk, "Look, I know I owe you my life Augustus, however when it comes to registering possible fighters, I'm not going to risk my neck, nor the lives of the viewers."

"I get that, this is your income Gerard, and this is a Registered Sanctuary for those Unnaturals deemed too aggressive to even be considered as a patient at any Institution: however, the least you could've done was forewarn me of your plans," I growled, slowly helping the struggling woman back up to her feet, only to have the bodyguards take custody of the still fighting woman away from me.

"Augustus, let us just get this over with."

Crossing my arms, I took a long sigh, "Fine."

Gerard from there leaned down into the lower drawer of the computer desk, and removed a long needle syringe full of what I

185

could only guess was either a pheromone upper or a sedative, judging by its transparency and CC dosage. As he stepped towards the woman whose arms were being restrained by the two burly men, I watched her try to fight against their brute strength. Cinder's fears of needles and drugs were overwhelming the exhaustion that had swept over her entire frame. "Hold her steady." Leaving one of the men to hold her arms and the others to hold her avoiding neck, I further observed the Man remove the syringe's cap prior to injecting the long needle into the woman's neck. Introducing the liquid straight into one of the undamaged nerves left in her body, he announced to the world. "There we go." The syringe was quickly emptied and was just as quickly began to consume the fair-skinned woman, Gerard proceeded to communicate, "In a few seconds, she will change forms."

As soon as he had said that, the woman's body began to indeed shift. The bodyguards dropped her bi-pedal form onto the ground to allow the change into the large, one-hundred-pound Beauceron canine from that was a part of her Hellhound gene. The black and tan pelt taking over the smooth pale skin, covering the old scars. Fighting to regain her sapped strength, Cinder began to struggle to get back on her four feet. The snarl sounding completely savage and overrun with more anger than fear. As she managed to finally falter on her massive paws, I observed the bodyguards pick up two catch poles that were leaning off to the side of a passageway door.

"This is not going to end well," I told myself.

Chapter 35

Augustus

The metal wire loops were easily draped down the thick canine's muscle neck before both catch poles simultaneously tightened, further restraining the transformed Unnatural. Cinder while exhausted, still fought just as much as I had expected her to. Throwing all of her weight up onto her hind legs, she flung her head backward and began expressing one of the most savage snarls I had seen since I had been physically in her life. The sound that was coming from deep down in her throat made my breathing monetarily stall. It was a dreaded sound I had only heard a couple of times prior, and those other times came from the capture of Lord Zachariah's other Hellhounds. It was the sound of a true monster.

"Woah, there's the monster." Gerard cooed, his voice expressing the obvious sound of excitement by the sudden motion of the forcibly transformed woman. "You did not tell me about this side of her, Augustus."

"To tell you the truth, this is the first time I am seeing it," I replied as I also observed the canine's erratic behavior. Cinder threw her front legs over the angled poles to fight the transferring weights that the bodyguards were trying to maintain over the drugged animal. We all knew that all they had to was ride out the fear, let the drugs seize their hold over her, and eventually, the large one hundred-pound Beauceron submitted. Her body collapsing onto the wood floor yet again. The legs barely holding her up as her tongue rolled in and out of her mouth at a speed that made me worry over her respiratory system.

"Well, there she goes. Finally settling down, are you?" the casually-dressed man questioned, his hazel eyes locked in a cold stare down with the fiery blue. "Those eyes and that fur, who would've thought that this is what Hellhounds are supposed to look like instead of those pictures in fables."

"Yeah." I sighed, passively agreeing while Cinder bickered, her tone having unchanged.

"Alright, now onto the fun part: moving her."

"I want to see where you will be holding her," I ordered the human.

"What you don't trust me?" Gerard laughed.

"Not really." I chuckled back as I kept one eye out on the Hellhound and her well-being. "I want to make sure that everything I asked for, is being accommodated to."

"Fine, fine." The human gave in, raising his hands in the same playful manner. "Follow me."

Following in behind the Pit Owner, I kept my eyes out for the bodyguards as they proceeded to drag the still-fighting Cinder down the same pathway. Heading through the secret passageway, we were led down a flight of stairs, escorted through a landing where I saw rations of straw, mulch bedding, rows of metal food dishes, and several fridges full of what I assumed were collected venison and beef. The place hadn't changed in the years since my last visit. Leading the animal down yet another set of stairs, I noticed that there were newer surroundings. "You've updated the pens since my last visit, haven't you?"

"Yeah, had to. We had some breakouts with the old cages a couple of years back, so we decided it was time to upgrade the fencing, as well as the ground in which the posts are dug." Gerard explained, allowing the two employees to take the final lead and pull Cinder towards wherever they were going to be containing the threatening creature. Discerning the new chain-link fences that stretched possibly ten feet tall, I eyed that there were chain-link ceilings attached to the tops of the cages. The sizes of the kennels ranged from seven feet to ten feet across, allowing the varying shifter species a chance for some comfortability, if it allowed. As our group finally neared her assigned cage, I noticed that not everything had yet to be set up.

While Cinder heavily applied the brakes, I growled to the leader, "Why hasn't everything I paid for been done?!"

Not skipping a beat, the guards moved continued to drag the struggling one-hundred-pound animal up into her assigned 'kennel'. The poor employees had to use all of their strength just to get the beast onto the slightly raised concrete platform and inside the cage. Watching the men still fight Cinder, I heard Gerard's excuse, "Well, we got it started, but..."

"Do not bullshit me."

"Look, we got caught up in some shit with the 'legality' of our holdings." Gerard hastily admitted, creating bold excuses like he always did in order to save himself. "So, I haven't been able to have my men put the tarps over the faces of every kennel. Hell, I don't even know why you want them up in the first place?"

"I need them up for reasons I prefer to not tell someone as conniving as you." I hissed back as the guards had finally won their seemingly endless match with Cinder. Once more eyeing the kennel up and down, I saw that two out of four of the blue tarps had been hung. Each wall of chain-link that separated the fighters from one another had been covered. Separating the Reaping Hellhound's sight from a Kitsune, and a Cat Magus. Both exotic shifters who could've met a painful demise per the choice to tease the Hellhound with a rare Blood Trait. Neither the ceiling nor the face had yet to be covered. "I want them covered before I leave here."

"Alright, I'll have them finish the task once they are finally able to remove the catch poles from our little fighter," Gerard submitted, crossing his mildly covered hairy arms, the muscles flexing. Once the catch poles were released from the Beauceron's neck, I watched Cinder turn around and begin to pace around the kennel, her fangs trying to reach for the employee's hands as he attempted to lock the chain-link gate.

"That's enough, Cinder," I ordered the woman. Her blue eyes flashed at me and she snarled, but surprisingly the Hellhound listened. Falling onto her tired legs, I watched her continue the pace for a few minutes longer.

"Why couldn't you have done that earlier?"

"Well, because I wasn't entirely sure she would've listened to me." I huffed back.

"Anyways, once she finally settles into her temporary home, we will finish with our end of the registry," Gerard spoke up, slightly altering the subject on me while the two bodyguards advanced to covering the remaining walls of Cinder's cage. Using a latter to climb the chain-link and blanket the ceiling with the blue-tarp, I watched the men dangerously step on top of the fence, completely expecting it to break. "Don't' worry, it's made to hold up to eight hundred pounds of force." He described as the men began tying down the tarp. Climbing back off the ceiling, I relieved one long sigh, as did Cinder, who returned to pacing the front wall. "We have to leave the gate open by code, but we can cover up to five feet on the front-facing."

"Cover as much as you can. I do not want it one hundred percent covered, just enough to block out a majority of the prying eyes."

I answered back, this time being the first one to alter the conversation's subject. "About the registry, what are you all going to be doing?"

"We'll first check for tags, then we will do an overview of both her physical and emotional health, before clipping those nails that scratched up my new floor, and finally marking her with our regular protocol collars. All in all, it shouldn't take more than a couple of days unless we find tags, then we have to go through the process of removing them and the recovery that follows in suit." Gerard continued to thankfully answer. "She is set to be here for a few months, right?"

"Five months. Seventy-two fights." I recalled, choosing to go against Zachariah's orders by a few months so Cinder wouldn't be entirely exhausted. "I will pay everything per month as it says in the contract."

"Good, and I already have your first month's bill paid in full." The human now chuckled, stepping up to the gate to stand over the Beauceron, who was still pacing the exposed chain-link. Spinning in anxious circles to continue stalking the little bit of still exposed fence line, she flashed her fangs at him somehow managing to not make a single noise. "It's going to be fun having someone as challenging and willing to fight for one's survival as she is. Hopefully, the Pit's don't break her too soon." Gerard now jibed as he teased the furious canine, jabbing his fingers through the chain-link.

"Yeah, I hope so too," I growled under my breath, of course, however my hushed thoughts were still audible to Cinder's heightened hearing.

"Now that everything has been set up, let us return to the office and get that contract finalized." The Pit's Owner enthusiastically exclaimed as he walked away from the cage's gate, the snarling canine pursuing his movements with her hunting gaze.

"I will be up there shortly, just give me a minute with her." I sighed.

"Do as you wish; the door will be left open." The human sighed, leaving Cinder and I alone.

Coming down to Cinder's level, I watched the dog's pacing calm before it had stopped altogether. Those cropped ears flattening against her head before she pushed her large muzzle through the small gap that separated the gate from the adjacent fence post it locked to. Hearing her let out a half growl, half cry, I couldn't help, but feel her pain. Rubbing my fingers down her soft short-haired muzzle, I quietly apologized, completely expecting her to ignore the apology in her typical tease. But Cinder lightly huffed another growl, her eyes intensely eyeing me, silently articulated everything that I knew she was attempting to say in that mute language of hers.

"Okay, okay." I chuckled, removing my hand and bracing my forearms on my knees. "You're going to stay here and collect the souls that Zachariah needs to be claimed. It is your assignment to collect seventy-two souls. No one in particular; all of these souls are at their end one way or the other. Now, I would prefer that you behave while you stay here and don't kill anyone you are not set up to meet inside the ring." I explained. Catching the eyes blink and dance around, I could tell she was not only digesting the verbal information but the visual as well. A small whine of complaint emerged though, it fell short telling me that she reluctantly understood. "Thank-god." I happily exhaled.

Chapter 36
Cinder

"Alright, come on Hellhound." I heard Gerard call from the other side of the chain-link wall that separated my fangs from ripping into his jugular. The bodyguards again entered my personal space, throwing those cursed catch poles over my neck. I could have fought back, but what was the need to, when I now knew that this was part of my 'assignment'. This was a job I had to complete, or I would further risk 'their' lives.

Following the men outside of the covered dark kennel, I over-heard the little cross that was wrapped around my neck jingle, as my hung head allowed the metal to jam back and forth over my fur-covered chest with each gait I made. Recalling that it was a way for the angel to apologize, I rolled my eyes, and huffed a deep exhale to my memories, "For now, I don't forgive you, you asshole, but I will try to keep the collateral on the down-low." Deciding that I would yes behave in my own way, I fell in line. Keeping my eyes locked on my changing surroundings as I was led back down the hall in the same direction I had come from only hours earlier, I began to mem-orize the layout.

Analyzing the other shifters who were also stuck in their genetic mutated forms, I hastily noticed those who were attempting to challenge me and those who're attempting to already submit to my intimidating size and power. Easily hearing the uniform animalistic language, I perceived that those around me could already see who and what I was without me ever announcing my title. Challengers shouted their threats, refusing to believe I was the one told in legends. While the followers retreated, asking for me to take their life or spare mercy, no matter who it was, they were all calling me by the title, 'Reaper' and it was starting to piss me off; I was becoming so irritated that I was beginning to forfeit the promise I had made moments earlier.

"Hey there, sweet-cheeks." I could hear a snarky creature call. The tone hissing such a deep form of masculinity that it could potentially challenge Masters's angry voice. Flashing my eyes in the direction of the call, I marked that I was on my way to prowl past an Unnatural Shifter who I could not name with what little knowledge I knew on the breed, though I didn't really care either. Craning my left cropped ear into his direction, I paid closer attention to the teasing animal. "Where is all that spitfire you had earlier? I never knew that the 'Reaper's' spirit could be tamed by men, so easily." He laughed, flashing fangs that were longer than my own from his feline muzzle. Flashing my own fangs back, I kept my mouth shut while his pacing faded red and white furred body paralleled itself with my exhausted physique. "Huh, sweet-cheeks?"

Having enough of the name-calling, I swiftly turned inward towards my left, the adjacent pole jabbing itself deep into my shoulder. Pushing through the pain, I mustered up all of the faded strength I had and charged for the large kennel. My fast speed burning the poles out of the bodyguards' grasp. Taking advantage of the little freedom I had, I charged the cage. Feet before I reached the chain-link wall that separated us, my body was jerked back. Lifted onto my hind legs, I huffed a low cough mixed with the snarl I was swallowing deep down. Retaining my focus on the large feline with shocking amber eyes, I dropped all of my weight back down onto the floor. My front feet touching the concrete floor as I steadily dragged myself forward step by step towards the Unnatural who was now excitedly awaiting my arrival. Pulling the lasting inches, I fought against the fatigue and heightened my flashed snarl. "You do not want to see what I really am, cat!" I chomped. My jowls snapping together with such force they produced a vocal clap.

"Oh, and what is that sweetie?" the shifter probed, his snarl mimicking mine. "You do not seem as 'demonic' as the stories that have been told."

Summoning my Blood Scythes, I began attempting to swarm into the darkness of my psychotic itch, calling for a little bit of its' aid, hoping that I would not become too consumed. However, before I could manage this, my body was thrown down into the ground. Falling on top of the Scythes, I forced myself to hastily sheathe the Iron Blood weapons before they could have the chance to injure their host. I could feel the wire loops tightened like a noose around my throat, the weight crashing down on my windpipe. Savagely bellowing out in agony while the catch poles were stabbed deep down into my makeshift collarbone to hold me still, I overheard the Pit's Owner tiredly swear.

"Jesus Fucking Christ." Gerard cursed. "Well, there's the 'Demon' I was told to watch for." The human once more exhaled as his bodyguards harshly dragged my body around the floor. Pulled in a direction away from the cage of the Unnatural who had taunted me into this predicament. "I was hoping to not have to use this, today." Feeling the needle get jammed into my haunches, I instinctively threw my head up, attempting to once more fight the swarming people who circled tightly around me. Stopped by the poles, I dropped my head down onto the floor and fell back into my own promised submission. "I should have figured that you two would not get along so well."

195

"What is wrong with you? Why do you give up so easily to them?" I heard the cat now question me as he paced from the safety of his kennel. Taking my chance, I finally noticed the feline's size. This Unnatural was three times larger than my enlarged form. His eyes were an orange amber, mimicking a similar color to the other Hellhound I once had in my life.

"You try-" I paused when my voice strained. The words slurred and I knew that my mind was fraying itself over the fight against the drug that was recently injected into my veins. I again attempted the statement, but fatefully failed at it. Rolling my eyes, I submissively followed the lead of the catch poles. Standing up on my tired feet, I limped myself back between the two bodyguards who followed behind their employer and continue to journey towards the upcoming stairwell.

"I will see you again soon, 'Reaper' and the next time will be in the Pits." The feline shifter swarmed.

"Get her on the table before she collapses on herself." I heard the man order his lackeys as he speedily walked off to the side of the room and out of my peripheral vision. Feeling the poles tighten their hold on my neck, I was lifted onto my hind legs and steadily dragged onto the cold metal examination table. After I fell into an uncomfortable lying position, I locked my preserved sights on Gerard as he stormed around the small room. If I had to guess, this used to be an office but was turned into a medical ward once more Unnaturals had filed into the ring. Eventually, the lean man came back out within my murderous fangs, and hastily began to run through the same old, same old examination I had gone through countless times. His fingers slipped their way under my lips as they pried my jowls open so he could survey the interior of my mouth. Too exhausted to fight back, I allowed the man to do every task that was needed for the ritual checkup, wondering softly in my head; did he have the same experience with us Unnaturals like the Doctors at the Hospitals, or was it with the exotics like the Zoologists and Veterinarians had? Feeling myself steadily lose consciousness, I barely heard Gerard's last words; "Everything looks good so far. You guys can go ahead and remove the catch poles, she is barely conscious now. If I need you, I will call you back..."

Chapter 37
Cinder/Augustus

As I came back around, I felt miserable. Every bone and muscle in my body stung for some reason my still waking mind could not hypothesis. Scanning around the same surroundings as when I had passed out, I hastily noticed that more men were surrounding me than before.

"There she is." My stunned hearing caught Gerard's voice mockingly jab, his callused hand once again scouring through my fur, running its way down the side of my stomach in a painful way that made it seem as if he was claiming ownership over me. Refuting my opinion, I tiredly drew back my lips, flashing my white fangs that hid underneath.

"Well, you haven't broken her will yet." I heard another voice mock. The familiar tone of the Archangel's voice ringing deep down into my fatigued soul.

"Give it some time, and she will stop playing her games," Gerard answered back to the Deity's Angel.

Observing the blonde-haired green-eyed Unnatural step into my line of sight, I watched him as he stood over me and present his softer masculine touch. The fingers grabbing and pulling on my right ear that for some reason hurt really bad. Yelping out the sharp shear of agony, I again threw my head up, my jowls almost catching flesh.

The hand swiftly released from my soar ear as Augustus apologized. "Sorry Cinder, I didn't know that was the ear."

"There's a little bit of cartilage missing from where we had removed one of the microchips."

"Microchips?" I wondered. "One of them?! How many did you find?"

"One of-?" Augustus returned, also asking the same question that I too was wondering.

"Well, there were three in total. One in her leg tagged to an Institute in Colorado, and one in her neck that was tagged to the Institute you mentioned earlier." Gerard answered, his explanation stammering out.

"So, what of the ear?"

"It's not exactly a tracking chip as one would think. I would assume that it's one of those newer chips that act more like a USB or a memory card."

Confused, I kept my wandering questions to myself while the Valkyrie continued to inquire many of the same thoughts. Asking, "What exactly are you trying to say?"

"I'm surprised that someone as intelligent and as tech-savvy as you don't know?" Gerard chuckled, returning to the same serious toned voice that could still mimic Peylith's tone. The human put his hand back down on my fur, pressing the skin against my shoulder before further clarifying, "She must have been one of the first ones they implemented this experiment on." The man paused before venturing back out of my sight for a moment.

Observing the man come back up to the exam table, I noticed that he had something in his hand. His fingers doing what they could to hold onto a little black object that easily resembled the newer models of a SIMs Card. While in the spec of his palm was the fine microchip that allowed the ability to track the location of our little female friend who was surprisingly behaving herself quite well despite the nasty stink-eye she was flashing at the two of us.

"That's the chip?" I asked, taking the little black chip that had to be cut out from her flesh and ended up leaving a missing piece of cartilage in the outer rim of her ear.

"Yes, it is. I had my technicians run it through their computers to make sure it works the way it's supposed to, and we received much more than expected."

"How much more?" I probed.

"Go ahead and take her back to her cage," Gerard ordered, his eyes avoiding its contact with mine. "She's all set anyway. Just make sure the monitor is activated before you leave." The bodyguards without saying a single word-wrapped the same catch poles around her neck. Easily slipping the wires over her head and the thick three-inch high-rise black collar that was buckled around her neck instead of the simple nylon choker that was there the day before. Although still dancing around her neck as she stirred herself off the table was the cross necklace I had gifted her.

Watching her leave the room with little to no argument, I quietly pondered, "What are you thinking about inside that crazy head of yours? You never just go along with things you don't want to do-"

"Here, Augustus." Geared bluntly called, his hand outstretched with a different object now in its grasp. Coming back to reality, I journeyed my sights down to the extended object, catching the flash of the blue nylon waving around his wrist. "This is hers, right?"

"Yeah, it is. It belonged to the Syndicate she was sanctioned in before she arrived in my life." I sighed, receiving the object. "But I do know that it has an important significance to her."

"I wasn't going to throw it away, I just wasn't sure what you wanted me to do with it," Gerard explained.

"I'll take it." I acknowledged before inquiring in on another thought, "Speaking of collars, those are also new, right?" Recalling the sleek shine of the nylon collar that had what appeared to be some sort of black box on it, the type of box that resembled a shock collar.

"Yeah, each one costs a little shy of seven-hundred dollars due to all of the advancements it has."

"Advancements? It looks like a basic shock collar." I shockingly recoiled, following the man back into his office on the upper level.

"Well, it does have that for control reasons, however, it also has a few sets of cartridges in it that contain small vials of leaking seda-tives, or any typical drug we want it to possess, as well as a small monitor that reads heart rate and blood pressure." The man ex-plained as he settled down into his office chair. The serene silence making this room seem much eerier than it should have been. "It's all for the safety of the fighter, my employees, and the guests here."

"And who's the one that is tech-savvy here?" I teased, uncon-trollably mocking my own foxy smile. The two of us chuckled to-gether for a moment as we relived our alluded brotherhood.

"I guess, for now, I am just trying to assure you that all the pre-cautions have been made to ensure that that fucking gorgeous monster is in good hands." Gerard happily howled, his facial expres-sions reading the taste of pure thrill at the mention of Cinder's ap-pearances. "Seriously, Augustus, how the hell did you come across someone like her?"

"It's a long story that I do not have the time to tell." I excused, recollecting that I could not let Zachariah's name escape my mouth in front of humans, even if it was one whom the Deity had saved. Returning my attention to the small SIMs card chip I was handed, I changed the subject of our conversation and requested the information the human knew was on the device.

"I will let you see for yourself, Augustus. I don't have that kind of patience to review the hundreds of pages and thousands of other files that were on that little thing. Besides, wouldn't that be a complete invasion of privacy? It's already bad enough that my Pits are being related to the same care that the Institutes give."

"Well, I can see the relation, though I also can't." I jabbed, once more before standing back up from the leather seated chair that sat in front of the desk at a thirty-two-degree angle facing the desk. "I will go ahead and research this in my free time. Until then, allow me to say a few things to Cinder before I leave."

"Why couldn't you say them before we came up here?!"

"Just allow me the access, Gerard, after all, what am I paying you for if I cannot have access to my 'Hellhound'." I asserted.

Chapter 38
Cinder

"What do you want?" I lowly growled in the desired canine language. I was still so frustrated with him. I was so angry at the Valkyrie for not at least telling me beforehand. Strolling up to the front of the chain-link front wall, I locked my gaze with the angel's while he knelt, coming down to my eye level.

"You're still pissed at me, huh?" he chuckled. "I guess I had it coming, huh?"

"Yeah, you did." I barked back at him, reflecting a few of my long canines at him.

"Anyways, I came to tell you that I will be going down to Florida for a couple of months, I got a few clients to take care of down there."

"Why tell me?" I wondered quietly. "Did you think that this was going to bring back the little amount of trust I had in you, the trust that you broke?"

"I would prefer if you would just comply, and whatever you do, do not let Gerard break that perfect will of yours. Don't let that asshole win." Augustus continued, slowly straining his hand through the gate's post gap, the soft skin rubbing along the side of my still face.

I was unsure whether to rip his fingers off or to listen to his words and indeed behave myself.

"I wasn't planning on it." I snarled, pulling away from his comforting touch. My exhausted body fighting to stay conscious, let alone standing. The legs furiously shaking.

"There's the Cinder I remember." The archangel praised, removing his hand. Standing back up, he straightened out his back before the smile faded, returning to a sympathetic apology. The changing demeanor disturbing me. "Before I leave though, I do want to let you know what happened to you while you were out, and why I am holding this-" Augustus reported, dragging out the nylon collar that was supposed to be around my neck. Immediately rushing to the front of the cage, I snapped my jowls together, however, the man stood firm. Unshaken by my charge. As I attempted pacing the wall that separated us, my neck stung. Stung so fluently that I cried out in savage pain. The volt of shock ran through my entire nervous system, momentarily freezing me, "It had to be removed to put that on you."

"Put what on me?!" I snarled, refocusing my attention on the disguised human. "What the hell did you let them put on me?!"

"That collar is a revamped shock collar. It gives enough electricity that has been said to break the trance that you shifters tend to get locked in-" I overheard the deep-toned human speak up, stunning the angel who now turned around to lock gazes with Gerard.

"I thought I told you that I wanted a moment alone before I left," Augustus growled, his soft tone darkening into one I did not recognize.

"I just wanted to come down and make sure that her collar worked properly," Gerard explained or rather lied. His excuses were just as bad as my babysitter's. "The collar also has a few other tricks up its sleeves."

"Tricks?" I panted, finally able to gather my breath after the electric volt had shorted itself out. "What tricks?!"

"Which should start taking effect right about now–" The human continued, "Ah, there it goes." Before my body could even grasp the apparent situation, I collapsed down onto the floor. My unsteady legs giving out from beneath me. Fighting every numb nerve in my body to get back up to my feet, I angrily snarled at the two men who stared back down at me.

"You knew about this didn't you, Augustus?!" I wheezed, locking my blue eyes onto his apologetic glare. The blonde-haired man's green eyes seeming unusually soft.

"I told you that if anything happens to her, you should start planning your funeral, Gerard," Augustus warned, his eyes again darkening into such a dark color it petrified me. The human quickly submitted, retaining his place in a hierarchy I could not see nor understand. Augustus returned his stare on me as I finally mustered up the strength to stand back on my feet. "I will be back in a few months and remember what I told you."

"Yeah, yeah." I snarled between pants. "I get the drift, I cannot make a one hundred percent promise on it, but that man will not break me, not when I have this assignment to do, Valkyrie." The man removed his presence followed by his passive-aggressive associate, leaving me alone in this tarp-covered kennel that blocked out nearly all available surroundings.

Finding the strength, I limped over to a comfortable corner hidden away in the shadows of the tarp and collapsed once more down onto the cold concrete floor. Finding the back of my eyelids with ease, I sunk away into a hefty slumber, one that was for once not accompanied by the haunting nightmares of those recent events a few months ago. A slumber where I could finally get some rest.

It was awhile before I was finally allowed venue outside of the kennel. The lights that filled the hallway seared my vision as I was dragged out of the darkness. The catch poles' wires tightly ripping into my skin, irritating the mid-length fur as I was pulled further down the corridor in the very direction my mind dreaded going, in the direction of the Pits.

The closer I got to the ring, the louder the cheers of the crowd got, the louder the screams became. Their Auras ringing heavily through my nose as I collected every one of their scents. Their taste for the bloodshed, the lust for the fight was not only raising the desire to not be standing in front of these cruel men, but it was also rising the undesired feeling of the 'thrill of the hunt'. That psychotic itch I did not want to lose control over. Biting down on my tongue, I fought the urge to maintain some self-control knowing that I had to complete seventy-two fights, collect seventy-two souls. I had to bear it, as much as I didn't want to.

Reaching another wall of chain-link that separated us, I felt the poles change direction. Going from pulling me to pushing me, the poles pushing deep down into my shoulders. Rising my lip, I snapped my refusal but quickly reigned myself back in recalling the electrical shock that could send heavy volts through my out entire body if I tried to push anything any further. Getting pushed past the now open gates, over the threshold, my worn paws felt the change in terrain. The concrete exchanged itself with the collection of pounds of blood-stained dirt and sand. Trying to attack the catch poles, I finally felt the wires' stiff hold lessen, and the loops slip free from around my neck. Once free, I hastily pivoted in a tight circle and launched myself for the wall. The gate was slammed shut in my face just as I had kicked myself off the ground to lunge for the nearest guard. Parkouring off the wall, I returned all fours onto the ground whose scent was loaded with the stench of both old and fresh blood. The red liquid had obviously been splattered everywhere around the large fighter's ring. Ignoring the stench, I tried my best to collect my riled nerves as I awaited the Pit's next move.

Cursing to myself as I passed along the fence, I observed the two men take their leave. Their brutish gait sauntering back to who knows where. Still trying to center my nerves, I fought the rising fears and did what I could to understand that my only way out was to fight and kill my opponent. Preparing my still 'intoxicated' physique to fight whoever my opponent was set to be, I snarled out to the world, "That was your goal, right Shadow? Force me to fight, to kill my fellow kin? Force me to give in to this craze of enjoying the thrill?" Making my way to the center so I could alert my presence to the eager crowd, I continued, "Or is it that you want them ALL to see who their maker is? Well, whatever you got planned in that insane head of yours, I will do it as long as you live up to your end of our bargain, Shadow." I then ordered as I locked my sights on the other Unnatural who too, was being dragged through the gates on the other side of the square ring. The sight of my opponent further triggered the psychotic itch of mine, triggering the color change of my pupils.

Chapter 39
Cinder

Examining the creature, I studied the tall build, lean muscles, an intense number of scars that rode his neck, face, legs, and stomach. It was a sign of just how thick his muscle was, considering I could see that there were hundreds of tooth and claw scars running over the beast's vital spots. Dropping into a hunting prowl, I continued to quickly examine this creature's breed.

"The stench of a Lycan." I snarled, licking my lips I recalled the taste of both Calem's and Logan's blood in my mouth.

"I'm going to enjoy playing with you, mongrel." The wolf-shapeshifted Unnatural barked, his long fangs breathing in the chill air of this summer night. Those amber eyes of his were intensely locked on me and stuck out like a sore thumb to that brilliant white fur, which greatly contrasted against my soot-black coat. Holding my ground, I surveyed the wolf's shoulders roll before he charged straight ahead. His endured muscles shining under the shiny summer coat and bright lights.

Lifting my head up from its lower position of studying my opponent's traits, I bared my fangs back at the soon to be collected victim, and called out, "Let us see how far your play can get you, wolf."

As the wolf jumped for my smaller frame, I darted forward, slipping right on by the left side of the transformed Lycan. Swiftly veering around him, I prepared myself to jump onto the wolf's back, however, the white fur retained nothing more than a blur as it ran out of my line of sight. Coming to a halt, I attempted to steady my worn sights while maintaining a glimpse on the turning legs, but before I could even finish resetting my intoxicated sight, I was feeling fangs rip into the top of my neck. Throwing myself around, I hastily busted through the grip. Tearing the skin away from his fangs' deep hold, I held down the urge to shout out in savage pain, I regained some distance. Placing several feet in between us, I decided that with this established Unnatural who was used to this line of dirty fighting, I had to devise a worthwhile plan.

"But why can't I think of anything?" I silently pondered. Glancing over to the wolf, I remarked that yet again, his enormous size was closing in the distance. Locking gazes, I noticed that there was a familiar flicker in those amber eyes. A gaze I knew all too well. Quickly computing the situation with such few seconds between this Lycan and me, I finally figured it out, "That's what it is! Drug us, so we fight on primal prognosis." Dodging the next toss from the creature, I cringed at the thought of having to do the worst available trick I had, while I felt my eyes begin to sting. Knowing their color was darkening, I swore, "I will let you out..." Telling my darker temptations that it was okay to let loose. "For now, I will let you have control of my domain," I called out, again feeling the familiar break in my conscious. That shattering glass feeling in my mind.

Pushed back behind the arousing urge, I felt my jowls uncontrollably cling to its target as I was thrown down into my primal instinct. Feeling the blood spray onto my jaws, I observed from the sidelines, my possessed build release its hold and kicked off the wolf. Again, placing the distance between the wolf and me, I licked the side of my lips and turned around in the traditional circle to evaluate my next attack. Unknown to my conscious self my 'itch' had ripped open one of the heavy scars that had adorned itself under the wolf's right eye. The blood drooling down the white fur heavily staining its snow-white opacity. Strolling around in the invisible circle, I preyed on the wolf who followed my hunting prowl with a gaze of his own. Finding a decent spot for my next attack, I charged forward. The Unnatural turned around to face me, yet because of his massive size, he was still too slow to outmatch my speed. Springing open my long jaws, I chomped them down on the back of the wolf's neck. Slamming the front of my chest into the side of his shoulder. I braced my front legs down into the massive muscles and proceeded with the next primal action. Ferociously shaking my head from side to side as I stood on my hind legs, I could taste his blood flood it's way into my mouth, its strong taste overriding the animalistic taste buds on my tongue. With the Lycan howling out in agony, trying his best to escape my grip, I continued to shake while simultaneously drove my one-hundred-pound weight into his left side. However, my grip was short lived and I was forced to let go a few minutes later. Snapping my jaws at the wolf as he swarmed over the top of me, his height towering inches over my smaller frame, I hastily scanned his strong physique for the next opening.

With the scent of the blood casting an overpowering spell on my consuming psychotic itch, I fought to retain some control. Barely keeping my head above water, I scanned over the surroundings that spanned around the cage-shaped ring for a specific detail in the ground. Eventually locating what appeared to be a fool's hill, I charged off in that very direction with my opponent chasing after me. Dodging every attack the larger canine made, I sidelined all of his thwarts for my head. Praying as I approached the hill that the sand would make the perfect trap for his massive size.

Approaching the small hill, I then craned my head around to attack the wolf, who I had intentionally allowed to catch up with me. Making my attempt predictable, I permitted the Unnatural an opportunity to parry my fangs. Jumping forward a few feet, I watched his front left paw catch itself on the hill. Losing control of his footing, the estimated two-hundred-pound wolf fell over onto the hard ground. Not missing a beat, I pounced on top of the Unnatural and attached my fangs hastily onto the now wounded neck. My fangs tearing right through the swollen flesh, diving further down into the muscle. Although my body was too excited for the chance to claim my first kill on this assignment, I overthrew my weight and tumbled over the top of the wolf. Forcing my perfect hold to let go or else I would be threatening to break my neck. Rolling in the sand, I felt the rough substance catch on my fur and connect to the skin lying under my double coat. As I rolled back onto my feet, I wasted no time to return to the forefront and neither did my opponent it seemed. With the wolf having difficulty collecting the lost air I had shoved out of his lungs, I yet again threw my leaner weight into him. His tiring frame crashing into the ground with my fangs relentlessly baring their full potential into his thick fur coat. With my jaws tightly wrapped around his neck, I brought one of my large paws in and commenced pressing down on the trachea. The wolf slipped free from my hold, his body tossing around like a fish out of water, fatally trying everything he had in his fight-or-flight instinct to get his opponent off him. Shaking my head, I warned the creature to not move as the jaws reached the final stretch, finally ripping through the underlying muscle.

The wolf submitted, screaming out in pain. The shriek of unbearable agony flashed my conscience back into control, reminding me of all the other memorable screams I had heard during my institutionalization. Attempting to maintain control, I also recalled all the others whose lives were on the line here. Softly growling to the heavily panting creature, I confessed. "I apologize for this." Fighting through the tiring drugs, I spawned the Blood Scythes out from the imagined source. Allowing the heavy iron to coat my teeth and extend the bones' length by inches so it could reach much deeper than what was believed to be applicable. While my curved incisors pushed themselves through the muscle and tendons and down into the veins lying beneath, I also moved my free paw and pushed along the pressure point connecting the wolf's neck to his shoulders.

Dropping my crushing weight down onto my opponent's lengthy physique, I summoned my remaining strength and succeeded in creating a third Blood Scythe from behind my wrist. The blood-made weapon easily penetrated the muscle as I pushed my leg further down, swiping the foot-long blade through the muscle and into the organ that lied underneath the rib cage. "Again, I apologize." I snarled as he screamed out in more agony from my vicious assaults. Pushing past the encroaching thrilled crowd, I hurried my mercy along. Releasing my Blood Scythe's all together, I stood myself back up and waited the few seconds it took for his heart to bleed out before mimicking the final blow. Shaking my head, I shook the throat as I watched the wolf attempt to lengthen his life while the ember glow steadily fled those hunting eyes.

Losing control over my conscience once more, I proceeded with pressing my head against the larger wolf's head. Inhaling his last breath, I watched a strange green glow escape his mouth. Assuming this was his soul I was to collect, I accepted the collection as it absorbed through my skin and into the unknown. With the crowd digesting the results of our duel, I glared over the surveying humans, their greedy glares' locked on the two of us canine shifters. Observing the cheers rile my hackles and the still fighting will of that psychotic itch, I cursed, "Fowl humans, you are all so disgusting." Upon finally having my keen sense of smell returned to me post its fulfilling meal of enticing blood, it caught onto the stench of men begin to saunter their way into the massive chain-link cage called the Pit.

Seeing the same employees cautiously approach, I bared my fangs, fully prepared to semi-aggressively admit my hold in the ring, however, I felt another strong volt of electricity run through my nervous system. Freezing the thoughts, I yelped my frustrations while I fought to stay grounded. The catchpoles were easily thrown over my neck and I was effortlessly removed from the deceased Lycan. My numb legs struggled to stay working with each passing step, but I stubbornly remained on all four feet until I passed over the threshold of the cage I was to call my own. From there I dropped onto the now straw-covered concrete floor and submitted to the drugs while they eagerly sapped away my remaining energy. Once the poles were released from my neck and the gate was slammed shut, the chain-link crushing into my fur-covered flank, I conceited defeat to powerful sedative.

Hearing the humans chuckle at me and congratulate me on my first win, I refuted their sarcastic praise. Reminding the two humans, that I was still coherent and still capable of being a threat. The warning was enough to shut the men up and enough for them to thankfully take their leave. Forcing myself to stand back up, I strolled into the awaiting darkness to find a more suitable position to lie in as I listened to the dimming crowd again get swooped off their feet by what I assumed was another round of Unnaturals fighting. "So disgusting." I again cursed.

Chapter 40
Augustus/Jakob

Slipping into one of the two seats I had bought per my first-class ticket to Atlanta before taking a layover for Miami, I proceeded with pulling out my laptop from my carry-on and began to set myself for whatever news I was going to find out upon skimming over this file Gerard had found in one of Cinder's chips. Planting the small SIMs card into the chip and finally into a corresponding USB Drive before the final resting place inside the port, I took a long exhale followed by a few swallows from the complimentary glass of sparkling water. The water soothing my underrated thirst as I pulled up the files residing inside the SIMs Card.

"Holy shit." I quietly murmured as I drug around the laptop's mouse and proceeded with finding the first file that caught my attention. Eventually finding one from the list of hundreds, I was vacuumed into another massive compilation of folders containing: base information, growth photos, medical charts, surgical files for every procedure that they had done on her and complimenting assigned photos, filed attacks, and more photos, and finally Government contracts. Personally, it was a mess of work, but it was nothing I couldn't control. Now, if only they had hired me instead of whoever they had probing around this mess, I could've easily made the drive a lot more aesthetically pleasing. "Oh, the choices I have." I grinned as I reread through the long menu, deciding to start with the simplest file which was labeled 'Base Information.' Taking another sip while the inner document slowly loaded up, I began wondering the endless possibilities and horrors I was about to unfold. "What information was I about to see? What information was I about to see that I could no longer un-see?"

With the file finally uploading, I noticed that it was a simple three-page dossier. It was printed with good fonts, making it very legible instead of the disguise that lingered from the typical Doctor's signature. Inside the file, I quietly read the contents to myself:

"Patient's name was Cynthia Swallow. Patient's Identification Number was 0497." I read before skimming over the sex, age, date of birth, and social security number, I continued, "Parents' names were Nicholas Swallow and Cassidy Swallow." I paused recalling file reports on these two per 'his' orders. "You, sly piece of shit." I smeared, taking a minute away from the file while remembering the details I had exhumed on the report of Cinder's parents. "If I remember things correctly, Nicholas had an undiagnosed Blood Trait, the same Blood Trait that lured Zachariah further towards his chosen 'Reaper'." Looking back over the bright computer screen, I further read the report, beginning to understand more and more why the Deity had urged Cinder to be under his care. Skimming over their social security numbers, I hastily wrote down the given address and phone number that had stupidly been jotted down. "You guys were sure thorough with your research on her." I chuckled. Finding a good spot to pay attention to, I studied the next line that told me that her assigned 'Doctor' was, "Doctor Shane Masters. An Unnatural Genealogist with over twenty years of experience in dealing with new breeds." Recalling the time, I had also been ordered to overview this man's track record. "Why did you want me to overlook that again?" I wondered as I finished surveying the first page. Glancing over phone numbers, rooms, and granted access to so-and-so, I then moved over to the next page. "And here is the contract they signed," I said as I read over the title of the legal custody contract that her parents had so easily endorsed. Noticing inside the labeled print they were allowing access to the horrible treatment that Cinder, aka 0497 was put through in those sixteen years of Hospitalization. Allowing the treatment of hundreds of untested drugs, plenty of surgeries, horrible experiments and other things I could only assume were too much to bear on a grown adult, let alone an innocent child and especially a child who knew no better. "You guys really did not read through everything." I sighed, cringing at the faults lining the fine print of this checklist. "You surrendered your only child to the worst possible treatment man could give. Why?"

I knew it was useless to wonder aimless questions, so I took another sip and quick exhale before closing the file to examine the next one down the list. The one labeled, 'Growth Photos'. Expecting to relive through the same photos I had seen from the file I kept locked in my office, I opened the Window's Photo Viewer to make sure there was nothing I had missed. As soon as the first photo came up, I rolled the laptop's screen towards the jet's window so I could keep the petrifying photos away from the prying eyes of the stewardesses and the passing passengers. As I scrolled through these photos, I came to realize that these were much darker than the ones I had seen from the 'confidential folder'. In many of the photos, I could see these thick burly hands holding up a barely conscious female child by her arms and the back of her neck. Her bright blue eyes looking dull and watered over. Grabbing at my mouth to keep from gasping, I hastily scrolled through the slideshow. Flying through the array of familiar photos, I noticed that the pictures were timestamped six months apart. In two minutes, I once more watched Cinder grow up. Observing the tiny child develop into a teenager and finally into the woman I now knew or the one I thought I knew. Staring at this woman who no longer even had the will of life flashing in her dead eyes, I also noted her dirty blonde hair had turned black, her face was pushed exposing the lining of her petite skull underneath, her collarbone was sunken in along with her eye sockets. Holding everything together, I swallowed risen vomit as my sights digested everything they had just seen.

"How was it even possible that the Vampirics were able to pull someone who was as malnourished and ready to die as she was, out of that darkness?" I whispered with deep inquiry while the slideshow also began to oversee the damage her previous life had done to Cinder's other form. Barely able to hold down the vomit, I chugged hard on the sparkling water I was given before calling the flight stewardess over to my seat. "Get me something stronger, some whiskey or scotch, if you don't mind," I ordered the middle-aged woman who was flashing the fakest smile I had seen in a long while. "I'm going to need something stronger to deal with the rest of this shit." I slyly smiled, closing down the photos to open the next file.

"Jakob, hey Braedon wants to see you." I heard Mhykal call out, his voice shaking me out of my deep wondering thoughts while I sat in 'her' room on the little bench positioned at the end of the bed.

"Tell him to 'Fuck Off,'" I growled, glancing back over to the other Vampiric I desired to still call my friend, yet wondered if it was possible given the recent incidents.

"Look man, I get that you are upset about what happened, but we still got things that take priority and that includes the safety of all these other Unnaturals we house here. We did that to protect them as we attempted to create a stable enough alibi for Cinder's sanity-." Myhkal attempted to apologize, his eyes softening in hope of making me see his sympathy.

"I don't care, Mhykal." I still refused. Standing up from the bench, I repeated, "I don't fucking care."

"No, right now you don't care because that woman had cap-tured your heart. But you have to fucking remember she almost killed you, Jakob!" Mhykal snapped back, his fists clenching.

"Cinder had to do what was necessary to save me!" I argued, vividly remembering the saddened face she had on.

"No, Jakob you don't get it! Cinder was doing what she needed to do to save herself..."

"Yeah from killing me, you, and everyone else!"

"I do not know where you had gotten that idea in your head, but from considering everything we had interrogated out of her-"

"INTERROGATED?!"

"Alright interrogated was the wrong word of choice, I see that now, but from everything we could get her to tell us, it seemed she was more focused on getting herself out of the Syndicate rather than apologizing for what happened to you, Peylith, or I! Get it through your fucking head, Cinder was out for her own gain, whether or not she was afraid of some punishment by that 'Shadow' or something completely other, she was out for her own life, Jakob!" Mhykal con-tinued, bursting out what seemed to be bearing down on his shoul-ders for the longest time. Taking a long steady exhale, he softened his words again, "Look, Jakob please understand where our concern for you is coming from..."

"I don't care, Mhykal. Tell Braedon whatever the fuck you want, but I will not speak to him, not now, not for as long as it has to do with his fucking gain." I snarled, storming past my younger friend who I had helped sire and out of the room that was on its way into transitioning for another Unnatural to take its key.

"Jakob-"

"TELL HIM TO FUCK OFF!" I growled over the back of my shoul-der while I began to walk towards the hidden staircase that I knew would lead me towards the room I have had in my possession for almost one-hundred years; hoping that if I was hiding in my room no one would bother me while I continued to try and sort through this mess. I wanted to trust Cinder, although I couldn't help but forget the words my fellow associate had told me. I knew Mhykal had nothing to gain from lying to me, so why couldn't I shake his words loose.

Chapter 41

Augustus

Arriving at my deluxe hotel suite that overlooked the stunning high-rise view of the bright Atlantic, I dropped my suitcases and once more grabbed out my laptop to finish reviewing the endless abundance of files. Though I was slightly intoxicated from the alcoholic beverages consumed on both flights, I barely managed to finish the list of medications and experimental drugs they had put Cinder on before I had to take a break. There were so many drugs that it was easy for me to justify the Hellhound's dislike for drugs and needles.

Reviewing the file one more time, I rolled my green eyes over the lists of separated and categorized charts. There was a table for sedatives and painkillers, listing the ranging dosages per year and the different doses she received pending the Blood Moon's unusual lunar phase and the time of day. The next table recorded all of the food additives that the Doctors were giving her after Cinder had dived into her shock paralysis state. Sure she was alive on the outside, but on the inside, she was gone. Scrolling down the fourth page of nothing but large tables, I proceeded with the fifth and sixth tables which were filled with nothing but tracks of records of experimental drugs. Many were drugs still not yet recognized by the Federal Drug Administration, nor the Unnatural Health and Science Organization. The doses ranged from moderate to extremely high, and besides each dosage count was a synopsis slot, a place for a quick summary over the effects each drug had on her for the first initial treatment.

"How could they do this to her?" I wondered aloud while my heart momentarily ceased beating and my gut churned with such a vicious tendency that I thought I would need to call an ambulance. None of the drugs I read through gave good synopsizes. All of them had either induced seizures, heart attacks, respiratory problems, heightened blood pressure, sores, rashes, fevers, illness, broken bones, internal bleeding, and even cruel flash changes. "How could they even attempt these?" I infuriatingly interrogated, pausing when my eyes had read over one specific drug that had a decent synopsis. "HNPA" I read over the name. "So, no long unreadable translation." Pulling up a quick google search, I got company names over and over, however as I scrolled down the fifth item on the list was a site, I weighed judgment on the link's summary. Having little to no luck with the rest of my search, I clicked on the Wikipedia link and prayed for the best. Hastily reading over the long website, I stopped when I read over the description:

'HNPA is a drug that is concocted of Sodium Chloride, Diazepam, and Thiopental. The drugs react in a way that would typically kill man, however, through unregistered testing in Unnaturals, it was found that those with the Shapeshifting Genes and those of Demonic Breeds were easily sedated and controlled. Depending on when the medication was injected into their bloodstream, the forms would vary.

Changing tabs, I pulled up the charts, and read that synopsis, "Came clear. Sedated and Controlled. No complications." Looking over to the internet's webpage, I moved onto the next paragraph:

'However, if not supervised the drug can become toxic the longer it is in the Unnatural's system. Stopping the circulation of ions in the Blood while simultaneously shutting down the white blood cells that protect living beings from infections as well as corrupting the control over the red blood cells and allowing the blood to severely clot."

It was hard to evaluate the pros and cons of this drug. Glancing over at the chart again, I saw that on the list of daily drugs they decided to put the young woman on, the medication had been used for the last three years of her Institutionalism. Using it especially on Blood Moon dates. Each time the drug, while painful, eliminated the 'change' the woman needed to complete while she was under that horrible Red Moon, it too gifted the Doctors the ability to keep her body in such a stalled state of paralysis for both mind and body. It was cruel treatment, pure abuse.

"Cinder, how could you have lived for so long in this life?" I wondered aloud to myself as I sat down on the lounger that sat out on my private balcony and enjoyed the warm tropical breeze that swarmed my soft skin. "How come Zachariah didn't liberate you then and there?"

"Because, Valkyrie, the Sodium they unknowingly put in the 'Reaper's blood blocked my chance to procure control." I heard the cold creeping voice inform.

"Sodium? Salt blocked you from taking control over her?" I smirked at the Deity who appeared beside me. The absolute black mass not even allowing a single ray of sun to create highlights or shadows. Stopping as soon as I realized that was a stupid question, I promptly questioned, "Control? What do you mean by control her?"

"That scar does more than just bind her to me, Valkyrie." Zachariah snarled.

"So, there is more to that scar than just a contract bind?" I alluded to myself. "Anyways, what do you want?"

"I would watch your tone." He warned, his voice sending chills down my spine. "I am here for a report on my beloved little 'Reaper'."

"Cinder is in the Pits now. She's been registered, all her tags have been removed, and if I had to assume, by now, she has already had her first fight. Now, I had to come down here to complete some jobs, but I will head back to New York after a few weeks." I reported per his demands.

"Good, and I assume what you are overlooking is not for your clients?"

"No, it's not." I returned. "Those bastards hid all of her files in a tiny chip in the underlining of her left ear. So, I'm taking my chance to review the information I wasn't able to before. However, my Lord, after reviewing as much as I have, I wonder why didn't you react? Why, besides those drugs they put in her, did you not use the power I know you have collected over the last two hundred years and at least return the favor to those humans? What made their existence so important that it delayed your ability to retrieve your 'Reaper' for sixteen years?"

"Curious huh?" the Deity teased. "Their existence proved to be an aide to her progress. They fueled the hatred I needed to install into her head about humanity. Fueled the kind of hatred that I could not install myself." The shadow then paused for a quick second as if to find a unique way to explain whatever he had planned for the Hellhound behind my back. "To answer your question, yes, I could have used the power I had gained from our past trials to eliminate those few souls; however, what you're not seeing, my stupid Valkyrie, is that it was that same power the others had given me that I was using to keep my little 'Reaper' alive."

"So, you let them do all this to her when we could've easily found another 'Reaper' for you to misuse and abuse?" I returned, standing up from my lounger to debate my point. "What the hell makes her so fucking special that you chose her?! What makes her so fucking special that you let sixteen years of torture happen instead of ending her miserable life-?!"

"Watch your tone!" The Deity snapped, his harsh red eyes darkening, alerting me that this was my final warning. That this was where I needed to check myself. "The reasons I chose her should not be of your discernment. Do your job, and as it goes, I will reward you when I finally reclaim my throne. Do you understand me, Augustus?!" Zachariah hissed. Those haunting eyes of his intently glaring down at me, leaving little to no room to refute.

Looking away from the god, I answered the words he wanted to hear. Watching the Deity vanish into thin air as he usually did, I resumed my reading. The further I went done the list of files, the more I felt repulsed by the type of life Cinder had been forced to live. Past, present, and what was yet to come, yet I knew I had to do this for my survival. I knew that she represented the best chance to change our horrible lives for the better, but was it still worth all this? Was putting her through this, keeping her alive for sixteen horrid years, really worth where we stand now?

Chapter 42

Cinder

"How are you doing, Cinder?" I overheard the human leader call out to me from the safe side of the chain-link. The same annoying tone, stimulating my deepened hatred for his kind. Snarling my refusal, I walked out of the darkness towards the gate. Keeping control over my nerves, I lingered on all fours and paced the chain-link wall that separated my fangs from sinking into his neck. "There you are. God, how is it that you are still so gorgeous after fifty-three fights?" Gerard cooed, his hand pushing through the chain-link gate's gap. Chomping my fangs down on his fingers, I was immediately stopped by the heavy volt shooting through my body. On instinct, I swarmed around to attack at my own body, my fangs trying to reach for the collar that I now knew was the source of these annoying electric volts, even though rationally, I knew that in this form it was useless. "It seems that we have yet to break your feisty will."

"And I will not let you." I returned, swinging my jaws back around to face him, my shepherd-like muzzle slipping between the gate's gap.

"It's alright the crowd loves your fighting spirit anyway, so what's the use in breaking you." The man continued while standing himself back up so his employees could now storm the gate and assumingly proceed with the normal weekly checkup. Maintaining some control over my shortened temper, I permitted the men to slip those dreaded wire loops over my neck. With the help of their steel poles, they dragged me out of the tarp-covered kennel and towards the makeshift medical room upstairs. Following in behind the employees, giving them little struggle as we walked towards the routine location, my eyes scavenged over the same feline creature who always had something on his mind every time I made this journey.

"How much longer are you going to keep playing that game, Reaper?" The cat hissed, his black striped orange fur seeming freshly stained with the familiar sticky red substance of blood.

"How much longer are you going to keep teasing me?" I shot back, flashing my eyes over off to the left so I could survey his behaviorisms.

"As long as it takes, sweet cheeks." The cat snickered, his long fangs peeking out from under his lips, absorbing the fake luminescent lights from above the kennel.

Rolling my eyes, I exhaled a long sigh to alleviate the urge to react upon his name-calling. However, after the third time, I could no longer take it and pulled in the opposite direction. Thanks to their experienced grip, I was thrown up onto my hind legs as I fought to get free.

"Every fucking time!" I heard Gerard complain over my loud snarls. Seeing a glimpse of his shiny black phone, I instantly knew what this godawful human was going to do and conceited. Dropping back onto all fours, I fell in line with the role I was to play.

"Coward." The tiger snapped.

"Shut up!" I bared back, shining my fangs back at the shapeshifter.

"There we go, much better girl." Gerard smiled, hinting towards the employees to continue their trek towards the exam room. "It took you a few times to realize where it was coming from, but a few times was better than the countless times it took Khalar." His gaze locking with the Unnatural who often teased me. Scanning over I oversaw the cat bare his fangs, but thankfully he had ceased his jabbing and name-calling.

"Fowl humans, you should have just let the Hunters kill me." The Unnatural named Khalar muttered.

"Then why do you continue to win your fights, if you want to die so much?" I thought as my body once more synced its movements with the two guards.

"Now that that has calmed down, let us get this over with so we can return her to her cage for the night." Gerard huffed as he resumed the lead.

Returning to the cage was easy when I noticed that Khalar was out of his kennel. With no one teasing me, I was more capable of staying in control of my nerves while I was being led back to the chain-link, tarp-covered kennel I had been calling my bed for the last two months. Passing over the threshold, I waited for the catch poles' loops to be removed from around my neck. Once I was freed, I wandered deeper into the darkness where like always, I would succumb to the black shadows hidden inside.

"While your checkup came up clear, you won't have any fights for the next couple of weeks. If Augustus found out that in three months, we rushed fifty fights down your schedule, man, would he have my head." Gerard sighed.

"Making excuses for yourself." I declared as I kept my back turned towards the Pit leader. "I may have no idea what made the Angel save your life, but I assume lying to him won't get you far." Finding a half-decent spot where the hard straw collected itself, I laid myself down in the back corner of the cage, keeping my frame parallel with the gate. Staying alert, I observed the humans collect

227

alongside the cage and waited for them to take their leave so I could fall into yet another deep drug-induced slumber.

"The sedatives seems to be working, surprisingly." The lead human continued with another heavy exhale. "Alright, I will leave you to your slumber, Hellhound." He ended, finally strolling away from the kennel-side.

"Thank-god." I tiredly moaned, dropping my head into my paws and easily slipping into the sleep that called out for me.

"Hello there, brat." My ears heard before my eyes had the chance to observe. Immediately establishing the source of the voice, I shot my pupils open and stood myself up. Although, my legs immediately gave out from under me. Falling straight down onto the hard concrete beneath me, I screamed out a yelp of sheer pain. "Oh, where's the fight I know you have in you?" The man mocked. "Come on, come for my head like you normally do!"

As my sights adjusted to the dim lights, I noticed that the being standing in front of the fence was the cruel Shane Masters. His slick back, sheer blonde hair reeked of more gel than what I last remembered. Dressing in surprisingly casual jeans and a grey shirt with an unusual decal, I wasn't sure whether or not I was truly matching the voice of one person to the sight of another. But as I took in the familiar stench and work I had done to his neck and face, I no longer had any further doubts. Baring my long canine fangs at him, I angrily howled, "How the hell did you get down here?!"

Chapter 43
Cinder

Trying to fully digest all the horrible possibilities and reasons for this man's arrival, I savagely fought to stand myself up off the cold concrete floor. However, with the drugs staying steady in my system, I barely managed to maintain my hold.

"Oh, what's the matter, brat?" The mad scientist cooed. His voice only further enraging my desire to fight against these sedatives and volts of painful electricity shooting throughout my large muscular canine frame. "Come at me-."

Before he could finish his statement, I found enough energy to give into my blinding rage. Charging straight for the chain-link fence, I jumped up along the gate. Standing up on my hind legs, I threw all my weight forward, watching the latch barely hold my attempt. Of course, the bastard didn't even flinch at my incoming attack. Using the chain-link fence to keep upright, I noticed my vertical height put me two inches shy of six feet, allowing my eyes to remain fixated on his familiar hazel-green gaze.

"Oh, man!" Masters smirked, flashing his sly-tooth smile. Poking his fingers through the chain-link to tease the snapping jowls, I barely managed to hear his next statement over my primal instinct.

"There's that hatred! Those damn eyes of yours, oh how do they piss me off!"

"Then come in here!" I barked back at the man, my deep canine voice echoing off the concrete walls. "Let me show my hatred for you! I promise that I will kill you this time and make it very slow and painful for all the years of abuse you gave me!" I now swore, feeling my blue eyes mutate into the burning orange while my energy filled the rage of the other Pit Fighters. Riling them up. The howls, snarls, and calls of each shapeshifter echoed throughout the concrete hall, matching the cheering and booing of the crowd watching from the floor above, where they were supposed to be.

"Tempt me all you want, you damn bitch, but I am not that stupid to get that close to you again without prior precautions." He continued, shying away from the chain-link fence. "However, as suiting as this is for someone like you, I am curious what made those fucking Rebels turn their backs on you after one of them nearly killed me that day?" Masters asked while I returned to all fours and resumed with the more obsessive pacing. Still pulling all the stops I could to fight the medicated fatigue, I furiously increased my pacing, watching every single movement this man procreated.

"What the hell are you doing?" I heard a voice command. Unsure of who it was thanks to the covered tarps around the chain-link that concealed my sights, I awaited the character to wander into my line of sight. "Spectators are not allowed down here."

"Sorry, I got lost." Doctor Masters excused. "I was looking for the bathroom, and one door just led to another-"

"That is a load of bullshit." I snapped, again throwing my weight onto the gate before once more shooting back up onto my hind legs.

"Whatever." Another man sighed. "Just get back upstairs."

"Before I do that, I'd like to talk with the owner of this Unnatural here." Masters spoke up, pointing his fingers back in the direction of the kennel that I had been calling my temporary bed. "I am curious how an Institute Patient arrived here after she was kidnapped..." The Doctor now once more lied. I had not been a Patient to anyone in almost six months, and I was not kidnapped by anyone, I was liberated. If I was kidnapped it was by the Hunters and by lying bastards like him.

"Fine. Lucas, you stay here with..."

"Doctor Shane Masters." Masters announced. "Unnatural Genealogist for Salam Hospital and Rehabilitation Center."

"Stay here with Doctor Masters while I go retrieve Gerard." One of the assumed bodyguards expressed.

"Alright." His co-worker attended, finally stepping into my line of sight, the employee a much-needed comfort beside this man who I completely despised.

Dropping down onto all fours, I proceeded with watching the white-blonde haired casually dressed man try to strike a conversation with the employee. Attempting to make himself less of a possible enemy to the humans. Eyeing all of his haunting movements, I perceived the man inquire, "How did you guys get them all to calm down, especially that one?"

"It's the collar they wear." I now heard the annoying tone of Gerard explain. "Each collar has a Disciplinary Box on it that emits both drugs and electric volts. The drugs don't make them comply as much as the volts do, right Cinder?" the leader to the Pits jabbed, his hazel eyes locking with mine. Folding my ears back, I retreated the fiery orange eyes, replacing them with the infamous blue gaze as I stepped away from the fence line. "That's a good girl." Gerard then praised. His 'new' habit. Although it pissed me off, it was more tolerable than those annoying pet names.

"Cinder? You know that is not her name." Masters corrected.

"Yeah, I kind of figured, but it's the one she responds to, so it's the one we use. Now, what are you up to?" Gerard said, quickly getting to the point.

"I would prefer to not explain in front of that one." Masters excused, again pointing at me from the other side of the kennel. Still refusing to see me as an individual.

"It can be said here. I think it is just a waste of time for me to come down then head back up there, then back down here. I am a busy man, Doctor."

Masters growled but submitted to the man in charge. "While I usually come here in my days off, I was taken back to see her fight with the Chimera. To see one of my patients here fighting against other Unnaturals."

"Get to the point."

"She is Federal Property and was stolen by a Rebel Syndicate almost three years ago and was again stolen a little over six months ago."

"Stolen twice?" Gerard sighed. "Federal Property? I thought Unnaturals were considered underprivileged citizens, not property?'

"While they are, the Courts allows Institutes to claim ownership over dependents once they prove useful to scientific advancements." Masters explained.

"Well, I apologize for the fact she was 'stolen' from you, however as you should know the way the Black-Market works: once someone's 'property' is brought here, the only way to get it back is to buy it back," Gerard explained, the sternness in his voice not coinciding with his casual smile. "Warrant's don't work, even the Courts will tell you that. And to buy that one..." The owner pointed down at me through the chain-link gate that still separated my fangs from ripping into both of them. "You will have to contact her current 'owner'."

"Aren't you the owner?"

"Far from it, I owe the man a favor, and this is a contract ownership, so I have custody, but I am not the owner." Gerard returned before he gave silent cues to his employees to grab those dreadful poles.

"I do not want to leave this cage." I rejected, slightly baring my teeth while the men followed their boss's orders and proceeded to enter the kennel, catch poles in arms. I argued my refusal, but upon seeing the slight glare of the light echoing off his phone. The same phone that wirelessly controlled when I received those agonizing high-wattage volts. Containing my rage, I proceeded to fall in line, allowing the wires to once more slip over my neck. Tightening along the fur, so I couldn't slip my box-shaped Beauceron head out of the metal loop. Submissively following in behind the two body-guards/transporters, I once more played the game. Playing the exact same game I used to, so I could imagine the Shadow was not haunting me, only this time it was to imagine that Masters was not conversating with Gerard as they followed in behind. Realizing I was being led back to the exam room, I questioned Gerard's plans. Something was up.

Chapter 44

Cinder

"Get her up onto the table." Gerard ordered the two employees, following his previous orders to have me muzzled and sedated.

"What are you doing?" I confusingly growled under the nylon muzzle that was tightly wound around my mouth, restraining any possibility of my jaws chomping down on human flesh.

"Wow, I would have never guessed that her fur would have been this soft." Masters cooed, rubbing his hand down my rib cage. Reacting out of hatred, I flung my muzzled head up towards his arm, already knowing what to expect. The nylon restrained my jaws, while the short chain-lead kept my head from rising more than three inches off the metal table. All of that was soon followed by the dreadful volts of electricity that had zoomed its way throughout my lean canine form.

"Most of the time, the sight of my phone stops her, but whoever you are and whatever you did, she really hates you for it." Gerard returned. "I know Cinder dislikes men, men like me, I mean she hates me, but she contains that hatred pretty well for her level of ferocity."

"You could say it's more than hatred, I guess since her parents abandoned her, she was always been out for my head. Blaming me for it all."

"Well, you probably were at fault. After all, you work at an Institution." The owner chuckled while he now rubbed his hands along my left ear, pulling away at the little divot that the surgeon had created when they had removed my trackers. His finger's softly stroking the inner ear in an unfamiliar pattern yet somehow felt much more comforting than I had initially anticipated. It was much more comforting than the other human's hands that were now running against the flow of my long canine hair along my back.

"I guess I was, but I think it was the time I spent as her assigned physician that rose her animosity towards me. Sixteen years is a long time to hold a grudge."

"Yeah, that is quite the time."

"However, who is it that I must contact to regain custody?" the cruel Doctor inquired, removing his hand from my scarred skin while Gerard maintained the hold on my left ear, still rubbing the inside of the cartilage.

"That would be Augustus Gale. I do not know how she went from being in the hands of a Syndicate to his hands, but that is who you should contact. And as of right now that man is in Florida."

"A man as famous as him is her 'owner'?"

"Famous?" I wondered to myself. "How famous was Augustus, that even this man knew who he was when I had never even heard of the man until my time in the Lycan Syndicate?"

"Yeah." Gerard chuckled. "Hard to believe, isn't it?"

"Well I assume by the favor you owe him; you must have a decent relationship with him?" Masters tried to ease in.

"I am not going to be used as some telephone." The Pit owner rejected, removing his fingers from my cropped ear. "If you want to get a hold of him, come back in a month and ask him yourself."

"Well, that is what you do not get, I don't have the time to waste, and nor the money. We are wasting taxpayers' hard-earned money on tracking her down, let alone for the experiments that we have succeeded in finalizing since she was signed over to the Federal Government."

"Well they already fuck taxpayers over with everything else, so why not waste a few more dollars on another month of waiting." Gerard coldly theorized, giving Masters little room for further debate. "And you have to remember where you stand, Government has no rule here."

"Right, I could have everything closed down with one phone call." Masters threatened as his tone darkened, his cruelness poking through the casual attire he wore.

"And I could have you killed, and your body disposed of with one phone call." Gerard returned, his own sadistic cruelness coming out of the darkness. I knew something was lurking under his already crazy stern maturity, but I was not expecting it to be this. The way the statement had rolled off his tongue with such coolness it overrode my rage with fear. It even froze Masters for a minute. The small exam room filled with silence for a few seconds before the Pit Owner with the nice build spoke up. "I would like you to leave. Gentlemen, could you escort Doctor Masters back to the front. Don't worry about Cinder, I will take her back myself."

"You will?" I questioned, deeply confused by his sudden takeover.

"Do you want one of the catch poles, sir?" asked the employee called Lucas.

"No, a simple leash will do. The sedative I had Brian give her was more of a top-up." Gerard informed.

"I will return here every week-!" Masters snarled as he was being pushed towards the staircase that led up into Gerard's office.

"Fine by me, as long as you pay your admission, there is nothing I can do to stop you; however, if my men find you back down in the kennels, I will throw you into the ring with the very Demon who hates you so bad it even terrifies me." Gerard once more threatened. "And I will make sure that the drugs that stall her rational thinking are not pushed into her system so she can physically enjoy ripping you to shreds."

"The crowd-"

"Pfft." The Boss now busted a laugh. "The crowd has seen people get murdered down there all the time, matter of fact we allow Mobs to respectfully dismiss enemies and traitors here quite often. And if you tell the Government about that, I will not only be forced to tell your buddies that you severely abused one of your patients beyond the loopholes of the Second-Citizenship Laws in place for Unnaturals, but I'll tell my friends in the Mob to deal with you in their unique fashion, as a favor to this obedient, sweet, Hellhound." Gerard threatened the cruel Doctor as he looped one of the nylon rope leads around my neck and unmuzzled my mouth. "Now get him the fuck out of my sight!" He proceeded, coldly ordering his employees, whom both were sweating profusely from their employer's threats. With such a strong stench emitting off their skin, I knew that it meant Gerard's threats would be promises kept. Keeping myself in line, I marched alongside the man as he led me back to my kennel, and the serenity I was hoping would wash away the rest of today's chaotic events.

Chapter 45
Augustus/Cinder

"Holy Shit!" I cursed as I walked through the front doors of the Pit's Coliseum. "This place is packed!" I continued to think quietly to myself while I parted through the thick crowd of cheering and booing spectators. I couldn't see who was in the Ring that was hyping the humans up so much, however judging by the sounds of the growls and snarls coming from the epicenter of the lower floor, I had to assume it was a Cat Magus; a species that were popular for their unique feline forms and supernatural elemental culture. Pushing through the crowd, I ventured towards the staircase where the VIPs were observing the same fight. Stopped by the two bouncers at the base of the top step, I spoke up. Screaming over the shroud of the ecstatic crowd, I was barely able to announce my name. "Augustus Gale, here to see Gerard."

"Go on." One of the bouncers granted, pointing behind him offering me clearance to pass and head up onto the upper balcony. "He is in the office."

"Thank you." I sighed, stepping past the two burly men and onto a more organized floor plan. The spectators up here were calmly observing the fight from below while they sat at high-rise bar tables and were served top-notch service. Pushing past the urge to observe who was inside the large ring, I ventured down the runway and into the office, complaining as I stepped over the threshold, "It's a madhouse out there."

"That's bound to be expected." Gerard cruelly smirked, standing up from his office chair. "Especially with everyone's favorites down there going at each other's throats."

"Everyone's favorites?" I repeated.

"You didn't look, did you?"

"No, I am here to pick up Cinder, it's been five months since I dropped her off." I longingly sighed.

"Well, you should have looked, because Cinder is one of the Fighters that the crowd is cheering so hard for." The Pit owner answered, now stepping away from the office and towards the door. "I don't know what it is about her, but these guys love that Hellhound of yours."

"I am going to kill you, bitch!" Khalar violently shouted, swinging his head around to snap back through the sand cloud his massive size had summoned.

Dodging each attempt, he made with either his long three-inch claws or his two-inch fangs, I teased back "Well that's if you can catch me first." Flashing a sly snarl, I parried a left and swung my neck back around to attach my fangs once more to the back of his neck. Getting easily thrown off his neck, I spaced myself out once more and pushed for another opening. Peering into my strategizing thoughts, I pondered what were the available tactics I had yet to try. "I cannot let this fight go on for much longer." I impatiently grimaced as my left eye starting to do a familiar burning sensation. "I cannot lose control. Not yet."

"What's wrong, Reaper?" The Tiger Cat Magus now mockingly questioned. Observing the damage I had done, I looked through the red-stained orange fur and saw the small puncture holes on his neck and flank. It was difficult to penetrate his thick muscle and previously scarred tissue, but the attacks were slowly fatiguing the Cat Magus. "Are you finally out of ideas?"

"Damn it." I snarled, keeping my color-changing stare locked on the feline. Rushing in headfirst, I decided to embark on this last tactic I had. A reckless move I had not used since my one-sided brawl with Logan and one I dreaded the after-effects of.

"Head-first." Khalar smiled, raising his head to mock my reckless attempt. Unthwarted, I steadily reached for the underside of his neck where very little muscle resided regardless of the Specie and Breed. "Like that is going to work." He continued to yammer, throwing his head back down to block my thwart.

Smiling back at the feline, I exposed my fangs and the under-lining of my thinned pink gums as I came within range. Quickly increasing my speed, I danced around those huge fangs of his, which were trying to bear down on my scruff, and finally attached the white teeth to the designated target. The blood once more coating the interior of my mouth, satisfying my craving taste buds. Tightening my hold of the flesh, I ignored the pain of Khalar's fangs grabbing onto my skin, as we locked ourselves in a momentarily stalemate.

With both my opponent and I stalled, I began endeavoring ways to kill my current target without paralyzing myself; although the more I tried to think of something, the more my worst fears were starting to rise from the abyss. That psychotic itch's dark voice ordering me to let it consume my conscious. Trying my hardest to not befall the heavy blood lust, I vigorously shook my head, not only working to overthrow the holdings this Magus had on my back, but also attempt to maintain the firm hold I had on Khalar's throat. Feeling the color-changing steadily consume more of my flawless blue, I mentally swore to my subconscious, "You stay the fuck out of this!"

"Something's not right," I murmured aloud as both Gerard and I peered over the second story's railing to safely observe the fight. With the final dust cloud fading, I noticed that the two Unnaturals were in a stalemate.

"What are you talking about? Don't worry man, that beautiful woman of yours has this. She has used this tactic on a Chimera last week and she easily..." Gerard returned, temporarily taking those stern eyes off the fight.

"No, it isn't that I am worried over the move." I interrupted, straining my eyes to see if what I feared was coming to fruition. Once my vision had adjusted, I, unfortunately, realized my gut was right. The fears were not of my imagination. "You need to stop this right now!" I urgently ordered, trying to maintain the calm stability in my voice.

"What? There is no way in Hell I am stopping this! There is too much money at stake here." The Pit leader refused. "Besides Pit Rules are that the only way to exit the ring is to win, be completely immobilized, or die. You know that just as much as the Fighters do."

"Damn it! Would you just listen to me?!" I hissed back. "Your undefeated Cat Magus is in worse danger than losing his first fight." Peering back down at the fight that was finally returning to its wild pace, I noticed the horrifying changes not only occurring in the Beauceron-shaped canine but also in our surroundings. While Cinder's entire physique altered, the change in her build, and the change in her spinal structure, yet so did room temperature of the entire building.

"What are those?" Gerard concernedly shouted over the noisy crowd as he began to sweat profusely. "Why aren't the drugs working on her–"

"It's that 'Itch'-" I murmured once more under my breath. "She let her blood lust take over again."

"Her what? Augustus, you better start explaining what is going on real fast!" Gerard hissed, the sweat starting to collect in his neatly trimmed facial hair.

"As I said, stop the fight now-" I attempted to yet again order the Pit Leader, but was cut off by the fierce howl of a deranged animal screaming over the deafening noise coming from the excited humans. I didn't need a second glance to know who made that cry or what it meant. With the echoing roar of the Cat Magus savagely wailing back, I again ordered back to the Pit Leader, "If you do not stop this now, you will not only be putting that Cat Magus life at risk, you will also be putting the lives of all these spectators at risk."

Chapter 46

Augustus

"Don't you think that was something you could have told me earlier?!" the dark-haired human snarled as he reached for his cellphone.

Naturally assuming he was grabbing for the device to set off those shock collars wrapped around the Unnaturals' necks, I hastily grabbed the man's hand. Causing his actions to stop. "If you activate those collars, it will only further enrage her."

"Well, what else would you expect me to do?! I'm presuming that if I send my men down there, that too will 'enrage' that bitch of yours-"

"Hey watch your language!" I bit back before thinking about the consequences.

"Oh, defending her now. You are a severely confusing, man, Augustus." The Pit Leader taunted, locking those dull and difficult to read eyes back at me, however, that was also cut short when another scream echoed from inside the Ring.

Peering down below, we watched the Beauceron with her savagery now standing on top of the Tiger. The Cat Magus howled out in what I could only assume was frustration as he tried to dance around in his skin to escape his opponent's grasp. But the Hellhound was much faster, her petite frame retaining control over the massive Magus's size. Recognizing the posture from Cinder's fight with the Lycan Leader, I abruptly swore, "Shit! We need to hurry up."

"Augustus, what are you talking about?!" I heard Gerard furiously suspect.

"What Cinder is about to do next, is the same move she used against..." My voice was mumbled by the uproar of the crowd while they also continued to watch Cinder repeat the deafening shake of the Cat Magus's neck. Grant it the male feline had a great amount of muscle, which helped drown out the extensive damage her fangs were capable of, I knew by the way he was crying out in agony that the Hellhound was penetrating his airways, crushing his vocals. Regaining my voice, I clarified, "It's the use of her Blood Trait. It nearly broke my hand when she was unconscious,..." Once more, I was hushed by the crowd who were being drowned out by the wolf-like call of the victorious Hellhound. "We need to stop her now!"

Stepping away from the railing, I ran for the office and it's lower levels where I knew I could get inside the chain-link ring. "Augustus, where are you going?!"

"I'm going down there to distract her-" I shouted back, knowing that the Human was attempting to follow me. Turning around to stop him, I continued. "If you follow me, she will for sure kill you! The Blood Lust is already wrapped its tight leash around her neck! I need you to try to get her as sedated as possible while also taking out your contender's body! If we wait any longer, Cinder will cremate him alive."

"He's still alive?" Gerard said, looking back over the railing towards the Pits, completely bewildered.

"For now, but we need to hurry," I called back.

"Okay, I will get the men in position." My long-time associate growled before taking off in the opposing direction.

Proceeding to run down the stairs and into the caged barracks where the Fighters lived, I began to strategize a way of distracting the Reaper, however, all the only thought that kept coming to me was, "Was this really just a portion of her potential? Was her power really this underestimated?" Reaching the fence line that separated me from the Ring, I noticed the Beauceron was already locking her sights on the spectators surrounding her, hunting for her next target while she continued to stand over the top of the orange and black-striped feline, who was gradually bleeding to death. Quickly glancing around the upper walls of the ring, I caught onto shimmers of snipers locked on the Great Dane sized beast. Their guns armed with heavy sedatives, poised to strike once I had gotten Cinder's focus locked on me. Scanning over to the Ring's second entrance that was on the other side of the Pit, I noticed six men ready to run in, collect the nearly deceased Tiger, and run like hell. Nodding my head as we acknowledged one and another, I placed my hands on the chain-link simple gate-locking mechanism and flicked it open. The noise triggering the sensitive hearing that Cinder had, causing her to look in my direction, locking those fierce eyes on her next opponent, me.

"That's right, Cinder, come at me." I teased while I slowly locked the gate behind me, simultaneously keeping my eyes locked on her movements. The Hellhound so far had only turned her attention around to face me but had yet to leave the Tiger's fallen body. "Come on, baby-girl," I called, trying to egg her on. Hastily registering that although the Blood Lust had taken its control over her, Cinder still despised being called by pet names. Once more calling her out, I finally got the riled beast to leave her prey. "There we go."

Raising my arms to defend myself for the head-on collision I knew she was going to do, I gave the signal to the awaiting men on the other side of the Pit. Being sure to keep my eyes locked on the fast creature, I barely avoided her jump for my throat. As I evaded, I noticed that her Blood Scythes were dancing like Sabers out of her mouth, coating those sharp fangs of hers. Being careful to avoid the bone spikes coming out her spine, I grabbed for her scruff, but before my fingers could even feel her blood-stained black fur, Cinder had danced herself out of my reach. "Damn it-!" I cursed. Before I could parry the next attack, she was attempting, I was thrown onto the ground. The one-hundred-pound weight crashing directly on top of my chest. Using my arms, I barely managed to successfully block those flying jaws of hers.

"Hurry up!" I urged the men. Staring into her sharp eyes, I realized that the infamous blue she had was gone. Instead, the pupils' color had transformed into a deep red. It was the exact same demonic blood-red hue, Zachariah had. Locked in the memorizing gaze, I failed to block the incoming swing of her jaws as they swam for my neck. Preparing for the agonizing pain I knew was going to receive, I flinched. Surrounded by darkness, I was taken back by a surprising howl. Forcing my eyelids open, I surveyed the Hellhound had her sights locked on another person.

"Oh, thank god." I praised, continuing to stupidly watch the unfolding scene, I noticed that embedded in the upper part of her left shoulder were several tranquilizer darts. The aimed snipers had successfully shot the Hellhound with some of their heaviest ammo. Howling out her frustration once more to the now silent world, I observed the Hellhound return her focus on me. "Great-." I groaned. Fully expecting to brace myself for another swarm of encroaching fangs, I was surprised to suddenly see those red eyes fade away and that deep, vivid blue eyes swimming their way back to the surface. Cinder was returning from the dark subconscious abyss she had been thrown into.

"Aug-Augustus." She softly called, her ears folding flat against her skull. A telling clue that her Alter Form had diminished, the drugs which were injected into her system before her fight finally allowed the return of her humanized lingual. Although, it was still quite broken.

Relaxing my fists, I opened up my palms and softly stroked the Hellhound's cheeks, my callused skinned hands feeling the sticky cold red liquid run over each pore. Sighing a long-awaited exhale, I explained, "It's alright, Cinder." Before I could get anything else out of my vocals, Cinder had collapsed on top of my chest. Her exhausted body succumbing to the after-effects of fighting the Itch and the quick effects of the anesthetic sedatives. Fighting my body out from underneath her massive frame, I once more coaxed her soft but filthy fur.

"I apologize about what has happened tonight, folks, but as you know sometimes there is only so much someone can take." Gerard's voice cooed from the announcement speakers. "I will waiver ticket and bar fees this weekend to accommodate the loss of wages and excitement you may have suffered from tonight's match."

Barely managing to pick up the Hellhound, I carried her out of the ring, thinking to myself along the way, "You sure know how to win over the crowd, but I guess when it comes down to this, you have had your years of experience, haven't you, Gerard Hunter."

Chapter 47

Augustus

"Well, that went worse than I had expected," Gerard smirked while both unconscious contenders had been brought into the examination room. "Candice is on her way, so please get Khalar ready for surgery." The Ringleader then ordered his employees before returning the entirety of his focus on Cinder and me.

"Candice?" I questioned while I rubbed my hand through the canine's blood-soaked black fur. "I haven't seen her in a long time."

"Since you broke up with her for that model, Theresa."

I choked back. "Is she still mad at that?"

"Beyond pissed, but I mean you can always find out for yourself." Gerard gently mocked as he began to feel over the Hellhound's wounds. Modifying the subject of the conversation, he discoursed, "Most of these seemed to have healed up."

"I wouldn't be surprised, Cinder does have advanced healing capabilities, even with the drugs you have slipped into her bloodstream, it barely slowed her down. Just be glad that she didn't have enough power to completely transform into her 'Alter' Form." I paused for a moment, my mind traveling over the idea of seeing that image Lorde Zachariah had envisioned. "If she had, I doubt things would have gone as smoothly as possible; hell, I know for sure that your Cat Magus over there would be dead."

"Augustus, I know you are here to pick your precious Hellhound up, but we have a few matters to discuss first."

"A few matters?" I questioned.

"Go ahead and return Cinder to her kennel, when she regains consciousness..."

"Just return her for now, once I'm finished, I'll take her home. I'd prefer her to wake up back home, rather than for her to walk back out of the Pits and have to walk through the Black Market yet again." I explained.

"Alright, fine. It's not our customary tradition, but she is your Unnatural."

"Why do you keep saying it that way?" I hastily interrogated the Ring Master. "I mean yes, I signed over custody so that she could be registered here, however by all means the real owner of Cinder, is she, herself, and her Deity, you know that just as much as I do."

"Yeah, I know that." The human paused, daring to not utter that Cursed God's name. "I keep bringing that up because a few months after you had left Cinder in my care, we had a man coming in saying that Cinder was 'stolen' government property."

"Stolen government property?" I chuckled.

"Augustus, I know that my holdings over the Unnaturals here are legal by both the Government and Syndicate sanctions, however, if that man had come up in here with a warrant to reclaim her, I would have had to oblige."

"Though you would have never obliged."

"While that may be true, and I would have thrown his ass into the Pit with Cinder, I'm just telling you about the situation we are currently facing. Although, curiosity does have me wondering;

Where the hell did you get her? Where did he get her?" Gerard asked, now leaning against the counter and crossing his large arms. His hazel eyes glaring back at me with a look I saw quite too often. The look that he wanted to get to the bottom of a messy situation he had been thrown into. Let the interrogation begin, I guess.

Taking a heavy exhale, I replied, "I cannot answer how he had received Cinder, but I do know that yes, she was institutionalized, however, I never got her from any Institution."

"So, where did you get her?"

"She was exiled from not only one, but two Syndicates." I sighed. "I received custody shortly after she had banished herself from the Lycan Syndicate."

"Ouch." Gerard sneered. "It takes a lot to be expelled from a Syndicate, but frankly speaking, I can also see how it could be possible, that bloodlust of her's is beyond recognition. Even in the eyes of a place like this, that specializes in working with those kinds of Unnaturals, I don't think I would've been of much use."

Taking in the movement of his subtle feature changes, the softening of his stern facial expression, I took over the interrogation. "Now answer me this, Gerard, who exactly came by telling you this tale?"

"He called himself, Doctor Shane Masters."

"That asshole?" I snarled.

"Oh, so you do know him?"

"Personally no, but that SIMs card you gave me told me everything I needed to know about the man," I responded as calmly as I could, trying my hardest to retain control over my unleashed frustrations. Taking another long sigh, I pressed on, "Did Cinder see this man?"

"Do you need to ask me that?" he hastily jived, his body language suddenly turning ironic yet aggressive. Placing his hands on the marble countertops to help holster his balance, he proceeded. "Cinder nearly incited a riot just by charging the gate. It took her seeing my cellphone, just to get her to stop trying to break through the chain-link fence. Though, it did little to stop her from vocalizing her disgust. Your Hellhound's hatred for that man is beyond reasoning and goes even beyond my disciplinary tactics."

"That doesn't surprise me, either. Masters is the only person she hates more than all of mankind, and that alone goes pretty deep." I snickered, recalling Zachariah's reasoning for the Hellhound being institutionalized for so long.

"I did tell this man that when you came back to pick her up, I would let the two of you discuss Cinder's predicament."

"Well, let me speak with this 'Masters,'" I ordered the Leader of the Pits. Getting called upstairs and into the office, I fell in line, wondering along the way: How was I going to explain the situation without giving away the truth? How was I going to lie to a man that lied better than I ever could in my two hundred-years of experience?

Stepping up the last step and through the secret door's threshold, I finally laid my eyes on the man with sheer blonde-haired man with similar bright green eyes who called himself a Doctor. It was obvious that the man had already tasted the Hellhound's fangs, judging by the deep scar that had broken his soft-skinned face. The tissue had healed over, however, even from where I stood, I could see that he would be forever adorned with a memory of nearly being killed by a child.

"So, you are the famed, Augustus Gale?" the human's annoying face jabbered, stretching out his left hand for a formal handshake. "It's nice to finally meet you and may I say, I appreciate someone like you taking such good care over, oh what's her name now, Cinder Salam?"

Not even daring myself to touch his filthy hands, I swiftly saw through the act, "Cut the fucking sweet-talk."

Chapter 48

Augustus

Retaining from sitting down in the chairs adorning the outside of Gerard's desk, I overheard the boss order his men, "I want you three to stand watch over Cinder's Kennel, now."

The men obeyed and swiftly left, of course, the lunatic doctor also perceived the same orders and had to put his few cents in. "What? Do you think that I'm only here to distract you?" His small chuckle that followed making me grind my teeth in fervent anger.

Finding a statement to combat his quirky tease, I threatened, "If that were true, it wouldn't be my guys who your men would have to fear."

"Oh, and what do you mean by that? Cinder? She's still unconscious, right? I watched her topple over the top of you in the Ring, so I'm doubtful she's able to refute anything."

"It's not the Hellhound you must fear, it is the Entity that watches over her that you must fear. You know he exists, the poor woman can't stop talking about him." I attempted to remind, or should I say lie. I knew that as a child, Cinder complained about a Shadow. I saw it in those reports, but I could not let the fact that the

Shadow was Zachariah, nor the fact that I too could communicate with the Deity just as much as she, get loose in this man's ears.

"Oh, I'm so afraid." Masters ridiculed. "Anyways, back to the matter at hand, I'm here to reclaim custody over the Hellhound."

"Do you have a warrant?" Gerard questioned, now understandably stepping into the conversation. Besides Cinder, Gerard had the most to lose, so he needed to keep the legalities out of here as much as possible.

"It is in progress, right now. Of course, 0497, stands as a 'High Security-Risk' that is on the loose-"

"High Security-Risk?" I interjected with an uncontrollable laugh. Thinking to myself, I muttered in my head, "You have no idea how much of a threat she truly is to the world." Retaining control, I took a long sigh and proceeded. "Look, I get that Cinder was in the care of two Institutes, however, I wasn't the one who stole her from you guys." I said emphasizing the word 'stole' with finger quotations. "I wasn't the one that broke in and took her from those cruel conditions you had her living in. I ended up sanctioning her after she was kicked out of two Syndicates." I recapitulated the fable. "Nonetheless, if you want to take her from me, I can always play the fact that you are indeed breaking one major Unnatural Citizen rule."

"Unnatural Citizen rule?" Masters questioned with a low growl.

"Do you think that someone as famous as I wouldn't have contacted a lawyer to be on the safe side in case you guys came crawling back to attempt to recapture her?" I interrogated. "Do you think that just because I don't work for the Government, that I'm stupid?" Watching the man bite his tongue and lock his jaw, I knew I was hitting another soft spot. "Do you need me to explain?" I hit back, adding a bit of sarcasm to the tone in my voice.

"No!" Masters shouted.

"Yes, I need some clarification. After all, I do play third-party here." Gerard interjected the Human Doctor, again maintaining the legal side of this meeting.

"Well, the Unnatural Citizen law requires all Citizens who're tagged as Unnaturals to receive regular Citizen care, and while they may not receive all the same equal rights as their human counter-parts, they still get many things that someone not registered gets. One of those things is the freedom of not being hunted down like a damn rabbit by you guys. It also refrains the fact that you guys can't make her do anything you want even without her consent." I paused for a moment before exchanging glances with Gerard. "It also means that if someone was once a patient, they can leave whenever, or for instance, if they are out of the care of the physician for six weeks, they are no longer the Institute's problem. No matter if they are sto-len, a runaway, an escapee, it persists for any 'case'."

"Make sense." Gerard playfully shrugged, his shoulders rolling. "Wait! So that's why you had me take care of her for those few months?"

"Yes. Of course, as my lawyer said it's a recent law, so it is bound to be expected that someone like Dr. Masters wouldn't know all of the loopholes and quirks this law carries."

"Do you even have the paperwork for it?" Masters bit back.

"Of course, I do," I smirked, taking the paper out of my back pocket. Unfolding the piece of paper right in front of the two hu-mans, I showed them the certification of Citizenship for Cinder Salam. "As you can see, Cinder is marked as an Unnatural Citizen. So, the law hereby stands in favor of the Hellhound you were trying to capture, and because she is unconscious, she cannot give you her consent. Now, to make it all easier for you, because I am marked as her 'Guardian', my consent can stand in for hers; and I hereby tell you, to get the 'Fuck' out of my sight!" I bit, still trying to keep my anger on its short leash.

"Fine, I will leave, but if I were you, I wouldn't expect that law to stick for long." Masters angrily bickered as he began to storm towards the office door, where two more of Gerard's guards were prepared to escort him off the premises.

Once we were sure the Doctor's ears were far enough outside of the parameters of our conversation, I finally took that much-needed breath, "Thank fucking god that is over!"

"Yeah, thank god." My good friend agreed. "Now, onto taking her Home, right?"

Nodding my head, I agreed. "Time to take her home, and then get back to work."

As we proceeded back down the steps into the examination room beneath the office space, I overheard Gerard hypothesize, "Although, if I were you, I would limit her work because I believe that you have not heard the last of that man, nor the Hunters."

"Yeah, we will be taking the added precautions." I acknowledged. "Although, I would have never thought you to be so worried over Cinder?

"She grows on you, but it's not like it was just her life on the line: my life is also on the line here, you know."

"It is hard to believe how much she does grow on someone, even for someone as sly as you to say that, must mean she really has won over your heart."

"The beautiful and elegant way she fights, and her overpowering will, I guess you could say those help-" Gerard paused for a quick moment as he made a sharp right for another door off the side of the examination room.

"Where are we going?" I questioned, interrupting the few seconds of silence.

Getting welcomed into the off-set room, I saw that it was a safe room where there were numerous computerized charts and tables full of placed bets. There was earned money and even lost money, characterized per fighter. As my eyes scanned around the room, I saw the piles of money being compiled into a large iron safe.

"Jesus fucking Christ, Gerard," I said in awe.

"This is the main reason why Cinder grew on me." The Pit's owner exclaimed, "Since her third fight, she's topped the charts, and she has had eighty-seven fights since then, including today's fight with Khalar."

"She had ninety fights?" I questioned. "I only requested seventy-five."

"Don't worry, I still gave her adequate breaks between fights, however, if we waited too long, Cinder would let us know that she despised waiting in that cage."

"You did it for her sanity?"

"I guess you could say that." Gerard chuckled. "Although I cannot say that all those fights were good for her bloodlust."

Recalling the moment she had lost the reigns on that 'Itch' of her's back when she had murdered Calem, I agreed, "Yeah, she's always had a problem with controlling herself when it came down to the kill." Coming back to reality, I pondered what exactly was going on when my arms suddenly became heavy. Looking down at the medium-sized, black duffel bag that was now resting in my arms, I demanded, "What's this?" Zipping it open, my eyes were hastily met with large bundles of money, a wide variety of twenty, fifty, and even hundred-dollar bills.

"That is your share of the money, or well, her share. Remember when you signed the contract, you receive thirty percent of all winnings. Well, that is seventy-five thousand dollars, right there."

"Jesus fucking Christ." I again muttered, this time softly under my breath.

Chapter 49

Augustus

"Now where are we going?" I questioned as I still followed the owner of the Black Market's infamous Pits in the opposing direction of Cinder's kennel. We were still in the basement, however, instead of heading in the direction of the Ring's entrance, we headed in the opposite direction.

"We had to move Cinder around after the whole Masters's fiasco, and her continuous arguments with Khalar," Gerard answered. "I don't want to say it's special treatment, but having that creepy bastard and his Hunters strolling around the lower levels, awaiting their chance to steal her while my life was on the line with, well, you know where this is going."

"Yes, I understand, and I appreciate what you did to keep her in your custody during my absence." I gratefully confessed. Following my long time associate down a dark corner, I soon realized we were heading away from the main kennel lineup that circled the ocular build of the Ring. "Are these the new kennels you had put in?"

"They are. This is where we also tend to hide our more aggressive and larger Unnaturals." Gerard rambled. "The material we use for these cells are secured with a stronger molecular bond to help keep the links from being ripped through, ah, here she is."

"Still unconscious huh?" I smirked as I once more fastened my gaze on the dark soot-black fur with the gorgeous rottweiler-like tan markings. Her large rib cage rising and falling with a casual ease that relaxed my anxious mind about the unfolding chaos we had been thrown into.

"You speak as if you were expecting her to be up and moving around by now?"

"No, I was anticipating her to be unconscious, but now that I am thinking about transport, I was hoping for her to be awake." I chuckled.

"We can still hold her here for the night, this section of kennels gets locked behind an iron gate with a keycode after hours. We had that extra security put in right before you left her here."

"I know it wasn't for her."

"A week before Cinder arrived here, I had twenty of my top fighters stolen out from under me by Hunters, and of course by legal means, the Institutes won the civil suits," Gerard answered me as he dutifully began to unlock the padlock that bound the gate.

Stepping inside the kennel, I began to step around the sleeping Hellhound so I could easily slip my hands under her large one-hundred-pound frame and hastily pick her up. Cinder's body retaining the dead weight, went limp the second her body left the concrete floor. Releasing a deep exhale as my knees straightened out, I again left the kennel.

Making our back up to the exam room, I overheard Gerard speak with an unusual sternness in his voice, "Augustus, how much of that 'Law' is true?"

"What are you talking about, Gerard?" I answered with a follow-up question, my hand's grasp on the shifter's fur tightening.

"I never heard about an Unnatural Citizen Law, until you brought it up today, and you know that I follow all the Unnatural Laws as much as possible." The Owner honestly implied.

"Well," I began as we finally reached the hidden parking garage at the back of the building where I had parked. Looking for the right words to answer his deep interrogation, I explained, "The law does exist, however it varies from state-to-state, and New York isn't a state that has it legalized yet. The Lawyer and Judge I had contacted were both licensed in the state of Florida." I paused for a quick breath. "They were the ones who helped me get the Certification, and all the necessary info I needed." Exhaling another heavy breath, I began to wander towards my newly bought 2018 white four-door Dodge Ram truck, stopping to look back to my fellow associate.

Thankfully, he took over holding Cinder while I reached inside my jean's pockets for the vehicle's keys. Unlocking the truck's doors, I took back the comatose Hellhound and began to slowly push her into the back seat of the driver's side. Once I had her unconscious frame appropriately positioned in the seat, I proceeded to hear Gerard's now say in his traditional ironic tone. "It is hard to believe even with how big your truck is, she still practically takes up the entire back seat. Did she get bigger while she stayed here?"

"It looks like it, but that doesn't surprise me. Hellhounds are a large breed of Shifters, and unfortunately, they don't stop growing." I honestly answered, too noticing the change in the Unantural's physical traits. There were parts of her body that seemed thin, but I could tell it was from her growth and not from malnourishment, rather it was due to the rapid speed at which her skeletal and muscular frame had developed. "The other Hellhound that was staying at the Vampiric Syndicate stood at over four feet tall in his canine form."

"Cinder could get that big?"

"While her distinct Rank doesn't get that big, it is still a high probability that she could get as large as him," I said before recognizing the large black shock collar she still wore wrapped around her

261

neck. "Should I take that off?" I inquired, pointing to the three-inch collar.

"No, don't worry about it. I was planning on giving it to you anyway. She responds better to it than one would think."

"Okay, well how do you expect me to keep tabs on her if I don't even have the same device," I remarked.

"It isn't that hard, Augustus. Everything is run through an app on my smartphone." The human explained as he took out the cellular device. Pulling up the app called, 'Shock and Discipline, he proceeded to scroll through the list of different product numbers until he found the one, I assumed Cinder had around her neck. "See, after you get the app, you add in the product number on the underside of the box, and from there you can control when to shock, how many volts are used, and you can also survey the current heart rate, blood pressure, and blood sugars of the person who's wearing it. It's not that complicated, Augustus, and believe me, the collar has come in handy with that one."

"I can only assume so, she can be quite the handful to keep control over." I expressed, graciously accepting the gift. "Thanks for the gift, man."

"No problem, oh and here." Gerard paused as he began to shift through his pockets again. "I took this off her not too long after you had left. Sorry, I did that, but we don't allow other forms of collars and necklaces when they fight as contenders." He said as he exposed the cross-necklace I had given Cinder prior to my departure.

Taking hold of the object, I again heavily exhaled to the human. "Yeah, I should have known better, however, I think she needed it to know that I wasn't going to leave her there."

"Like the others did to her in her past?"

"Yeah, like the others." I reluctantly agreed.

"Are you sure that you aren't being that soft because you're feeling something else for her?" I heard the man probe with a foxish glare and clownish tease.

Retaining my short tension to beat the human, I put my guard up and barked back. "I'm not in love with her, if that is what you're implying, Gerard."

"Sure seems like it to me."

"Bite me, Gerard."

"Can't. Someone else beat me to it."

"FUCK OFF!" I snapped, stuffing the necklace into my jean pockets before proceeded with finally shutting the driver's side back door close and storming towards the front door. Climbing into the vehicle, I slammed the door shut and swiftly put the keys into the ignition. Cursing to myself as I started up the truck, I looked back over to the unconscious Hellhound and stupidly mumbled aloud, "Alright, let's go home, Cinder, we still have a lot of shit to do."

Chapter 50

Cinder

"Where am I?" I questioned to myself, while hastily finding that my surroundings were utter darkness. I was wrapped inside the shrouds of the endless abyss. Seeing a glimmer of a familiar red amber glow, I pressed forward. Bringing my left paw forward, I stopped when my paw felt heavy and the familiar rattling of the irritating metallic chain links. "What is going on?" I anxiously snarled, snapping at the chains that left the shadows, their white metal glimmering under a false light catching my well-trained hunter's eyes. The endless links had surrounded me. They were wrapped around my neck, chest, legs, and hips, their heavy burden clamping down into my flesh. Biting my lips, I again cursed aloud the continuous questions wandering through my mind.

"Well, I was wondering when you were going to finally come around." A voice echoed through the bleak. It was a familiar-sounding tone with a tad more rasp than what I had remembered last time.

"Who are you?" I demanded. "Where am I?"

Stepping outside of the shadows, the unknown being too exposed itself to the false lighting in this questionable room. The creature looked the same as I, well at least while I was in this cursed form. "To put it bluntly, as you can see I am another form of you-"

Finally acknowledging where I knew the voice from, I interrupted, "That voice! You're the owner of that maniacal itch!"

"In a way, yes, but 'itch' is putting it coldly. I am in the form you wish to see me in, but I would prefer to be known as the Fiend."

"Fiend?" I questioned, folding my ears back with a bit of suspicion and fear. "What do you mean?"

"I am the voice of your bloodlust, your darker side, your lust for power, I am the voice to it all."

"You are the one I risk losing control to," I responded in between pauses.

"Somewhat. I take control, so neither one of us risk losing rationality. Although, you are more of a tight ass, than I." the Fiend sneered, stepping closer to where I remained chained to an unknown source. It's size almost double that of mine, its fangs showing from its long jowls without baring a single snarl: all this telling me that while it may look like me, it had differing traits from me. "I am what stands between you and losing your sanity. I would not be here if it wasn't for that event earlier on in the year."

"SHUT-UP!" I ordered, charging to the end of chains that burned their way through my coarse short hair and scarred flesh. Biting my tongue, I hissed back at the chains, wondering aloud why I was still tied to these posts.

"Because I still want my fun." The beast whispered into my notched ear.

"What?!"

"You gave me control remember, with that fight against the Cat Magus, and well, I am not yet ready to turn over the reins. Not until I show that Valkyrie that stopping us from obtaining our kill may very well be his death sentence." It continued to speak, now distancing itself from my free face and clapping jaws.

Recalling the event, I told myself, "Augustus separated us from that for the safety of the humans."

The 'Fiend' must have heard what I thought to myself in my head because it's facial expression changed to a more intimidating flashy smirk prior to speaking, "The safety of those humans? I know that you want to rip your fangs into them just as much as I do, and I would have let you keep control to do that if you so desired it."

"Not all humans deserve to perish, eventually death will come for them, and it will be ME that will be their 'Reaper.'" I snapped back at the creature called the 'Fiend', feeling a few chains snap loose from around my paws. Relaxing my newly freed feet, I redirected the subject of the conversation back to its main course, however, inside my conscience, it was deeming itself the rightful heir to attack the fallen angel who fulfilled his agonizing promise to me. "Augustus is off the table for you, if anyone is going to rip their fangs into his olden flesh, it will be me! The conscious version of me, and not the blood-lusted version of you!"

"Ouch. So, you aren't a complete pushover. Although, I will not give back these reins- "

Fighting the lasting chains around my neck and chest, I charged at the taller creature who seemed to still be exposing hidden secrets from the surrounding darkness. "You will give me back my body, and will only ever be given control over MY body when I see fit."

"You mean, when 'he' desires fit." The Fiend softly growled to me, not at all phased by the tethered charge.

"No," I muttered.

"Yes, you know just as I, that the person who has the real control over both you and I, is 'him'."

"The 'Shadow'." I presumed from inside the depth-defined conscious inside my head.

"Yes, him."

"Stop reading my thoughts!" I snapped.

"No, it is too much fun to stop now." it laughed.

"Give me control! This is my body!"

"Make me, little 'Reaper'." The creature again chuckled, exposing fangs a few centimeters longer than my already long canines. Standing over the top of me, I finally felt the true size and intimidation this being held: the Fiend was double my size and twice my power. Looking over his build, I saw that everything was the same between us, everything from our markings to our scars, our collars, our fur; the only difference was its red eyes, the boney spikes protruding out of its' spine, and the appearing scarred wolf skull that I had stolen off of Calem's corpse.

With the monster in my range, I jumped up at the extended neck. My teeth fell short of my victim by mere inches before the chains tightened, the metal digging deeper and deeper into my flesh. The creature burst into another fit of laughter at my entanglement. Furious, I charged once more towards the being where again, I missed, but this time it was because the Fiend had diffused into a mass collection of bleak shadows. "Stop playing games and let me have control again!"

"Fine!" It agreed finally. "However-" It paused. "this little feud between you and I is far from over. I will get to have my fun again, little 'Reaper', and the next time I get the reins, I will not hand them over just because you asked so nicely." The words echoing into the black abyss as it finally disappeared, the chains following not long after.

Stretching my neck out, I took a nice long sigh before muttering aloud once more, "God, that was completely exhausting." Sitting on my haunches, I took another sigh as a bright light filled the room defeating the shadows and allowing my conscious to return to the realm of reality.

Chapter 51

Augustus

Pulling up around the large marble Spanish fountain sitting center stage on the stone-paved circle drive, I parked the vehicle adjacent to the large iron manor doors. With a thankful sigh, I glanced up into the center mirror to see that the 'monster' was gratefully still comatose. The mixture between electric shocks and powerful sedative anesthetics had kept the Beauceron Hellhound unconscious during the long drive between New York and Florida, between the darker side of Stanton Island and the outskirts of Miami. Of course, I knew that this was only part one of moving. I still had to relocate Cinder from the truck to one of my newly bought properties.

Turning back around to face the sleeping canine, I wondered whether it was a promising idea to move her or not. Deep down, I was still concerned that at any moment she could awake and very likely rip those long fangs finally into my flesh. As I imagined the horror, I relived the moment I laid eyes on that haunting gaze of hers. They were such a vibrant dark red that I felt my skin crawl at the idea of even attempting to reminisce the memory. Shaking loose the residing emotions of fear, I decided to indeed attempt to move Cinder from one place to another. I had to because if I didn't and she woke up and ran, I would be the one meeting my death next. And that was something I was not yet ready to meet.

Stepping out of the truck, I played with the keys in my hand as I walked towards the large double glass doors adorned with rustic black Spanish iron rods. The rounded top had an extended three-foot-tall glass window to help bring in more of that natural Mediterranean sunlight to the blended warm white walls and dark oak-stained wood floor in the foyer. Placing the front door key into the keyhole, I unlocked the door and swung open the left door with ease. Staring inside the modern twist foyer, I examined the large spiral staircase off to my left with matching iron railings. My sights following up the steps towards the rustic grand black chandelier and down to the glass-top pedestal that had fresh cherry blossoms from the recent Open House. With a relaxed breath, I inhaled the air-conditioned serene air prior to migrating a contained demon into the open eight-thousand square foot manor. Placing the keys on the pedestal beside the glass flower vase, I turned back around and went back towards the truck.

Opening the back-passenger side door, I came face to face with a still unconscious transformed Unnatural. Keeping my phone handy in case she awoke, I proceeded with reaching for the dog's scruff. Tightly grasping the thick shock collar she wore, I dragged her body towards my chest. As her head fell off the seat, I slipped my hand under Cinder's muscular neck and pushed my other hand under her hips before finally removing the beast from the truck. Breathing another elongated sigh of relief, I used my back to slam the truck's door shut. "Thank fucking god Gerard knows how to make a good sedative." I jabbed. Wandering back towards the manor, I hastily entered the foyer and carried her into the family room that was in the back of the house; where it observed the large back patio and the beautiful length of coastline beyond partially landscaped stone walls and lightly-covered iron fence to mark where my property met the beach. Placing her down on the same dog bed that Theresa had made me buy the Hellhound months ago, I left the canine to lock up the white four-door truck followed by the stunning front doors.

Reentering the foyer, I watched as driving up the driveway was a way too familiar car. A vehicle I was desperately hoping wasn't going to arrive while I stayed here.

"Why?!" I complained aloud, banging my head against the flat smooth-sided glass front door. After three heavy hits, I questioned, "Why is she here?"

The expensive sports car sped up the drive, parking beside my truck before the woman I had been calling my girlfriend stepped out. The model strutting her highly feminine attire up the small path connecting the drive to the house. I had to admit that her clothes fit her body accordingly, but for some reason in my head, as hot as she was, her beauty failed in comparison to the natural beauty of the sleeping transformed woman I had tucked away deep in the family room.

Unlocking the door, I reluctantly invited Theresa inside the manor. Observing her excited gasping mouth as she spun around the foyer, I upsettingly asked my girlfriend, "What are you doing here?" while openly greeting her with an amorous hug.

"I thought I had seen your truck a few months ago here in Miami, so I asked around and saw that someone online had posted that the infamous Mr. Gale had bought one of the most fabulous homes in Florida." She exclaimed, giving me a quick peck on the cheek.

"Fucking realtors." I silently cursed in my head. "I thought I had told them to keep my purchase confidential." Leading Theresa down the hall into the large sleek modern kitchen that absorbed all the beauty of the beach, especially as the sun rose along the coastline, I continued "Ah well how long will you be here?" Trying to not rush her back out, at least not rudely rush her out.

"Well I finished with my shoots today, so I thought I could stay here for a couple of weeks until my runway show in Japan next month. Why do you ask? Don't you want me here?"

"No, I do." I lied, again crediting that the Beauceron was unconscious or else I would be hearing about my blunt lies. "It's just I got a busy schedule and I wouldn't want to miss out on precious time with you babe."

"While that is sweet honey, but it's alright we can still sit by that pool or walk down the beach when you get home from your business meetings." Theresa eagerly planned with a deafening glint casting in her gaze. "There are other things we can do to maintain a relationship besides always having sex and going out on dates, you do know." The woman laughed before catching onto Cinder's sleek black coat along the white-furred dog bed.

"Yes, I do know that there are other things than those." I hastily brought up before changing subjects. "Um, babe I wouldn't wake her."

"Why not?" Theresa barked, her hand inches away from touching the Hellhound's most likely still-blood-stained coat.

"Because she's been sick, and I would hate to-."

"Alright, I get it."

"Thank god." I sighed. "That could have been a disaster if she found more blood on her or if Cinder woke up on the wrong side of the bed."

"So, what do you want to do, Augustus?" she asked.

"Why don't you get your suitcases and get them settled in the master suite? It's the last room on the right upstairs." I replied.

"Sure." She agreed, standing up from beside the dog bed to return towards the front doors.

Once she was out of the house, I returned my gaze onto Cinder, murmuring to myself, "Well, this sure got a lot more complicated."

Chapter 52
Augustus/Cinder

"So, why did you decide to move out here?" Theresa questioned as she tore pieces from a freshly baked bagel she bought from the nearby city.

Sipping a nice cup of coffee, I hesitated to tell her the true answer. Swallowing the hot beverage, I finally explained, "It's for her." I pointed with my free finger from the tough grip around the mug. "Cinder deserves to be able to have more room than my penthouse could offer."

"Yeah, I can only imagine. After all, she is a large dog-"

"She's still growing." I interrupted, taking another sip. "I looked for some properties on the outskirt rural parts of New York, however-." I delayed, hastily realizing I was coming too close to spilling the beans behind my real reasoning. Swiftly coming up with another blunt lie, I continued, "However, I couldn't find any properties, nor space that would fit my taste."

"And you went south?"

Chuckling, I agreed. "I don't know how she'll like it here, but I'm sure it won't take her long to adjust to living here."

"It normally doesn't take them long."

"Well, that's where she's different from the rest of them."

"Oh yeah?" Theresa continued, now attempting to change the subject on me with the aid of her body. While I could feel it indeed start to work, I caught a familiar rising glimpse out of the corner of my eyes and managed to fight those masculine urges back down.

"Alright, Theresa, I've got a few phone calls I have to make, could you please excuse me." I lied, breaking away from the countertop and wandering down the large and well-adorned hallway towards the large office containing more secluded views of the beach and front drive at the same time. Stepping over the double door threshold, I hastily locked the doors behind me and growled frustratingly beneath my breath. "Couldn't you have picked a better time to decide to appear from the shadows?"

"Valkyrie, do you have to be so rude?" the shadow slyly smirked. "You were in the middle of an enjoyable conversation with your enticing mate."

"Why did you show up now?" I interrogated. "I thought you were going to show up after she awoke?"

"Ah, well time is shrinking."

"Shrinking? How? Is the Council finally catching on?" I paced towards the luxurious black leather office chair. Frustrated, I sat down on the comfortable seat and rested the right side of my head in the palm of my hand. "So, what do we do now?"

"Proceed with the plan," Zachariah replied. "Though be more observant, they are moving far faster than once anticipated and I have yet to figure out a way to fool them."

"Okay." I acknowledged, trying to keep my building frustrations on the down-low. "But because they are moving faster, does that mean we will have to increase the number of her assignments?"

"Not yet. We are close enough for now-"

Recklessly interrupting Zachariah, I questioned, "What else do you have planned?"

Receiving that haunting glare of red death, I held my breath for the god's usual frozen threats that came after. "It is none of your concern what I have planned. Keep my little 'Reaper' contained, for now, I will let you know when the time comes for us to go into the final phase."

"Phase? You mean when you drain her dry." I exhaled coldly. "Or, do you mean the phase where you change her once more?"

"When she awakes get her set up for her next set of assignments. Those should keep her pre-occupied until I return."

Catching on to my Lorde's plans, I leaned forward in my chair and placing my elbows on the glass desk, I stared directly into the eyes of Death once more. "You have someone else collecting souls for you, do you not?"

The cruel skeletal smile faded, his eyes darkened and for a single moment, I felt my heart stop beating. Controlling my heavy pants, I listened to Zachariah snarl. "Augustus." Calling my name out with the taste of death coating each syllable. Taking a soft exhale, I submitted to his gaze. "Stop doubting my decisions and continue forth with the plan."

"Yes, my Lorde." I bowed, returning my gaze with him for a single glance. "So, besides Cinder collecting a few more souls, what else do we have left to complete?"

"Just make sure that when the time comes for the ritual, her heart is still in the right place."

"Meaning I should continue with building up her level of trust in me?"

"Yes." He simply answered for a momentary pause. "You need to be the closest person to her for this to work, or else the ritual and this entire experiment will be a failure."

"The experiment to make a 'Fiend' whose blindly loyal to every command and at the same time will ensure your 'ascendance...'" I began, but before I could even finish the Deity had already vanished. I knew there was an urgency to get this done and get Zachariah back to his original form before the Council caught on, but could we really do it? Could we really finish our mission before it was too late? We didn't even know if Cinder could handle the 'Ritual'. Leaning back in the office chair, I frustratingly threw myself forward and banged my fist on the glass with such force that it cracked the thick glass. "Fuck! Fuck! Fuck." I stopped when my ears heard someone knocking on the mahogany doors.

With no words being spoken, he simply vanished. The actions alone told me that I would be in for hell once he regained his Deity Form.

"Babe, is everything okay?"

Feeling a familiar cold rush over the top of my head, I slowly opened my exhausted eyelids. "Ah, you're awake my sweet 'little' Reaper." I heard his cold voice echo into my cropped canine ears.

Attempting to get up from the lying position I had been propped in, I attempted to speak. Yet, nothing would work. No words would come out.

"Those drugs that idiot gave you will take longer for your body to wean off." The Shadow responded. "I am assuming that it will be a few more hours before you will be able to walk again let alone speak."

Taking a long exhale, I spoke the same question in my no longer secluded thoughts. "So why are you here now? I know you had me sent to the Pits for a mass collection, so now what?"

"While you did exceed the quantity, I desired we need to make some alterations to your 'assignments.' We need to slow down the rate of her 'Reapings', so for now, I will have someone else collect souls." The Shadow responded after he had read my thoughts, his boney fingers petting the top of my head and rubbing the inner part of my left ear. "However, there are still some precious souls I want you to collect until I return. And Augustus will oversee those hunts."

Silently nodding my head, I proceeded to mentally communicate with the Deity. "I understand." Feeling the god softly pat me on the top of my head and praise my submission, I then wondered, "Who's next?" just as my nose caught onto the awfully smelling flowery stench that Augustus's girlfriend wore. Pushing past any curiosity, I stayed entuned with this Shadow being. Unusually desiring to focus on reaping rather than interacting with that woman.

"The Immortal Drake, Saylene, and the leader of your ex-syndicate group Braedon." He answered.

"Braedon?" I questioned, allowing my exhausted soft voice to speak up once I had realized that it was just the two of us in this massive room. "Why him?"

The cruel Deity vanished, leaving behind the echoing words: "My 'Reaper's questions she seeks answers to will soon appear."

Chapter 53
Cinder

Throwing my head backwards, I collapsed back onto the still ever so surprisingly soft white faux fur dog bed. After months of lying on the cold concrete and hard straw, the Tempurpedic mattress was a welcomed luxury. Scrolling my weary eyes around the unfamiliar floor plan, I saw that the dog bed had been placed between the large open floored living space and sleek modern kitchen. Craning my neck to straighten up into a one hundred eighty-degree angle, I noticed that I was lying against a wall full of Spanish floor-to-ceiling arched windows adorned with iron rods. I couldn't move much more without causing pain to my exhausted body, so I decided to put exploring the admirable property on hold. Puffing a long sigh, I brought my head back into a more comfortable position before once more closing my eyes for a short and finally quiet nap...or at least tried to.

The moment my eyes shut, my sensitive canine ears were flooded with loud shouts and curses, so loud that they echoed off the bland white walls, leaving a horrible ring deep in my eardrums. Sitting back up, I fought my sore body up to an upright lying position to focus my curiosity more on this arousing argument.

"Theresa, just stay out of it! It has nothing to do with you!"

"How does it not have anything to do with me, when I heard you shout with someone about 'gaining her trust'?! Who is this woman?!" I heard the familiarly annoying high pitch of the Archangel's girlfriend. While I was curious why she was here, wherever here was, I was more interested in observing this argument unfold. Judging that this argument aroused because of the Shadow's appearance, I stressfully groaned. "HAVE YOU BEEN CHEATING ON ME AUGUSTUS GALE?!"

"Ouch." I cringed to my thoughts before quietly chuckling to myself, "Augustus cheating? Oh, come on."

"For the last fucking time, I am not cheating on you!" Augustus shouted back as they came into my line of sight past the long white 'U' sectional sofa. "How many times have I told you that I would never cheat on you!"

"Well you still had to be doing something you shouldn't have with another woman!" the model continued to argue, her body arched in complete aggression. Her hip swaggered out, her finger pointed directly at his chiseled chest.

"FOR THE THIRD FUCKING TIME, I WAS NOT DOING A DAMN THING THAT HAD ANYTHING TO DO WITH YOU THERESA!"

"Then who did it have to deal with!"

"IT HAD TO DEAL WITH CINDER! THAT'S THE 'HER' WE WERE TALKING ABOUT OVER THE PHONE! IT WAS ABOUT A DOG!"

"Oh." The now dyed blonde softly murmured, her voice softening into a very hushed voice. "I didn't know."

"No, you didn't, and if you would have given me a moment to explain instead of blowing off my head, then you wouldn't be feeling like such an ass." Augustus sighed, his shoulders relaxing while his testosterone and other raging hormones raced into highly elevated levels.

"I'm sorry babe for bursting like that." She paused, pulling out one of the dark cedar wooded bar stools. "I just saw in the news that you were considered as one of the states' most eligible bachelors and I just-" Another pause occurred. Tilting my head in curiosity over the juicy gossip, I wondered what was going to come out of her mouth next. "I mean, why would they think that, Augustus? Haven't we been dating for these past few years?"

"Maybe it's because when I'm seen out in public it's always alone." The Angel spoke in a slightly foreboding tone. "Every time I try to invite you out to a benefit, or a charity event, or to do something, you always have a show or a shoot, or an audition, or something has come up with your family and it makes it difficult to maintain the dating image. Even if I do tell reporters that I am no longer single, the story only sticks for a few days, and then they think it's some lie or that I'm dating a different girl every time they ask."

The model smiled prior to emotionally breaking. Her frustrations melting away with the tears that seemed to smell too salty to be healthy. "Well, I will try to make more time for us, but I can't make any promises."

"I know, but at least you can finally drop the whole cheating thing now. I have told you that I would never cheat on you, especially when you are the only girl fit for me." The Angel returned with an obvious lie that made my hackles rise out of pure disgust.

"So, what were you discussing things about Cinder?" Theresa now asked, wiping away the tears from her cheeks as she attempted to change subjects.

Augustus exhaled a long breath, creating a long pause. "It's a long story, but the people who once 'owned' her are now trying to regain custody of her for their cruel means. And I've told the lawyer whom I hired to help me end this tyrant that the damage they did to her was so great that she's just now starting to trust me. I can't imagine losing someone who has entered my life and given me something important to look forward to, that I wouldn't know what to do if I lost her-." He paused as his eyes finally met mine. Observing his expression, I immediately read the 'oh shit you heard that' facial remark.

"You are such a shitty liar, Augustus. I know you were talking with 'him' and not some lawyer." I softly growled in the canine language to continue playing the lie that I am just a 'dog'.

"Oh, you're up Cinder." He returned, changing the subject once more.

"Yup." I meekly smiled. "And I heard everything you two were arguing about."

"Sorry girl, did we wake you?" Theresa exclaimed with deep concern in her dumbfounded eyes. Standing up from the stool, she strolled over to where I remained grounded, lying on the large dog mattress before stroking the top of my head.

"Fortunately, no." I sighed. "Somebody else did." Accepting the affection, I proceeded with gingerly shaking my head before laying it back down on the bed.

"It will take a few hours till those drugs finally wane its everlasting effects out of her system, so she will be drowsy for a little while longer," Augustus spoke up over the short tranquil silence. Bending down to also place his hand on my head, the Valkyrie too patted me before he hurriedly stood up and wandered towards the same room, I saw the couple exit from minutes earlier.

"I'm sorry for what you had to hear, and I am sorry for whatever life you had to live in the past," Theresa apologized. "Not all humans are evil, I can promise you that, Cinder."

"Sure." I reluctantly agreed, rolling my blue eyes at the statement this foolish female human proclaimed. "You're just as bad of a liar as he is."

My eyes followed the movement of feet as one set disappeared from my line of sight and another came back in. The difference in size and shoes alerted me to the identity of whom it was. Glancing up, too exhausted to lift my head, I barely made out the blurred image of Augustus's hand approaching my neck. His hand poised in a way too familiar pose that it now arose my own anxiety and emotions.

Folding my ears flat, I listened to the man explain, "Gerard told me that this would help you come out of the sedative faster and regain some of those lost valuable nutrients from your 'stay' at the kennel." While he moved his hand closer to my neck, speedily injecting a syringe needle into my bloodstream that hopefully contained exactly what he had stated. "We should start seeing a difference in a few days-"

"WAIT A MINUTE, AUGUSTUS! YOU LEFT HER WITH GERARD!" Theresa shouted, deciding to start yet again another argument.

Chapter 54
Cinder

"Here we go again." I sighed, rolling my eyes once more. "Although, this one could get interesting," I told myself as I watched the couple get closer to one another for some odd reason.

"Yes, I left her with Gerard!" Augustus shouted. "I had to! I wasn't going to leave her in my Penthouse by herself for five fucking months! Do you know the damage she could have done to my place in that amount of time!"

"Well, you aren't exactly lying." I chuckled, weakly crossing my left canine leg over my right as elegantly as I could manage.

"So what! You could've called me and I could've had her with me-"

"Yeah, no." Augustus quickly shot down his girlfriend in a tone I had yet to hear come from the Archangel.

"WAIT! What did you say?!" Theresa loudly shouted in that annoying voice of hers. "What, you don't trust me?!"

"Not exactly. We may have been dating for a while, but Theresa you don't know how much of a hassle she can be!"

"HEY NOW!" I growled back. "I am not that bad!"

"She's just a dog! How hard can it be to dog sit?! Cinder seems well behaved."

Watching Augustus's body language change, I began to wonder if I was seeing the limit of his patience. Was he finally at his limit? "This just keeps getting more and more interesting," I smirked.

A lasting silence overcame the unfamiliar house it even altered my demeanor on this debate. It wasn't fun anymore. Folding my ears back, I lied my head down onto my crossed paws, I was too familiar with the raging hormonal scent. So familiar with it that if my legs were working, I would have left the house and run as far away as I could, as fast as I could.

"Augustus?" Theresa softly asked, her tone hushed, making me suspect she had read her boyfriend's tense body language.

The Angel turned and left the tight circle the two made to scream at one another, disappearing into what I could only assume was the foyer by the direction of light. Watching with an intense level of concern, I surveyed a change in the opacity of the sunlight glow then dim followed by a heavy slam. Immediately, I knew that he had stormed out the front door.

"Augustus?!" she loudly yelled from where she stood. Turning over to glance in my direction, I saw that in her heavily eye-lined hazel eyes, she was questioning if she had pushed him too far. I could see the hundreds of questions fill her head. Our soft exchange only lasted for seconds when both of our ears caught onto the roar of the vehicle, I guess he had used to drive here. It's heavy roaring only growing louder as he burned the rubber of the tires on the drive. Observing the horror and anger in the model's eyes arrive I knew what she was going to do. Once more screaming out the blonde-haired Valkyrie's name, she raced in her tall heels towards the same door seconds earlier he had fled from.

"WAIT!" I cried, trying to force my tired body up to a standing position, so I too could follow them. However, my body was not allowing me to complete any actions I desired. Attempting it for a second time, I stopped when I heard the woman scream out his name and the door to the house slam shut once more. Her voice was barely audible over the screeching tires and roaring engine. Another failed attempt, I cried out in pain as the joints in my legs halted every nerve in each appendage. "Damn it-!"

"GOD DAMN IT AUGUSTUS!" the woman's voice cursed as she stormed back into the kitchen. Grabbing her luxurious leather purse, Theresa then too angrily fled, her heels clicking loudly on the wood floor with long strides. Again fighting through the pain in my body, I began to argue against my tight muscles to finally stand myself up. Making headway, I sprinted after the human until I was stopped by the massive glass door getting slammed shut in my face. In between the iron rods that adorned the glass which obscured my adjusting vision, I watched Theresa get into her sportscar before she too raced out the cobblestone paved circle driveway. Her car's tires also screeching while they rode over the stones.

I may lack experience with these kinds of arguments from my childhood, but I had plenty of experience from my time in the Institutes, as well as multiple memories of heated debates that I had observed between Mhykal and Yalu, arguments unfolding over the Vampiric, Vixen, and their Syndicate Leader. Recent memory told me those arguments were over me proceeding the 'Incident'. Though regardless of the subject, I had learned early on that chasing after someone was a bad idea. As I recollected the same raging hormones, the same raging anger, the same raging stench of fear, it sent my body into a fit of anxious fear and shocking worry. With my collection of memories replaying, I was reminded that when somebody chased after the other, it generally left at least one side of the party either emotionally or physically hurt. I knew that I had to do something, but my body was unable to do what I desired.

"DAMN!" I snarled, trying to find some way to open this door without being able to transform. Stupidly scratching at the door, I cursed aloud over and over again. "DAMN IT! DAMN IT! DAMN IT!" Getting no luck, of course, I sat down in front of the doors, childishly hoping for them to drive back any second now. I knew they weren't going to come back, and I knew that when either one of the two returned, I was going to be blamed for this stupid argument the couple had gotten into.

As the sun worked on its final seconds of setting in the horizon, casting its rays directly into my face, I reluctantly remained in front of the door. Feeling completely useless and depressed as, yet again in my life, I was unable to do anything. With my exhausted body beginning to win control over my hurting heart, I loudly collapsed onto the floor. Recognizing that I wasn't going anywhere anytime soon, I decided to wait for their return, for someone's return, for his return. Switching positions, I made myself comfortable on the harsh wood floors while my exhausted eyes prowled the long yet beautifully landscaped Mediterranean driveway for a single sign. Telling my body that regardless of what it wanted, I was going to lie here and wait until then.

With another long hour slipping by and still not a single sign that either one was coming back through this door any time soon, I rolled into another position on the floor. Finding one that was a little more comfortable, I curled my large black-furred body up into a ball, covering my face with my tail to block out the bright moon who had recently taken charge, guarding the night sky, and easily drifted off.

When I awoke, I saw that the bleak house was coated with more sunlight. Its warm rays echoing off the large windows from the back part of the manor, peeking through the spaces of hair on my tail. Craning my head around, I unwrapped my tightly formed sleeping position to see if the driveway had been filled with at least one vehicle. But it wasn't...

Chapter 55
Cinder

The day speedily swept by as I continued to watch for someone's return, for anyone's return. The sun had set as soon as I had found it arisen, the moon too. Yawning out my depressed frustration and endless loneliness, I stared up at the gorgeous white moon who beat its matching cold glaze onto my fur through the glass.

"I'm glad you aren't red tonight." I teased the moon.

"Gone to talking to yourself, haven't you?" I heard another familiar voice coo in my ear. Of course, I recognized the voice as my own. Its short burst of sanity and demonic conscious talking back to itself.

"What else do I have left to do?" I responded with a weary sigh.

"We can hunt, or reap, or anything else but..." the voice attempted to persuade, offering up various tasks it enjoyed.

Closing my eyes, I envisioned it again, the other version of me, the Fiend. "I'm not doing anything else, but..." I coldly affirmed as I reopened my heavy eyelids.

"BUT WHAT WAIT HERE!?!" it teased in my head.

"YES!" I proceeded to shout inside my deranging mind. "Besides...besides I can't do anything else, I can't change back, I can't move from this cursed spot!"

"And even if you wanted to, you wouldn't because you feel blame for their fight." The Fiend surprisingly declared in a softer tone, respectably discerning my reasons.

"Why is it always me?" I asked the cursed itch as I broke down, placing my head once more into my paws and onto the cold hard floors. "Why?"

"It's the curse of being a 'Reaper'." The other version of I called.

"Leave," I demanded the being, shifting myself around to attempt to ignore the darker image who was still trying to steal my conscious.

"Fine, I will leave for now." The Fiend's voice coldly whispered deep down into my left notched ear.

Flickering my ear to block out the colder demonic voice, I rolled my eyes before once again allowing slumber to take the reins. Content that my conscious was quiet, even if my heart was aching.

Upon opening my eyes for the twentieth time, I noticed the black sky. As my pupils adjusted to the dull color of the cloud-filled sky, my sensitive hearing detected the heavy patter of the rain. Craning my head over to look out the front doors of the large house; I had not yet gained the ability to rummage through, I saw under the solar-paneled garden lights outlining the driveway, that it indeed was pouring rain. Pouring rain in such a depressing manner it matched my current mental status. With a bright flash of blinding purple and white light followed by one of the loudest booms of thunder I had ever heard, I unexpectedly jumped up. Hastily rising onto my feet, I watched as another flash of blinding light pressed itself against the glass. As my heart anxiously pounded, I began to feel my worry over the locations of my 'babysitter' and his 'annoying' girlfriend deepen. Dropping back into a sit, I returned to tiredly watching the driveway while the intense thunderstorm kept shooting out heavy rain and eons of bright light out over the property.

However, the longer I watched the storm dance under the night sky, the more I was beginning to grow more anxious, more fearful. Memories came flooding in like waves of all the other days the weather was horrible, all those days where obscenely cruel treatments happened, all those days where I was alone, alone just like I am now.

"Was I always meant to be alone?" I wondered aloud to the empty house. "Is this what I am to expect for the rest of my life? To be alone? Alone like this?"

Expecting an answer, I received nothing. Nothing but the echo of the thunder who stood as my only form of company. I was even expecting an answer from the Fiend or the Shadow, but no one called back. Of course, when I needed someone here for me, no one showed. Nothing new.

Ultimately, I lost track of time the longer I watched the same routine of a bright flash of light and a loud boom repeatedly strike. Locked watching its natural beauty, I ignored all my canine instincts and focused more on my human emotions. Hoping it wouldn't last much longer, I moved around on the floor, changing positions to allow me to once again lie down on the cold hardwood paneling. Falling back onto the side of my stomach, I laid my back against the back of the glass front doors. Dancing my head through several various positions until I found one I could call comfortable, I eventually passed out or at least tried to.

Feeling my heart grow colder as the darkness surrounded my pupils who now hid beyond my still heavy eyelids, I continued to listen to the thunderstorm and its heavy downpour for a few more minutes. The sound of the drops of rain heavily slamming into the stone pavers and the roof above, helped soothe my rising anxiety. Allowing me to finally drift off into yet again another day alone.

Coming back around, I didn't fuss with changing positions, nor with my surroundings. Why bother with it? Just why? Huffing out a deep breath, I could tell that the storm had lightened up at least. The rain had lightened up but had yet to go away and with its ever-lasting grey hue, it made the house feel all the emptier. Hearing my stomach growl, I moaned my complaint for it to shush up yet it only groaned louder. The noise-making me wonder the last time I had eaten, but that worrying thought was pushed further back to the endless line of other questions and worries I was suffering from, hunger was the last thing on my mind, reaping was the last thing. My draining insanity was no longer even a concern to me. I just didn't want to be alone anymore. I was done with it.

Managing to stay awake for who knows how long, I listened more to the light rain patter on the stone pavers and just processed more harmful thoughts. While they started to take more control over my exhausted body, I felt a familiar ting come from my back. A pain-ful burning sensation coming from that horrible cross-shaped scar resting along my spine.

Bellowing in pain, I demanded, "WHAT DO YOU WANT?!" Knowing who exactly was making it hurt so bad.

"I will not let you think so coldly of yourself, my Reaper." I heard the Shadow's voice call from somewhere out of sight. "I will not let you bring harm to yourself, not when we are so close to finishing our task." Futilely attempting to ignore him and the pain he was pro-voking, I painfully tuned back into his endless rambling. Listening to that deathly cold voice of his, "My little Reaper remember this: You are my way back to the being I once was, you are my way 'Home'. You still have a purpose to fulfill, and I will discuss it with that stupid 'Valkyrie' of mine. Neglecting his posts over human emotions when he knows there are more important things to do."

291

Swallowing my anxiety, I bit down and asked the question I had hanging over the top of my head during these past days. Lifting my head I saw that indeed his shadowy presence was kneeling beside me. Bowing over me. Pushing my head into his exposed skeletal palm, I asked, "Zachariah, why me?"

"Sleep now, my 'Reaper."

Chapter 56

Augustus

Upon finally calming down, I steadily drove back to my newly bought mansion. Driving up the solar-lit driveway, I came back to the house foolishly expecting it to be lit with someone angrily waiting on my return, but of course, it was as dark as the everlasting beachfront property. It seemed she too had left. Changing the gears to park, I took out my keys and began my walk towards the front doors. Reaching for the door handle, I proceeded to check if it was locked or not, unsure if that damn woman had locked it when she had left. My grip easily twisting the unlocked French outer doorknob arose one worrying thought that had pushed its way up to the surface of my exhausted mind:

"Please tell me she didn't get out?" I wondered.

Pushing the door opened, I was immediately greeted with a block, it wouldn't budge. Firmly pushing once again, I received the same results.

"What the hell is going on?" I noisily shouted.

"You finally came home." Someone interjected. The voice interjecting my train of thoughts.

"Look, I don't want to talk about it. There-" I returned, not turning around to look back at the person.

"I could care less about your argument with that filthy human." The voice now snarled, its tone much darker than a few seconds ago.

Finally acknowledging the husky scarred voice with its death-filled tone, I froze. Shakily dropping my hand from the doorknob, I began to find a way to excuse my erratic behavior. I had only heard that low of a tone once before in my time with this Deity, and the last time he almost killed another God. Swallowing, I hesitantly turned around to face the black robe wearing shadow.

"My Lorde-" I paused, seeing his dark red eyes peering right through and beyond me. The rage he held sending utter chills down my body.

"I can see you, now remember where you stand, Valkyrie." Zachariah snarled.

"Why are you here?" I stupidly questioned through the endless silence.

"I am sure you can figure it out."

"Look I needed to leave for a bit to clear my head."

"Again, I can care less about why you did it. I care about what you did."

"What I did?" I questioned, completely confused by my actions. "What did I do?" I continued to think in my wandering thoughts.

"You know full well." His deep voice echoed. "Fix your mistake and I may give you mercy."

"My mistake?"

The creator of the infamous Book of Demons simply pointed back towards the front door of the mansion as he returned to the nothingness he had risen from... His words coldly whispering into my right ear. "You will soon see for yourself, my very stupid Valkyrie."

Standing on the small entryway, I attempted to calm my scared body. Trying to contain and control my vigorous shakes, I took a hard breath as I realized how close I was to becoming nothing more than dust in the wind. Exhaling another heavy breath, I slowly turned around to face the glass door, and there beyond the iron decorated glass door I had attempted to open, I saw a heavy black mass placed against the hurricane proof door. "Shit-!"

Pushing more weight against the door, I attempted to yet again get the front door open, however with her dead weight body pressing against the glass, it proved futile. Stepping away from the door, I took a small breather before heading in for another try. Pulling out my supernatural strength this time, I kept my hands planted on the glass and began applying more momentum in my legs. The unconscious Unnatural on the other side started to creep along the wood floor. It may have only been a few inches at a time, but it was working. Once the door had creaked open a gap large enough for my body to slip through, I without wasting a second squeezed through. Finding the dimmer switch to the chandelier that hung over the foyer, I took a few moments to survey the assumed to be sleeping Hellhound.

Observing her lungs rise and fall at a steady rate, I took a long thankful sigh. Finding little to no problems at first glance, I decided to creep closer. Squatting down onto my knees, I softly put my hand on the large square head of the Great Dane sized Beauceron and slowly swept it down her neck onto her chest. Feeling her slow and steady heart rate beat against her ribcage, I promptly realized that she had lost much more weight than I had last recalled. Bracing my elbows against my knees, I huffed another deep sigh before standing back up to quietly shut the front door and lock its uniquely hidden deadbolt system. Cautiously stepping over the Hellhound, I proceeded to begin with turning on all the other lights in the house, so I could track my path around the yet to be memorized floor plan.

Eventually coming back to the foyer, I was once more greeted by the sleeping Hellhound. Heading over to pick up Cinder, I was met by something else. Before I could react, a massive black mass swarmed up off the floor, followed by a flash of white and swirling surroundings. The hundred pounds of weight smashed right into my shoulders and throwing my body tumbling backwards before finally hitting the hardwood floor. Flinching at the impact, I mistakenly shut my eyes. Shooting them open when my body forced instinct to take over and expose my sights to these fast unfolding events.

Adjusting to the bright lights that hung over the top of us, my eyes portrayed the image of one too many fangs standing inches from ripping into my face. Focusing on the blurred image while it steadily brought the shadow into the foreground, I saw that standing on top of me was the large dog-shaped Demonic Unnatural. Her short-furred box-shaped head covered by the way too familiar shaped wolf skull she stole from the Lycan Syndicate. The same skull I had left back in my Penthouse, locked inside my office. Confused about how it came to sit on her head with the same posture alignment that I could stare directly through his eye sockets and into those familiar blood lust red-orange.

"Cinder-?" I attempted to question. Hastily cut off by a deep savage bark and a spray of saliva from the massive jaws, I hushed up. Listening to the snarl echo from within her throat before escaping out of her lips, I once more tried to call out the woman's given name, and again I was silenced, but this time, it was by a different sound.

With her massive size standing over the top of me, I watched the massive paw release its firm grip on my shoulder and begin to approach my face. The limb changing shape as it came down on to my throat. Glancing back up for those red eyes, so I could continue to call out for the creature who had yet to break that ravaging stare, I was greeted by the change of forms. The Beauceron replacing itself with the female human form lying beneath the sleek black coat, wearing the same out she was back when I had left at the Pits. My eyes in a state of confusion and fear raced to survey every single movement she made, quickly observing the petite woman lean back on my chest, her legs stretching out over my shoulders and her right hand steadily reaching up towards her still skull-wearing face. The long fingers grabbing at the scarred bone, fingers spreading far apart to grab the eye sockets by her thumb and pinkie. As the skull danced off her smooth-skinned face, I was greeted by a colder stare, a stare so cold it sent familiar chills down my back of my neck.

The same crackle echoed once more throughout the foyer, and before I could place the soft tone of its unusual noise, I surveyed the blood-red scythe growing out of her right wrist. Her long black hair falling out from behind her ear to hide half of her face and a newly noticed sly smile. Putting her voice and the quiet laughter together, I again attempted to call out her name this time with more worry.

AGAIN, I WAS INTERRUPTED! Though this time, it was by the push of the blade millimeters shy of carving into my throat. The message was clear to me, forcing me finally zip my mouth shut. Watching the woman lick her lips while she leaned her arched malnourished body towards my right ear, I quietly listened to her voice softly whisper, 'Gotcha."

Chapter 57

Augustus

"What?" I frantically thought. Swallowing for a breath of relief as the hairs on my throat felt her blood scythe release its edge from slicing into my flesh, I softly interrogated, "What the fuck?"

Cinder straightened herself, bringing her back to an upright position still expressing the same sly smile. She gave no spoken answer. No, the only response the woman gave me was a fit of laughter.

"What the fuck!?" I repeated, trying to fight myself free from her hold.

"Hey, don't yell at me!" the woman quickly snapped, redrawing that same blade preparing to again go in for the killing technique, I assumed her Vampiric allies once taught her.

Trying to maintain my anger, I took a quick breath before attempting to politely ask, "What do you mean-"

"I gotcha. I was able to make you feel the same fear I felt during your temper tantrum." She coldly returned, her tone no longer sounding childishly amused.

"Fear?"

"You don't get it, of course, you don't." Cinder growled, sheathing her blood scythe and weakly standing herself before straying off.

"She felt fear?" I wondered aloud to myself. "Why would she be afraid?"

"I can hear you, you know." The Hellhound snarled from the living room.

Standing myself back up, I hastily followed Cinder. Coming into the living room, I hoped I was able to get some answers out of the woman, as well as hoped I could calm my swiftly beating heart. "You're right, I don't get what's going on, but if you can explain it to me-"

"You left me alone for days on end. Something you as my 'babysitter' is not supposed to do."

"Look, I didn't mean to leave you, I just needed to get away from Theresa-"

Interrupting me she blurted, "I GET WHY YOU DID IT!" Taking a quick pause, she then spoke in her normal uniquely soft feminine voice, "I just don't get why you left me for days. It could've been a few hours, that I would've understood, but you left me for so long I lost count of the days and judging by your current expression; as well as how he spoke of you before putting me to sleep to ease my wandering conscious. I assume you also didn't realize the length of time you left me alone. You left me alone, locked away in my canine form with no way of taking care of myself in your absence."

"Theresa was here, she could've taken care of you."

"No, she wasn't."

"Huh?"

"She left right after you did. Matter of fact she left so she could chase after you. Why else would the front door be unlocked?"

"Oh." I expressed with a stupid choice of following expressions, trying my hardest to adapt to this level of observation she was exposing.

"Yeah oh." Cinder snarled, turning herself around on the island stool to face me. Her elbows braced against the countertops and her left leg crossed over her right with a very calm and yet stern look on her face. Watching her roll her eyes, I proceeded to listen to the Unnatural speak, "Look, I wanted to get you to feel the fear I felt every day I was locked up in the institute praying for the day of my death to finally come, every day I was locked up in a cage as I used as a Harvesting Vessel, every day I was locked up in a cage at the Pits forced to fight and kill innocent Unnaturals for Mankind's' enjoyment; for every day I was locked up here alone with nothing but myself to talk to."

"Cinder, I don't know how to say I'm sorrier than I am, but-"

"There's no point in being sorry over what you couldn't control, however, you did promise me that you would return and bring me home, and yet." She paused as she stood up and brought herself closer to where I stood a few feet away, her blue eyes finally returning to their normal hue while they stared up into my green eyes with a cold gleam. "And yet you still broke that promise and left me."

'Look, Cinder, I am so sorry that I did that, but I had a lot on my plate between bringing you here, after driving all fucking night, and all my Client calls and making sure we weren't followed."

'We all have a lot on our plate, still doesn't mean you had to leave me alone." Cinder depressingly expressed, her eyes glancing away from me in such a submissive behavior that it seemed oddly unfamiliar.

"Cinder." I tried to call out as she walked away from me, heading out to the backyard through the sliding glass door. Stopping myself from chasing after her for a moment, I allowed myself to collect my thoughts. "I get that you felt alone, but there is something else about the way you keep saying that word that it seems as if it's about something else. What were you so afraid of from being alone?"

Observing the beautiful woman wander over to the patio furniture where she elegantly sat and looked out towards the stunning night coastline, I debated whether I should head over and ask her about it or not. Would that be overstepping her boundaries? After a few minutes of sitting on the number of questions I had nestled in my mind, I took a hopeful sign that the Unnatural wasn't going to rip my head off and embarked outside as well.

Sitting down on the wicker patio chair, I placed my elbows on my knees and rested my head in the palm of my hands as I asked, "I understand why you were so afraid all those times, but the way you said you were left 'alone' has me confused. Why were you so afraid of being alone Cinder, when we both know quite well about how you also enjoy your alone time."

Turning to look back at me, I surveyed the change of emotion dance in her eyes. "Augustus, I am afraid of being alone because for the second time in my life I have a person who can keep my sanity in check, a person who can keep those voices away, someone who...someone who helps me keep control over that...that 'itch'."

Observing her tear ducts start to fill, I stood myself up and ventured over to the couch where she was relaxing. Comforting the Unnatural, I proceeded with giving my sorrowful response. "It's alright Cinder, I'm here and I know I may have not kept that promise I made to you earlier, but I will try to not leave you alone without telling you where I am heading, or without a way of contacting me." Keeping the woman close in a tight hug, I felt her arms finally embrace my touch as she tightly wrapped her small arms around my back. Resting my head on top of hers, I then wondered quietly in my head, "It's not so much that you fear being alone, as it is you fear the dark abyss of your "Fiendish' conscious consuming you. And while your version of trying to get me to understand how afraid you were was childish, I can't hold it against you as you have not learned any mature ways of communicating your feelings." Taking a moment, I quietly whispered aloud, "You sure do have the heart of a child, Little Reaper."

Chapter 58
Jakob/Cinder

"Jakob, are you coming or what?" Mhykal questioned slightly louder than normal.

"Yeah, I'm coming." I sighed, taking one last glance at the enormous Red Moon that stared coldly down at me. Its orange glow haunting the night-filled environment reminded me of all those times she had been harmed by its unusual lunar powers. Speaking to myself, I called out, "Cinder, wherever you are, I hope you are holding up." It was all I could think up. I had forgiven Cinder for the incident, but I had yet to forget its traumatic events, and still could push the thoughts of worry about why she had done what she did out of my head.

Strolling over to my longtime friend, I returned another sigh as he held out a familiar item in his right hand, revealing the same casual expression, "Glad to have you back, man."

Taking hold of my black long trench coat, I easily slipped my arms through the sleeves and returned with a matching tone, "It's nice to be back." Changing tones, I took the lead of our small raid party, "Alright, now here's the plan..."

"Alright Cinder, I'm heading out. I should be back later tonight."

"Okay." I acknowledged, waving my hand over my shoulder to the Archangel. Hearing him lightly chuckle as he left me able to return to my solemn meditation on the back patio. It had only been a few months since my fight with Augustus, and he had indeed begun to change. Telling me when he was leaving, or what plans he had, and going even to the point of involving me or informing me on some of his ordeals. Taking a long sigh, I stood myself up from the lounge chair's footstool and wandered over to the soft grass patch that resided in between the house and the beautiful coastline.

Taking a stance, I began to recall all the times I had sparred with my old friends back at the Syndicate. Remembering all the advice and all the input that Yalu had taught me, all the silly missteps and important flaws that Mhykal had made, every spar I had competed in with Peylith. I was able to evoke every single movement that all three of them had made, and just as my memories replayed, my body instinctively danced like a puppet on a string. Although shadowboxing with myself proved more self-loathing than normal today, it felt more boring, more unfulfilling.

"What's the point." I sighed as I broke my stance.

"What is the matter Reaper?" I heard the familiar voice of the Fiend call, using that annoying pet name he had given me.

"There's no point in doing this anymore," I growled aloud. Talking to the voice in my head while speaking over the roaring of the saltwater waves that were lightly besieging the coast.

"There is a point to everything we do. You need to stay on top of these humanoid combat skills, in case the day comes you cannot change forms into your Primary Form."

"My Primary Form? What are you saying?" I verbally interrogated the silent being, staring out at the coast, trying to hold back a small snarl of anger for my bloodlust subconscious, knowing more about my own body than I.

"When he returns ask him, he will explain it."

"Why can't you?!" I snapped, closing my eyes to envision myself talking to it.

"Because I don't necessarily know myself." Its reflection smiled, mirroring the same image of me. Its face mimicking my 'kind' soft smile in such an irritating smirk, it alerted me to the fact that this was just another tease, another joke it was playing to make me lose control over my rationality.

"Go away, now." I snarled in my head. "I have had enough of your games for one day."

"Jeez, learn to take a joke."

"NOW!"

"Fine." It sighed, disappearing into the black abyss that was my mind as I once more opened my eyes. The bright afternoon sunlight blaring deep into my pupils and penetrating its gorgeous warmth through my scarred skin. Taking a long deep breath, I decided to take its advice. Standing still in that laxed manner I was told I had, I proceeded with the next round of shadowboxing. Pretending that my invisible enemy was coming closer to me, completely unaware of my sheathed weapons. Changing my choice at the last minute, I enclosed my bare fist and brought in a deep southpaw. Backing up the impact with another charged punch, I pretended that my enemy was staggering back and began to configure another strategy.

"Focus," I ordered myself, knowing that I had less than three seconds between the recollection of my enemy's surroundings, I hastily centered myself and began to summon a single scythe on my right wrist. Taking the weapon made of heavy iron concentrated blood, I lightly slit my lower forearm, cutting at the skin away from the major artery. With the blood oozing out along my hand, I grabbed at the blood and outstretched my arm. Solidifying the finally healthy and drug-free cells into a long black rod. Applying the images of the desired weapon, I brought the complete rod out away from my right wrist. Swinging its tip away from the skin, spraying the particles outward, I forced the diffused particles to stretch and collect. Instructing it to reform itself into the scythe blade image, I had become so used to creating but this time attached to the last five inches of the rod. Ordering myself to remain focused, I then stretched out the density of the blood clot back to the blade to reinforce the strength of the large scythe I had grown. Taking another deep breath, I observed watched as my body began to falter, swaying side to side. Using the six-foot-tall rod, I used it to brace my tired physique; however, a second later the ground came crashing towards me with the sound of the blood collapsing onto the grass beneath my feet. Catching my exhausted self, my arms and knees shakily managed to hold me up.

"DAMN IT!" I cursed, punching the blood-stained grass, I uttered the words once more. "DAMN! DAMN!" Dropping down onto the floor, I rolled onto my back and stared back up at the bright sun that stared down at me. "I thought I had it that time." I vocalized as my head attempted to wrap around everything that had gone wrong in that test. I had been attempting to make a Grim Reaper's Scythe for an entire month, but I always got so tired after creating it that I failed time and time again. "Why can't I seem to figure this out?" I sighed before exhaustion completely overtook me.

"Well, that went faster than expected. Nice job everyone." I praised my team upon completion of our safe return home. We had finished such a decent raid that it was in almost record time.

"It only went so well because you were here." Mhykal jabbed at me, expressing his same jokester smile as he picked up sweet little Mhykila.

The infant looked so much like Yalu, but with her father's unusual ex-human eyes. She was born with a full head of pitch-black hair, and a mixed shade of pale Vampiric skin and soft Caucasian skin. Words could not express how happy everyone was when Yalu and Mhykal had finally had their child, mostly because Yalu's pregnancy hormones were becoming insufferable during her third trimester, although there were also no words for how great of a father my friend had become. I personally couldn't be any prouder.

Following the Vampiric, over to our common lounge area, I heard him ask, "Although what made you decide to come tonight?"

"I don't know." I sighed looking away from him.

"It's because of her, isn't it Jakob," Peylith interjected as he sat down on the sofa across from us, his back pressed into the far corner. One of his dark jeans-wearing leg crossing over the other with the sock-wearing foot resting on his thigh, while his left arm braced the spine of the sofa. For an eight-hundred-year-old Pharaoh, he had adapted well to masculine laziness.

Staring into those haunting amber eyes the Hellhound had, I swallowed as I felt the stare run right through my immortal soul. "I don't know," I repeated.

"Man, how can you forget what she did you?" Mhykal hissed while handing the infant child back to its mother, his voice telling me he was also reading through my unprepared lie.

"I didn't forget it." I returned as sternly as possible. "I mean I am forever scarred by her actions that night." Rubbing my hand over the toothmark shaped scars on my neck. "But I also do not hold her actions against her."

"STILL?!"

"So, you forgave her?" Peylith inquired, changing his position to a forward lean with both feet planted on the ground.

"I haven't forgiven her either! I still want an answer, but I know that Cinder would not want me to depressingly mope around this place, not when there are so many Unnaturals who are still suffering out there, just as she once was. I know she would want me to return to freeing those that cannot free themselves." I coldly spoke to my comrades, my tone telling them now to drop the subject or regret it. Standing up from the couch, I began to wander towards the staircase that led up to my bedroom, murmuring "Think what you wish, but I'm going to bed because unlike you sorry pieces of shit, I have work to do tomorrow."

Chapter 59

Augustus

"Hey, I'm back," I called out as I strolled into the open-spaced living and kitchen. "Sorry it took a little longer than normal, but I forgot to make some errands-" I paused mid-sentence. Something was amiss. Glancing around the room, I easily noticed that the Hellhound was nowhere to be found. Normally when I came home, she was either outside meditating, lounging, or she was inside watching the sunset from the u-shaped sectional, however, I didn't see her anywhere. "Cinder?" I again called, pacing around the large mansion. "Cinder?" Ascending the stairs, I tried to think of all the places the woman could've been.

Coming up to the door of her room, I saw that the door was ajar, alerting me to the fact she had not yet come to the massive bedroom for her normal evening ritual, or for some time alone. Concerned for the location of the Hellhound, I decided to peek inside just in case she hadn't shut it, but just as I put my hand on the door to push it open I heard a woman's voice call out my name.

"Augustus, where are you?" The feminine voice called back from downstairs. Recognizing its soft call, I took a deep sigh of relief thankful for her safety.

Now descending the staircase, I saw that in the foyer was the black-haired, blue-eyed woman staring up at me with that observant glare. The type of stare that could read every single movement I was going to make. Cautiously approaching the question, I answered, "I was upstairs wondering where you were."

"Oh, I went out for a run." She said, walking down the hallway towards the kitchen. Surveying her outfit which consisted of a black sports bra, matching capris leggings, and soft gray Nike sneakers, I judged her statement to be true.

"Where?" I dumbfoundingly questioned. The question slipping out before I even knew what I had said.

"Don't worry, I just strolled down the driveway, and halfway down the block before coming back around. I stayed in this form the whole duration." Cinder calmly replied while she grabbed a glass cup out of the clear cabinet to fill with water from the tap.

"Don't worry? Cinder it doesn't matter what form you were in; you can't just be out jogging whenever you feel like it!"

Finishing chugging up the glass of water, and putting the glass down the counter, the beautiful woman locked glares with me. I knew we were about to go through another argument, but I still had to make my point of concern clear. "Augustus, I know you are supposed to be my babysitter, but I am going crazy being stuck here all the fucking time!"

"She beat me to the point." I thought to myself. I hurriedly raced to find another point, hoping for one where she wasn't going to have a comeback. "I get that you are going crazy being stuck here, but-" I stopped. I was out of ideas. Out of words to finish my point. Dropping my shoulders, I caved into the debate. "Look, just be careful when you go out."

The Hellhound's eyes softened, and her eyebrows raised in bewildering confusion as she cautiously countered, "You're not going to scold me?"

"There's no point." I sighed. "You're still going to do it."

"Yeah, I still am." She smiled.

"How long have you been jogging around the neighborhood?" I probed, desperate for an answer to at least one of my questions.

Her eyes glanced up at the ceiling as her forefinger tapped her chin. "Uhm, about a month. I don't know how long really." Cinder answered, returning those blue pupils to lock onto my glare.

"And no one has tried to talk to you?"

"A few have. Some nice people."

"And what did you tell them?"

"That a friend and I had moved into a house down the street, and we were going to be staying here while he finished up some work contracts." She responded, the comeback shocking me once more. "Don't act so shocked, Augustus, I do know how to tell a few white lies here and there."

"You didn't give them any reason to ask you about your species?"

"If I was human or not? No, they didn't."

"And you stayed in your human form the entire time?"

"Yeah, I'm not stupid enough to change in front of humans without their acknowledgment of who or what I am." She snarled, her tolerance for the interrogation becoming a thin sheet of ice.

"Okay, I'll stop asking questions." I conceded.

"Thank you, now I am going to take a shower." She graciously informed, putting the glass into the sink before strolling back towards the staircase where she was going to head to the privacy of her room.

"Thank god that's over." I sighed, flopping down on the sofa. Leaning against the spine, I tossed my neck backward to stare up at the modern three-winged ceiling fan hanging directly overhead. Closing my eyes for a moment's rest, I reopened when I felt my cellphone vibrate from my front jean's pocket. The repetition alerting me to an incoming call. "Who the fuck is calling me now?" I hissed, taking my phone lazily out of the pocket. Seeing the contact name, I continued to painfully complain, "Why her?" Deciding to decline the phone call and allow it to go to voice mail, I told myself that I would deal with my crazy girlfriend later.

It had been a few hours after the discussion had unfolded before I decided to check in on the Hellhound. The sun had set and judging by her past schedule, I was expecting her to be asleep by now. It was like clockwork every night. She was up early and was in her bed by nightfall. I couldn't tell if it was from her short childhood with her parents, the long suffrage with the Institute, or if it was her even shorter time with the Vampiric Syndicate, but whatever it was, it made me feel like I was living with a child. It was very regulatory and annoying.

Coming up to the bedroom door, I saw it was still cracked ajar. Pushing it open slightly, I spied inside the bedroom. The white moonlight entered her large bedroom from its Spanish second-story balcony, easily illuminating the very scene I was expecting to observe. Well, sort of expecting...

On the queen-sized bed, lying on top of the white fleece throw blanket, sitting on the edge of the light beige comforter was the large canine. Her still growing body taking up a little over a third of the bed. The black fur resembled a show-dog quality with its impressive sleek and shiny coat as it rose and fell with each breath she took. Though I was taken aback by her taking on the Beauceron canine form, I was also overtaken by the serenity of the sight of such a beautiful creature sleeping before me.

Cutting the moment short, I pulled myself back out of the entryway and brought the door back to its ajar position. Heading towards my room, I too embarked on my normal routine before I too retired. Tossing my cellphone onto the bed, I proceeded with switching out my casual attire of a white V-neck shirt and faded blue jeans for something more comfortable. Leaving my chest bare and shifting my worn legs through the soft pantlegs of my long black sweats, I returned to the bed. Sitting down on the King-sized mattress, I began to start the final task of scrolling through my phone for all of its missed messages. Seeing her missing call, I frustratingly ran my hand through my blonde-hair to attempt to calm myself. Seizing the movement mid-stroke when my neglected Unnatural instincts caught a change in the serene presence. Someone had broken through the barrier I had placed around the property.

"For fuck's sake!"

Chapter 60
Augustus/Cinder

Opening the front door, I noticed that the being who had invaded my front yard was none other than the Deity Zachariah. It didn't come as a surprise to me, after all, it had been a little while since he had checked in on us. Closing the door behind me, I tiredly yawned, "What do you want?"

"You usually don't' catch on to my presence."

"Why did you cut your normal dialogue?" I asked, attempting to keep down another yawn.

"Time is becoming of the essence." The skeletal shadow answered.

"The Council, or?"

"How are things coming along with the Draconic?" the god hastily interrupted.

"It is more challenging to get your Reaper into another Syndicate especially after what happened to the Lycan," I protested with an exhausted sigh.

Appearing in front of me, the depth of his black shadows blocking out the backdrop of the moonlight. Making his red eyes gleam with much more burning red passion and some other emotion I had not seen in almost two hundred years; concern. Before I could speak, my engraved tattoo ravaged a burning sensation throughout the entirety of my arm. Our eyes were locked in a stalemate. "Get it figured out soon, Valkyrie, or else you, I, and even her will all meet our end."

Acknowledging the order, I nodded my head in agreement as I awaited the painful attack on my nerves to subside. "I understand and will get on it as fast as possible." I complied.

"Good." He hissed, flashing me one of those paralyzing smirks of his and fading back into the dark abyss of the nightscape.

"Great." I once more complained. Turning around to return my attention to heading off to bed, I wondered aloud while my hand reached for the matching rustic doorknob, "Now how the fuck am I going to get someone as crafty as Saylene to accept a Syndicate fugitive? This is just fucking great-"

"What is honey?" I heard someone else's voice speak from behind me.

"FUCK ME!" I growled, immediately recognizing the voice. Turning around to face yet another trespasser on my property, I resumed "Why me! Why is it always me!"

'She said that the target should be around here." My ears caught on to an unusual voice muffle inside the house. The depth and masculinity of the voice forced my subconscious instinct to remain inquisitive. As the long-cropped cartilage filled with more voices, I felt the nerve spasm and my ear twitch. Rising my head up off the plush throw blanket, I brought rolled over onto my stomach and awaited the voice of my babysitter, whom I was hoping was still somewhere inside, but other unrecognized voices spoke in its place.

"This is a two-story mansion-"

"Split up. Beta, check the first floor, while Alpha, survey the second floor. The target has to be in the house."

"Shit!" I cursed, forcing myself to stand up. "Where are you stupid Valkyrie?!" Examining the door to my room, I noticed it was ajar in the same way where Augustus had peeked. A position too close to the entryway that it would stop me from being able to use my paw or muzzle to slip out of the room. "I would have to change forms to slip by, but I can't risk any visual evidence-" I attempted to strategize but halted mid-way through once my ears twitched to the loud echo of more undesired noise. "Shit!" I again profaned, realizing the humans were coming closer to my room."

Panic rising, I jumped down off the bed and began to hastily scan around my room for a place to hide. Of course, thanks to my tedious habits and Augustus's horrible rules on décor, I had nothing in my room but the large bed to hide under, and of course, with my large canine form I couldn't fit underneath the box spring let alone slip past the lip of the bed's side rails. Hearing the heavy footsteps creep closer, I took my chances with the most obvious place. Darting around to the other side of the bed that was hidden from the door's face, I proceeded with crouching down on the dark-brown and white geometric pattern rug and ordered myself to center my panicked breathing.

Counting the footsteps, I counted at least three men who were ascending the spiral staircase. "It's hard to tell how many men each team contains, however, 'three' in this confined space will be hard to fight especially when I am stuck in this limited form. Damn it!" I stopped when I saw the glow of their flashlight stop at the door.

"That flashlight's going to give away our location!" I now heard one voice cry.

"Don't' you think I know that!" I silently agreed, allowing my deep canine growl to slip out of my throat, thus giving away my location.

"Target's in here!" a man excitedly spoke to his team in a loud whisper. Swinging the door open, I observed the light hastily fill the entire room. Knowing there was no more time to waste with thinking of a strategy, I reacted. Charging out of my stupid hiding spot, I dashed around the corner of the bed and jumped for the lead man's throat. My back legs with their strong muscles, easily allowing me to close in the space to my target from a far distance. In milliseconds my body encountered one of the men who were dressed in familiar black tactical gear, my fangs striking through what little exposed flesh he had. My tongue being drowned with the taste of the blood, I reluctantly craved. In the passing seconds, the first target dropped, his body following the laws of physics.

Locking sights on my second target, I released my hold on the injured man before swinging around for my second victim. Yet as I leaped, I watched this brute's arms come in front of his vital arteries, protecting his fate from my powerful jaws. Dancing around his arms, I continued to try to go in for my next kill, but each time my fangs were met with the unusual fabrics of the sleeves protecting his arms from breaking under my supernatural bite pressure. Focusing on his unusual mixed expression of calm calculations and fear-ridden anxiety, my neck felt a drastic pull against my vocal box. The blue choker I still wore was being used by design to remove me from this man's ally, but I held firm. Both my mind and fangs had locked on this target.

"Hold on Damian, they're looking for his phone to get the code!" I overheard the man behind me worriedly conveyed.

"WELL, HURRY UP!" the man beneath my hundred-pound body ordered. Frustrated, I morphed my fangs, coating them with the sharp blood scythes. Throwing my head forward, I finally felt the surge of blood once again fill the inside of my mouth. It wasn't my intended destination, but it was still a viable wound that was close to a major vein. "FUCK! DREW! DREW! DREW! JUST SHOOT HER! SHOOT HER!" Damian yelled to his partner as he was barely able to manage to keep his left arm from hitting his forehead.

"Theresa, what are you doing here?" I yawned.

"Well, I'm here to talk to you." The now dyed dull dishwater blonde teased, waving her hand through its long locks.

"About what?" I interrogated. "The fight we had or the fact I said I wasn't going with you on vacation because I had no one to watch Cinder?"

"I'm here to talk about why you chose to lie to me." The woman growled.

"Lied? Lied about what?" I mocked back.

"About?!" the woman argued. Finishing her statement before a trio of loud pops came from inside my house. "Looks like they found her."

Chapter 61

Augustus

Ignoring my model girlfriend, I rushed back inside the house. Entering the foyer, I overheard agonizing screams of an injured animal, sounds so bone-chilling it sent my heart free-falling into the bottom of my stomach. Forcing my legs to work once more, I charged upstairs as the agonizing cries began to turn into a much darker call. The familiar sound of snarls so savage it ran chills down my spine. Sensing the tattoo on my arm burn with extensive rage, I immediately stopped at the top of the stairs figuring out that the Unnatural had morphed herself into a darker form. However, after a few shouts from the shocked men, I heard a loud thud hit the hardwood floors. My heart hastily rose into my throat with such speed it made me want to vomit while I observed two more men wander into her bedroom.

"No!" I quietly murmured to myself, demanding my heavy feet to saunter closer towards the second bedroom. "Don't be dead! Don't be dead! Don't be dead!" I repeatedly prayed per step.

"Woah, sir you can't go inside!" one of the broad men wearing thick protective gear ordered me.

"Move aside," I ordered.

"Sorry, we can't let you in." he continued.

"MOVE THE FUCK ASIDE!" I snapped, throwing my fist into the man's face, making contact with his unguarded nose and easily breaking it. My victim fell to the ground, recoiling in pain, allowing me to catch a glimpse of the creature I was looking for. "Cinder?" I called out, observing all the blood that had splattered itself on the five-hundred-dollar rug. Stepping around the injured man, I observed the Hellhound's chest speedily rising and falling as she fought with every inch of her conscious to get up to her feet. Her paws too shaky from blood loss and shock to grasp onto the blood-soaked fabrics. "Cinder." I again called, now passing the threshold of the door. Continuing to observe the condition of her body, I noticed that my intuition had been right, that she had transformed into that form. The Hellhound was wearing the white wolf skull, and her back was protected by the long-curved spikes that accentuated her spine. Inching ever closer to the Hellhound, who was finally making her way into an upright position, I witnessed her body tense up before yet again collapsing. "CINDER!" I shouted, now rushing closer to her side.

"Stop him!" a man ordered.

My arms were quickly locked behind my back, and before I knew it, my body came to a complete halt. I knew I could expose my secret; however, I couldn't risk the same consequence. So, I had to unfortunately stay human. Furious, I angrily demanded, "GET THE FUCK OFF ME!" Struggling to get free I watched one of the free-handed men begin to wrap white zip ties around the Hellhound's legs, tying her wrists and ankles together. "WHAT THE FUCK ARE YOU GUYS DOING TO HER?!" I again shouted out to the men, finally realizing that they were Hunters! Hired Hunters!

"Don't worry, your precious pooch is fine." Theresa's voice spoke up over my loud shouting, her fake-model body coming out of the now dimly lit hallway.

"IT WAS YOU!" I snarled, struggling to get out of the hunter's immense lock they had on my arms. "YOU HIRED THESE ASS-HOLES?!"

"Yes, I did." The woman answered, striding past me and closer towards the bleeding and unconscious Unnatural. "How many times did you shoot her?" She now questioned the man who was standing over Cinder.

"Three, and then we had to shock her twice before she finally lost consciousness." He obediently replied with an exhausted sigh before handing over an object that resembled the cellphone I had left on my bed.

Taking my phone, Theresa proceeded to ask, "Can you remove that?" pointing to the large wolf skull that had magically spawned on the Beauceron's square-shaped head when she had entered that form. Turning back to me, Theresa then inquired, "Augustus, can that be removed?"

Shaking my arms free from the Hunters, I darted for the sleep-ing Unnatural. Halting a foot away from her body when my eyes saw my crazy girlfriend's thumb inches from touching the screen of my smartphone. "What the fuck do you think you are doing?" I growled.

"Do NOT think that for a moment that I am afraid of shocking her until her heart stops!"

"You!" I stuttered, tightly clenching my fists together until my knuckles turned a bright shade of white.

"We will discuss this on the way to my dad's house, honey, until then, let these men finish the job which I had hired them for." The-resa coldly told, keeping her thumb still too close to the stun button on the shock collar's app. "Now answer my question, can the skull be removed?"

Finally shutting up when the sound of low whimpers could be heard filling the tense room. The thankful noise that 'she' had yet to stop living. Watching the black holes of that skull's eyes fill with the dark blood-red hue, I observed Cinder attempt to fight back to her feet once more. The zip ties only tightening their hold on her legs, their plastic material ripping into her swollen skin. "Cinder?" I quietly called to the Hellhound as I was cautiously creeping closer.

"Augustus, think of what you are about to do!" Theresa snarled back.

Ignoring the petite woman, I was now figuring out to be truly crazy, I sternly ordered the Hunters. "In the left end table that's in my room is a mixed sedative. One of you go, get it now."

"What are you doing?"

"Just shut the fuck up!" I snapped, quickly calming my voice I proceeded to coldly speak, "Shocking her again will only kill her, and I cannot have her dying on me." Kneeling in front of the Hellhound, I slowly grabbed at the Lycan skull and begun to remove it. Exposing the box-shaped head to the artificial light. Cinder snarled, exposing all of her blood-covered teeth and gums from her successful attacks in an attempt to warn, but I remained unphased. "Shhh, it's alright Cinder, I know these Hunters here hurt you, but it's okay. Everything is going to be okay." I soothed, holding her large head in my hands and petting the top of her temple. Working my way up towards her chipped ear where I could begin easing the enraged creature. "I don't know why they are here nor what is going to happen, but I will get it figured out, alright?"

"Augustus?" Cinder quietly panted the red hue fading from her eyes, the soft sincerity in her voice making my hurt heart skip a beat.

"Here's the sedative."

Not even giving my gratitude, I slowly put my free hand behind my back and accepted the syringe. Patiently bringing the needle around to inject it in the major artery that ran in the canine's shifted neck, I resumed, "It's alright. Everything will be alright." Steadily injecting the drug cocktail into her bloodstream, I carefully continued to soothe the woman who was closing in on losing control over her sanity. Understanding solely from experience, not even bleeding out would stop her from murdering everyone and everything in her path. Once she had become truly unconscious, I looked back up at the woman I had been calling my girlfriend for these past few years and gave her one of the coldest glares I could. Returning my focus to the Hellhound whose head had dozed off into my lap, I broke the eerie silence and declared orders. "Now, your Hunters will have six hours to finish transporting her before that wears off."

"Augustus, leave them to their job." Theresa defied.

Knowing she had the power to still give Cinder almost seven-hundred volts of electricity in a single shock, I hastily snarled back, "Shove it, Theresa! As you said, we can discuss what the fuck you did when we are on our way to your dad's place, but until then, I will not leave her side."

"Ugh! Fine!" The woman gave in, storming out of the room.

Now free to overlook the wounds Cinder had suffered by the Hunters without being persecuted by that bitch, I began to medically survey every inch of her body. Under the bright warm light of the room's hanging lights, I saw that bullet holes were piercing the strong muscles. One was in her left hind leg, and the other was in her upper shoulder. She had been shot by two hunters, one off to the side of her and one directly in front of her, whose aim was thank-fully off. The amount of blood oozing out of these wounds were so severe that it had left a red stain on her soot-black fur, a noticeable stain.

"Sir, we need to muzzle her. Precaution." One of the hunters softly spoke up, breaking the silence.

Lifting the canine's head, I held it steady while the man rolled what appeared to be a nylon lead over her muzzle before wrapping the leash around the back of her skull and slipping the lead through the leash's handle. Tightening the strap so it could remain firm around that unusual shape, it left about eighteen inches of the material and the metal clasp to be used for who knows what means.

"Alright, she's all set to be taken down to the truck." The man whom I assumed was the leader of the small group of six, or should I say four people spoke.

Two men came up beside the sleeping animal to pick her up for transport, which I reluctantly allowed. The shock in my body made my muscles too exhausted to pick up the large canine. Returning my focus to the leader who followed his men out of the room, I asked, "Do you have any I.V.s set up for the trip?"

"Yes, we have I.V. drips all set up. Our employer expected the target to be a fighter and didn't want any significant harm to befall it either."

"Significant harm? And you wouldn't call shooting her full of bullets significant harm."

"We had little choice."

"If she had threatened me first, before allowing you guys to break into my house, I could have dealt with Cinder without having you guys spook her."

"We were just following her orders."

"Right." I countered, rolling my eyes as we finally approached the three-vehicle caravan. A truck, an SUV, and Theresa's fancy red Mustang had miraculously showed up in my driveway. Unfolding the tailgate to the truck, I watched the men slip my Cinder into what looked like a titanium crate large enough to fit three dogs of her size inside. "That's what you are transporting her in?" I asked surprised, as my eyes watched the straw they had filled the bottom with turn a bright red under the shining light of the bright moon, alerting me to the fact that she had another grievous wound which had remained hidden from my trained vision.

"Yes, it's one of the best carriers to transport a shapeshifter, Institutions all over the country are using them now for transport. The bars are thick enough to stop even the strongest of Unnaturals from breaking them. And the locking mechanism on it is efficient enough to keep even the most talented lockpicks and codebreakers out." Theresa answered, coming up from behind me while the lead Hunter put in a keycode to the numb pad before locking it with his thumbprint. When the man had turned to acknowledge the insane woman, Theresa exhaustedly spoke "Now that that is all done, how about we start heading out."

Rolling my eyes are her, I returned with a snarl of my own, "Let me go lock up the house and grab some clean fucking clothes first." Holding both my anger and the harsh words I wish I could say down, I ventured back towards the Spanish manor I had bought less than ninety days ago.

Chapter 62
Cinder/Augustus

Feeling my senses return, I swung my eyelids open, instantly re-living the last memory I had. The one where I was attacked by Hunters. Attacked by Hunters in my own home! With my eyes adjusting to the bright light of the sun that bore its warm rays down on me, I surveyed my new surroundings. Or should I say surroundings I had become too familiar with? Back behind bars. Caged. The painted white bars while new to me still felt no different than the bars I was behind at the Pits, nor the bars I was behind at the Lycan's Syndicate, nor the chain-link I was behind at the Institution in Colorado. "It was all the same." I depressingly moaned.

Forcing my drained body to move around in the large crate, I instinctively came to a stop when something cut into my wrists. The humans had tied my feet together. Irritated, I huffed another complaint before just allowing my body to continue to lie on its side, further allowing the sharp edges of the hay to stab itself into the side of my body that was hidden away from the humid rays of the mocking summer sun.

Glancing up at the passing scenery, I saw that there were many passing vehicles and the outstretch familiarity of the long highways. Moments later, the heavy sound of traffic faded away and the serene sound of the rural landscape took its place. Observing the array of beautiful trees hang their amassed branches overhead, I couldn't help but wonder where these people were taking me. "Was it another Institute?" With the flash of the bright sun coming in and out of the tree's shadow, I unwillingly recalled the memory of Augustus's last words to me, remembering that it was Theresa who had hired the team of Hunters and not some random group of cruel doctors and scientists. "No, if she is involved, I doubt he would let them take me to another place like that, but then again, that asshole did drop me off at the Pits for five months." Further recalling the statements and promises the hidden Archangel had made to me, I once more recalled, "No, he seemed too shocked for it to be another one of his acts, and considering that he is a horrible liar, I doubt this is another one of those things." Opening my jowls to the limit the nylon loop wrapped around my muzzle would allow, I took a long exhale, "So where is it they are taking me? I guess I will just have to wait and see."

It felt like forever before the truck that was transporting me had finally come to a complete halt. Thankful to be under a collection of soothing willow trees, I awaited the arrival of undesired humans. Preparing myself for the mental and physical torture that was going to unfold, I suddenly fell ill. My body felt like it was overheating, sweating profusely. Beginning to pant uncontrollably, I watched my vision blur, my tear ducts filling up the tears only accompanied by extreme pain.

Watching through the blurred vision, I observed the black tailgate lower, returning to its flat position. Still panting, I counted the enemies who were present before me, eight in total. Locking my sights on a familiar broad-shouldered, blonde-haired silhouette I cried out for help, however just as I allowed the whimper to slip out, my throat burned and before I knew it, I vomited. "Shit!" I cried as another slip of burning stomach acid filled my canine formed mouth and my lips rose in a snarl to allow for easier regurgitation.

As Theresa's car drove finally to a stop, I watched the group of hunters surround the cage in the bed of the truck, surrounding the Hellhound who by now should be waking up from the cocktail sedative. Hastily exiting the passenger side of the vehicle, I ran up to the truck. Something felt off. Something deep down in my gut was putting up major red flags about this scenario.

"Augustus, where are you going?!" the crazy nuthouse I refused to listen to on the seven-and-a-half-hour journey to her father's house out in the rural suburbs of Savannah, Georgia demand.

Continuing to ignore her mad calls, I finally reached Cinder's side, questioning the humans what was going on. Before they could answer me, my eyes were already surveying the scene. "Oh, Cinder." I expressed, watching the canine-transformed woman continue to vomit liters of blood and stomach acid out of her mouth. The brownish-red color verifying my fears. Watching her lips curl so high it highlighted her white gums, I proceeded to observe her lower jaw spread open until the lead stopped it, seconds before another round of aspiration. "Hold on." I hurriedly sighed, bringing my hands up to remove the leash from around her muzzle, the lead easily slipping off the bridge of her nose. Rubbing my hand through the short-fine hairs on the side of her cheek and up towards the same chipped ear, I continued to soothe the Beauceron. Her blue eyes were full of so much fear and concern for life, I couldn't help but feel truly horrible about the situation. "It's alright." Returning my attention to the hunters, I took the lead of the scenario while my mind called through all the medical knowledge of the Hellhound form, I had learned over the last two hundred years. "She's begun to aspirate, and her body is becoming so dehydrated that if we don't get her some medical attention now, she will die soon." Pausing for a moment, I now coldly threatened, "And if she dies, you will face my wrath." while an unusually bitter gale burst through the weeping willow trees surrounding the large circular pebble stone driveway. I had mistakenly allowed my powers to slip, however with-it being elementally related I guess the stupid humans did not realize who created the quick forty-five-mile gust.

"I wouldn't go threatening anyone anytime soon, honey." The model with a silver spoon recoiled, coming into my line of sight, her buttery fingers still holding tightly onto my cellphone. "Remember, I am the one who holds the power over that bitch's life."

Stepping out of the target range of Cinder's projectile vomit, I also allowed Theresa to see at first hand the painful suffering my girl was going through. Watching the dyed-box blondie attempt to hold back her own vomit, I passive-aggressively submitted to her threat. Although I did thoroughly enjoy her seeing reaction, I needed to remain calm and find a plan that would successfully free Cinder from this torture. Glancing back at the heavily panting animal, I returned to her side and began to take the creature out of the titanium-steel crate. Her open wounds still oozing mass amounts of blood on to the straw as I slid her death-ridden body out. "Where is the doc here?" I asked aloud to the open world.

"Oh my." I now overheard a shocked voice exclaim. Looking away from Cinder's groggy head, I saw standing before me were Theresa's parents. Recognizing the voice to that of her brunet-haired mother, I once more listened to the woman exclaim in a heavy southern accent, "Our on-call vet is here giving check-ups to the others. She can help treat that one. She's out back, Matty can show you."

Giving my thanks, I raced after the young teen who was speed walking around to the back of the property. Observing the characteristics of the young woman, I noticed the family trait of dark-brown hair. Except unlike this one's mother and sister, the teenager had a short almost tomboyish haircut, and while, yes wore today's fashion statement, she seemed to be more like her father than her sisters. "You're him, aren't you?" the girl with a raspy voice and a soft feminine tone inquired.

"You mean, your sister's boyfriend? I don't know how to say it?" I answered, readjusting my hold of the hundred pound and barely conscious canine while avoiding the Hellhound's large bone spikes that had yet to shrink back into her spine. "After today's events, I wouldn't call us intimate."

"Good." Matty coldly quoted. Then before I could respond, the assuming thirteen-year-old girl had stopped at the side entrance of what appeared to be a heavily landscaped and enclosed courtyard. "Dr. Lillian, we got an emergency."

Chapter 63

Augustus

"Put her on the table." The vet swiftly ordered as she paced around the small yet very modern room that had been refurbished into a small treatment center. Hastily obeying, I gently put the Hellhound on the cold metal table before I rushed to the sink to begin to wash the fresh blood off my hands and arms. "Why do you idiots always use such harsh treatments with these innocent creatures?!" Dr. Lillian yelled at me as she took some plyers out to cut the zip ties wrapped around Cinder's legs.

"Doctor, you're blaming the wrong person," Matty spoke up in my defense. "This idiot here was the one dating my sister. It was her and the Hunters who did all that to it."

"Forgive me."

"No. No apologies needed. Just save her." I sighed, watching the woman wearing a white lab coat with what appeared to be a traditional plaid button-up shirt and faded work jeans under, complete her work. Evaluating Cinder's condition, the vet hastily worked through checking all the bullet holes that had been pierced into her skin.

"She isn't a miracle worker, but I have seen her treat some of our more severe cases of abuse and neglect, so I wouldn't worry too much." The young woman now spoke up in defense of the Doctor's reputation.

"There were other cases?" I remarked.

"Yes, Doctor Lillian successfully treated every single Unnatural we have on the grounds."

The statement shocked me, sent uncontrollable rage through my body. Trying to hold it all deep down for Cinder's sake, I bit my tongue.

"Judging by your expression, I doubt my stupid sister told you that we own twenty-two Unnaturals."

"Twenty-two?" I angrily questioned.

"Don't be too dramatic, all of the Unnaturals living here are here by choice or are here because of their inability to live independently," Matty explained with a roll of her unusual green eyes.

Managing to calm down, I wondered, "It's because of the Unnatural Citizen Act that you are caring for them?"

"That law was only recently put into effect, some of the Unnaturals here on the grounds came to us fleeing Institutions, or Syndicates, or..." The teen sighed. "Or were brought to us by Hunters too soft to send them back to their employers."

"And you have been treating all of them?" I proceeded to ask the vet. "And how is it that you have been treating them when they are Unnaturals?"

"Dumbass." Matty chuckled.

"Matilda," Dr. Lillian scolded. "What did I tell you about cursing in my office?" Watching the woman set up for what appeared to be the most obvious treatment to save my girl, I continued to listen to her highly educated voice ramble, "I have been able to treat them because just like this one, they are all of the Shapeshift Class. Or to be more precise, they cannot change at all to their humanoid form, however, sir-."

"It's Augustus, Augustus Gale," I interjected.

"Mr. Gale, do you know if they gave her any drugs besides the I.V.?"

"I gave her a sedative cocktail," I answered. "It contains a downer, a painkiller, and a little bit of sodium besides the sedative."

"How were you able to mix so many medications?"

"Why did you give it to her?" the teenager hastily interrupted the vet, her expectations of the current situation evolving. "I thought you were the caretaker?"

"I am, I had created the cocktail in case she had lost control."

"Control? As in like primary control?" Dr. Lillian answered.

"Yes." I simply answered back. "Once in a while, she loses control over blood lust, and for safety, I created that. It keeps her sane while also limiting her powers and treating the pain those limiters put on her."

"I see."

"It wore off along the way here, as its max duration is six hours."

"So, she will need another anesthetic before I begin."

"Cinder?" I murmured, coming away from the counter I had been leaning on for the duration of the conversation. The Hellhound was now fighting her way back to the world, using her regaining strength, she slowly began to stand back up on her feet. However, before the legs could lock-in, they gave way. Rushing to her side, I eased the fall and returned to soothing the confused animal who was snarling at the two women she did not recognize. "Cinder, it's alright, they're just trying to help."

A savage snarl sounded for a quick second but hastily changed to a pain-filled yelp, a cry of acknowledgment and submission. Crawling closer to the edge of the table, Cinder pushed her head into my stomach.

Petting the Unnatural's head, I soundlessly soothed her while vocalizing to the Doctor, "Yes, she will need another sedative. As well as a downer, if you have one."

'We don't have any downers?"

"Saltwater will work," I answered. "About fifteen CCs should hold over till the end of the surgery."

"Okay, I'll start making it now."

Cinder whined her refusal, but I remained firm. "It needs to be done. You know just as I that your blood is toxic to living organisms outside of their host." Again, another refusal but this time it was thankfully short-lived. Taking a sigh of relief to avoid an argument, I proceeded with introducing the two humans to the surprisingly barely breathing and conscious Hellhound. "That girl by the door goes by Matilda, Matty for short. And the Vet who will be removing the bullets you were shot with is called Dr. Lillian..."

"You know she won't remember this when she wakes up, right?" Matty mocked.

"You don't know her well enough." I jabbed back. "She has a much better memory than I." Continuing to soothe the Hellhound, I attempted to distract Cinder from watching a long three-inch needle stabbing a major vein in the canine's front leg, but those blue eyes were locked on their target. Her body spasmed instinctively, in an attempt to foolishly escape. Keeping my arms locked around her head, I held it firm for the few seconds it took to inject the anesthetic, as well as the saltwater concoction.

"In about three minutes she will be asleep, and I can finish getting her set up for what I am expecting to be a long surgery."

Chapter 64

Augustus

"I'm surprised by their level of content," I declared, putting my hand through the strong iron bars and running my fingers through the white fur of an extremely rare Kitsune fox. Examining the Victorian style 'exhibit', I noticed that its corners were professionally landscaped with gorgeous ivy and bright yellow roses.

"As I said prior, most of these Unnaturals are here by choice. Some of them were brought here against their will, such as that, what is she a Hellhound?" Matilda returned, slipping to be what appeared to be pieces of bacon through the bars. The white five-tailed fox vigorously yet gently taking each piece.

"Yeah, Cinder is a Hellhound," I clarified, removing my hand.

"Well just like her, Myst was brought here against his will, but in time he learned that this was better than his previous life and stopped fighting."

"Well, I don't how well Cinder will take to that."

"So, you weren't sending her to us?" Matty asked, wiping her hands on her skinny jeans free of the heavy grease.

"No, Theresa went behind my back." I snarled, following the calm teenager around the courtyard full of other exotic shapeshift Unnaturals.

"That's my sister for you." She chuckled. "Don't trust anything she tells you."

"I can see that." I also laughed back. "But I did not give Cinder up, so she could live her life stuck behind more bars even if it is a place as peaceful as this."

"I see. Well, even if you didn't intend to give up the custody of your Unnatural, the two of you are still here." Matty truthfully exclaimed as she slipped more slabs of bacon to what I presumed were a pair of Serval Catamancers. With no comeback to her cold examination, she made another light chuckle, "Cat got your tongue, huh? I can tell you though, while she stays here, she will receive the same care and spoils that the rest of them do. You'll just have to pay my father back for the boarding fees."

"Boarding fees?!" I laughed, catching onto the sarcasm in her tone. "Judging by your parents, I doubt they will allow me to maintain custody over her especially when Georgia has no Unnatural Citizen Law."

"True, but knowing him a simple conversation will easily do the trick. Dad always fixes my stupid sister's problems. He even pays for her three condos, all her travel expenses, and horrible spending habits." Matty tattled, the tone of her voice changing. Going from enjoyment to pure jealousy.

Attempting to change the subject, I kept the idea of having a private conversation with the owner of this massive Southern Colonial Mansion hidden. "So where will Cinder be held? I asked.

"I'm surprised you didn't ask to keep your beloved mutt indoors."

"Indoors?" I questioned, avoiding the same sense of returning cold sarcasm.

"We have only a few that live inside the Mansion, but they are how to put it." She paused, putting her thumbnail in her mouth and flicking it against her front teeth. "Have you heard of Unnaturals born with no human identity?"

"I have. They're animals born with the same supernatural gene making them creatures with strong powers and DNA similar to Unnaturals." I responded. "I have opened reservoirs and sanctuaries to specifically ensure they live the rest of their lives happily."

"Yes, we have sixteen in total. Fourteen of them are equines, but the two in the house are small breed dogs. The only reason we have them not caged up is that, well society-"

"Society views them as unique designer breeds, and not 'monsters'." I interrupted with a sorrowful explanation.

Matty simply nodded in agreement before stopping at what appeared to be a set of paved stairs leading up to an open gate. "The kennel in the center of the courtyard is assigned to her." Looking up at the Victorian themed atrium/gazebo styled cage, I observed the familiar décor and landscaping. Ivy flowering white roses wrapped around the rounded corners. The cage was lifted about eighteen inches off of the floor, and the foundation was marked with matching pave stones resembling broken red bricks. "The floor was compacted with three inches of concrete, then filled the rest of the way with some of the freshest dirt and fertilizer before crabgrass, young aspen trees, and edible flowers were finally planted. Then once they grow to our desired premise, we put in the last missing part."

"The Unnatural," I answered, my eyes examining the length of two tall aspen trees that were planted inside the assigned atrium. Their branches growing either through or around the small spaces between the rod-iron roof. They were giving off enough sunlight but also protected shade that it made me wonder, "She would've enjoyed this more if it wasn't a cage."

"Theresa told us that 'Cinder' enjoyed being outdoors."

"She does." I smiled, feeling the warm sunlight once more brush against my face. "Cinder would enjoy a place like this much more if it wasn't for how she got here, or that it was still a cage."

"Well, we will soon figure out how well she likes it," Matty said just as her parents walked into the courtyard.

"So, I see, Matilda gave you the full tour of our beautiful courtyard." The fifty-year-old man exclaimed, his salt-and-pepper streaked dirty-blonde hair surviving well in the small breeze working its way around the amass three-faced room.

"Yes, she was just telling me that this was where you guys had planned to hold Cinder," I answered, shaking the man's hand in acknowledgment.

"Oh yes, this was the only one we thought would befit her after Theresa told us about her behaviorisms." Doing my best to hold my anger back, I just nodded my head. "I'm surprised she didn't tell me about your Unnatural sooner-"

"Yes, my Unnatural." I sighed.

"I'm sorry, I didn't mean to-" The surprisingly considerate man apologized. "I just thought that this was a way to help thank you after my daughter had informed me about how well you have not only been treating her but how hard you have fought to change the way Society is treating Unnaturals."

I remained silent as I tried to think of a way to explain my reason for acting out, but before I could even speak up, Theresa's younger sister spoke. "He's just mad at Theresa for hiring those men and hurting Cinder. He's also afraid of losing custody over her."

"Mr. Gale, is that true?" Theresa's mother spoke up her voice sounding extremely harsh.

No longer hesitating, I answered, "Yes, I mean I'm glad that you are willing to go so far to give not only Cinder but all these Unnaturals such a happy and fulfilled life even if it is behind bars; yet it doesn't waiver the fact I am infuriated with Theresa. I know she's your daughter and all, but..." I paused when I watched flaunting out of the shadows of the covered patio surrounding the courtyard was Theresa herself. "I would prefer to discuss this with you in private later, Mr. Englishmen.

"Yes, that is fine with me." The patriarch of the house gratefully agreed. "So how is the young Hellhound doing?"

"She's still in surgery," Matty answered. "Dr. Lillian said that it was going to a few hours yet."

"Augustus, I am so sorry for those men shooting Cinder." Theresa now apologized, her voice rising to such a high-pitched tone it only further enraged my already short fuse. "I wasn't expecting them to do that, honestly I wasn't..."

"Whatever." I sighed, deciding to not start an argument with her in front of her parents. I had to at least hold some decency while I stayed at their home, even though I was obscuring the fact that she was holding Cinder's life hostage for my affection away from her parents.

"You know that is a crock of bullshit, Theresa!" Matty cursed. "Everyone knows that when you hire Hunters, they shoot first and ask questions later! I swear you are the stupidest bitch I know!"

"Matilda, language!" Mrs. Englishmen scolded.

Chapter 65

Augustus

"Oh, there you are Mr. Gale."

"Dr. Lillian," I called back to the vet who had strolled into the living room where I was playing the PlayStation with the younger sister Matilda to distract my worry-ridden mind. And to of no surprise, she was kicking my ass in Counter-Strike. Putting our face off on pause, I once more devoted my anxiety back to the only subject that mattered right now, Cinder's health. "How is she?"

"Still in critical condition, however, I do think she is out of immediate danger." Taking a fresh breath of relief, I gave my deepest thanks to the Vet who had successfully treated a nearly deceased Hellhound. "It was a tough surgery, but Cinder pulled through."

"You act as if you weren't expecting her to make it?" Matty questioned.

"To tell you the truth, I wasn't, Cinder was severely anemic and dehydrated. Besides being shot in her hind leg, and her front leg, the bullet that had been shot into her chest cavity caused one of her lungs to collapse. I was barely able to remove that one but I managed to, and for some reason, once they were removed the lung healed."

"It's not surprising." I smiled. "It's because of that Blood Trait she has. It amplifies her healing powers so much so that even with sodium in her veins, it still heals at ratio speeds about five times faster than the average human." I explained to them. The shocked expression on the Vet's face making me even prouder of Cinder's mysterious yet rational pull through. "But even with that amazing ability, it will still take at least a few days of fluids and transfusions before she regains consciousness." I exhaled, remembering the truth and extent of her genetic limits.

"I see. Well, that makes it less shocking." Doctor Lillian digested. "So, do you want to see her?"

"More than you-."

"Honey it's late, why not see her first thing tomorrow?" Theresa interrupted, inviting herself into the conversation while she attempted to play sexy in an almost completely see-through negligée to turn my attention onto her rather than the still very ill Unnatural, I noticed she still had that annoying Shock Collar app open. However, this time it was on her phone. This was not surprising, considering she had returned my phone earlier in the day after completely erasing the app and its saved data on Cinder's collar, of course, the blabbermouth had transferred the data to her cell-phone. Knowing that I still had my hands tied behind my back, I painfully submitted to her passive order.

"Don't worry Augustus, I'll check in on her before I head off to bed," Matilda interjected as she kept adding more kill shots to her score.

"Thank you, Matty." I painfully submitted, depressingly following the crazy woman to her room where I would play her game for now, even though every ounce of me made me want to vomit in disgust.

Once alone, I heard Theresa murmur, "Now remember, just comply and your precious mongrel will live out a happy life here for the rest of her days."

When morning finally came back around, I hastily cleaned myself up before wakening the crazy woman, whom I had regretfully fornicated with. Every single fiber in my body felt filthy, and no matter how much soap or steaming hot water I used, the feeling wouldn't leave. After my shower, I dressed with one of the hurriedly packed outfits in my suitcase and rushed through the hallway eager to check in on Cinder. Of course, though I was stopped by Theresa's parents before I could make it out the door.

"Mr. Gale, why don't you join us?" Mrs. Englishmen asked as he was just finishing up his breakfast, the voice of the matriarch reminding me of the eldest offspring. Sending horrible chills down my spine.

Accepting the invitation, I sat down beside Matilda, who looked barely awake but was dressed for what I could only assume was a boring day at school. Receiving a full plate from one of the hired cooks, I thanked them and began to swiftly devour the Belgian waffles with an appropriate side of scrambled eggs and sausage links. The meal coldly reminding me of all the breakfasts I had cooked for Cinder in the recent three months.

"Hungry, aren't you?" Matty snickered.

Nodding my head, I grabbed for the recently filled cup of coffee and sipped away. The hot beverage helping me swallow the bland comfort food.

"I'm surprised you are up so early." Mr. Englishmen expressed, trying to break the silence at the little four-seated breakfast nook.

"I guess you could say I'm a recently acquainted morning person." I sighed, swallowing another large sip of the smooth coffee I had sweetened with a dash of cream.

"Oh, from taking care of that 'Unnatural'?" the wife spoke up.

"Yeah. Cinder is used to a specific schedule, and I had to adapt to it so I could sufficiently take care of her." I explained, attempting to ignore the tease. "I still sleep in from time to time though. Even though most of the time I'm up a few hours earlier than this."

"Talking of her, Matty and I were going to stop by and see how she was doing after surgery." Mr. Englishmen spoke, trying to lighten the tension felt between his wife and me. "Would you care to join us?"

"Yes, I would also like to see how she is holding up." I responded while thinking to myself, "I was already planning on it the minute I finished eating."

"Courtney dear, care to join us?"

"No, I will see that monster once she gets moved into the exhibit." The woman snarled while she collected the empty plates. Mumbling under her breath, "That bitch deserves to be locked behind bars anyways."

"Bitch?" I questioned, stopping when I felt a hard pinch to my forearm. "Ow."

"Just ignore mom. She tends to think that way of all Unnaturals, besides her precious beasts." Matty quietly refined.

Arriving at the small shed that had been remodeled into a vet office, I was immediately greeted by a surprise. She was awake! I couldn't believe it. She was awake! I couldn't believe that my Cinder was once more conscious.

343

Chapter 66
Cinder/Augustus

"Alright, hold on." The woman wearing the ugly white lab coat told me as she began to inject a hazy but clear liquid into my front leg. I wanted to pull away with all my might, but it was taking everything I had, just to keep my head up let alone remain conscious. "There we go, it should take effect soon."

"Mmhmm." I sighed. "You all say the same thing." Allowing the woman to stroke the top of my head, I began to recall all the events that had happened who knows how long ago. Hunters had invaded my 'home'! Hunters that were hired by her! They had shot me and shocked me! And had almost killed me! All the memories came flooding back while I lied my head back down on the cold metal table.

"Oh, hey you guys." I heard the Doctor call out to presences that I was too tired to even worry about sensing.

"How is our new guest doing?" an older middle-aged man's voice asked.

"Fine, she just regained consciousness and is surprisingly quite calm right now."

"Calm?" I mocked. "Right. I'm too exhausted right now to care." Of course, though, with being trapped in this form and on so many familiar downers the humans couldn't understand a single word I articulated. However, it seemed to me that they knew I was an Un-natural and not some crazy large dog.

"That's good news. So, when do you expect her to be ready to be moved?" the man then questioned.

"Maybe in a few hours."

"Moved?" I wondered, folding my ears back at the many other memories that came flooding back to me of others who had asked the same questions. My mind quickly shot back to reality when a tall jean wearing figure came into my view. Glancing upward to see whom it was now standing in front of my limp body, I slowly recognized that it was none other than 'him'. The man who was supposed to be babysitting me and not letting this type of shit happen to me! The Archangel.

"I'm so happy that she pulled through-"

"Shut your trap!" I grumbled just as I could no longer keep my eyelids open.

"Cinder?" I asked, watching the blue eyes fade under the heavy black eyelids. Smiling once I heard her produce a heavy exhale, I relaxed my nerves.

"I gave her some painkillers about an hour ago, and just finished giving her another 'downer'." Dr. Lillian told the room.

Clenching my fists, I tried to hold back my anger. "There was no reason for her to get hurt," I repeated before raising my voice and angrily stating. "There was no reason why your daughter couldn't have let me deal with Cinder!"

"Mr. Gale?" Mr. Englishmen softly asked, the sorrow in his voice telling me that he at least agreed with me on that.

"If Theresa had told me her plan, I could've had Cinder set for transportation without a single injury happening to either party." I resumed, now relaxing my fists and rubbing my hand over the Beauceron's smooth black fur. Feeling her skull also push against my recently tanned skin, I felt my anger wash away because although she was once again listless, the Hellhound was happy to have me by her side.

"I don't understand why she did it either but knowing my stupid sister, all she ever cares about is herself, and Unnaturals let alone other people hold second place to her." Matilda snarled, carefully pacing up closer to the sleeping Hellhound. "Although I have to admit, now that I am seeing one up close, I am completely overwhelmed by her sheer size."

"Yeah, she's about a hundred pounds, maybe one hundred and twenty pounds at the most." I guessed. "Feel free to pet her. Take advantage of her being asleep because if she figures out your related to Theresa, she just may hold a grudge against you."

"Well, I'll just have to bribe her to like me then." The cheerful Matty snickered, slowly running her hand down Cinder's back, her fingers grazing over the missing bone spikes. "Hey, didn't she have these white spikes protruding from her back?"

"They most likely retracted not too long after she regained consciousness," I answered. "They only come out in times where she feels that she's in grave danger. They act as a shield, so they can protect her spine and vital nerves while also serving as powerful weapons."

"Cool!"

"Scary." I quietly cringed at the human teenager's thrill over the Hellhound's unnatural adaptations. Shaking loose the thought, I now voiced, "I believe that we should move her before she wakes up. Cinder hates being put in cages, even one like that."

"Okay, we can do that." Mr. Englishmen said. "Anything else you should tell me about her?"

"Cinder will need to remain on the downers and light sedatives in the least." I answered before mumbling beneath my breath, "Until, I can get this fucking problem solved." Speaking back up, I continued, "She may like the 'exhibit', but Cinder has a rough past with 'cages' so keeping her drugged will help keep her contained in case she ends up having a flashback."

"What about the sho-" Dr. Lillian went to inquire before getting interrupted by her employer.

"You can finish telling me about them once I get back from taking Matty to school, okay Mr. Gale?"

"Yeah, that's fine." I returned, still petting the sleeping hellhound whose head had slumped over the edge of the metal examination table.

Immediately after the father and daughter had left, the Vet once more asked, "What about that Shock Collar that she was wearing when she arrived here?"

"I knew I should've taken it off her when I regained custody over her." I regretfully sighed.

"When you regained custody?"

"Yeah, I had no one to watch her while I had to attend some important meetings and I couldn't rely on Theresa when she was overseas, so with no one left to watch her, I regretfully loaned her to a friend of mine who let's just say does a familiar thing to what Mr. Englishmen does but a tad bit crueler."

"Crueler?"

"He holds and protects Unnaturals with high aggression and are unfit to belong to Syndicates or other Sanctuaries."

"He owns a Fighter's Ring?"

"Yes." I simply answered the cold question. Ignoring the harsh glare, I continued, "I hated putting her in a kennel next to screaming humans, and Unnaturals fighting for their enjoyment, but I didn't know there were other places like this." I continued to lightly lie.

"I see."

"And when I returned to reclaim her, I found that he had put that on her. My friend also told me that it had come in handy when she had lost control over her rational side."

"Lost control?"

"Cinder has a high Blood Lust that sometimes lets loose from time to time, and even I quickly caught on that the shock collar helps snap her back into place when other things like sedatives and downers could not."

"And you don't want it removed?"

"Preferably not, I know it should be, but it has held better benefits than I could even attempt to explain." I returned, deciding to keep the fact that if it was removed without being disarmed the collar would send electric shocks to not only the one wearing it but the one who was attempting to remove it. And with that bitch holding the code to remove it after changing the pin code to her cell phone, I had little to no choice but to fall into line or else risk losing not only my precious girl but my life and soul as well.

"Okay, anything else?"

"Besides the Blood Trait, her dislike for needles, cages, humans, and being told what to do, there isn't much else."

Chapter 67
Cinder

When I came around yet again, it took me a minute before my spinning world stopped and I noticed that I had been moved. As I lied on the side of my stomach, I saw that above me were the scenic surroundings of gorgeous white-barked tree branches covered in healthy green leaves, beautiful blue skies filled with seamless white clouds, and the familiar warm rays of the sun. However, as my still waking senses continued to observe the vast forest, my eyes surveyed the undesired sight of black bars intertwining with the smaller branches of the Aspen-trees. The forest I had woken up in was a fake.

Furious, I swung my body into a standing position. Nausea overwhelmed my legs, urging them to shake while my head once more spun. Regaining control over my exhausted body, I overlooked the entirety of the cage I had been thrown into, it was a Victorian Style atrium modified to hold a large creature such as myself, however, it still felt confining. The trees, the planted rose bushes, the strategically placed boulders, and hanging vines all made the cage feel so small. I could make out about twelve feet of open walk space on all rounded sides, though the corners and rounded tops were covered by either large ivy-leaves or oval groups of tree leaves. Surveying beyond the bars, I counted four other similarly designed cages put into each corner of this paved courtyard. Each cage too contained Unnaturals of similar shapeshift species, a white fox with five-tails and violet eyes, two sibling Serval Catamancers, and two other creatures that for some reason my subconscious knew but I did not. One looked like a soft brown, extremely fluffy raccoon dog that kept ringing the name 'Tanuki' to me. And the other resembled a medium-sized weasel with rough-coated fur like a hedgehog, whose name echoed through my ears, 'Kamaitachi'. They were all strange to me, but I guess I was just as strange to them, judging by their facial expressions and shocked exclamations.

Ignoring them, I began to wonder, "Where was I? Where had my useless bodyguard gone off to? Where had the Doctor who treated my wounds disappeared off to? Why were all these Unnaturals so calm here? What was this place?" The questions were running through my head one after the other and my head just couldn't keep up.

"Why is the Reaper here?" I heard a mimicking chatter of a raccoon question. Assuming he too, like I and the others were stuck in their animal forms with powers limited.

"Who's on your list this time?" one of the Servals now hissed.

"Brother, if she were truly here to take someone out, the Reaper would not have been caught." The other mocked, the voice registering to me as the female of the two Catamnacers were probably siblings of the opposite gender.

Taking a long exhale, I lied down under the crossing shadows of the two Aspen trees. "I am not here to collect anyone's lives." I sighed. "My assignments are elsewhere."

"If so, then it still doesn't explain why you are here?"

"If I knew, I would tell you." I snarled back to the meddling Unnaturals. I understood their prying, but I hated being interrogated.

"You are with that worrisome blondie, aren't you?" the weasel now cooed, his tone telling me he felt attracted to Augustus.

"Worrisome?" I now inquired. "Worrisome is the last word I would use to describe him."

"Well, he was gravely concerned over your well-being Hell-hound. He even checked out that cage to which you were supposed to be held in." a soft male voice spoke up. Spinning my head around to locate the voice, I locked glares with the very calm and serious violet eyes of the white Kitsune.

Huffing a chuckle, I told myself, "I hardly doubt it was for my sake." Placing my head into my large paws, I then gave a long exhale before thinking to myself, "However where are you, Augustus?" Recalling my memories, I continued "Weren't you the one who told me that you were going to figure this out?"

"Hellhound, since you are here you mind giving us your name?" the fox addressed as he sat in front of the bars, his five tails sitting around his clean snow-white frame.

Staring once more into those auspicious eyes of his, I upsettingly answered when I just wanted to be left alone. "My name is Cinder Salam."

"A pet name." The Kamaitachi laughed.

Locking eyes back at the weasel, I bared my long fangs and hastily snapped, "IT IS NOT A PET NAME!"

"Whatever it is it's unusual. Not something you were born with." The Tanuki too chuckled.

"I don't remember my birth name." I softly argued, glancing away from their still prying eyes. "Why am I even talking to you guys?!"

"I'm sorry if we are intruding, but it has been a while since we have seen a newcomer." The female Serval apologized. "Talking to these guys after a while gets bland. The only fun that ever happens is when the sisters get into their usual arguments."

"Don't worry." I sighed, again lying my head down in my paws. My free jowls feeling the soft brilliant green grass. "It's not your fault for what happened in my past."

"We all have our horrible pasts." The fox calmly de-escalated, "However, here we have been able to live without facing further trauma."

"Lucky you," I mumbled.

"Anyways, it only sincere if we too introduce ourselves. The raccoon-dog goes by Hanzo, although the humans call him Tom. The weasel is called Joker, but his real name is Rhames. The twins were born here so the humans gave them their birth names. Ha'kira is the sister, and Ha'taru is the brother. And while they call me Myst, my real name is Shusui." The fox informed, giving formal introductions to his fellow kin. "There are many others that live here, but we aren't allowed outside of these four walls."

"Only because the matriarch thinks we are too dangerous for those pampered monsters." The weasel Rhames hissed.

"Pampered monsters?" I questioned, my attention returning all of its focus back onto the conversation.

"There are two little dogs who were born with supernatural gifts. The fat orange hairball who goes by Maximus has a form of Telekinesis. While the tiny short-face, black-furred, pig-tailed canine has the ability of Psychokinesis, and he goes by Prince Charleston or Charli. Those two get away with everything and anything, and all-day we can hear the matriarch or eldest female child yelling at them to come or to behave." Shusui explained. "I'm sure you will see for yourself soon enough and understand the group's dislike for them."

"Dislike is not the word we would use." Ha'taru's voice growled from behind me. After a pause and the sound of leaves shaking, it recapitulated, "It's more like hatred."

"I see," I responded. "I know that feeling all too well."

Chapter 68
Augustus/Cinder

With time where I was finally able to be apart from the crazy wench, I strolled back through the house and into the courtyard, very eager to see how she was responding to her current treatments. According to the vet who was still observing Cinder in case the drugs continuously being pumped through her bloodstream gave severe reactions, she was doing alright. As much as I hated that collar, deciding to keep the unique object on had proved quite useful. Because we had to keep her powers limited until I could figure a way to get her out of here, we were using the dosage control to inject the desired medication, but I was unsure for how long that was going to work.

Stepping out under the cloudy skies, I surveyed the vibe of the outdoor holding facility and noticed that all of the rare Unnaturals were resting. The Servals were grooming one another. The Kamaitachi was perched on one of the landings in his large enrichment station. The Tanuki was also doing similar behaviors, however, he seemed to be maintaining a stern stare with the enclosure meant to be Cinders, making me feel unsure about what possible events had unfolded in my absence. From where I stood, I could also make out that Myst was lying against the front wall of the exhibit almost as if napping. Strolling around the exhibit that I had helped moved the previous unconscious Hellhound into, I finally caught glimpse of the black fur. Her dark soot color blending into the shadows of the Aspen tree where she was casually lying.

Before I could call out the 'Reaping' Hellhounds name, she was on top of it. Those oceanic eyes already locked on me and whatever movements I was preparing to make. Expecting for her to chew my head off in the English language, I swiftly remembered that the downers we had been slipping into her had enforced the more animalistic side of her breed, henceforth limiting the Human Language. Taking a long exhale, I stepped closer to the cage wall before finally speaking up. "I'm so relieved that you are okay."

Awaiting the soft acknowledgment, I watched Cinder hastily bare her fangs in my direction. The ears lying flat against her head. The hackles raised. Curling her lips even higher to the point where the bright pink of her gums was exposed, I began to fret if what I had done was wrong or had irritated the savage Hellhound beyond what I assumed was her current level.

"Cinder-" I tried to call out yet was interrupted by a chortling click noise that arose from behind me. The vibration sounded familiar to that of a raccoon, I soon realized the source was coming from the Tanuki behind me and observed the large Beauceron charge the iron-barred wall. The rods stopping her charge while her muzzle inched outside the barrier. The long fangs inches shy of ripping into my face once more. Confused, I attempted to theorize what had caused the sudden change in her behavior, however, I stopped when I noticed the brilliant blue eyes were locked on something besides me. The deep cold stare casting its spell of aggression and endless pain right through my soul.

"OOOOO, I'm so scared." The Tanuki called Hanzo laughed, his irritating coo enraging my instinct to rip that vocal box right out of his fat throat.

"Just be glad this fucking cage is stopping me from tasting your blood-" I barked back, smacking my jowls heavily together as I withdrew my muzzle from the other side of the cage wall.

"Hanzo, stop teasing the 'Reaper'. Testing her tolerance of your impudence will only grant you a mortal death to your immortal life." Shusui sighed from out of my line of sight. "And Cinder, please talk with that man, we all can tell he hopes the best for you."

Looking down at the Archangel whose eye level was slightly higher than my own due to the raised foundation the cage was built upon, I took a painful sigh. Thinking quietly to myself, "Right, all he cares about his survival. If I die, he will get killed by the Deity who turned me into his 'toy', that's all there is to it. Faking a relationship to keep me on his tight leash, so he can ensure the longevity of his life." Taking another long sigh as I recalled his promise, I finally relaxed my heightened tension. "You better get me out of here in the least, Augustus."

The blonde-haired Angel's hand slipped through the bars to once more stroke the side of my face, my strong sense of smell noticed that there was a change in his endorphins. High-level concentrations could be snuffed steadily dancing throughout the entirety of his body. Listening to the fast-paced beating of his Immortal heart, I began to wonder if the others were speaking the truth.

"Was he honestly worried over my health?"

"Cinder, I am working on finding a way to get you out of here, but please bear with me." He softly mumbled, his voice so hush that my trained ear was able to pick up the statement. The words causing my recent beating organ skip a beat in shock. Sitting on my haunches, I decided to continuously listen to the Unnatural talk, this time his voice speaking at a more audible level. "However, at this rate, it looks like we will be stuck here for a little while."

"Stuck?!" I snapped. Hastily standing back up, I furiously shook my head, trying to shake loose the craving to rip my fangs into that thin set of skin wrapped around his trachea. "I am going to be stuck in this fucking cage, while you get to freeload off these horrible bastards!" Almost losing my cool, I elected to walk away and proceed to hold onto the thought of Augustus's previous promise coming true.

"And of course, she's mad at me." I sighed, dropping my head as I watched the large canine wander away from me. "I swear sometimes it's easier to talk to a fucking wall than it is you."

"God, she hates you." I heard Matilda's voice tease from behind me, her words jabbing deep into my side. "Then again, she's been just as cold with the rest of us." Staring over at the fifteen-year-old teen girl I saw that her eyes were full of amazement and curiosity over the still unknown variables Cinder continued to hide. "But then again, I would be pretty pissed off if it were me who had been shot at for protecting your home, then kidnapped and brought to an unknown place while your own blood is suffocating you. And when you finally wake up, you find yourself locked up behind bars while the person who is your guardian is on the other side of the bars moving freely."

The words that Matty spoke of was as if it were coming directly from her mouth. Another painful jab to my side. Observing the Hellhound lie down under one of the openings in the tree's foliage where an afternoon sunray was peeking through for a few seconds, I eventually found some words to extend the conversation. "I see what you're saying, but I'm trying to find a way to get her back home. You know this isn't her home and won't be her home."

"Yes, I know that, you idiot! I'm the one who told you to talk to my dad about boarding, remember?" the teenager sarcastically inquired. "But the question is, how much longer do you plan on playing Theresa's stupid game?"

Again, I was astounded by this child's ability to read the room. She was much more intelligent than her elder sister. Speechless, I took the seconds it was taking my brain to find a comeback and surveyed the Hellhound who was now coldly staring at us. Her blue eyes attentively observing every movement we made like a predator did their prey, it sent chills racing down my spine. I knew that look all too well, and it wasn't good. Continuing to watch the eyes, my supernatural vision caught onto the color change of those memorizing pupils. "Matty get back!"

Chapter 69

Augustus

Hastily pushing the teenage girl away from the wall of black iron rods beautifully overrun with ivy, I barely managed to get the human out of the way. "Augustus, what is-?!" Matilda urgently exclaimed. "AUGUSTUS!"

"I'm fine!" I shouted back to the young woman, my free hands trying to grab at the fangs that were painfully penetrating the flesh between my neck and shoulder. Grimacing as all my pain receptors were filled and broke, I hastily shut my eyes and attempted to center my breathing. Quietly retelling myself, "I'm fine, Her fangs only broke through the muscle. If I would've moved any slower, her fangs would've been wrapped around my neck." Feeling the teeth dance around back and forth in the wound, I shot my eyes open to see those dark red eyes of the Hellhound staring back. "How was it that she was able to even reach us? Were we that close to the bars? No, her skull is too large to fit between the-" I paused when I had realized my mistake. "That was when she did it. The moment I had pushed Matty behind me, I stepped closer to the exhibit, and I had sealed my fate with that stupid mistake." Feeling the fangs once more dance, I watched the Unnatural's head begin to shake back and forth. Her muzzle rubbing along the bars, creating such friction that it rubbed the skin raw. Observing the blood oozing down her nose, I hastily reacted, "Shit, if it drips down into my wounds-"

"Augustus!" Matilda again called.

"Stay out of this human child!" The familiar female voice ordered and in the Human Language. The words were muffled by the amount of skin she had in her mouth, but I knew all too well that it was Her voice. It was Cinder's voice, although something felt off about it. "This has nothing to do with you."

"She's right, Matty, I'm fine. Just go get Dr. Lillian now!" I ordered, keeping my eyes locked on those red-tinted pupils glare at me. Maintaining a lookout on the blood that was dribbling down the brown muzzle. So captivated by their ember flame, my body was thrust forward, and before I knew it, my face was slammed into the iron rod bars. Within seconds a burning sensation was hastily spreading across my face. Scanning around, I began looking for any rational signs for the heated metal but unfortunately found none.

"Augustus!"

"Damn it, go now!" I anxiously shouted. Another round of shaking quickly transpired, and before I could tell what was next, I felt the fangs pull upward and my body follow. Cinder's weakened body was slowly dragging me up off my feet, her large human-sized paws were using the heated bars as grippers. The metal conforming to the weight of her long legs. "Shit." I thought. "I need to find a way to stop her, now." My mind working in overdrive began to try to strategize and play out as many plans as possible for the best result, but with the loss of blood, as well as the essence of time, I could only come up with one solution. I had to once more call upon that power.

Centering my breathing, I put my tired arms up along the bars and spawned the shadow of my glorious wings, I only needed a fraction of it. Pulling back the muscle, I forced the wings to create a powerful wind gust. The wind rushing into the Hellhound, her fur blasted backwards following the airflow, but she remained un-phased. Every muscle in my body was ordering me to stop, however, I knew I had to give it a bit more power and try again. Summoning a little bit more power, I again created the same gust. This time it succeeded, but barely. Cinder's fangs were rushed out of their holds, heavily tearing away the skin and muscle residing beneath. Scream-ing out in pain, I hastily regained my momentum and kicked off the cage, my body following the backdraft. Swiftly hiding my wings once more, I began to regain my footing. Looking over at Cinder who had been thrown a few feet backward, I observed her haunting eyes still preying heavily on me.

"Coward." She huffed with a sly smile seizing her lips.

"Call me what you wish." I sighed back to her as I collapsed onto the pavers. Bracing one leg up so I could put my uninjured arm on the same knee, I took another long exhale of relief. Content to be a few feet away from Cinder, unsure if it was her who had attacked me or if this was the Fiend bearing its ugly head.

"Asshole."

"That's her alright," I told myself, recalling the fact that the Hell-hound had picked up my foul mouth since staying with me. Her Childish mind easily digesting all sorts of language behaviors and all I had were nasty ones. With another sigh of relief, I watched the Hellhound pace back and forth along the wall. The heat along her body raising not only the surface temperature of the bars but chang-ing the molecular structure and the surrounding air temperature. "How long has it been since the drugs wore off?"

"They haven't."

"What?" I blurted. "How is that even possible? Those drugs were measured out by me, twice!"

"I kind of figured that out."

"Mr. Gale, are you okay?!" Doctor Lillian shouted. Looking over at the Vet and young woman who both were running up behind me, I scanned my vision back over to the Hellhound. "Matty told me everything. I have to say, I'm surprised by her sudden erratic behavior."

"I'm not. When she's had enough and when she is given the chance, she will resort to this." I defended. "Isn't that right, Cinder?"

"Hmph." I heard her mumble as she began to wander away from the barred wall.

"Isn't she still drugged? How is it possible for her to do all this?" Matilda questioned, walking closer to the cage once the Hellhound was a good distance away. Placing her hand near the bright orange bars, she astoundingly resumed, "It's so hot! So, this is the power of a Hellhound's Flames?"

"Just a fraction," I answered, forcing myself to stand back up.

"Mr. Gale, please don't move too much with that wound." Dr. Lillian ordered, her hand firmly pressing a blood-soaked gauze along my shoulder.

Glancing over at the countrywoman who was frantically trying to digest the situation at hand as she simultaneously tried to treat my grievous wounds, I lightly snickered, "I thought I told you to call me Augustus."

"Sorry- but, Augustus, we need to get you to a hospital now."

"No, just get it bandaged up."

"Huh?" the two girls spoke in unison.

"This kind of thing happens a lot, Cinder isn't the only Unnatural to bite back, and this could've been a lot worse if her blood had reached the wound," I responded.

"What do you mean?"

"I told you about her Blood Trait, the other ability it has is to create mass pressure on any surface it comes in contact with. It can

362

break and even fracture bones without ever being ingested." I clarified. "Well, I hadn't learned of its traits until the last time she had bled, and it created several multi-fractures in the top of my left hand."

"Wow." Matty softly mumbled. The tone of her voice telling me that her unusual rebellious side was in love with the chaotic gifts and curses the 'Reaping' Hellhound possessed.

"Scary." Dr. Lillian muttered.

"It's very scary, but alright we need to hurry up and get this bandaged up before the rest of your family finds out, especially your sister." I returned walking out towards the converted Vet's office building. "Cinder doesn't deserve to get hurt for what she did."

"Of course, she does!"

"No, she doesn't. You see, I told you all that she hates cages and people like Theresa, matter of fact, I could go as far as to say she hates nearly all humans. Her first reaction when she is given the chance is to fight and ask questions later. It is how she has survived all this time, and you only encouraging to punish her for her reaction makes her reasoning to hate humans even more logical." I answered before quietly thinking to myself. "Although, if that bitch hadn't hired those Hunters none of this shit would've ever happened!" Sitting down on the office stool so the Vet could begin triaging my bite wounds, I glanced over at Matilda who seemed still in awe and shock. As I grimaced at the pain of having the wounds get flushed clean of any bacteria that had transferred from Cinder's fangs and saliva by rubbing alcohol, I told my suspicions, "This is probably her first time seeing an Unnatural react in that particular way. But it was only a matter of time before she came face to face with the hard-cold reality of an Unnaturals' hatred for their normal counterparts." With the wounds finally being stitched together, I called out to the teenager, "I know you are worried, but I need you to do me a favor, Matilda."

"A favor?" she asked, her voice sounding a bit stunned.

"Yes, I need you to get a hold of the Draconic Syndicate."

Chapter 70
Augustus/Cinder

"Okay, it's done, Augustus," Matilda told me as she wandered into the indoor pool where I remained, recalling the day's events.

Looking up at the teenager who stood over the top of me as I lied on the wicker patio sofa. "Thank you, Matty." I happily exhaled, now sitting up. "Now, when are they going to pick her up?"

"Yeah, about that. They told me that it was still going to be a couple of months before they would have room for her. Emergency or not."

"I see." I sighed, feeling completely crushed about the delay. "A couple of months, does she even have that amount of time?" I wondered to myself aloud.

"Huh?"

"Oh, don't worry, just thinking aloud." I chuckled, quickly attempting to put the young woman's mind at ease. "How are you holding up?" I then asked, wondering how Matilda was doing after seeing me get attacked by the one-hundred-pound animal who only a few days ago was unable to move her head.

"I'm okay." Matty swiftly responded, sitting down beside me. "You know though that if Theresa sees that bandage on your shoulder, she is going to blame Cinder, right?"

"Yeah, I know, that is why I wanted to get her out before your sister returns from her day of shopping." I breathed, indeed fearing the worst for the beautiful Unnatural. She had already been through enough and being electrocuted would not make it any more convincing that I was indeed trying to get her out, let alone convince her to remain civil. "Alright, now to relay the news to her, and your father," I informed, standing myself up and grimacing at the pain of my wounded arm.

"Whoa, who would've thought the Reaper would attack her Babysitter?" I heard that damn raccoon coo, his voice further enticing my boiling rage.

"Shut-up, Hanzo or do you want to die?" the female Serval Catamancer hissed. "Please forgive him, Cinder, he has that ability to get on everyone's nerves."

"I can see that." I huffed, licking my lips. My tongue tasting the drying blood that was caked into the short strands of fur on my muzzle. Recalling the attack, I cursed. "Damn it, if he hadn't have done that maneuver with his fucking wings, I would've been free of this prison."

"Indeed, we would've been free." I heard the dark version of my voice echo in my head. "You should've let me have the reins."

"No, if I loaned you control, it would've been fatal to him, and torturous for you and I." I snarled to the Fiend who I had grown to have regular conversations with since the night Augustus had abandoned me. We seemed to have created a certain level of understanding between one another, but I still didn't trust the blood-crazed version of me, that lunatic side that he had encouraged me to create. "If we had killed Augustus, then Zachariah would've punished us."

"Well yeah, although you do get scolded a lot by him, so what would it matter if we had killed the Angel." It reminded. My voice beginning to irritate the living hell out of me.

Biting my lip I refuted, "You are talking of the same being who has helped him stay alive for the past two hundred years, and has helped not only him but-"

"But you." The Fiend coldly answered, the words echoing throughout my head. "Why are you talking so much about him all of a sudden?"

"I can't get his promises out of my head," I grumbled, rolling off onto the side of my stomach. Feeling not only exhaustion creep in but also the drugs starting to take their hold on my body, finally gaining control over my body. "It's just like back then." I continued, exhaling another breath before closing my eyes.

"You mean back when you lived there?" it asked. "When you lived with them?"

Reopening my eyes, I stared out at the beautiful flowers that were growing around the ivy and iron bars held inside this horrible cage. Responding with a soft agreement. "Yeah."

"Well, you know that he is only doing this because he is being told to?"

"Yeah, I know."

"And you know that it is only a matter of time before he also shows his true colors."

"Yeah, I know."

"So, what are you going to do?"

"I'm going to play along," I answered. "I need to, but it will be my way."

"Well, how long are we going to play this game then?"

"Until he's done with me," I growled, now readjusting myself around the soft crabgrass as the Valkyrie wandered into the courtyard.

"Speaking of which, here comes the Black Angel." The Fiend laughed, its mimicking voice fading away into the darkened abyss beneath my subconscious awaiting its next turn to fight for the reins.

Flashing my fangs at the blonde-haired coward, I snarled, "Now, what do you want? Weren't my fangs ripping into you once already enough for you to get the idea?"

"Ouch, so she's still mad." I cringed in my head. "Well, that's bound to be expected." Surveying her behavior, I noticed she wasn't moving much. Alerting me to the fact she was finally feeling the exhaustion of her reckless actions. The drugs were finally working. Finding my words, I finally spoke up, "I came to relay some news to you."

"What?"

"We managed to get in contact with the Draconic Syndicate," I answered, watching her eyes glint at the statement. Pressing on, I further explained, "They will take you in..." Pausing for a moment, I observed her eyes slant with a stern look and a flash of pink gums.

"But..."

"But they won't be able to take you in for another few months."

The statement obviously infuriated her because before I knew it, the drugged Unnatural had charged the barred wall. Her healed muzzle flying between the bars. Her jaws smacking with such power

I could hear the clapping sound of her fangs clamping against each other. "SO, YOU ARE TELLING ME THAT I AM GOING TO BE STUCK IN THIS PRISON FOR ANOTHER TWO FUCKING MONTHS?!"

"Unfortunately, yes," I answered, looking away from the deep blue gaze. "But I will be talking with Theresa's father about ways for you to be out of this prison even if for short durations."

"You know full well that if I am in the same room as her..." Her words stopped, stopped midsentence. The statement became flourished with a deep utter growl. Telling me that the rest of the sedative had taken its final hold on her, but I knew exactly what she was going to end her threat with.

"Yes, I know what you will do to her, however, think this through." I sighed, but before I could finish the rest of my statement the Hellhound was already strolling back over to the shade of the Aspen tree, completely ignoring me.

"That didn't go so well," Matty interjected, stepping out onto the paved cobblestone pathway.

"No, it did not."

Chapter 71

Cinder

Time smoothly flew by succeeding my attempt to escape the prison, and I had somehow managed to slip out of any kind of punishment. Knowing that Archangel had something to do with it, I wondered what he would be scheming up for me to do in return for him concealing his wounds from that crazy psycho. With all this endless time to think of everything he could be planning, I kept coming back to the fact that I had to endure two whole months locked behind this cage before I would be relocated to the Draconic Syndicate and most likely held behind more bars.

"There are just so many possibilities that I cannot think of a clear path to complete that assignment." I sighed aloud after strategizing a hundred different plans and probabilities over the last ten days. Glancing up at the passing storm clouds hanging over this large property, I continued to wonder aloud, "I guess I will just have to wait until the day arrives and what events unfold so I can come up with a specific strategy to deal with Saylene and her followers." Dropping down onto the planted grass that grew over the foundation of this iron-barred prison, I rolled over onto my left side for a better position. Exhaling a long breath, I rolled my eyes while expressing a small grin, "Although I still have yet to input what you will be also planning, huh, Augustus?" as I watched the blonde-haired man stroll into my line of sight.

Locking our gazes for a minute, I now eavesdropped into his conversation with the older looking but much younger Patriarch of the household:

"I see, so that's what going to happen." The man chuckled with the Valkyrie. "It's a shame that it is still so far away, but I guess it can't be helped when she is as powerful as she is."

"Yeah, Cinder is quite a powerful being and is only getting stronger by the day. The time delay could be very likely related to that." Augustus returned with a mimicking laugh and relocking that green gaze of his with me. Baring my fangs at him, I relinquished my smile and rolled my body over to the other side to look away from that charismatic gleam.

"She's still mad at you, huh?"

"Yeah, she is, but I don't think it is over the delay, as much as it is over the fact that I didn't drop dead from her attack the other day, or over this whole situation she's stuck in."

"It could very likely be all that combined. I just want to say I am sorry over how that went down."

"It isn't me who you should be apologizing to, but Cinder herself, and I don't think an apology from you would change the fact that she is still stuck behind those bars," Augustus returned.

"Well, if anything-."

"Oh, Augustus there you are!" the irritating high-pitched voice of the woman who put me here in the first place shouted. Spinning my body up around to an upright lying position, I rushed to lock my eyes on Theresa. Surveying his psycho girlfriend run towards the undercover Unnatural and filthy human who had helped create that horrible being, I bared my fangs. "I need to talk to you! In private! Now!" She sporadically panted.

"Okay." He painfully sighed in agreeance. "If you could excuse us, Mr. Englishmen."

"Sure, it's about time I go pick up Matilda anyway." The Patriarch dismissed. "We can talk later, Mr. Gale."

Once the man was a good distance away, I then heard the Angel question, "Now what did you have to so urgently discuss?"

Theresa's eyes quickly shot over in my direction, locking enviously with my own for a hasty second. Her face made an ugly snarl of disgust before the glare danced back towards the man who was far from hers. "I don't feel comfortable talking about it in front of these beasts, especially in front of her."

"Alright fine, we can talk inside the house. I don't see why you are so afraid of talking in front of them when they can hardly do anything to you in their current state." Augustus questioned with a complaining sigh.

"Let's talk in my room." The model loudly cooed as she dragged him behind her back into the large house and out of my enhanced hearing.

"WHAT!?"

"Sounds like something is going down." I heard that damn Tanuki fuss.

"I wonder what caused it this time?" the male Serval questioned his sister.

"If it involves her, it could be anything." Shusui sighed.

"I wonder what it involves though..." I stopped midsentence when I recalled the last argument that I had seen involving Theresa. The results weren't good. He had walked out. Biting my tongue, I snarled to my now anxious conscious, "Don't you dare do it again! Don't you dare leave me again!"

"Cinder are you okay?" the female Catamancer softly asked with deep concern in her eyes.

"I'm fine." I snarled, giving acknowledgment to the Serval sibling, as I stood myself up onto my exhausted feet.

"You aren't going to lose your cool again, are you?!" Rhames hissed from his perch high in the tiny Aspen tree. "That last time could've been deadly for you."

"I won't make any promises, it all depends on how this goes." I returned, feeling an exertion of my powers escape their drugged induced cage. The air temperature once more changing around me.

"WHAT THE FUCK ARE YOU TALKING ABOUT?!" Augustus's voice broke through the thick walls of the house. The tone in his voice once more forcing my mind to revisit that incident not too long ago. Feeling my ears old flat against my head, I uncontrollably began to feel my body begin to quiver as it was overrun with anxiety. Hearing doors slam shut, and more shouting between the two ruined couple continued to drag my mind back and forth between the memory and reality.

"Augustus just listen to me!" Theresa's voice called out as she chased after the image of the Angel storming behind the floor to ceiling colonial windows wrapping around the courtyard. His silhouette dancing in and out between the sheer curtains. "AUGUSTUS!"

"WHY SHOULD I LISTEN TO YOU?!" He angrily called out, his feet pivoting as he swung around to face Theresa. "WHY SHOULD I HAVE TO ADHERE TO ANYMORE OF YOUR LIES?!"

"IT ISN'T A LIE!"

"WELL, IT FOR SURE AS HELL NOT MINE!"

"WHAT is going on here?!" My ears caught onto the surprisingly authoritative voice of the Patriarch, Mr. Englishmen.

"Sounds like Daddy's home." That damn coon now jabbed in.

"Would you just shut the fuck up!" I demanded Hanzo. Chomping my jowls together as I proceeded to worry over the results conceding this argument.

"Make me Reaper!"

"I wouldn't tease her too much, Hanzo," Shusui spoke up, his voice still as calm as ever.

"What? She's behind a cage just like the rest of us."

"Yeah, but that Reaper did almost break out of it last week," Ha'taru responded. "So testing her when she is already worrying herself over that man, will only further entice her to kill you-"

"Would you all just shut up!" I snapped. My burst releasing the small amount of heat I was trying to keep contained in a circumference around my body. The wave erupting through the iron rods and hitting each Unnatural within the radius around me. "Please."

"Forgive their intolerance Cinder." The white Kitsune attempted to apologize in place of the others. However, I was so focused on the passing shadows and their heavy shouting I zoned it out.

"I need to focus, to calm myself," I told my warring mind. "Breathe. Don't lose control..."

Chapter 72
Cinder/Augustus

Seconds later, Augustus came storming out of the house's sliding glass door connecting the residence to the patio, and the scent that was wavering off him immediately told me the extent of this argument. The level of anger was unmistakable.

Shortly after the woman who had started this heated conversation came charging out, pursing the Archangel. "Augustus! Damn it, Augustus, wait up! Let me explain!"

Swiftly pivoting once more on his heels he, yet again, came face to face with the female human. "EXPLAIN WHAT, THERESA!? What the fuck is there to explain!?"

"PLEASE!" she panted, trying to outreach her hands in an attempt to grab at the blonde-haired man, but he wasn't having any of it. Throwing his hand out, he slapped away her attempt to grab at his fitted arms.

As soon as our skin came in contact with each other, I saw a flash of black come charging out of the corner of my peripheral vision. A heavy smack of one hundred pounds of muscle hitting the iron rodded bars soon followed. A glimpse of spraying saliva shot in between Theresa and me, making her fall flat on her ass. Turning my head over, I came face to face with the horror I had imagined. Bright red eyes were staring right back at me. The glare lasting for less than a second before it shot over to Theresa, and the canine began attacking at the bars that separated its fangs from ripping into her flesh. Furious, the Hellhound released her hold on the bars leaving behind deep heat penetrated puncture holes in the iron and began to angrily bark at the woman.

"Her humanity is gone." My mind hastily conjured.

"Keep..." I heard the familiar female voice order. Its tone so utterly deep and authoritative it rose all the hairs on my arms, making them stand on end. "Keep your..." It continued. "KEEP YOUR FILTHY FUCKING HANDS OFF OF HIM!" The voice eventually finished as the Hellhound began to rise on her hind legs, making her body much larger and intimidating than it already was. The devilish eyes locked on Theresa with killing accuracy.

"No, that's her." The words told my conscience. "She's just pissed off," I remarked, watching the black iron change colors again, becoming a bright blue, then orange, and even white the longer her paws remained on the metal. Glancing my sights over to this lying son of a bitch, I saw that written all over her face was the expression of absolute fear. Her eyes were bulging out of their sockets, unable to take a single blink, too afraid to look away from the creature who was once more living up to her 'God-Given' Title.

Although, the fear lasted only for a few seconds when the crazy woman brought out her cellphone from her back pocket. The screen had cracked from her falling hard on the paved cobblestone pathway. Exposing it to the Hellhound only made the creature more furious. Her snarl rose even higher. The heat surrounding her increased in temperature and began to waft over us as well. "Try keeping that threat when you are convulsing on the floor!" Theresa now threatened Cinder as she pressed down on the shock button held in the app.

"THERESA!" I shouted, trying to grab for the phone. Cinder didn't budge. Her posture held firm. I saw no shaking. Heard no voltage release. "Did it not work?" I wondered with fear. "Was the collar broke?"

"Why didn't it work?!" the insane woman threatened, now standing back up on her feet as she again pressed the button three more times! "WHY WON'T YOU DROP DEAD?!"

"THERESA STOP IT!" I shouted, attempting to grab for the phone. The subject of our prior argument momentarily diverted.

"TELL THAT FUCKING BITCH TO STAY OUT THIS!" she now barked, dancing the cell phone around to keep it out of my grasp. "IF IT WEREN'T FOR HER!"

"If it weren't for Cinder, I would have still been blinded by your numerous lies." I calmly exclaimed, watching the image of her father come up behind her, his hand swiftly grabbing the phone. Succeeding in taking it out of her evil clutches.

"DAD!" Theresa screamed, trying to take it back from her father's surprisingly stern grip. "GIVE IT BACK!"

"Mr. Gale, go ahead and calm down your Unnatural before she does manage to break out of that cage and cause more damage than just concaved bars." Mr. Englishman calmly ordered. "That should give us a moment to calm all of our nerves."

"Okay." I attempted to speak before I was interrupted by the low bark that came from deep down in Cinder's throat. She was still trying to find a way to break loose so she could very likely 'kill' Theresa.

"DAD! WAIT, WHY DOES SHE GET-?" Theresa now angrily complained. Her face inches from her father's.

"Because she is a guest here at MY HOUSE!" he coldly remarked. "And because I know when my daughter is up to no good."

Proceeding to listen while I stepped closer to the barred cage wall, I called out to the Hellhound. Still keeping her haunting eyes locked on the woman, Cinder broke from her stance. Returning to all fours and pacing over to where I stood. The snarl fading, but her overprotective behavior remaining headstrong as she stood by my side. Hackles raised. Tail standing straight up on edge. Ears pitched flat against her skull.

"I am not!" Theresa refused.

"Yes, you are. I should've known you had something planned when you hired Hunters to capture her." Mr. Englishmen clarified as I gently pushed my hand through the bars to attempt to soothe the raging emotions Cinder was combating. The Hellhound fought back; however, she eventually retreated her fangs. Her gaze only lining with mine for a quick second before the eyes returned to hunting her target. "I also should've known something was up judging by Mr. Gale's demeanor towards you." Glancing over at the Patriarch of the large estate, I listened to his authoritative behavior tell me, "I will come for a proper explanation once I have dealt with her."

"Okay." I again muttered, this time stopping when my hand felt a vigorous vibration run through my fingers. My mind returning to the Hellhound as it presumed, "So it did work. You just are so stubborn and loaded full of raging endorphins that your body is just now suffering from the tazing."

"Wait, Dad, we aren't finished!" Theresa piped in, her spoiled attitude raging back to the surface.

"Yes, you are, now get your ass in the house!"

"You can't tell me what to do!"

"Well, then I'm leaving!"

"Fine by me, but I'm keeping your cell phone, after all, it is my name that's on the contract."

"Whatever!" this crazy woman snapped, storming back into the house.

Mr. Englishmen took a long exhale, breathing a heavy sigh before his wise eyes shot back at Cinder and me. "I know my apology won't hold, but I am sorry for what she did to your Unnatural."

"You can say it to Cinder, she is her person." I sighed, feeling the Unnatural's tense body begin to relax. Or at least start to.

"I am sorry for everything my daughter has done to you, Cinder." He ended simultaneously dismissing himself from the scene.

Once alone, I too took a sigh of relief. Happy that for at least right now, the argument had been put on a temporary hold...or....

"So, what was that about?" I heard Cinder's voice question. This time much calmer, but still pretty stern, her red eyes coldly staring back at me, demanding answers.

Removing my hand from the cage for safety reasons, I painfully moaned, dreading the response that was yet to come. "Well..." I began. Pausing as I recalled that she could read my lies so easily, and if I had attempted to lie, the Hellhound would very likely attack me. "Well, she says that she's pregnant."

Chapter 73

Augustus

"What news." Cinder snickered, her shaky legs finally winning the fight against her stubborn mentality, forcing her to collapse down onto the hard ground beneath her. Examining her chest start to rise and fall heavily, I knew that the adrenaline was fading. The reparation of all those shocks was finally sinking their teeth into her nerves. Hearing a small cough, I overheard the Hellhound again tease, this time in a calm collected tone, "Is it yours?"

The words stung my heart. The rage came boiling back to the surface as my mind tried its damnest to find the right wording to answer the question. Thinking, however, "How was she able to come up with that conclusion?"

"It's not, huh?" She now asked, answering her question. "I can tell by your raging scent, and your hesitation."

"How?" I asked as I now tried to again calm myself. Turning around, I leaned my back against the cooling iron before falling onto the pavers. My knees pulled up, allowing me to brace my arms flat out on them. Feeling the strong wave of heat wafting off of her body against my sweating neck felt oddly cooling. Soothing even. Comfort enabled me to find my ability to speak again. "Yeah, it isn't mine."

"So she's trying to play it off..."

"Again, how do you know this?" I interjected, leaning my head backwards, turning my nose up to the sky, and allowing my eyes to lock with the still ember red glare that stared back at me.

"It isn't that hard, especially when you were shouting on and on about how it wasn't yours, and that you weren't going to listen to her explanation." Cinder calmly replied with those haunting eyes reverting to their memorizing deep blue. "My question although, is still how?"

"That I don't know. I tried asking her." I argued. "But she pushed off my questions."

"The math doesn't add up."

"I know it doesn't," I growled, bringing my head back so my eyes could stare straight down at my feet. My hands covering my face as my mind began to recalculate the passing time. Recalculating the equations.

"Although, it does explain the erratic behavior."

"What?"

"I may not have been in the outside world for long, but I have been out long enough to understand all the changes an impregnated woman goes through." The Hellhound clarified, her tone full of sorrowful memories.

"You are talking about that woman from the Syndicate-?"

She said nothing.

"I know it's hard to talk about..."

"Let's just focus on you for once." The Beauceron quietly muttered.

"Okay." I reluctantly agreed. I would have preferred to change subjects, but going down that road for her would not be good for the both of us.

"Were you guys having sex while I was in the Pits?" She bluntly interrupted.

"Well, you sure have learned some bad habits in your time on the outside." I swiftly jabbed, trying to avoid answering such a bold question.

"I can blame many people for them." Cinder huffed, her beautiful feminine voice sending more soothing chills down my spine. "But seriously, Augustus, were you?"

"No, I was in Florida, like I told you I was. I had three clients and in between all that, I was working on getting those legal papers set aside for times like what happened with that crazy Doctor." I harshly answered. "The last time we had any intimate relations was before then, on that blood moon."

"That was almost nine months ago."

"Yeah, I know that."

"And since being here, I know you been having intercourse with her." Cinder continued to boldly speak aloud in front of the other Unnaturals I was certain were eavesdropping in our conversation.

"Yes, we have, but it was only-"

"Only to meet her demands of being a loyal boyfriend."

"She knew." I quietly theorized in my head prior to attempting to test it, "You knew?"

"Not really, but you were assigned by Him to be my babysitter, and doing anything that could cause my demise without orders by him, would only cost you your own life. At least, that's how you have explained to me."

"Yeah, she had the code to that shock collar-"

"Which by the way, why do I still have it wrapped around my neck?" Cinder snarled.

"Gerard gifted it to me, saying it could come in handy."

"That asshole. Should've known."

"I debated removing it, but before I could finalize my thoughts this happened."

"She stole your phone and the code."

"Yeah."

"You owe me." The canine shifted woman demanded.

"I know. I know." I painfully complained, standing myself back up. Surveying the Hellhound still lying down on the grass, her eyes watching every move I made.

"Well no matter what way you add it up, it isn't yours."

"Thank fucking god somebody else sees." I blissfully cursed.

"I am only agreeing with you because I hate that woman."

The answer was not all that surprising to me. "Well, now that you seem to have calmed down, I should go talk with Mr. English-men." I sighed, gently slipping my hand through the bars.

"I'm as calm as I can be for now." Cinder confirmed as she pushed her forehead into the palm of my hand. Rubbing it back and forth for a moment before quietly delivering, "Thank you for staying with me." The words were only audible for the two of us.

Taken a bit back, I hesitantly agreed. "Yeah, no problem, but what made you react like that in the first place?"

Removing her head, the large dog then began to saunter back under the shade of the small Aspen tree. Along the way, calmly answering, "It's because you made a promise to me, Augustus."

Chapter 74

Augustus

"Has she calmed down?" the patriarch in charge of the property asked as I walked into the large living room.

"Well, she is as calm as she'll ever be, but I think I'll have Dr. Lillian check her out in a little bit," I responded taking a deep sigh as I plopped down onto the sofa across from where Mr. Englishman sat.

"Again, I want to apologize for all the pain my daughter has caused not only you but that beautiful Hellhound of yours."

"Some of it was my fault." I jabbed, rubbing my hand against the back of my head as I avoided eye contact.

"What do you mean?'

"I was debating removing that shock collar on Cinder prior to the incident." I hastily answered, adjusting my position on the sofa. Placing my elbows on my knees and leaning forward, I painfully explained, "I know I am known famously known for being a Sympathizer all around the world, but I'm sure you also know that Shapeshift species can be difficult to handle on the count of their primal instincts."

"Yes, I know that quite well." Mr. Englishmen agreed. "However, my work fails in comparison to yours, Mr. Gale."

"Yeah, but what you are doing is still amazing. The sanctuary you have provided for these Unnaturals is remarkable, but this isn't fitting for someone like Cinder." I continued, evoking the memories I had when I had reviewed the countless photos and files on the Hellhound's past. "It just isn't right for her."

"So, you kept that collar on her to maintain necessary control over her when she loses control."

"Unfortunately, yes," I defended. My gut spinning in circles as I felt like what I was doing to her, what we were doing to her was exactly what they did to her, what everyone had done to her.

"Well, it is understandable. Everyone needs a check once in a while, even we humans, do from time to time." Theresa's father surprisingly advised, taking a swig of whiskey. "At least, for now, she has calmed down. I only came in at the end, but I still saw the power she has. Even being as drugged as she is, and being shocked multiple times, the fact that Cinder managed to keep such an intimidating image terrifies me." He lightly chuckled, putting the glass down on the glass coffee table.

"If only he knew the truth," I sarcastically joked to my conscious. Speaking aloud, I then lightly huffed, "She sure can be a monster when she wants to."

"Judging by the situation, she was reading your emotions and reacted in order to protect you. The relationship you have with her is surprisingly strong, so strong in fact, that I am beginning to understand my daughter's jealousy. However, talking about the situation, I do want to have a full explanation as to what the two of you were arguing so furiously about, Mr. Gale."

"Well-" I began, leaning my back into the sofa's cushion. "This feels like the type of thing that Theresa should be telling you."

"She isn't here right now, and my daughter tends to be a profane liar."

"Let me just start with that there is no way it is mine."

"Okay? What isn't yours?"

"Theresa told me that she is six weeks pregnant." I boldly answered, leaning even more forward on the edge of the sofa so I could brace my elbows on my knees, my chin in the palm of my hands, and my eyes staring directly into his buzzed gaze.

"SHE IS?!" He ecstatically shouted, his voice full of mixed emotions. Nodding my head in agreement, I patiently awaited his next response. After a few seconds had passed, Mr. Englishmen finally questioned, "And you say it isn't yours? Are you positive? Theresa has told me that you two have been together for a couple of years now."

"Yes, I am positive," I answered. "Before coming here, the last time we had any kind of intimacy was shortly after I had obtained custody of Cinder, and that was almost nine months ago."

"I see."

Surprised by his second reaction, I cautiously asked, "You believe me?"

"Well, not entirely. She is my daughter, after all, even if she does lie. But if what you are saying is indeed true, she would've had already given birth, or at least have been close to going into labor."

"Yeah, that was exactly what I was thinking." I sighed, also agreeing with the easy math equation laid out before us. "If anything else, I'm sure you can always view her credit card statements and her call log, after all, you do have her cell phone."

"That is true, I could do that. However, I won't do it right now." The Father remarked before taking another drink.

"It's a lot to take in, I know, but if it was indeed mine, I wouldn't have reacted the way I had."

"I can understand that. Anyone with the right mind would've reacted the same way you had. They would ask the same questions. Follow the same math. Even I would react the same way."

"Mr. Englishmen, I know I shouldn't be talking about your daughter and grandchild like this in front of you, but there is no way in Hell that is mine." I once more testified. "After she had tried to call me out for cheating, then two weeks later she returns with this?! Coming out that she is pregnant with a child who I KNOW IS NOT MINE! IT JUST PISSES ME THE FUCK OFF!" I snapped. Angrily shouting at the top of my lungs.

"While it hurts to hear you speak of her in that way, and a child that isn't even yet born in this world, I will not blame you for your reaction."

"God, it's no wonder she is a spoiled lying brat with a father like him." I recklessly thought in my head.

"Although there are some things I am still confused about."

"And that would be?" I stupidly asked.

"Why would she believe you cheated on her?"

"How the fuck am I supposed to know? I still don't know how she found out Cinder was an Unnatural in the first place!"

"Well, there's a reason."

"Huh?" I again stupidly asked. My subconscious already explaining that reason to me. "Oh, right."

"Why would you lie about that?"

"For both of their sakes. For the sake of everyone." Silence reverberated back to me. Rubbing my hand through my streaked back blonde hair, I continued, "The fewer people that know Cinder is an Unnatural, the better."

"Why is that? Anyone knowing an Unnatural is putting themselves at risk, that's the unfortunate society we live in today."

"True, but Cinder is beyond that."

"What do you mean by that?"

"Let's just say you should be glad the Hunters she hired were freelancers and not government contractors," I informed. Once more silence echoed, so I further refined "Cinder, was once considered Federal Government property." The news utterly shocked him, making me wonder if he was about to have a stroke or a heart attack. "She was liberated by a Rebel Syndicate, then when things got dangerous for her there, I was contacted, and she was put in my custody." I partially lied.

"I see, now." Mr. Englishmen panted. "I can see why it is better off having so few people know."

"Yeah, so I lied to Theresa about her being a regular overgrown mixed breed. Matter of fact, it was Cinder's idea to play that out. Although I don't know how Theresa found out the truth."

"Now, that's a question for another time Mr. Gale." Mr. Englishmen exhaled another large breath, attempting to change subjects. Reverting it to the main subject at hand, Theresa's pregnancy. "Now before we end this 'exciting' conversation, are you sure there is no other reason why that child is not yours?"

"Yes, there is." I painfully sighed. I did not want to have to tell anyone about this. I didn't want to bring up my horrible past, but here we go.

"What is it?" the man authoritatively interrogated, the tone in his voice very demanding.

"There is no way that child could ever be mine and that is because I'm sterile."

Chapter 75
Augustus/Jakob

"Excuse me?" The man questioned with a deep snarl in his throat, believing what I hold him was a lie.

"I know you don't believe me, but it's true. I wouldn't have told you this if it hadn't been for today's incident, it's very emasculating." I sighed as I avoided eye contact.

"I just can't believe someone as famous as you and as generous as you would be-"

"Well, I am. So again, there is no way that the fetus growing in her womb is mine." I once more swore. "If you still don't believe me, I can give you my medical records."

"No, I trust you, however, my question is, what are you going to do now?" Mr. Englishman calmly requested.

"I don't know. I really don't know."

"What are you doing?' I heard Mhykal happily questioned Mhykila, the almost year-old toddler, who was attempting to crawl around inside one of the large cardboard boxes that once hid her toys. Three large bows were stuck to her luscious ebony black hair.

"She is a spitting image of her father." I teased before taking a sip of my blood-filled whiskey glass.

"What does that mean?" my Vampiric friend snarked, his mimicking human brown eyes staring coldly at me. Taking a bow out of his daughter's hair, he now calmly affirmed, "It's nice to see you coming back to your old self."

"I don't feel like myself, though." I returned while avidly watching the innocent child crawl back out of the box to play with a different one.

"You may not feel like it, but we all are happy to at least see images of your old self flashing back to the surface. Although I'm also seeing other images of your older life coming out of the abyss as well, fragments of who you were once were." Mhykal perceived. "And that has me more worried-"

"That's all in the past though." I denied, recalling the moments of our history.

"No, it isn't. Not when it is a part of your character."

Leaning back against the antique victorian sofa, I extended my arms, wrapping them around the spine while sitting my left foot on my right knee. Holding the whiskey glass in my left hand as it hung off the edge, reflecting the warm white light of many little bulbs wrapped around the glorious twelve-foot Christmas tree. The tree elegantly sitting behind our little set-up common room, its ornaments, and lights allowing our darkened Manor to feel cozier as it lit up the two-story space. Locking my eyes with the beautiful white porcelain angel sitting as our tree topper this year, I wondered aloud, "It's hard to believe it has been almost a year since our first Christmas."

"HEY, DON'T IGNORE ME, JAKOB!" my friend shouted in his anguished teasing manner.

"I'm not ignoring you, just choosing to not pay you any mind." I groaned, returning my glance to the Vampiric who was sitting across from me.

"That's the same thing!" Mhykal continued to drag on, eventually dropping his head in comical defeat and exhaling a deep sigh. Glancing up at me, he exclaimed, "But, I do agree, it's hard to believe how fast time has slipped by."

"I hope you are doing okay, Cinder." I quietly transpired to my depressed self, taking another long sip of the thick red liquid. "Mhykal?" I now called.

"Hmm."

"Would you believe it if I were to tell you that she could represent the end to Mankind?"

"What are you talking about?"

"You know exactly what I'm talking about?"

"Her again?" he lowly questioned. His newly attuned fathering tone emanating. "How many times have we told you to just forget about her?"

"Just answer the question," I sternly ordered. "Would you believe it or not?"

"To tell you the truth, after what I saw 'that' night." Mhykal paused for a moment. "Yes. I do. But why are you asking?"

"It's been on my mind for a while now," I answered.

"That doesn't help me."

"Just forget it." I coldly dictated, now standing up and heading back towards the kitchen for my next glass.

"Jakob." He now called out to me.

"What?"

"You need to stop feeding so much, or else you really will turn back into..." Another pause. Turning my head around so I could lock my gaze with my fellow kin, his image coming into the side of my peripheral vision.

Before he could finish his statement, I childishly returned, "And what if I don't."

"Jakob-."

"Yalu," Mhykal shockingly derived, looking up at the mother of his hybrid child. "You're back already?" he now inquired while the other members of our little family began to pile into the common area.

"Yeah, we're back now. Valeryie decided against going to the mall." The eldest Vixen explained while I turned my head back around and continued my venture towards the kitchen.

Entering the recently renovated kitchen, I strolled towards the fridge where we Vampirics held our necessary bags of blood. Grabbing a bag, I swiftly refilled my glass. Sitting down at the island, I felt my mind aimlessly wander about her health, mentally and physically. Feeling a shifting presence come in behind me, I snarled, "You followed me?"

"Well, because I'm worried."

"Oh, it's you." I sighed, recognizing that it was the Vixen who had followed me and not her boyfriend.

"Jakob, I get that you are suffering, but if you go down that dark road you are not going to find the answers that you are so deeply seeking." She wisely lectured, staying in my blind spot.

Slamming my glass down on the counter, I swung around to face her, my six-foot height towering over her. "How the fuck can you say that? Weren't you at one time her closest friend? How can you so easily forget about her?"

"I haven't forgotten about her, I've just moved on." Yalu coldly claimed, her amber fox color eyes harshly staring back at me. "You need to move on too." Turning back around to sit back at the island, I continued to listen to the woman talk. "Just because you move on doesn't mean that you have to stop trying to find her or stop loving her." Drinking more blood, I remained quiet. "Jakob, please say something."

"Could you leave me alone?"

Chapter 76
Jakob/Cinder

With the New Year having come and gone, some of the tension that hung around the manor had dissipated. It never failed, Christmas time was always a rough and tense time. We were overfilled with many Unnaturals, and to add on to it, we were on a much tighter watch with the increased sightings of Hunters around the City. Strolling out of the shower, I began to dry off my soaked skin. Calmly putting on my collected clothes, I stopped when I felt a sharp painful shock in my neck, my fingers hurriedly grasped the spot. Rubbing the irritated wound, I recalled the location. Lifting my fingers, I saw my reversed image in the mirror expose the punctures and scrapes scarred around the left side of my neck. The scars caused by her, caused by Cinder. Wounds that even Viktor's advanced healing could not restore. Shrugging off the pain, I finally put on my long sleeve snug u-neck gray shirt and strolled out of my bathroom, ready to start another day.

Stepping out of my room, I was immediately called by the ex-Pharaoh. Glancing down over the balcony, I noticed that the 'Guardian' Hellhound was in his tall human form staring up at me. Wearing a white 'affliction' shirt that revealed his golden arch tattoos wrapped around his arms, and a pair of dark blue faded jeans. His short cut hair forming his face quite well, and even making his animalistic amber eyes seem all the more suspenseful. Leaning over the banister railing, I listened to Peylith inquire, "Are you ready for today's mission?"

"Not really," I responded, tiredly recalling that today we were heading up into Maine to break into another Institute, our fifth one in the last six weeks. "But the sooner we can get this over with, the better," I complained, beginning my descent down the stairs. "Who are we still waiting on?" I wondered as I strolled into the common area descending the final step.

"Mhykal and Yalu." The Hellhound answered with a snickered grin.

"Mhykila keep them up again?"

"I assume so."

"Well, hopefully, they'll hurry up. We're falling behind schedule." I pestered as I again rubbed at the scars on my neck.

"Are you alright, Jakob?"

"I'm fine." I returned. "It just aches for some reason today."

"You're thinking about her too much."

"You're starting to sound like them," I growled, my eyes hinted at the arriving shadows of our comrades. Changing the subject, I took the position as the Leader of this raid, "Everyone finally ready?"

"She's in the center cage." I heard the voice of the younger sister speak, my ears catching on to the subject before my eyes could. "Just be cautious in how you approach, as her owner currently isn't here."

"Augustus left?" I questioned, standing myself up from my normal post beneath the center Aspen tree. "I'm going to rip him a new one when I see him again," I vowed to myself while Matilda and her guests cautiously strolled towards the wall of iron bars. Using my nose, I absorbed the newcomers' scents. I wasn't familiar with them, but I was still aware of the basic stench wafting off them. Their species' scent. These guys were Draconics. I had only recalled the scent for a brief time from Colorado, but it was forever entwined in my vastly growing mental library. Baring my fangs at them, I wondered to myself in the canine language, "Why are they here? The Draconics were not supposed to arrive for another week, so why now?" I speedily thought. "Was it because he wasn't here?"

"Any medications we should be aware of?" the taller Draconic requested as our eyes locked for a fleeting moment. This male stood around six foot three with his long black hair pulled back into a neat man-bun. Keeping the healthy locks off of the dark blue suit he wore.

"Unfortunately, I am not too well aware of what Dr. Lillian and Mr. Gale have been pumping into Cinder," Matilda answered. The sweet girl who had often brought human food around for us at random times throughout the passing days now seemed anxious. I had to assume she was intimated by their massive size.

"Mr. Gale was the one whom you called in the favor for, right?" the taller one persistently interrogated.

Continuing to bare my fangs, I barked my warning flare as the slightly shorter and assuming very young Draconic who was around the same age as the wench's younger sister, expressed, "If I were you, Shaun, I'd back off on the intimidation factor. You're scaring her, and it's not working too well with any of the other Unnaturals here. I can sense their lust for our blood, especially hers." The assuming young yet wise Draconic pointed directly at me, his reddish gaze flashing and setting off my Demonic glare.

"Cinder, I'm okay." Matilda calmly told me, her voice remaining firm. Flattening my ears against my head, I relaxed my snarl but kept my hunting gaze fastened to the men. I knew I was to be taken to their Syndicate, but if they put a child's life endanger in front of me, I was not going to stand so idly by. Human or Unnatural, a child was a child. "As far as I know, it is mild to strong sedatives depending on the day, and regular doses of Blessed Salts. That's as much as I know."

"Just like Saylene had told us to expect," Shaun responded. "Alright, when does Mr. Gale return?"

"He should be back in about a half-hour," Matilda answered.

"We can wait. It'll give us some time to communicate with the Unnatural herself." The younger Draconic addressed.

"You can talk to her, but I am going to speak with this Doctor Lillian. If you won't mind introducing me."

"Yeah, yeah." The human girl snarked, rolling her eyes at the pair. A sign that her normal rebellious self was returning and the intimidation was fading. "Come with me." Matilda called, leading Shaun out of the Courtyard, stopping a few feet away from the gated exit, she then forewarned this youngster, "Just be careful how you talk to her, Cinder does have a quick temper and has almost broken out of that cage twice while drugged."

"I will take that into consideration, thank you miss." He graciously accepted, his mannerism surprising me. The way they acted was similar to the other Syndicate members, but unlike the Lycans who were straight forward, or the Vampirics who were generous and calm, these guys seemed to be very formal. Formal, in such a way that not even I recognized it, making my anxiety stand all the more on edge.

"Damn it, Augustus! Where the fuck are you?!" I furiously snarled.

Chapter 77
Cinder

Anticipating all possible movements, my eyes heavily surveyed every single move the remaining Draconic made. Taking in his figure, I overheard the man calmly jab. "The reports weren't kidding when they said you have such cold haunting eyes." His words attempting to fray my gaze. "Such a deep blue."

Lifting my head in amusement, I snickered, "Let me guess, those reports came from Joseph and Lucious."

"I'm surprised that you remember their names." The shorter one whose name I had yet to figure out, snickered. "After what you did to their Leader and all."

"You're missing some vital information." I cynically informed. Lowering my head, I locked my gaze on his arms while he sauntered closer to the caged wall. Holding my breath, I impatiently told myself, "Wait. A few more steps and he will be within range."

The man stopped a few feet shy of the wall, a bit shy of my long fang's reach. "Oh, and what would that be?"

"For one, I have killed two Lycans, and for two, that man was a despicable being, a false Immortal," I answered, snapping my jowls together with much anticipation.

"Oh, that's right, the half-breed that attacked that Vixen child." The Draconic snarked, a sly smile seizing his face as he finished speaking those words in an antagonizing tone. A type of tone that was so easily able to push my short temper over the edge. Raising my hackles, I proceeded with simultaneously curling my lips to expose the bottom ridge of my gumline while digging my long nails into the hard dirt beneath my canine frame. Continuing to listen to the Unnatural tease. "Oh, that's right, that place holds deep memories to you."

"If I were you, I would shut your trap," I warned, attempting to remain as refined as possible.

"And what if I refuse-?"

"Sam!" I now overheard Shaun's deeper voice call, his tone breaking our momentary feud. "What were you told about egging her on?"

"Sorry, Shaun. It would seem she was already on edge before our conversation. Everything I tried to tell her she returned with that." The shorter Draconic answered, rubbing the back of his short black-haired head, acting the same way, a child did when he was being scolded by his parent.

"Bullshit." I cursed, easily catching onto his lie.

"It would seem she has a different story," Matilda spoke up as she too wondered up from around the outskirts of the courtyard, Dr. Lillian not far behind.

"Anyways." Shaun then redirected, turning his attention to the Veterinarian turned Unnatural caretaker. "We should get on with this, Lady Saylene only moved the date ahead because of the suite we had managed to free up. And although her current guardian is not here, the one who made the appointment is, so we have all the necessary clearance, all that's left is to ensure a safe voyage back."

"I'm not going anywhere without him." I voiced, my mind digesting the unusual change in his dialogue. The formalities returning as the Draconics refocused their minds on the mission at hand.

"If we just kill them, then we won't have to leave without the 'Angel.'" I heard a voice coo into my right ear. It was my voice, or rather the voice of that 'blood-thirsty' being held deep within my conscious.

Craning my head away from its invisible presence, I directly commanded the Fiend, "No. I can't do that. They aren't our targets. Just their leader. And they can lead me directly to her."

"Then why won't you leave without that promise-breaking fool." It snarled in retaliation while I returned my attention to the collection of people who were attempting to devise a successive plan for the exchange of custody. "He'll just be in the way."

"I won't leave without him." I refuted "Now leave."

The voice faded without a comeback. Returning to the endless black abyss that was my mind.

Taking a breath of relief, I now attempted to soothe my rapidly beating heart and scared nerves. "Now think." I proceeded to order myself as the group began to walk towards the cage door, bolted to the south end of the cage. "THINK!" I once more ordered, this time more frantically as the human teenager began to unlock the door. "Judging on past events, the Draconics will most likely try to distract me while that doctor loads up that tranquilizer gun she has in her hands." I thought as the two indeed began to wander up the foundation steps. "No, I'm sure he's already thought of that! Damn it, Augustus, where are you?!" Lowering my head closer to the ground to protect my neck and chest from any impact, I kept my sights locked on the two men who were much broader than I had originally anticipated, as well as the approaching doctor. Centering my breathing, I continued to formulate my thoughts, "He most likely has a hidden sedative somewhere within his suit, knowing that I will keep an eye on Dr. Lillian." With the men steadily approaching the line where my personal space existed, I knew I had to hastily devise a plan, even though this was already looking futile no matter what I came up with. "Come on, think! Think of something!" I snarled to myself, my eyes momentarily shutting as I cringed in horror, of yet again being taken somewhere I do not want to go. Upon opening my eyes, I promptly noticed the gap they had enclosed in the split second my lids were closed. "SHIT!" I cursed. My mind now desperately allowing instinct to take the reins.

"Watch it, Shaun! Her eyes changed color." Sam warned, his body language changed from a calm stance to a defensive one.

"I know!" Shaun shouted as my body came thrusting forward for the two. Lifting off of my hind legs, I leaned my torso towards the space between the two. With my body slipping between the two men, I released one of my warm heat waves. The dry heat quickly mixing with oxygen surrounding me and with the wind made by my moving figure, hastily evolved into a wall of bright orange flames. Coming in for a landing, I surveyed out of my peripheral vision as the flames hastily lost their power and changed into dancing embers. Not wasting a second, my body once more moved on its own and darted right for the gate. "Damn it! She saw right through our ploy!" I heard him continue to roar from behind me. "CLOSE THE GATE!"

"Damn it!" I snarled, watching the gate quickly slam shut just before my body prepared for a lunge past the two women. I knew if I braced enough of my weight, I could easily break through the wall, but the minute my eyes observed Matilda stand in front of the way, her body propping the gate shut with all of her might in anticipation of my lunge, I stopped. My paws skidding along the fake grass. Releasing another strong wave of warm air as I hastened to a speedy halt.

"I'm sorry Cinder!" she hastily apologized. The girl's sarcastic tone was replaced by a concerned one.

Folding my ears back in response, I felt my mind snap back as it regained the reins. Turning my head over to stare at the two Draconics who were too locked in this outdoor cage. Surveying the damage my flames had done, I noticed that their hidden traits had surfaced. In place of the burned skin were silver scales mimicking the shining light of the sun poking through the foliage's shadow. I knew that they had a sort of immunity to fire just like Hellhounds did, and it seemed my stupid slip up was not hot enough to cause significant damage. Debating on what to do next, I turned myself back around to face them. I could either challenge them, which would only end up hurting me in the end, or allow them to take me. My stomach suddenly twisted on me at the thought of surrendering so easily. "Damn it, this would have been so much easier if you were here!" I mumbled to myself. Watching the men cautiously wander closer to me, I continued to debate on my next move. But before I could choose an option, my body was tackled to the ground.

"CINDER!" I heard Matilda cry, her voice informing me of how afraid she was of this kind of circumstance.

With the heavy weight of the Draconic crashing down on my rib cage, I snapped my fangs up towards Sam's face. My teeth inches away from clashing with iron-clad scales. Soon finding out how futile that also was, I dropped my head down on the grass. As I listened to my steady heart erratically beat out of control, I began to feel my surrendered mind start to panic. The feeling of being alone in enemy territory terrified every fiber in my body. "Damn it, where are you?" I cried, shutting my eyes in anxious fear.

"Seems she's not as violent as they say." I heard Sam's voice tell his associate, his hands tightly readjusting their grip around my neck while a third hand tightly clasped my front left leg.

Shooting my eyes open the minute I realized what was coming next, I began to struggle once more. Twisting my body around in the tight and heavy hold, I howled out my refusal. Yet again, it proved useless, just like always. "You spoke too soon, idiot," Shaun responded, his grip too remaining quite firm on my leg.

"Hold still!" the shorter one aggressively demanded of me as I observed the long needle pierce my leg before invading the vein lying beneath.

"It'll be over in a bit, Cinder." I heard Shaun empathetically apprise. Seconds later, the needle was removed, and my body was released from its restraint. Allowing my head to fall again on the prickly grass, I stared up at the sun's rays that beating down on my befallen body. Feeling its mocking warmth on my black fur, I continued to listen to these confusing men. "By the time you wake up, you will be back in a warm bed, safe at our Syndicate."